PRAISE FOR
THE TRIALS OF NIKKI HILL

ALSO BY CHRISTOPHER DARDEN

In Contempt

ALSO BY DICK LOCHTE

Sleeping Dog
Laughing Dog
Blue Bayou
The Neon Smile

THE TRIALS OF NIKKI HILL

CHRISTOPHER DARDEN

AND DICK LOCHTE

WARNER BOOKS

A Time Warner Company

WARNER BOOKS EDITION

Cover design by Andrew Newman

Warner Books, Inc.
1271 Avenue of the Americas
New York, NY 10020

Visit our Web site at
www.twbookmark.com

 A Time Warner Company

Printed in the United States of America

Originally published in hardcover by Warner Books.
First Paperback Printing: January 2001

10 9 8 7 6 5 4 3 2 1

To my wife, Marcia, and the baby Dardens—
Jenee, Tiffany, and Christopher, Jr.

C.D.

To Jane and Bryson, the home team.

D.L.

Acknowledgments

I would like to thank:

San Diego County Deputy District Attorney Michael Runyon and Alameda County Deputy District Attorney Patricia Ector, two old friends who were kind enough to read the early drafts of this text and offer their comments.

Special thanks to a lawyer with a conscience, my former boss, Head Deputy District Attorney Roger Gunson, Los Angeles County District Attorney's Office. We tried.

Dean Leigh Taylor and the faculty and student body at Southwestern University School of Law, for putting up with all the distractions.

Deputy District Attorneys Michelle Gilmore, Karen Nobomoto, Charlene Underwood, and Shante Penland, for your inspiration.

My good friend and mentor, Norman Brokaw, chairman of the board at the William Morris Agency, and my literary agent, Mel Berger. Thanks guys. We did it our way, with class and dignity.

My publicist at the Brokaw Company, Claudia de Llano. I can't help but laugh whenever I reflect on the way you took on the "big heads" at the Republican National Convention.

My friends and editors at Warner Books, especially Susan Sandler, who worked long and hard on Nikki's behalf. Thanks for everything. Larry Kirshbaum, you've made a dream come true.

A very special thanks to Dick Lochte, my new best friend. A great writer. Nikki Hill lives and breathes on paper. You have my endless gratitude. You, sir, are the bomb. Okay?

Finally, my heartfelt gratitude to the thousands of people who stopped me on the street to say "thanks," gave me the thumbs up on the crowded Santa Monica freeway, or who wrote me during difficult times. You helped make my life easier. God bless each and every one of you.

CHRISTOPHER DARDEN

THE TRIALS OF
NIKKI HILL

≡ PROLOGUE ≡

The way Jamal Deschamps saw it, life was a good news–bad news proposition. For example, the good news was bumping into a fine young sister at the 4-Speed Club on a slow Sunday night, having some drinks, talking some trash, and then spending some quality bump time in her bed until her roommate showed. The bad news was that he wound up all alone out on Dalton Street at around 2:30 A.M., which is when a black '63 Chevy filled with Crazy Eights gangstas rounded the corner.

Jamal did a swift backpedal into the nearest alley and tried to make himself small behind an overripe industrial-size faded blue Dumpster. His mind was filled with grisly images based on what he knew about the Crazies, the worst involving an acquaintance who'd had his hands, tongue, and private parts hacked off with a machete for daring to get too close to one of their women. He wished he knew a bit more about the history of the woman he'd just been with.

He strained his ears. And heard nothing. *They didn't see me. I'm too fast for 'em.*

Then he heard the Chevy brake at the entrance to the alley.

Okay, so they stopped. They'll check out the alley and I'm gonna be like Casper. They'll see nothing but empty space and be on their way.

He heard the Chevy door open. The pat of rubber soles hitting concrete. Then, oh, shit, the harsh metallic click of an automatic that damn well had to mean it was dying time!

Jamal squeezed in tighter against the brick building, trying to become a part of it. The gangsta came closer. *Pat, pat pat, pat.* He must've been right at the Dumpster. Another two steps and he'd be staring down and pointing his gun and . . .

Then Jamal heard the good news: a police siren a few blocks away, coming closer.

"Yo, Fupdup," someone yelled from the Chevy. "Get yo' ass back in here, bro."

Listen to the brother, Jamal begged silently. *Get your homicidal ass back in the car.*

"It's right here, sucka. Jus' be a minnit . . ."

The driver of the Chevy revved the engine. "We bookin'," someone called out.

"Bunch o' pusswipes," Fupdup growled angrily as his thick rubber soles pat-patted away.

A car door slammed shut and the Chevy roared off. Jamal rested his head against the brick wall and let out the breath he'd been holding for what seemed like hours. *Thank you, Jesus.*

His eyes wandered up past the buildings to the clear night sky. Stars were blinking way up there, without a care in the world. He knew just how they felt.

The police siren was coming closer, down Dalton. Jamal turned his head toward the street and saw, for the first time, something draped over the edge of the Dumpster. He blinked, his mind initially refusing to accept the image before him. But it was real. A human hand. A woman's hand. Not small, exactly, but delicate. White. It was the whitest damned hand Jamal had ever seen.

His immediate reaction was to move away from it, to put as much distance as he could between him and that got-to-be-dead-as-Dracula hand.

Then he saw the ring on her finger, its diamond twinkling like the stars overhead.

The ring posed a dilemma for Jamal. His brain was screaming at him to do a three-minute mile away from the dead woman in the Dumpster. But that ring sure as hell wasn't gonna be much use to her anymore.

Screwing up his face in disgust, he approached the lifeless hand and gingerly poked it with a finger. The hand felt cold, stiff. *Over the line. No fucking way do I touch that thing with my bare hands.* Near his feet was a Fatburger wrapper. He scooped it up and, using it like a glove, grabbed the corpse's wrist. With his other hand he gently tugged on the ring.

He hovered next to the bin, the garbage smelling so ripe a rat would turn its nose up at it. He didn't want to look at the dead woman, but he couldn't help himself. She was buck naked. Was a time she might have been Penthouse material, but not now.

His eyes traveled up the pale trunk, past the bruised chest to the face. Somebody had done a dance on baby's face, busted it up big time. But there was something familiar. He blinked. He knew that death created its own disguise. His daddy had looked like some other dude entirely, lying in his coffin. But this corpse . . . *Jesus!* he thought. *It's Maddie Gray.*

In a mild state of panic, he yanked harder at the ring, cutting his palm on the corpse's jagged thumbnail. The ring wouldn't move past the dead woman's knuckle.

The police siren was wailing now, really close. Too close. Almost on top of him. Shit!

He gave the ring a final jerk and there was a popping noise as the pale white finger broke, dangling like an icicle ready to fall off a roof. But the ring slid free. Jamal jammed both it and the burger wrapper into his pocket and started running down the alley.

A bright light caught him full in the eyes, blinding him.

"Hold it right there, boy," a voice shouted.

Jamal couldn't see a thing but the bright light. He didn't need to. There would be two big beefy white boys in blue drawing down on him, licking their lips at the thought of him making a move. He held it right there.

Good news—bad news, he told himself. *My life ain't nothing but good news—bad news.*

≡ ONE ≡

Nikki Hill awoke to colored lights dancing on her bedroom ceiling.

She raised her head high enough to glimpse a youthful Marlo Thomas on the silent TV, wearing a Peter Pan collar and a worried expression. *Just what I need,* she thought as she flopped back against the pillow, *a white-bread night-light.*

She was suddenly puzzled. *If the TV sound is off, what am I doing awake?*

As if in answer, the phone rang.

With a groan she shifted on the bed, sending *Witkin on Criminal Law, Volume 5* and several Manila folders and their contents tumbling to the carpet. Her "Liar For Hire" T-shirt, a joke gift that she perversely embraced, was sticking clammily to her body. At least she hadn't fallen asleep in her good clothes again.

The phone rang once more.

As she reached for it on the bedside table, she saw the time glowing on her radio alarm: 3:47 A.M. She cleared her throat. "This better be an emergency," she warned her caller.

"Nikki?"

The voice sounded vaguely familiar. "Yeah?" she replied warily.

"Joe Walden." It was her boss, the district attorney for the county of Los Angeles. "Sorry to wake you, but this *is* an emergency."

Her head was fuzzy. "Uh . . . right," she managed to reply, feeling a little embarrassed, as if he'd caught her doing something weird. Like getting a night's sleep. She turned on the bedside lamp, then grabbed the TV remote to send Marlo back to nostalgia heaven.

"You okay?" he asked.

"Sure."

Something caught her eye—Bird, framed in the doorway, observing her curiously, black curls obscuring part of his dark handsome face.

Nikki winked at him as Walden asked, "You familiar with Madeleine Gray?"

"Uh . . . sure," Nikki said. Her mouth had that dry, sucking-up-smog-all-night ashy aftertaste. "On TV. Big Viking of a woman. Whiter than rice with a mess of blond hair. Does gossip news. Interviews. Not exactly Barbara Walters."

"Lucky for Ms. Walters," District Attorney Walden said dryly. "Maddie Gray's big white naked body was found in a Dumpster in South Central a few hours ago."

Nikki forgot about the early hour, morning mouth, and nearly everything else except the voice on the other end of the phone.

"A suspect was apprehended near the corpse," Walden was saying. "They're getting ready to interrogate him."

Bird approached the bed, yawning.

"A couple million people watched Maddie Gray every night," Walden said. "The media jackals are going to dine large on this one. It's got everything. Sex. Drugs. Showbiz.

I want you to get down to Parker Center ASAP and keep tabs on Homicide's progress."

She didn't know Walden very well. She couldn't imagine why he'd phoned her—a midlevel deputy D.A. who'd been stalled at Grade 3 for three long years in Compton, the Siberia of the district attorney's office. But she wasn't about to question his decision. Any prosecutor with an ounce of ambition would slit both wrists for a chance to rub up against a high-profile case like this one. Nikki had more than an ounce.

"I'm your man," she said, trying not to giggle as Bird touched his tongue to a bare brown foot he discovered sticking out from under the covers.

"Good," Walden said. "I hope I'm not, ah, taking you away from anything . . . more pressing."

"What could be more pressing?" Nikki replied, reaching out a hand to grab Bird's curly head.

"Yes, well, as soon as you know something, I want to know it, too. Okay?"

"Okay," she said, scowling at the clock radio.

"Oh, and should the detectives handling the case wonder what you're doing there, tell them you're my special assistant. Assuming you're okay with that title."

It took a moment for her to realize she was being promoted. Not a major promotion—probably wouldn't mean more money—but it was a step up, and it made her feel the time she'd spent in Compton hadn't been wasted. "No, sir, no objection at all. Thank you."

Bird, who was not used to a subservient tone in her voice, gave her a questioning look.

"We'll see if you're still thanking me by the time this all shakes out," Walden said.

She replaced the phone, exhilarated. "Guess who's just been appointed the special assistant to the district attorney?" she asked Bird happily.

Bird yawned again, unimpressed. He didn't really get the gist of her question. Though he understood nearly fifty words, the only ones he really reacted to were "food," "walk," and "cat," and, of course, the special commands. He was a Bouvier des Flandres, a coal-black Belgian sheepdog weighing eighty pounds, much of it muscle. The full name on his papers read Charlie "Yardbird" Parker.

He had been the bequest of the only man Nikki had ever loved, and she couldn't look at him without thinking of his departed owner. Tony Black. She smiled wistfully. "Tall as pine, black as crow, talk more shit than radio."

Her first thought had been to find Bird another home. At the time, she'd been in no condition to assume the responsibility for a large animal who demanded a certain amount of attention. Especially one who would be a constant reminder of all that she'd lost. Something about Bird—her best friend, Loreen Battles, said he looked like a beautiful holy man in a dog suit—kept her from giving him up. In fact, Bird had helped her through that difficult period of mourning, had been a protector and companion and, on those long, lonely nights when she felt she had to talk to someone or she would freak completely, a doggy shrink.

That had been four years ago. Now, she could hardly remember what her life had been like before she began sharing it with the lovable, loyal, hardheaded, territorial, demanding beast who obviously adored her.

Bird was digging his nose into the skirt she'd dropped on the floor the night before. She grabbed it from him. "It's messed up enough without you slobberin' on it, fuzzball," she said.

He cocked his huge head to one side, staring—critically, she imagined—at the other clothes sharing the carpet with law books and files and scattered newspapers and magazines. "Okay, so I ain't Martha Stewart," she said, slipping her feet into her tatty but comfortable old Bugs Bunny slippers. "You're not exactly Lassie."

Bird followed along devotedly as she padded her way through the dark, mainly unfurnished ranch-style house they'd moved into only months before. It was much too big for just the two of them, about four times the size of her old apartment. But Nikki had always dreamed of moving up to this particular location—Ladera Heights, the black Beverly Hills. The deal had been one she hadn't been able to refuse. The Asian couple who'd purchased the place sight unseen had taken one glance at the cemetery just down the hill and raced away in search of better karma. Essentially, all Nikki had to do was take over the monthly notes.

She looked out of the kitchen window and smiled at the tombstones. "Roll them bones," she said, remembering the depressing little one-bedroom apartment that she and Bird had been sharing next door to the dangerous neighborhood known as the Jungle.

She left the window and turned on the sound system that the builder had thoughtfully wired into every room in the house. An all-news station was providing a litany of the previous night's tragedies. Fires, wrecks, robberies, drive-bys, carjackings. Murders. She wondered when Madeleine Gray would make the list.

Bird emitted his "feed me" yelp and Nikki responded quickly. Though most of the house was barren of furnishings, the kitchen was filled with enough pots, pans, gadgets, and instruments to pass for a Williams-Sonoma showroom. This was the result of a six-night cooking class taught by a local celebrity chef that Loreen Battles had dragged her to. "You know what they say about a man's stomach leading the way to his heart," Loreen had said.

While Nikki had never put much stock in that stomach theory, she'd gone along with her friend. And discovered the joy of cooking. Ever since childhood, however, she'd had a tendency toward obsessive behavior. Great for her career. Less great for real life. In this case it had resulted in an awesome collection of rarely used cookware that ran the gamut from a fuzzy-logic rice steamer to an Italian espresso machine so medieval it made only one perfect cup at a time.

She used her state-of-the-art Scandinavian can opener to trim the lid from a tin of the special food the vet had recommended for Bird's diverticulosis, plopped most of the can's contents into his bowl, and topped it off with a flea pill. While Nikki would have to be at death's door to see a doctor, Bird visited the veterinarian on an almost bimonthly basis.

One ear tuned to the news, Nikki carried the food and a water bowl out to the patio. The animal would have to dine outside and perform whatever daily rituals he found necessary without her assistance. She had no time for their usual morning workout.

She returned to the kitchen, set the glistening chrome and glass coffeepot to perking, took one final loving look at Bird hungrily devouring his food, and said, "Now for the hard stuff."

The bright bathroom light made her wince. Her image in the mirror above the washbasin made her wince even more. Her light brown face with its freckled, full cheekbones was puffy and pillow-wrinkled. Her dark brown eyes, which Bird's master used to rhapsodize over, were bloodshot. Her thick black hair vaguely resembled an unpruned shrub.

Damn, she thought. *I don't need a shower. I need that fountain at Lourdes.*

The shower helped.

Nothing else seemed to.

No time for a curling iron. Her last clean panty hose looked like a cougar had been pawing it. The cream for the coffee had curdled. Bird's flea pill was resting at the bottom of his empty bowl, untouched. And the four-fifteen news summary informed the world that "the battered body of television star Madeleine Gray was found several hours ago in an alley in South Central Los Angeles. The police have not released any further information, but we'll try to have more for you at five A.M."

Nikki knew that by five she'd better have discovered that information firsthand. After anxiously consulting her watch, she tracked Bird down in the yard and force-fed him the pill he'd avoided. Then she was on her way.

Her loyal Mazda RX7, as dependable as always, started right up. And, at four-twenty on the warm, dark Monday morning, she was zooming toward downtown L.A. along nearly deserted streets, confident she'd be on the job within minutes. That's when she noticed the gas gauge was on empty.

She swung into a service station. Only when she was parked did she realize this was one of the more dangerous stretches along Crenshaw Boulevard, particularly at this time of the morning. She placed her black coffee on the dashboard, tried to ignore the abrasive rub of her shoes against her bare heels, and removed her credit card from her briefcase. She hesitated, gave the area a quick scan, then took out her police special, too.

She was anxiously pumping gas when the man approached her. Another of the city's homeless population, she thought. Grizzled, grimy, ageless, and apparently aimless.

"You up kinda early, sistah," he said.

She casually dropped her right hand from the pump and slipped it into her pocket, wrapping her fingers around the gun grip.

"Don't worry, sistah," he said quickly, holding up empty palms and keeping his distance. "Juppy don't mean no harm, specially to a fine-looking woman like yourself."

Great, she thought. On top of everything, she was getting hit on by some raggedy-ass homeless man.

"Gals your colorin' we useta call Red," Juppy told her. "'Cause they redbone. Bet they calls you Red, huh?"

"No." It was a lie. Even her father had, back in the days when they were speaking. Maybe that's why she hated the nickname so. "And don't *you*, either."

The Mazda's tank was far from filled, but the man made her uncomfortable and she'd pumped enough gas to get to the office and back. She replaced the nozzle, keeping an eye on Juppy.

As she got into her car, he said, "'Scuse me for saying it, but you got a lovely ass."

"Oh? You don't think it's too round?" she asked sarcastically.

"Hey, can't *be* too round," he said, stepping closer to her open window. "You look like you a happenin' woman. Goin' up in the world. Juppy been up there, too. Think maybe you can spare Juppy a li'l somethin' somethin', sistah?" He held out his hand.

"I'm not your sister, Juppy," she said, staring into his surprisingly clear brown eyes. He *was* right about her being on her way up. The thought made her feel magnanimous enough to take a couple of dollars from her wallet and hand them to him. "Here's your somethin' somethin'."

"Thank you for your gen'rosity," he said. "You won't regret it, Red."

Damn, she hated that name. "I'm regretting it already," she said, jamming her foot on the gas pedal.

≡ Two ≡

The city was still cloaked in early-morning darkness when Nikki entered Parker Center, home of the Los Angeles Police Department. In spite of the petty annoyances that had been plaguing her since she'd gotten out of bed, she felt on top of the world. Nothing could dampen her spirits, not even the building's atmosphere of neon-lit, brusque indifference, nor the near-toxic smell of the cleaning crew's pine-oil disinfectant. She was the new special assistant to the D.A., assigned to what promised to be a major murder case. She was, as Juppy had observed, "a happenin' woman."

Still, as she waited for the elevator, the specter of doom flitted through her mind. Bad luck often traveled in the guise of good fortune, a fact she'd discovered the hard way the last time she'd been poised at the brink of success.

Three and a half years before, she'd been assigned a low-priority homicide. The defendant, a career criminal named Mason Durant, had stood accused of murdering the proprietor of a mobile lunch stand who dispensed hot dogs and other foodstuffs daily in Durant's neighborhood. Though there had been no witnesses to the actual murder, five schoolchildren and their teacher had heard the shots and observed Durant running from the dead man's "roach coach" with a gun in his hand.

Ordinarily, the trial would not have gone beyond page four of the Metro section of the *L.A. Times*. But Durant offered a rather unique defense: the gun six witnesses had claimed to have seen had actually been . . . a hot dog. A local television station used the declaration as a tongue-in-cheek "light side of the news" item. Then Jay Leno coined the term "weenie defense" in his *Tonight Show* monologue, turning the bright light of national publicity on Nikki's little trial.

It had been an almost perfect case for the prosecution. In addition to the ideal witnesses, the accused had been apprehended leaving his apartment building "lugging a suitcase and on the run," according to one of the arresting officers. The police lab had turned up traces of the lunch stand's brand of mustard on bills in Durant's wallet. There was only one small problem: the weapon had not been recovered. Still, getting a conviction looked like a walk in the park. Not even the accused's overworked public defender could mention the "weenie defense" without smiling. The jury deliberated for only two hours before finding Mason Durant guilty of murder in the first degree with special circumstances. Life with no parole.

The district attorney at the time, Thomas J. Gleason, a professional Irishman whose resemblance to the late John Wayne had convinced voters that he was a rawboned crime fighter, knew what to do with a media opportunity when one dropped in his large lap. He invited members of the press to "a simple lunch to publicly congratulate deputy Nicolette Hill on a job well done."

A photo of Gleason and Nikki dining on Nathan's franks

at the luncheon adorned a section of that Sunday's *L. A. Times* and even found its way inside *People* magazine. For about a week, television couldn't get enough of Nikki's sound bites. She was invited to an assortment of Hollywood parties where, to her surprise, the celebrities wanted to meet *her.* She was, in short, flying high. Then came the fateful day when the trial's evidence boxes were delivered to her office. While waiting for someone to remove them to the D.A.'s evidence locker, she idly lifted the lid on the top box and began browsing through the items in their protective plastic bags. One held the contents of Durant's hastily packed suitcase— a comb, a nearly empty bottle of aspirin, a razor, a dry shave cologne. She sniffed the pungent scent. *So that's what Hi Karate smells like.*

Bag two contained apparel Durant was wearing when apprehended. Rumpled black chino pants and a strictly seventies shirt, shiny dark blue synthetic with bright purple and red streaks, collar rolled up.

The third bag became her personal Pandora's box.

When she opened it, a ghastly odor chased away every hint of the Hi Karate. There was only one item—a tan poplin windbreaker. What was that stench? She felt a small, solid object in the jacket's inside pocket. Her fingers daintily searched for . . . *God!* She yanked her hand out. What had she touched? Something hard and furry.

Scowling, she shifted the jacket and shook the object loose.

It fell onto the floor of her office. The remnants of a moldy bun wrapped around a gaseous chunk of nearly desiccated meat.

Reeling not only from the odor but from the implication of her discovery, she pulled a Kleenex from the box on her desk and returned the remnants of Mason Durant's defense to the windbreaker's pocket, then shoved the jacket back into its plastic bag.

What now?

She had little doubt of Durant's guilt. She'd done her homework prepping for the trial. The witnesses had been certain that they'd seen a metallic gun in Durant's hand. He'd definitely been on the run from something. Though it had not been admissible as evidence, he had a long rap sheet and had previously stood trial for murder. That time, the jury had found him not guilty. But investigators had provided Nikki with a number of people, including the victim's widow, to whom Durant had later bragged that he had indeed killed the man.

Did any of this permit her to ignore the fact that she was in possession of evidence that might possibly have changed the outcome of the trial? While she wasn't sure what her obligation was to the law, she knew what her conscience was telling her.

Well, as Grandma Tyrell, who had raised her, used to say, the only way to handle bad news is to take off your gloves. She went to see Tom Gleason.

The district attorney was not amused. His ruddy, normally jovial face went purple with apoplexy. He took a small plastic bottle from his desk, removed a tiny pill, and popped it into his mouth. He grimaced, then demanded, "Who in their right mind digs through evidence *after* they've won? What the Christ were you thinking?"

"I sure wasn't thinking four-month-old hot dog," she told him.

He glared at her. "Well, you're not gonna like what *I'm* thinking."

He picked up the phone and dialed the number of his head deputy, Raymond Wise, who answered almost immediately.

Waiting for the call, Nikki thought. *Like Rover listening for his master's voice.*

Gleason explained the situation tersely, requesting that Wise join them. Then he strolled to his windows, where he remained staring out, ignoring her, until his head deputy limped into the room.

Wise was a pale, thin, unsmiling man in his mid-forties, with lank brown hair lying on a high forehead. His manner of dress was ultraconservative except for aviator frame glasses perched firmly on a long thin nose. He was the top prosecutor in the county, but his coworkers, though they envied his conviction record, considered him arrogant and egotistical, not to mention sexist and racist. The origin of his stiffened right leg remained something of a mystery. Nikki imagined he might have broken it trying to climb up Gleason's fat ass.

He stared at her blankly, then said to his scowling boss, "There's no legal obligation here. The acknowledged precedent in these matters, *Brady v. Maryland,* 1963, refers specifically to a trial in progress. Even there, the prosecutor must be convinced the evidence is exculpatory. I doubt a desiccated hot dog qualifies."

"C'mon, Ray," Nikki said. "You know how much emphasis was placed on the hot dog. It was Durant's main defense."

"You see, Tom," Wise said to the D.A. "That's exactly what I was telling you. We've got too many deputies like Hill who don't know what their job is."

"Hill knows enough about her job to recognize evidence when she sees it," Nikki said heatedly.

"Evidence of what?" Gleason asked. "That a murderer ate half a hot dog? Even if Durant's pathetic lawyer had dangled the sausage under the jury's nose, they still would have found him guilty. Maybe even guiltier."

"Why's that, Ray?" Nikki asked skeptically.

"Because, you, *People* magazine's sexiest D.A. of the year, would have explained that Durant was so cold-blooded that he calmly stood there eating his victim's hot dog while blasting him in the gut with the gun six clear-eyed witnesses saw him holding."

"Any way you slice the weenie, Ray, it's still evidence."

"You honestly think this scumbag is an innocent man?" Wise asked.

"No," Nikki replied, remembering the people she'd talked to who heard Durant boasting about beating the rap on his last trial. "I'm sure he's a murderer. And I'm about ninety-eight percent sure he's guilty in this case. But that doesn't change the fact that the jurors were not in possession of all the evidence when they decided to send him off to Folsom for the rest of his life."

Wise threw up his hands.

Gleason leaned forward and said in as calm a voice as he could muster, "Ms. Hill. Nikki. Thanks to your trial this office has been on the receiving end of some very beneficial publicity. We're not gonna dump that and run the risk of looking like donkeys just to satisfy some fucking schoolgirl notion you have about the law."

Nikki stood, tingling in anger. "We'll see what the court says about my fucking schoolgirl notion."

"No, we won't," Gleason said softly. "Because if you go public with this, I'll put you behind bars for the rest of your life."

Nikki couldn't believe it. He was threatening her. "What kind of bullshit is this?" she asked.

"Hiding evidence from a jury during a murder trial with special circumstances can put a prosecutor away for life," Gleason said calmly.

"You saying I hid evidence during the trial?" she asked, eyes narrowing.

"I'm saying you discovered that devil's own wiener in the midst of the trial, but failed to disclose it. You came to me today because your conscience has been bothering you.

"Isn't that right, Ray? Isn't that what you heard?"

Wise looked surprised and a bit shaken. He said nothing.

"Well?" Gleason prompted him.

"Tom, don't ask me to be a party to anything like this."

Gleason's eyebrows shot up. "Excuse me. I thought you were somebody I could count on. Somebody who knew how to play the game. Hell, this is all speculation anyway. I'm sure Nikki's bright enough to do the right thing, which is to flush the evidence of *her* crime down the crapper and go on about her business. Right, Nikki?"

The jive-ass son of a bitch!

Both men were staring at her. She wanted to scream. Or tear out their hearts. Something.

Gleason took her silence for affirmation. "Fine, then," he said. "Ray, you'll supervise the removal of the 'old business.' "

"Tom," Wise complained, "you're carrying this too far. Let's just put the fucking hot dog back in the box and file it. We're still on legal high ground there, but no matter how inconsequential the evidence is, once you start destroying it—"

"That's the point, Ray," Gleason said, grinning. "That's how I can be sure there'll be no more discussion of this matter. You two will get rid of the so-called evidence."

"I . . . I don't think so," Wise said.

Gleason stood, his face filling with angry blood. Then he seemed to relax. He slumped back in his chair and grinned at Wise. "That's a curious career choice, Ray. Just after I bumped you up to head deputy. Could be a short-term decision."

Wise blinked in surprise, and Nikki could tell by the change that came over his pasty face that he would be raising no more objections. Gleason saw it, too. "Good. Now that we're in agreement, be off with the two of you. When you're finished, Nikki, come back and we'll work out your reassignment."

"What reassignment?"

"I'm sure you'd be happier somewhere else."

"Where?" she asked coldly.

"You'll stay on here for a few months, closing out your caseload. Then when the media has forgotten all about the damned 'weenie defense' case, you'll quietly request a reassignment to Compton."

"You sorry sack of shit," she said.

"I love you, too," he said. "Now, why don't you and Ray get rid of that nasty old weenie."

They made their way to her office in silence, Nikki leading the limping Wise by several paces. When they arrived, she turned to him and said, "He's gonna be holding this over us for the rest of our careers. Even head D.D.A. isn't worth it."

"Grow the fuck up," Wise replied. "You can't beat Tom at this game. You do it his way, or you pay, as you are paying. I have no desire to wind up at the desk next to you in Compton. Besides, you know damned well Durant is guilty as sin."

"He is. But . . . aw, hell, what's the point of talking ethics to you? You want to destroy evidence, Mister Integrity, do it without my help." She sat down at her desk. "I'm already on my way to Compton."

She took no delight in the sight of Wise limping gingerly from her office, one hand clutching the rotten food wrapped in a Kleenex, the other holding his nose. When he was gone, she went to her bookshelf and pulled down a thick volume. She shuffled through its thin pages until she found what she was looking for. "*Brady v. Maryland*, U.S. Supreme Court, 373 OS.83 (1963)."

She scanned the words of the decision. "A prosecutor that withholds evidence . . . which, if made available, would tend to exculpate the accused or reduce the penalty helps shape a trial that bears heavily on the defendant, that casts the prosecution in the role of an architect of a proceeding that does not comport with standards of justice. . . ."

Wise had been right. She hadn't withheld any evidence. She'd turned over the jacket. It was not her fault that the public defender had failed to inventory the contents of its pocket. She'd had no legal obligation to practice law for the defense. But she still felt sick. To her mind, she was still in the position of being the "architect" of Mason Durant's fate. That did not comport with *her* standard of justice.

Glumly, she returned to Gleason's office.

Ordinarily, she would have waited for one of the secretaries to announce her, but her anger pushed her beyond that sort of formality. Gleason looked up from the magazine he was reading. "All done?" he asked.

"Yeah. And I quit."

"Oh? What are your plans? Gonna work as a cleaning lady? Drive a cab? Certainly nothing in law, nothing to compensate for all those years of study and struggle. Even if you managed to get as far as the personnel office of a firm, can you imagine the kind of reference I'd provide?"

"Why are you being such an asshole?" she asked.

"Because you disappoint me. Because I thought you were smart enough to know how the game is played. Because in this office defiance is simply not tolerated."

"Well, fuck you and your disappointment," Nikki said. "I didn't become a prosecutor so I could play games with the law. Ask Mason Durant what he thinks about your damned games."

"You want to set him free, Nikki?" the district attorney asked. "Would that be serving the society we're sworn to protect?"

Nikki remembered the woman whose husband Durant had bragged about killing, remembered her tears and bitter words. She shook her head, trying in vain to remove that sad image. "It's . . . not my call to make," she said, more hesitatingly than she wished.

"No it isn't," Gleason said. "A jury found him guilty and that's that. Know why? Because I say it is."

"That's fine for folks who don't have a conscience."

He grinned at her. "That's the other reason I'm sending you to Compton: punishment should put a little salve on that wounded conscience of yours."

"Who died and made you God?"

"I'm a self-made man," he said.

"Yeah, well, I'd rather drive a cab than spend the rest of my life working for you in Compton or anywhere else."

"Use your head, woman," Gleason growled. "We're not talking about the rest of *your* life. Just the rest of *mine*. I've got angina, I'm a hundred pounds overweight, and my cholesterol level is higher than the Dow. My doctor gives me five years tops, but I imagine he might be a little optimistic. If by then you've done the kind of job at Compton I think you're capable of, you'll be back here in a nanosecond."

She remembered her grandma telling her about school, how "smart learnin' is like carryin' a sword at your side, 'specially when dealin' with white folks who expect colored people, women in particular, to have heads full of cotton instead of brains."

That bit of advice had been given on a sunny afternoon on the front porch of Grandma Tyrell's little stucco cottage in

South Central L.A. a few decades before. The ashes from the Watts riots were still coating the bushes in the yard, and Nikki knew that she was going to need some weapon to get through life. Knowledge seemed like a good bet. So she ground her way through grade after grade, always excelling, always pushing herself.

Now here she was, facing the precise foe her grandmother had mentioned. She had the weapon: she was smart. Smart enough to know that what this devious and manipulative white man was saying carried a certain logic. She'd be around to dance on his tombstone.

"May not even be five years," she said. "They might vote you out, the next election."

"Not much chance of that," he said. "You'd be better off wishing me dead."

"No problem there," she said.

Tom Gleason's inevitable, fatal coronary had occurred near the end of her second Compton summer. The D.A. appointed by the Board of Supervisors, Seymour Kehoe, was apparently unimpressed by her superior record of convictions. Fortunately, he remained in office for only the final three months of Gleason's term. His defeat at the polls prompted her to apply to the man who beat him, Joseph Elijah Walden, the first African-American to be elected to that post.

Weeks went by without a response. She'd just about decided that Walden had filed and forgotten her letter when he phoned. He'd been on vacation out of the country, he explained, and had read her request only that morning. He'd be happy to meet with her to discuss the possibility of reassignment.

She arrived at their luncheon meeting feeling anxious and guarded. He put her at ease almost immediately by recounting an incident that had occurred during his European trip. He'd been trying to impress a woman he'd just met, but his less-than-perfect pronunciation had led to an embarrassing confusion between the French word for fish, *poisson*, and the American word *poison*. The self-deprecating vignette was only mildly amusing, but it served its purpose in relaxing Nikki to the point where she began to feel comfortable in his company.

Their resulting conversation had been wide-ranging, moving from the frivolous to the serious and back again. She'd left the restaurant quite impressed by the intelligent and charismatic district attorney. He must have been impressed, too, because one month later she was back on the job at the Criminal Courts Building.

Now she was in the thick of it, stepping eagerly from the elevator at the third floor of Parker Center, ready to begin her first assignment as the D.A.'s new special assistant.

≡ THREE ≡

The interrogation of the suspect, Jamal Deschamps, a twenty-five-year-old African-American apprehended near Madeleine Gray's body, was taking place in one of the small rooms off of the Robbery-Homicide bullpen.

A round, balding detective named Duke Wasson brought Nikki up to date while she poured herself a cup of black coffee. "Suspect's been in custody about three hours. He cried lawyer, and his low-rent mouth just got here 'bout a half hour ago. That's when the party started. Been goin' on ever since."

"Who's the attorney?" she asked.

"Bleed 'em and plead 'em Burchis," Wasson said, grinning. Elmon Burchis was well known for putting on an elaborate legal display until the actual date of trial, when he would invariably plead his clients guilty.

"High-level case like this," Nikki said, "maybe Mr. Burchis will change his game plan, get somebody a little stronger to come in with him."

"With what we got on Deschamps, they jus' gonna be walkin' the dog."

"What *have* we got?"

"Proximity, motive. Dead woman's property in his pocket. An', oh yeah, he's got banged-up knucks and his back looks like he's been wranglin' wildcats. Gotta be pieces of him under the vic's fingernails. Goodman and Morales are in there wearin' him down."

"Carlos Morales?"

"None other. Know him?"

"Uh huh," she said. "To know him is to love him."

"Then you see what Deschamps is up against," Wasson said.

"Who's Goodman?" she asked.

Wasson's expressive round face seemed momentarily puzzled. Then: "Oh, you musta met Morales back when he was partnered with Tony Black."

She nodded.

"Good guy, Blackie."

"Uh huh," she said, her mind recapturing the image of Tony seated on the floor of his apartment, Bird's huge head in his lap, both of them quietly listening to a cassette of John Coltrane and the amazing Johnny Hartman. She could hear the wistful strains of "Lush Life" . . .

"It's what fuels our fear," Wasson said. "Relaxin' off duty havin' a sam'ich an' some cranked-up punk-ass comes in wavin' a Heckler an' takes out half the tavern. Poor Tony didn't have a chance."

"I'd better get to work," she said.

"Be our guest," Wasson said. "Al'ays happy to cooperate with the D.A.'s office."

She took her coffee, and the memory of Tony Black, to a dreary room that hadn't changed much in three years. The same almost-orange wooden table and three matching straight-back chairs. The new addition was a puke-green leatherette couch that looked like it had last seen duty in a women's lounge where the women hadn't been too careful with their cigarettes. She stared at the furniture, but she was seeing Blackie's smile and humorous brown eyes.

"You okay, honey?"

The question came from a pale, skinny woman in jeans and a polo shirt sitting at the table, hands poised over a court stenographer's machine, looking at her with concern.

"Jacked as can be," Nikki replied.

The pale woman made a noise like "Hup," and her fingers began dancing over her machine's keyboard. She was wearing a cheap headset that was plugged into an ancient reel-to-reel tape recorder on the table, doing its job slowly and silently. With fingers flying, the steno moved her head to indicate a second set of earphones on the tabletop.

Nikki recalled how surprised and disappointed she'd been the first time she laid eyes on this room, when she'd learned that those cool, comfortable shadowy spaces with their one-way secret observation windows didn't exist outside of the movies. At least not in L.A. Maybe in New York, where they actually let the D.A.s participate in the interrogations. Here, you had to stand back and hope that the detectives asked the right questions. Which they did sometimes.

She placed her briefcase and coffee cup on the table, pulled over a chair, and picked up the headset. Satisfied that it was free from anything too communicable, she slipped it over her hair.

". . . the hell you think you kiddin', Ja-mal?" were the first words she heard. Morales sounded just as cocky and bullshit macho as always.

"Man, the Crazy Eights, they chased me into that alley. Like I said."

"Then how did the friggin' ring get in your pocket,

home-y?" Morales asked, giving the final word a nasty sarcastic twist.

"I resent that tone, detective." Elmon Burchis's overly dramatic delivery brought a smile to Nikki's face. She got her notepad from her briefcase, opened it, and slipped the pen from its leather holder.

"Excuse me, counselor," Morales said. "I din' mean to offend yo' altar boy client, who we all know is nuthin' but a fuckin' street rat."

"Sir, I am putting you on notice—"

"Everybody just calm down, now," came a new voice. Low. Resonant. Maybe a hint of the south. It must have belonged to Detective Goodman. "We're gonna be here long enough without the unnecessary rhetoric. Mr. Deschamps, I believe Detective Morales asked you about the object you had in your pocket."

"I tole you that already," Jamal Deschamps said. "I see this ring on her finger, looks like it worth some bills. So I take it. She already so dead she's stiff.

"Can't I go pee? My eyes got to be turning yellow. Lawyer man, don't I got the right to pee?"

"Indeed you do. I—"

"Okay, Mr. Deschamps," Goodman interrupted Burchis. "Detective Morales will escort you to the lavatory."

"You escort him, amigo," Morales drawled. "Up to me he could just piss in his pants. I'm sure it wouldn't be the first time."

"My God, you are a barbarian," Bleed 'em and plead 'em Burchis exclaimed.

Nikki removed the headset and walked to the door in time to see a tall, gaunt white man leading a smaller, much younger black man past the bullpen in the direction of the lavatories. The tall man was clean shaven, with longish, graying hair that stuck up in back as if he'd slept on it. Detective Edward Goodman.

As for the black man, she'd been expecting Jamal Deschamps to be dressed in bulky gangsta clothes, but he was wearing rumpled and dirty chino trousers and a maroon silk shirt with a rip at the right elbow. He looked a lot like the brothers who'd been in her law school classes.

Morales spotted her across the room and winked at her. A solid Chicano in his mid-forties, even in his boots he wasn't more than five feet eight, slightly shorter than she. He'd trimmed his Pancho Villa mustache since she'd last seen him. Aside from that, the years didn't seem to have changed him at all. Maybe obnoxious behavior kept you young. She'd have to try it sometime.

He strutted to Duke Wasson's desk, his thick torso shifting under his untucked pale blue short-sleeved shirt. He bent over the desk, his back to Nikki.

Wasson looked up, eyes shifting to her, then back to Morales. He mumbled something to the detective, who turned and ambled toward her. "Well, well," he said, "back from bad Compton country and already special assistant to our new D.A. You two must get along pretty good, huh?" He gave her a conspiratorial wink.

"Got something in your eye, Carlos?" she asked.

"Only your beauty," he said.

"I like what you did with the mustache," she said. "That and those high heels. And is that a rug you're wearing?"

"Ooohhh. Compton turned you mean, huh?"

"Mean? Little ole me?"

He cocked his head to one side and said, "It did do something to you, *chica*. An improvement, I think."

"We shall see."

"How you like our radio show so far?" he asked.

"I think you're ready for TV."

He smiled broadly, white teeth gleaming under the mustache. "Yeah. Us an' Maddie Gray. You ever watch her?"

"Once or twice."

"My wife was a big fan. Usually had it on at dinner. Maddie looked pretty fine, but she was a real ball buster. I never much cared for her."

"Maybe we should check *your* alibi."

"Now, Nikki, you know we got our killer. You prosecutin' this *pendejo?*"

She shrugged. Yesterday, she wouldn't have thought such a thing possible. But today . . . "That decision won't be made for a while," she said.

"Maddie had lots of fans. They gonna want our Jamal strung up by his *cojones.*"

"I think they stopped that particular form of justice a few years ago."

"Too bad. The mess he made of that woman, gas is too good for him."

"Assuming he did it," Nikki said.

"Yeah," Morales said, grinning. "Assumin' that."

≡ FOUR ≡

By seven A.M., when Nikki made her second call to D.A. Walden, several other facts had surfaced to strengthen the case against Deschamps. He'd previously been arrested for assaulting a young woman named Irma Childs. His day job, delivering and picking up mail for a production company in the San Fernando Valley, had taken him often to the studios where Madeleine Gray's series was taped.

Detective Morales eventually got Jamal to admit having met the deceased on the lot. He had, in fact, delivered scripts to her on at least two occasions that he could recall.

"She was a nice woman," he told the detectives. "Wacko, like all of 'em, but nice."

"All of whom?" Goodman asked.

"TV, movie people. All wacko."

"Wacko how?"

"You know. Kinda wired. Nervous, like."

"She gave people a hard time on her show," Goodman said. "Probably gave people she worked with a hard time, too."

"Not me, man. She was nice."

"Give you a big tip?" Morales asked.

"Tip? Hell, they never tip."

"But she was nice?"

"Yeah. Friendly."

"How friendly?" Morales asked. "Pet your pony for ya?"

"Jesus, man," Jamal said indignantly. "She smiled. That's all. Always real busy, but she took the time to smile."

"Maybe it was a special smile, huh?" Goodman asked.

"Naw. Just a smile."

"You're a good-looking young man," Goodman said. "Woman smiles at you, what do you think?"

"Lots of women smile at me," Jamal said. "That don't mean I'm gonna go beat 'em to death."

"What makes you think she was beaten to death?"

"I saw the way her body looked. I just assumed—"

"You were saying that lots of women smile at you, Jamal. But you don't beat 'em to death."

"Right. I mean, of course I don't."

"What made this one different?" Goodman asked.

"What? Huh?"

"Like you said," Morales pushed him, "the others you didn't beat to death. Just Maddie Gray."

"What? Shit, that's not what I said. I didn't beat anybody."

"Detectives—" Burchis began.

"Well, there's . . . wha's her name? Irma."

"You twisting everything. I didn't touch Madeleine Gray. Didn't touch her, understand? Didn't really know her. Didn't beat her. Sure as hell didn't kill her."

Nikki's steno roommate tapped her on the shoulder and waved good-bye. Her replacement was taller but otherwise the same—a drone doing her job in the hive.

In the interrogation room Morales once again took Jamal

through his whereabouts on the previous night, going hour by hour. Lawyer Burchis blustered that the questions had been asked and answered.

Nikki was yawning when the door to the room opened and a tall familiar figure limped in. He glared at her, nodded as if he'd achieved a goal he'd set for himself, and gestured for her to remove the headset. "You can go, Hill," Raymond Wise said. "I'm taking over."

Wise, who had retained his position as head deputy district attorney during two administrations after Tom Gleason's death, had reestablished their relationship her first day back from Compton. She'd bumped into him in the hall.

"Hi, Ray," she'd said. "Want to go grab a hot dog?"

"I never expected to see you here again," he had told her. "If Joe Walden had bothered to consult me about it, you wouldn't be here now."

"Kehoe asked you about me?"

"He did," Wise had said, "and, while I kept our filthy little secret, I could not in good conscience recommend a foolish and naive young woman who plainly didn't have what it takes to make the hard decisions."

She'd flashed him a wry smile. "Well, your man Kehoe is long gone and I'm back. And if you try fucking with this foolish and naive young woman, you're going to wind up limping a lot more than you do now."

The memory of that moment brought a smile to her lips as she looked up at Wise, standing before her in the drab room at Robbery-Homicide. "I'll take over now," he repeated. "You can go."

"Joe Walden wants me here," she said.

"What Joe wants," Wise replied sharply, "is for that dirtbag to be put away for the rest of his antisocial life. The only way that's going to happen is for you to hand over the earphones and let me start making my notes."

"I was given an assignment, Ray. If you want to hear what's going on in the interrogation room, I suggest—"

She was going to suggest that Wise try to talk Wasson into parting with another headset. But she was interrupted by the arrival of the district attorney.

He looked particularly formidable in a double-breasted dark blue suit that accentuated his broad shoulders. He raised a curious eyebrow at Wise and said, "Ray, what are you doing here?"

"Nikki's been at it for several hours," Wise replied almost sheepishly. "I thought I'd spell her. Let her get some of her own casework done."

"That was thoughtful of you," Walden said wryly. He turned to Nikki and asked, "Anything new?"

"Jamal Deschamps told the detectives that he's suffered from blackouts for a number of years. Possibly the result of drug use in his teens."

"A fugue-state defense?" Wise said, shaking his head. "That's pathetic enough to make my day. This'll be like catching fish in a bathtub."

Nikki was reminded of another seemingly absurd defense. She said, "There are a few . . . problem areas."

"Such as?" the D.A. asked.

"Deschamps is supposed to have brutally murdered one woman, dumped her body in a trash bin, then moved on to a nearby club where he proceeded to pick up another woman and have sex with her."

"Well, you know what Mick Jagger says," Wise smirked. "Some guys can't get no satisfaction."

"Mick say anything about why a man would do a dump job in an alley, then come back later and stick around for the cops to show up?"

"He returned for the ring," Wise said.

Nikki wondered how Wise had found out about the ring.

Had Walden already brought him up to speed? If so, why had her boss expressed surprise at finding him there? More likely Wise had his own private source in Homicide; one member of the good ol' boys' club helping out another. She supposed she could learn a trick or two from the man, if she could stand being around him for longer than a few minutes at a time.

"Then there's the anonymous caller who sent the police to the alley," she said. "Why didn't he leave a name?"

"Please," Wise said impatiently. "You live in that part of town, look out of the window and see a body, maybe you call nine-one-one. But you sure as hell don't give 'em your name, because in that neighborhood it doesn't pay to get mixed up with the cops."

"Call wasn't made from a private phone," Walden said. "It came from a pay phone at a service station about a mile away."

"Sure would be nice if the police could locate the caller," Nikki said. "Maybe he even saw who put the body in the Dumpster."

"The investigators are doing their best to find him," Walden said. "Meanwhile, if we're going to arraign Mr. Deschamps, we've only"—he consulted his wristwatch—"thirty-nine hours left. Opinions?"

"Is there any doubt?" Wise said. "Full court press."

"Nikki?" Walden asked.

She sighed. "He's what we got. But unless some really solid evidence turns up—hair, fiber, eyewitness—I wouldn't want to prosecute him."

"No chance of that," Wise said.

"You're forgetting, Ray, you're only the head deputy D.A.," Walden said. "If you'd like to make that kind of call, maybe you should think about challenging me next election. Until then I'll be the one deciding who prosecutes whom.

Now why don't we leave and let my new special assistant get back to work?"

Walden turned to her. "By the way, Meg's arranging an interview for you with the *L.A. Times.*" Meg Fisher was the office's public relations manager. "She'll let you know when." He smiled and added, "I like the bare leg look." Then he made his exit.

"Nice to know what it takes to get ahead," Wise said, looking at her legs.

Her first inclination was to tug down her skirt. But the hell with that. "I suppose this means you're not going to be wearing your socks tomorrow, huh, Ray?"

Wise grimaced and limped from the room. Nikki replaced the headset and went back to work.

FIVE

Detective Edward Goodman didn't much care for his partner, Carlos Morales, but he didn't dislike him enough to do anything about it. He figured that if he requested a new partner, he might just draw one he'd hate. Carlos was okay, so long as you didn't pay any attention to the bullshit that came out of his mouth all day long or you didn't try to buck him when he had his mind set on something.

Presently, Carlos's mind was set on building a case against Jamal Deschamps. This was fine with Goodman, because it would keep Carlos out of his gray hair while he looked into other possibilities. At the moment, his partner was rooting for clues at Deschamps's apartment, allowing Goodman to join his cohorts and the crime lab team as they searched for truth at Madeleine Gray's Laurel Canyon home. They had their job cut out for them. The building was a wanna-be mansion, a seven-thousand-square-foot, three-story collection of nooks and crannies perched high up along the canyon wall.

Goodman huffed and puffed up and down three sets of stairs and counted fourteen rooms, at least three of them offices. The largest office, at the rear of the ground floor, looked out on a slab of rock that surrounded a black-sand pool constructed to resemble a natural pond beneath a fake waterfall.

Maddie must have needed a map to get around the place, Goodman thought. Assuming she spent time there. He knew the kinds of hours TV people put in on the job. In the long ago, he'd been a technical assistant on a horseshit cop show, a thankless task since none of the information he provided was ever used. But it had helped send one of his kids—was it the one from his first marriage, or from his second, he could never remember—to college.

He paused at the threshold to a tiny study that the lab people had yet to invade. He was perfectly happy to wait for them to do their thing before he did his, but the messiness of the room intrigued him. Someone, possibly Maddie Gray but more likely her killer, had torn through it, opening drawers, scattering papers on the carpet, and yes, best of all, popping the lock on a filing cabinet. Definitely the killer.

Goodman squinted at the distant cabinet, hoping it wasn't just a trick of the light that the metal around the lock appeared buckled. He was about to enter the room for a closer look when Detective Gwen Harriman joined him, a lopsided grin on her suntanned face.

"Hey, pops," she said, "some pad, huh?"

Though he was approaching retirement age, Goodman was more amused than offended by the "pops" business. The previous year, when Harriman first joined Robbery-Homicide, they'd had a short romance. It had ended with him telling her to go out and find somebody her own age. Looking at her, with her red hair cut short now, curling around her sweet face, he was sorry she'd taken his advice. "The floor plans are a mite confusing," Goodman told her, "but this sure beats my little apartment all to hell."

"I sorta like your little apartment," Gwen said.

"At least you could tell right away if it was a primary crime scene," he said. The team had been going over the Gray house for nearly two hours without turning up enough evidence to indicate that its owner definitely had been murdered there.

"This room saw some action sure enough," Gwen said, scanning the study. "But no rough stuff. Furniture's too neat. Chairs are in place. No blood."

"It's a likely theft scene," Goodman said, moving toward the violated cabinet.

"Now, pops, you're old enough to know the techs haven't dusted in here yet."

"Never could resist a busted-open drawer," he said.

"Well, let me tempt you with something even more irresistible."

Goodman rewarded her with a suggestive Groucho Marx eyebrow wiggle.

"That's cute," she said. "Like Tom Selleck in the TV show about the private eye."

He sighed at the gap between their points of reference.

"Anyway, we got a room downstairs shows signs of a struggle. Wanna see?"

"Lead the way," he said.

The room was just off of a formal dining area. It was surprisingly bright, considering there was only one window and the walls were a deep dark green, broken by paintings of flowers in white frames. The polished wooden floor was bare. There were two stuffed chairs and a sofa, all covered with the same white material. A butler's table near the window contained various bottles of booze, a small ice chest, and an assortment of cocktail glasses. A middle-aged woman from the crime lab whose name he thought was Marcella sat on the wooden floor collecting scrapings.

"Blood drop," the woman told him. "More over there on that thing." She pointed to a metal sculpture, an orb, resting on the floor.

Goodman hunkered down and studied the brown smear on the orb's surface.

"Not much," the crime lab woman said. "But we're so good we don't need much."

"The vic's body says she really got knocked around," Gwen said. "I don't see it happening here. Floor's too unmarked."

Goodman studied the floor, which was surprisingly glossy and unscratched except for a worn area near the entryway. "I think we got a missing rug," he said.

Marcella agreed. "We'll check fibers, come up with a description for you."

"Body could've been rolled up in the rug," Gwen said.

"Maybe," Goodman said. "Yeah, I'm beginning to like this room."

"Was there a rug in that Dumpster with the body, Marcy?" Gwen asked.

"I didn't root through the garbage myself," the lab lady replied. "Seniority counts for something, thank God. But there wasn't any rug on the list."

Goodman looked at the table with the booze collection. "How many cocktail glasses come in a set?" he asked.

"Six, maybe eight," Gwen said.

"We got five here," he said, indicating the square faceted tumblers resting on their rims. "Water in an ice bucket suggests drinks were served. But no dirty glasses."

"They're not in the kitchen, either," Marcella informed them. She rose with a nearly polite grunt and placed her baggie with blood scrapings into a metal box. "Here's something," she said, plucking another baggie from the box. "Found it under the couch."

Gwen lifted the plastic container with latex-covered thumb and finger, studied it for a few seconds, then held it out for Goodman's inspection. He squinted at a dainty gold bracelet with a tiny gold charm in the shape of some kind of animal.

"That a dog?" he asked.

"A lion," Gwen said. "Dogs are the little critters, pops. Lions are . . . bigger."

"And the inscription on the bracelet's plate?" he asked.

Gwen squinted. "It says, 'Dear M. We'll always have Paris. Love, J.'"

"Hmmm. Find anything to suggest who 'J.' might be?" Goodman asked.

"Not yet," Gwen said. "We've still got about a dozen more rooms to check."

"Don't waste your time here, then."

"Right," she said, "but remember, Eddie."

"Remember what?"

"We'll always have the Buena Vista Motel in Hollywood."

≡ SIX ≡

One of several unpleasant consequences of Nikki being party to the destruction of evidence in the Mason Durant case had been an insomnia that neither prescription drugs nor whiskey was able to medicate successfully. As time passed, however, the feelings of frustration and guilt that were keeping her awake had begun to fade.

Then, nearly four months into her Compton exile, she had received her first phone call from Durant. "Do you accept the charge?" a disinterested operator had asked.

Nikki knew she should have said no. The man was a murderer and the world was better off with him behind bars. And yet . . .

"Hey, lady D.A." The voice was hoarse and phlegmy, barely resembling what she remembered of Durant's gruff bark. "How's it goin' in Compton? Guess you get to put away more brothers and sisters than Downtown, huh?"

"What can I do for you, Mr. Durant?"

His laugh ended in a racking cough. "I think you done enough, don't you?" he wheezed.

"What's the matter with you?" she asked, a bit more sympathetically than she'd intended.

"This place don't agree with me at all. Had a little trouble, uh, adjustin'. Lots of big white boys here in Fo'som. Got my arm broke. Some ribs. Restin' up from that in the hospital, I *con*tracted this lung problem."

He was a convict, she told herself, and cons, even the most brutish of them, had the uncanny ability to sense weakness and focus on it. "I'm sorry to hear you're not well," she said, back on guard now.

"Cough keeps the fags off my ass."

"Why'd you phone me, Mr. Durant?"

"Heard you put two more brothers in the joint yesterday. Was wonderin' why you do that, why you wanna play the white man's game like that."

"Those brothers killed a baby in a drive-by shooting, Mr. Durant. A little boy. He was a brother, too. Those two gangsta punks got what they deserve. They belong in the joint. Just like you."

"I don't belong here, lady."

"A jury believed otherwise." This conversation was useless, she thought. It was painful but it didn't qualify as penance. "I'm hanging up now."

"You took away my life," he croaked.

"Don't try calling me anymore," she said, her voice starting to shake. As she replaced the receiver, she could hear the echo of his wracking cough.

The sleepless nights started again. She considered sending Durant's public defender an anonymous note about the hot dog. Particles of it probably still rested in the pocket of the coat in the evidence box. The problem with that idea was that the public defender wasn't the sort of guy who'd put himself out because of an anonymous note. She doubted the judge would, either.

Maybe she *was* getting a little obsessive about the damned hot dog. It was not exactly a "Get Out of Jail" card. It didn't prove anything, really.

But what they'd done had been wrong, and she found herself unable to refuse Durant's subsequent calls. The best she could do was to keep her end of the conversation as chilly and noncommittal as possible. Durant didn't seem to mind. She listened to him, and that was apparently enough.

She heard from him five or six times that first year and less each year thereafter. But he never stopped calling.

"Yo, Nikki. It's me."

"I caught that right away, Mace," she said. She'd just stepped back into her office for a minute, to put on a pair of panty hose she'd purchased on the run from Deschamps's interrogation.

"You okay?" he asked with concern. "You sound a little stressed."

Lordy! Was he seeing a shrink? "This'll have to be a quickie, Mace," she said, tearing open the package. "I'm on my way out."

"Busy, huh?"

"Yep. Busy is the word I'd use," she said, holding the phone in place with her shoulder while she pulled on the hosiery. "What's on your mind?"

"I need some he'p with somethin'."

"What is it this time?"

"I been here at Fo'som more'n three years now," he said, "and I doan know as I can last much longer. See, the WABs got this idea I stuck this boy, Gerry P. On'y it wasn't me done it." Durant's persecution by inmate members of the

White Aryan Brotherhood had become a familiar tune on his turntable.

"Like I've said before," she told him, smoothing down her dress, "if somebody's on your case, I need a name."

"I can't do that," he said. "I don't flip off nobody, not even pale pig meat."

"Gotta go, Mace."

"Yeah, I didn't mean to hang you up with my problems," he said. "Guess you got more impo'tant things on yo' mind."

Why did she continue to accept his calls, she wondered? She knew that answer, of course. Still, her guilt was not overwhelming. "Good-bye, Mace," she said.

≡ SEVEN ≡

Jimmy Doyle had had a rough morning. The flight from D.C. had been crowded and noisy and the damned pilot had hit every air pocket the good Lord had placed in their way. Getting clear of LAX had been like treading through knee-high glue. The final indignity had been the bloody twisting and turning little streets and drives and avenues in the god-forsaken Pacific Palisades. None of them seemed to be on the bloody map he'd been given to the Willins home. By the time his rented Lexus finally entered the gate at 203 Bonham Road, the stocky man was about ready to explode.

When a guard seated in the wooden gatehouse requested his name, Doyle tried to keep his annoyance in check. It was time to lighten up, time to meet his new clients.

The guard was wearing some kind of space-age intercom headset. He muttered a few words into the mouthpiece, then gave Doyle the once-over before sending him down the drive. "Somebody'll be waiting for you at the main house, sir."

Somebody damn well better, Doyle thought. What he said was, "Thank you."

At the end of the drive, a young black man in a powder-blue jumpsuit hovered in front of the huge, yellow stone home. He was wearing the same sort of Star Wars headset as the gatehouse guard. Doyle supposed that with his ears full of plastic and rubber the man probably wasn't enjoying the crash of breakers and the squawks of seagulls in the near distance. He was too busy with other things, anyway, like directing visitors to park on a paved area just to the left of the house.

Doyle eased the Lexus into an empty slot near a gray Mercedes sedan with a vanity plate that read "HOBO1." That made it the property of Hobart Adler, the man who'd shaken his tree at six that morning, D.C. time.

Doyle stepped from the car, straightened to his full five feet nine, and suddenly was struck by the realization of what Southern California was all about. The sun. The cool, salt-tinted breeze wafting toward him from the Pacific Ocean. Colorful, fragrant flowers growing in abundance. And a house and property worth upwards of ten mil.

Just beyond the house he could see an emerald lawn and, past it, the ocean. On the lawn a chubby little black boy pedaled a tricycle furiously while a flustered young woman chased after him, shouting, "John Junior, you slow down, immediately." She pronounced it "ee-mee-jit-ly," which fit in with her dark blue dress with white collar, pale porcelain skin, and fine blond hair. A proper British nanny.

"Mr. Doyle?" The powder-blue jumpsuit was suddenly at his elbow. There was a bulge at the man's right side that Doyle assumed was a weapon of some sort. Maybe a space pistol. "Mr. and Mrs. Willins are waiting for you, sir." It was a polite enough command. "Go right into the house. Somebody will take you to the salon."

The "somebody" turned out to be Hobie Adler, the president of the Adler Agency, or TAA, as it was known in and out of Hollywood circles. His lithe, six-foot-three frame was neatly wrapped in a subdued dark blue British-cut suit that made him look more distinguished and wealthier than most of his clients, at least four of whom were among the twenty richest people in the world.

What always amazed Doyle about the superagent was that although he was handsomer than you and taller and certainly better dressed and more at ease with himself, and though he was as deadly as an anaconda, you still had to like the son of a gun. He shook hands with Doyle warmly. "I appreciate your coming here so quickly, Jimmy. I wouldn't have wanted to settle for second best. John and Dyana are eager to meet you."

As the agent led him down a marbled hall, Doyle's quick brown eyes evaluated the rich tapestries hanging from the walls. "The police have arrested someone," Hobie Adler said. "Good news, I think."

Doyle gave him a sideways glance. He couldn't remember having seen the elegant agent so much as frown before. This morning he was sweating a little.

John Willins and his wife were seated in the salon, an airy room with lots of window space and antiqued walls and a floor of pale green tiles that Doyle guessed had been imported from Spain or Italy. Willins was a big, strapping guy with black curly hair and a face so dark he appeared to be angry even when he wasn't. He was wearing black slacks and a black silk shirt buttoned to the neck. Doyle was guessing when he mentally placed his age in the mid-thirties. He could have been five years off either way. The fact that the man was CEO of a successful music company offered no hints. It didn't take a lifetime of work to make it to the top in that field. Not when your wife was Dyana Cooper.

She was not at all the waiflike creature he'd been expecting, possibly because he hadn't seen the action movie for which she'd literally changed the contours of her body, adding both muscle and a firm roundness. She was definitely something to see, a few steps beyond beautiful, with smooth chocolate skin and startling sea-green eyes. Not to mention cheekbones and ripe lips that had sold more silicone than Pamela Anderson's breasts. Her fitted jacket had a collar that reminded Doyle of those Nehrus that used to be hanging at the back of his closet. Her slacks were a matching peach color, snug enough to show off her supertoned body.

Willins rose from the soft, dark green sofa to shake Doyle's hand. Dyana Cooper nodded to him. Both were showing the tension they were under, but it looked better on her. Anything would. Even worry lines.

"Honey, maybe Mr. Doyle would like a drink," Dyana said.

"Not just yet," Doyle said.

Her gaze was unrelenting. He wondered what she thought she was seeing. Physically, he was nothing special. A thick-bodied guy with a round cherubic face under a full head of well-groomed hair. His clothes were expensive enough. He was clean cut. A redhead in D.C. whom he sometimes slept with once told him he had the pampered appearance of an overindulged child. He didn't mind that image. Mother love could be quite enjoyable. In any case, it wasn't his looks that impressed the paying clientele.

"We better get to it," he said.

"Hobie says you've . . . helped people out of this kind of difficulty before," Dyana said. Her voice was so mellifluous and sultry, she turned ordinary conversation into song.

"I've salvaged a reputation or two," Doyle said.

Willins said, "Hobie, maybe we're getting worked up over nothing. According to the TV, they picked up some young guy."

"Jimmy's here as . . . added insurance," Adler said. "Just in case."

Doyle lowered himself warily onto a soft plump chair near the woman. "Hobie has filled me in on the problem, but I'm not crazy about secondhand information. I'd appreciate it if you could indulge me by going through it all again."

Dyana told him of a meeting she'd had at Madeleine Gray's home on the day of the murder. Maddie had threatened her with blackmail. Angry words had ensued, followed by a brief struggle. Dyana had left, with Maddie shouting after her like a fishwife.

The tale took eleven minutes by Doyle's watch. When Dyana was finished, he asked several questions, ending with, "So, to your knowledge, the only thing connecting you to the late Maddie Gray is a Manila file containing material you'd just as soon not wind up on the cover of the *Globe*?"

She nodded.

Doyle turned to Adler.

"Being taken care of," the agent said.

"Good," Doyle said. "I'll have that drink now."

Dyana took their orders. She returned with an inch of bourbon in a glass for Doyle, a Perrier for Hobie, and iced teas for her husband and herself.

Doyle raised his glass. "To the State of California," he said. "May it find the poor bugger they've arrested guilty as charged."

"I'll drink to that," Hobie added.

Doyle downed his whiskey, enjoying the way it burned his throat, beating a molten path to his chest. He smiled at Dyana Cooper Willins and idly wondered what part of the story she had just told him, if any, had been the truth.

≡ EIGHT ≡

There was considerable LAPD activity in front of Madeleine Gray's canyon home as Nikki Hill drove up. She was showing her credentials to the cop at the door when Morales arrived behind her.

"Let this beautiful woman in," he told the cop. "She just happens to be the special assistant to our illustrious district attorney." This last was said with heavy sarcasm.

Inside the building, Nikki said, "You got some problem with me, Carlos?"

"No way, *chica*." He seemed genuinely surprised.

"Then what's with all the cutie-pie stuff at the door?"

"It's your boss I doan like."

"Why?"

He cocked his head to one side. "I got my reasons."

"Fine," she said, "but dislike him on your own time and keep me out of it."

He regarded her with such rare seriousness she almost didn't recognize him. Then he grinned and said, "Fair enough. Le's go see what my partner's been up to."

They found Goodman in some sort of trophy room. One wall was filled with certificates of honor and awards. On another hung glossy photos in uniform black frames—the late TV newswoman with a vast array of major celebrities and world figures, including the president and first lady, taken in the Oval Office.

"Maddie must have had a sense of humor," Goodman said. "She put this one of her and Clinton right next to this one of her and Saddam Hussein." He turned to Morales. "Find anything interesting at Jamal's?"

"*Nada,* 'cept the *pendejo* lives like a pig. Cock-a-roaches playin' soccer in the shower. Dirty sheets on the bed. Moldy dishes in the sink."

"But nothing in all that dirt to indicate he's our man," Goodman said.

"They still goin' over the place, but you don't need no microscope to know he didn't beat nobody up there lately."

Nikki was confused. "Wasn't the murder committed here?" she asked.

"That's one of the problems with body dumps," Goodman said. "Takes a while to find the crime scene. This may be the place, but the techs aren't sure."

Morales pointed to the wall of photos. "Jamal's got Maddie's photo on *his* wall, autographed."

"Well that's sort of interesting," Goodman said. "Any other pictures?"

Morales looked dejected. "The friggin' wall is just like that one. Covered with showbiz pictures. Mainly women, but some men. Even got a signed photo of Selena."

"We know he's not guilty of that one," Nikki said. One of the framed items on the awards wall caught her eye. Madeleine Penniston Gray had won a special certificate of honor for her work at the Florida State campus radio station fourteen years before. From Florida State to the White

House to the county morgue, in less than fifteen years. Fast traveling, but going nowhere.

"Mind giving me a quick tour of this place, detective?" she asked Goodman.

"If my knees can stand it," he said. "Lots of stairs."

He led them through the oddly designed building, waiting every now and then while Nikki poked around. He saved the possible murder scene for last. In the pale green room, he pointed out the metal orb that might have been the death weapon. Then he showed them the gold bracelet.

Nikki examined it, noted the inscription, and passed it to Morales, who studied it for a few seconds and said, with enthusiasm, "Aw'right. Now we got the *vago*."

"What're you talking about?" Goodman asked.

"Right here," Morales said, wiggling the baggie with the bracelet. "'M. We'll always have Paris. Love, J.' 'J' for Jamal."

Goodman shook his head. "That boy look like somebody who'd be rememberin' Paris with Maddie Gray?"

"Hey, amigo, we both been aroun' long enough to know these loco showbiz broads get a taste for somethin' different every now and then."

"Does Jamal strike you as the kind of dude who'd buy a little gold knickknack and put a tender inscription like that on it?" Goodman asked.

"You know, Eddie, you startin' to think too damn much. It's an old fart's habit—thinkin' 'stead of doin'."

Nikki saw color come to Goodman's cheeks. "Well, this old fart doesn't believe in tossing a guy in jail just to be doing something."

"Deschamps belongs in jail, damn it. You can't see he's dirty, you better get glasses. Whose side you on in this anyway?"

"Side?" Goodman suddenly shouted. "This isn't a fucking football game!"

The senior detective's outburst caught Nikki by surprise. She remembered the battles Blackie and Carlos would get into, but they were both aggressive and hot-tempered. Her initial assessment of Goodman was that he was the contemplative type. But Carlos could probably try the patience of a saint.

The two detectives seemed to be locked in a stare-down. "You boys decide to start whaling on each other," she said, "you might want to take it outside where you won't be bouncing against any evidence."

The older man blinked, shook his head, and casually leaned against a wall. He was breathing rather heavily.

"You okay?" she asked.

"Hey, amigo, you look shaky." Concern had swiftly replaced Morales's anger.

"I'm fine," Goodman told them.

Nikki wasn't so sure. The blood had drained from his face, leaving it an unhealthy pasty gray.

He straightened, assumed his usual laconic stance, and said, "Sorry about the show of temperament, Ms. Hill. Why don't we go consult with somebody who might give us some honest-to-God facts about the bracelet?"

"I doan mind facts," Morales said as they walked from the room. "Long as they doan get in the way."

They found Arthur Lydon, Madeleine Gray's assistant, in the office at the rear of the house, staring at the phone in frustration. He was a small man with short, spiked hair and a boyish face tanned so evenly it couldn't have been natural. He was wearing tight black pants, a lavender sailcloth shirt, and several tiny metal studs embedded in his right ear. "Ms. Hill," he said to her when Goodman had introduced them, "can you tell me how I might find out when Maddie's body . . ." He paused and almost gave in to tears. ". . . when she will be available for a farewell service?"

Nikki said, "The autopsy has been scheduled for tomorrow morning. You should be hearing from somebody after that."

"Mr. Lydon," Goodman said, "we'd like you to help us with something."

The small man's eyes brightened with curiosity as Goodman handed him the baggie containing the bracelet. "*Très* tacky," the young man said.

"Ever seen it before?" Morales asked.

Arthur Lydon shook his head from side to side emphatically.

"Check out the inscription," Nikki suggested.

Lyndon picked a pair of eyeglasses from his desk. They had round tortoiseshell frames that enhanced his schoolboy appearance. "Oh, I don't believe it," he said. "You're not going to tell me this trinket belongs . . . belonged to Maddie?"

"You never noticed her wearing it?" Nikki asked.

"Definitely not. Maddie rarely wore jewelry. Maybe a string of pearls."

"Nothing that she wore all the time?" Goodman asked. "Like a ring?"

"No way," the young man said. "She spent so much of her life in front of a camera. The folks out in TV land don't like their trusted newspeople to be too flashy. And this . . ." he handed the baggie back to Goodman. "This isn't her style at all."

"Was she in Paris recently?" the detective asked.

"Several months ago," Lydon said. "She had a week off and she up and went. Maddie was very . . . spontaneous."

"Go on a long trip like that by herself?" Nikki asked.

"To my knowledge," Lydon said, "and I made the arrangements."

"Couldn't she have changed your arrangements and taken somebody?" Goodman asked.

The young man considered the question and frowned. "Well, as I told you, she *was* spontaneous."

"She like black guys?" Morales asked.

Lydon looked quickly at Nikki and away. "Maddie was unattached," he said, pursing his lips. "She liked men. All kinds of men. Who doesn't?"

Morales rolled his eyes. Ignoring him, Goodman said, "There's a room upstairs, Mr. Lydon. Got a desk with a computer, filing cabinets."

Lydon nodded. "Maddie's private work space."

"Want to come up there with us for a minute?" Goodman asked.

Lydon's eyes dropped to the papers on his desk. "Sure. This can wait."

They trudged upstairs, gathering at the doorway to the cluttered room. "Wow," Nikki said. "I thought my place was a mess."

"Look around, Mr. Lydon," Goodman said. "Tell us what you think."

The young man took a step forward. "Let's just stay here," Goodman cautioned.

Lydon's eyes flitted around the room, finally setting on the filing cabinet. "It's a dreadful mess, of course," he said. "And someone's pried open that cabinet drawer."

"Not very professional," Nikki said.

"That's odd," Goodman said. "The lab folks haven't hit here yet, but I coulda sworn that drawer was open only a few inches last time I looked."

He moved past Lydon, putting on his thin rubber gloves. He used one finger to push the drawer open even more.

"What did your boss keep in there?" Nikki asked Lydon.

"I don't know. This room was off limits."

"Folders," Goodman said, staring into the drawer. "Folders labeled with nicknames. 'Hummer.' 'Jailbird.' 'Porn Pop.' 'Team Player.' 'Booty-Bandit.'"

He joined them, rolling off the gloves. "When was the last time you were up here, Mr. Lydon?"

"Yesterday afternoon. Maddie summoned me to say I could leave early."

"You usually work on Sunday?" Nikki asked.

Lyndon nodded. "Prepping for Monday's show."

"But yesterday she sent you home early," Goodman said.

"Every now and then she would do that. Other times she'd ask me to stay late. It evened out."

"Why do you suppose she wanted you out of here yesterday?" Nikki asked.

The young man shrugged.

"She expecting a boyfriend?" Nikki asked.

"I imagine she told me to go so I wouldn't know what she was expecting."

"Could she have done all this damage?" Goodman asked.

"Maddie had her paper-tossing moods. But she wouldn't pry open a cabinet."

"Did you know about those files?" Goodman asked.

"When I first started working here five years ago, Maddie made it very clear that this room was private. I was to enter it only at her request."

"Didn't that seem a little weird?" Nikki asked.

"Maddie's business was secrets. So, no, I didn't think it weird."

He paused, raised an eyebrow. "I wonder . . ." he began.

"What?" Goodman asked.

"I assume you think that whoever . . . killed Maddie also broke into the cabinet?"

"Possible," Goodman said.

Lydon took a step into the room. Goodman's shout to hold it stopped him in his tracks.

"Sorry, I just wanted to check . . . There's a hand-carved wooden box on the desk you might find interesting."

Goodman took a few steps to the desk. "Yeah. I see it." He lifted the box's lid very gingerly.

"Key to . . ." Goodman blinked and squinted. ". . . Bank of . . . Beverly."

"One afternoon," Lydon said, "while I was standing at her desk waiting for her to finish a phone call, I happened to notice that key in the box. She'd forgotten to close the top. She saw me looking at it and went a little postal. Slammed down the receiver. Called me a sneak and ordered me out of the house. Before I got to the front door, she'd calmed down. She felt so bad she gave me her tickets to a Liza concert. Maddie was like that. Big temper, big heart."

Before Lydon got too misty-eyed, Goodman said, "There's something else I want to show you."

They all moved downstairs to the room with the dark green walls. "Anything unusual?" the detective asked.

"The rug's gone," Lydon exclaimed. "Why would anyone want to steal that?"

"Why wouldn't they?" Goodman asked.

"It was just a modern Romanian copy of a Kashan. Couldn't have been worth more than six or seven hundred dollars."

"Could you describe it?" Nikki asked.

"Like I say, a copy of a Kashan. Basically red, with yellow and blue triangles around the edges."

"How big?"

"It was in the center of the room. I'd say eight feet by twelve."

"Anything like that in Deschamps's place?" Goodman asked Morales.

"Closest thing to a rug was the food on the guy's kitchen floor."

Nikki asked Lydon, "What was Maddie wearing yesterday when you left?"

The young man looked at Goodman. "I gave that information to the detective."

Goodman took out his notepad. "Red Dana Buchman suit," he read. "Silk paisley blouse, red and yellow. Black Ferragamo pumps." He looked at her as he put away the pad. "All missing."

"Lemme call over to Jamal's," Morales said. "See if they found the rug or the dame's clothes."

"Do it from the car," Goodman said. "We'd better get going if we expect to hit the bank before they lock up. You want to drive with us, Ms. Hill?"

"Nikki," she said. "Yes, I'd like to tag along."

"Fine. Thanks for your help, Mr. Lydon. I imagine we'll be talking with you again."

"Be still, my heart."

Nikki was surprised at how excited she felt at the opening of Maddie Gray's bank box. Sharing the small room with the two detectives and an officer of the bank, she was almost holding her breath as Goodman lifted the long metal lid.

"It's fulla cash," Morales said, staring down at rows of bound bills. He quickly began counting the packets. There were twenty, each containing twenty-five one-hundred-dollar bills. Under the last stack was . . . another key.

By the time they were finished, they'd opened four of the late Maddie Gray's bank boxes and amassed a total of two hundred thousand dollars.

"That must've been some rainy day Maddie was waiting

for," Nikki said. "I don't get it. She was making all she needed with her show. Why would she screw around with blackmail?"

"Control," Morales said. "Lady liked to make people squirm."

"I wonder why," Nikki said.

"Why? She was one mean bitch."

"What do you suppose made her that way?"

"Not our problem," Morales said. "We only care about who made her dead."

They replaced the boxes. Goodman told the bank manager that someone from the LAPD would be returning for the cash, which was now evidence.

As they drove away from the bank, Morales turned to Nikki on the backseat. "Like ole times, eh? 'Cept for Blackie not bein' here, of course."

"Except for that," she said. In truth, she didn't think it was like old times at all.

≡ NINE ≡

Jimmy Doyle spent the better part of the afternoon strolling around the Beverly Hills shopping area, checking out the boutiques along Rodeo and Little Santa Monica. He didn't have much else to do until the cops got their act together. If they ever did.

The sun was just starting to dip in the west when he was drawn to a shop called L'Homme Magnifique, where five years before he'd purchased a couple of three-hundred-dollar silk shirts that the buttons had fallen off of the first time he wore them. "So?" the salesman had told him when he'd complained. "Have your butler sew them back on."

Doyle was amused by that kind of brass. He looked around the small showroom hoping the snotty smart-ass was still there, but the only salesperson on the floor was a woman wearing dark green lipstick that made her pale face look like something out of a Stephen King novel. Good body though. He asked her if Harold was still working there.

"I don't know any Harold," she said, not giving it much thought. "There's a Raoul who does the books."

"It's not important," he said. "I'll just look around."

"That's what we're here for," she said, purposely glancing at her watch.

He was fingering a cashmere sport jacket so soft it felt like eiderdown when his beeper gave a chirp. The blinking number was Hobie Adler's private line. Doyle patted his breast pocket and realized he'd left the cellular in his hotel room.

"Got a phone I can use?" he asked the voluptuous ghost woman.

She looked at the little disk on her wrist again. "Sorry, closing time," she said.

They could be rude in other parts of the country, but no place beat Rodeo Drive for attitude. He loved it.

"Suppose I buy this?" He held up a silk tie—blue with tiny white dots.

She shrugged, then pointed a green fingernail at a telephone resting on a tiny counter at the rear of the store. "It only works for local calls," she said.

"This tie really two hundred and fifty bucks?" he asked.

"If that's how it's marked."

"Ring it up for me while I make my call," he said.

"Cash or card?"

"You get a lot of people plunking down two-fifty in cash for a tie?" he asked.

"You'd be surprised," she said, taking his card with a practiced boredom.

Hobie Adler seemed to be awaiting his call. He picked up on the first ring. "Me," Doyle said. "What's up?"

"I have the file," Adler said. One of his minions had removed the Manila folder containing Dyana Cooper's secrets from Madeleine Gray's home. "I don't suppose you want to see it."

"Not in this lifetime," Doyle said. "You take a peek?"

"No."

"Good. What you don't know for a fact won't lead to perjury. Give your shredder a workout."

"I gather there were a number of other files," Adler said.

"I hope your boy left 'em," Doyle said. "We want 'em found. We want the world to know the kind of broad she was."

Adler cleared his throat. "Ah, Jimmy, we've learned that the district attorney is probably going to charge the young man they arrested."

"Good source?"

"Hasn't failed me yet. So it seems unlikely we'll need your services. I just got off the phone with John Willins, who wanted me to convey how grateful he is for your help . . ."

There was a time when Doyle would have been happy to take the short-end money and head back to D.C. without having to lift a finger. But pickings had been slim for a while, and in truth, he'd been looking forward to the action as much as the cash.

"Is he thirty grand grateful, you think?" he asked.

Hobie Adler was silent for a beat, then replied, "That should be acceptable. John is sitting on top of a three-billion-dollar music empire."

"Then let's make it forty grand."

"Don't be greedy. We'll split the difference. You flying home tonight?"

Doyle looked at the saleswoman, who was shifting from one foot to the other impatiently. "Tomorrow morning, probably."

"Have dinner with me at Morton's."

"I'm a little tied up. Catch you next trip."

"You're not upset, are you, Jimmy?"

"Not at all," Doyle lied. "The situation changes, you know where to reach me."

He'd barely replaced the phone when the saleswoman was handing him a slip to sign. "Am I keeping you from something?" he wondered.

"Since you asked, yes."

"What?"

"I'm meeting a friend for drinks."

"Male friend or female?"

"Female."

"She as bitchy as you?"

She eyed him appraisingly. "At least," she said.

"What's your name?" he asked. When she hesitated, he said, "You've got mine on the card."

"Zorina," she said.

"Zorina what?"

"Just Zorina. You know. Like Madonna."

"You're not a dyke, are you?"

"A dyke?" She shook her head in mock disbelief at his naïveté. "You old guys are too much. You mean do I go down on women? Sometimes."

"But not exclusively?"

"No. Not exclusively."

"Good. Then why don't you and your friend have dinner with me tonight? At one of those hot new places where we can all smoke illegal Cuban cigars with our coffee."

"I don't eat red meat," she cautioned.

"Tell me something I can't guess," he said.

≡ Ten ≡

When Nikki returned home that night, Bird was waiting. It had been an exhilarating day, from Nikki's promotion to Jamal Deschamps's interrogation to the discovery of Madeleine Gray's secret cash boxes. All the Bouvier cared about was that it had been a long time since breakfast.

He yipped in delight at the sight of her, his nubby tail twitching like a pendulum as she bent to embrace him. "Sorry I'm late, baby," she said. "My hours are gonna get a little goofy from here on, but I won't forget to take care of my big boy."

When she stood up, she saw that he'd dragged his cedar-filled mattress into the otherwise bare living room. He marched to the lumpy, loud plaid object and plopped down on it proudly.

"Don't get too cozy in here," she told him. "Sooner or later I'm going to make it to the Furniture Mart. Then you and your bed get moved to the spare room at the back."

Bird gave her a skeptical look that suggested hell would

freeze over before she furnished the room. Then he growled that he was more than ready for dinner.

"Probably want a walk, too?" she asked.

He ate while she switched into her jogging gear. She selected a hot-pink outfit because it reflected automobile headlights. It almost glowed in the dark. By the time she'd double-knotted her shoes, snapped on her fanny pack, complete with Walkman, and downed a glass of water, Bird had finished his meal and was eagerly pacing the floor.

They'd gone about ten blocks when she heard her name on the Walkman. She'd been listening to one of the all-news stations, fully expecting more of the same Gray murder bulletins that had been broadcast during her drive home. A statement from the LAPD that an unnamed suspect was in custody, a sound bite from Arthur Lydon about what a caring boss Maddie had been, and several short eulogies from Hollywood celebrities who considered themselves to be "among her closest friends."

What the anchorman was saying now, however, was that "the district attorney's office has announced the appointment of deputy Nicolette Hill as Joseph Walden's special assistant. The career prosecutor's main assignment is to act as liaison between the district attorney and the LAPD Major Crimes unit working on the Madeleine Gray murder."

"So *that's* my main assignment, huh?" Nikki said. "Maybe if Joe Walden had let me know I might have been able to give that *Times* reporter at least one definite answer."

The big dog slowed his gait to look back at her.

"Don't mind me, Bird," she said. "Just talking to myself, like all the other crazies."

Two messages were waiting on her answering machine when she returned.

The first was from Loreen Battles. "Well, girl, you keeping secrets from me?" Though her best friend's raspy smoker's voice was no less harsh than a weed-whacker scraping the sidewalk, Nikki always found it extremely comforting. "Do I have to get my information about your new job from Channel Five?" Click. End of message.

The other call had been even more abrupt. A hang-up. No name. No comment. Nikki wondered if it might have been her father, though whatever gave her that idea she couldn't say. They hadn't spoken in over two years.

Loreen was at the beauty salon she owned and operated. Judging by the amount of noise coming through the phone, the place was jumping. It usually was until nine or ten at night. "Oh, it's you," Loreen said, pretending disinterest, "my suddenly famous friend who knew me when."

"I've been wanting to call you all day to tell you about the new job and everything. But I've really been on the run."

"I know," Loreen said. "I been watching the TV. Justice in L.A. has a new name. Nicolette Hill."

Nikki laughed. "I'm bad, huh?"

"You're badder than bad," Loreen said. "Pam Grier's got nothing on you."

Nikki carried the phone into the kitchen. While she searched the shelves for something that might pass for dinner, she filled her friend in on some of the day's highlights.

"What's the scoop on Maddie?" Loreen asked.

"Much as I love you, girlfriend, I can't get into that," Nikki said.

"Oh, Lord, the sister's goin' Hollywood on me."

"I knew you'd understand," Nikki said.

"Hell I do," Loreen said, only half joking. "You want to get some food tonight?"

Nikki peered into her nearly empty fridge. One solitary frozen fish dinner. "I'd love to," she said. "But I've got notes to type and I need some sleep. Been up since four."

"Fess up. You headin' out to Spago, right, with your new fast friends?"

"Hell, yeah. Then we might just jet off to Mah-zet-lan."

"I knew it. She's goin' Hollywood. Probably won't be able to make it to Juanita's tomorrow night, either."

Every month Nikki and the other women who constituted the Inglewood Money Mavens investment club met at one or another's home for drinks, dinner, gossip, and whatever news of their stocks and bonds the remaining time allowed. Nikki usually enjoyed the gatherings, but if Loreen didn't quite understand why she couldn't tell all about Madeleine Gray's murder, what would the rest of the Money Mavens think? That she was one stuck-up bitch.

Of course, they'd think that if she didn't go, too.

"I'll be there," Nikki said.

"Probably won't be as glam as a secret agent like yourself is used to."

"Girl, the day I outglam Juanita is the day fish stop swimming." Juanita Janes was a very theatrical actress, formerly of Broadway but for the last seven years a member of the cast of a popular soap opera, *The Power and the Passion.*

"Juanita's something all right," Loreen said. "Takes a special kind of woman to make a turban look like anything 'cept the result of a bad head wound."

"By the way, my title is Special Assistant," Nikki said, feigning annoyance, "not Secret Agent."

"'Scuse me," Loreen said, chuckling. "All your secrecy musta confused me."

≡ ELEVEN ≡

The morning was overcast and gloomy, a fitting backdrop for Nikki's arrival at the four-story building on Mission Road in downtown Los Angeles where the county autopsies were performed. A traffic snarl on the freeway had made her at least ten minutes late. That was only part of the reason for her anxiety, however. It was her first visit to the dreary facility.

She walked down a long hall, purposely keeping her eyes above the level of an incoming body bag. A confusion of people in a variety of uniforms moved swiftly around her. Nikki thought that if she worked there she'd keep on the run, too, to avoid having to think about the constant presence of death. By standing in his way, she got an orderly pushing an empty gurney to pause long enough to direct her to the elevators.

There, she waited beside a man smoking a cigar, its fumes adding to her general malaise. She was relieved when he took a car going up, but, descending alone to the second basement level, she longed for even his smokestack company.

She emerged from the elevator to face a sign on the wall reading "Autopsy Room." Her nostrils were assailed by a strange and powerful odor. Not a stench exactly. Something strong and . . . what? Malignant? She tried to find some category for it. A combination of Mr. Clean and collard greens? A mix of medicine and funk? It confused her senses and increased her apprehension. She remembered something Blackie had once told her about the way cops would soak their handkerchiefs in cologne before dropping in at the morgue. Good advice that came to mind too late.

She paused, poked in her handbag for perfume, breath spray, anything. Coming up empty, she gritted her teeth and prepared for the next sensory assault—the visual one. She told herself that if a wimp like Ray Wise could stand the sight of a body reduced to dead meat, blood, bone, and tripe, so could she. She made a silent prayer that her sensitive stomach would not betray her, clasped her leather briefcase close to her chest, and ventured forth. The words of the late, great King Pleasure never seemed more appropriate: "So afraid of where I'm going, so in love with where I've been."

A right turn introduced her to an amazing sight: a logjam of corpses on gurneys. She shivered. The chill she was feeling had more to do with emotion than air-conditioning. Head held high, she made her way through the corpses. Although she kept her eyes straight forward, her peripheral view took in the bodies. Male. Female. Fat. Thin. Black. White. Brown. Yellow. Stabbed. Shot. Beaten and bruised. Blood draining off in troughs along the sides of the gurneys.

She realized she was holding her breath. She paused, eyes on the ceiling, then continued on to the operating room.

The scene before her was worse than any nightmare she could have imagined. Surgeons in powder blue casually making "Y" incisions on corpses. Faces being pulled back. The top of one head being cut off, like opening a can of tuna. Brains being scooped out for analysis. Organs being removed, bagged, weighed, and labeled.

One of the masked men approached a body with an instrument resembling a bolt cutter. Nikki stood rooted to the floor, unable to look away as, with a crack as loud as a gunshot, he broke and lifted the breastplate of some hapless corpse.

Onward she moved, faster now. Passing organs being weighed. Blood being measured by a ladle. A brain being set aside for dissecting.

Nikki stopped at a table where a fleshy black woman was humming peacefully through her powder-blue mask while her latex-gloved fingers sewed up a long, gray male corpse with an instrument that looked like a thick crochet needle. "Excuse me," Nikki said to her.

The woman looked up from her work and nodded. "Minute," she said. She finished a stitch, and then, instead of merely setting the needle aside, she stuck it into the dead body's stomach as if it were a pincushion.

She yanked down her mask and said, "Now. How can I help you, sister?"

"The autopsy of Madeleine Gray?"

The woman gestured with a gloved hand. "Down that hall, the first door on your left. Dragon Lady's there, herself, so make sure you get suited up," she added, offering Nikki a wink as she adjusted her mask and withdrew her needle.

In the hall the prosecutor was struck by a wave of dizziness. She leaned against the wall and closed her eyes. *Damn you,* she cursed herself, *toughen up right now!*

It seemed to help. The wooziness passed and she entered the autopsy room, already crowded with powder blue people. In spite of their surgical masks she easily identified Ray Wise, Detectives Morales and Goodman, and the coroner, a bland, emotionless Asian-American named Ann Fugitsu, who stood back a pace, observing the pathologist and his assistants as they hovered over the remains of what had once been Madeleine Gray.

Nikki lifted a scrub suit from a hook near the door. One of the assistants got her a mask.

Dr. Fugitsu brought them up to speed in very little time. "It is our preliminary opinion that death was due to skull fracture causing injury to the brain," she stated without emotion. "There appears to have been a significant brutalizing of the body. Then a solid object, smooth rather than sharp, did the final job, cracking the back of the cranium."

Judging by physicochemical changes of the body and bodily fluids and the residual reactivity of muscles to electrical and chemical stimuli, she explained, they had narrowed the window of death to approximately three hours. "Between eight and eleven P.M. The body was, of course, in rigor when it was first examined in the alley."

The deceased had been legally inebriated. "Blood showed an alcohol content of point-one-four. There was some drug residue. Cocaine or some other coca derivative. We will send the usual sample to the forensic toxicologist. The vagina showed some irritation, and vaginal fluids were present but no semen was found."

"Meaning what?" Wise asked. "That she hadn't been schtupped?"

Dr. Fugitsu's normally unreadable face showed a flash of annoyance. "She apparently had been sexually stimulated prior to her murder. The stimulation did not go as far as orgasm. If she was with a man, he must have used a contraceptive, and one that left no traces of latex or lubricant."

Dr. Fugitsu noted that no foreign hair, pubic or otherwise, had been found on the body. "No flakes of skin, either," she said. "However, the fingernails on the victim's right hand yielded a small amount of blood and tissue. A slightly larger amount was recovered from under the left thumbnail."

Goodman asked about rug fibers.

"Numerous coarse fibers dyed mainly red and yellow were found on the skin and in the hair," the doctor said. "In addition, many other particles were clinging to the body, probably the result of the corpse's residence in the garbage bin."

While the coroner listed the various Dumpster contents found clinging to the corpse, Nikki's attention shifted to the doctor's assistants, who were busily photographing body samples and collecting fluids. Madeleine Gray's liver was thrown on a scale, then deposited into a plastic bag. Other organs were weighed and put in a larger bag that was closed and placed between the corpse's legs. The corpse was then cocooned in a material not unlike Saran Wrap. Finally, a rope was tied around the late Madeleine Gray's arms and shoulders. Why, Nikki couldn't imagine.

At the end of the ordeal the detectives put away their notebooks, and Wise, who'd filled several pages of a legal pad with his small, precise printing, clipped his pen to the pad. Nikki was startled to realize that her own pad was blank. She'd forgotten to take notes. She quickly zipped up her briefcase and hoped Wise hadn't noticed.

His interest was elsewhere. "When will we have the final results of your tests, doctor?" he asked.

"Two weeks," the coroner replied. "The DNA? You're talking more than a month."

"What about blood type?"

"I could have something on that for you today," she said.

Wise told her that would be lovely. Then he turned to Nikki. "Meeting in Joe's office in half an hour," he said. "Don't be late."

= TWELVE =

N ikki was impressed by Joe Walden's apparent calm.
He had less than an hour to decide if he should formally accuse Jamal Deschamps of murder or set him free. Still, he
was leaning back in his chair, chilling out while Wise relayed the results of the autopsy. When the head deputy finished, Walden sighed and focused on his spotless desktop.
Except for the fingers of his right hand doing a little dance
on the arm of his chair, he might have been a man with nothing of consequence on his mind.

Nikki, on the other hand, felt restless and uneasy, as if she
were several cups of coffee over her limit. The morgue experience had left its mark on her, its peculiar, funky smell
still clogging her nostrils. Then, the article about her in the
morning *L.A. Times,* which was waiting on her desk when
she arrived, added its own jolt of anxiety. Not only had it
carried the erroneous information that she was the deputy
"overseeing" the Gray investigation, it referenced the infa-
mous Weenie Defense Murder Trial, noting that "Hill refuses to discuss either the trial or why she chose to spend the

next few years out of the fast lane, serving in the Compton courts."

Just as vexing, the article mentioned her father, William Hill, citing his long and distinguished career as a member of the LAPD. Nikki had carefully stonewalled questions about her personal life and, much to the dismay of Press Relations Deputy Meg Fisher, had cut the interview short when the reporter had grown too insistent in probing into her upbringing. She had also turned down requests for interviews long or short from, according to Meg, twenty-six legitimate news outlets. Of course, to Meg, the *Globe* was a legitimate news outlet.

Ray Wise, perched beside her on an uncomfortable gray leather chair that was a twin of hers, cleared his throat suddenly. The noise seemed to shake Walden from his reverie. "I'm surprised more of the killer's flesh wasn't recovered," the D.A. said. "Judging by all the scratches on Deschamps's back, I was expecting there to be enough skin under the victim's fingernails to make a small boy."

"Deschamps says it was the other broad who tore him up," Wise said. "So maybe he wasn't lying about that. Anyway, there was enough for Fugitsu to work with. She said she'll have a blood type for us today."

Walden consulted his watch. "Any particular time today?"

Wise shook his head.

"Take us through the crime, Ray."

Wise plucked a yellow legal pad from a briefcase beside his chair. He flipped a few note-filled pages and began. "Sometime between seven and ten P.M. Deschamps and the deceased were at her place, probably playing some sort of sex game. There were booze and drugs, according to Fugitsu. But no semen was found in the body. So maybe Maddie tells the guy no and this pisses him off. The party gets rough. He belts her around, just like he's belted other women in the past. She doesn't like it, gives him some of it back and that pisses him off even more. He picks up something handy and uses it to crack her skull."

Wise's scenario was raising a number of questions in Nikki's mind, but she knew better than to interrupt him. Instead, she made notes and kept quiet.

"So there's Deschamps with a dead woman on his hands. In the woman's house. Still, he doesn't panic. It's dark outside. The house is secluded. He wraps Gray's naked tokus in a rug and drags it out to his car. He wants to dump the body ASAP, but he's afraid to take the chance of somebody seeing him. It's unfamiliar territory to him. So he drives down to an area he knows, South Central, where, even if he's seen, there's less chance anybody's going to report it.

"After he unloads the body, he feels wired, excited. He goes to a bar, picks up a bimbo," Wise consulted his notes, "one Dorothea Downs. They screw until around two A.M. when her roommate shows up and Deschamps takes a walk.

"That's when he remembers the ring on the dead woman's finger. A bauble like that's worth a few bucks. So he goes back to the alley. And gets nabbed."

Walden nodded, then turned to Nikki. "Comments?"

Her mind started to compose a diplomatic response, but Wise hated her guts anyway. So, the hell with diplomacy. "What makes you think the murder took place at her house, Ray?" she asked. "The police still aren't sure where it happened."

"Depends on who you talk to, sweetie," he replied. "The house is where they found the likely weapon. You know, the hunk of metal sculpture with blood on it. There's a missing rug Deschamps must've used to wrap up the body for delivery. And, there's the broken lock on the vic's office cabinet.

That might be considered a little clue, too, that the murder took place on the premises."

"What do you suppose happened to the clothes she was wearing?" she asked.

"Relevance?" Wise inquired.

"If she and Deschamps were engaged in sex play that turned deadly and if she wound up naked in an alley, wouldn't her clothes be in a pile near the murder scene?"

Walden gave her a smile of confidence and turned to Wise. The prosecutor shrugged his bony shoulders. "Maybe Des-champs folded them up and put 'em on a shelf."

"The clothes she was last seen wearing are missing. Shoes, too."

"So Deschamps dumped 'em in another alley."

"Why?" Nikki asked. "If he killed the woman in her own home, why not just leave the clothes there?"

Walden's head deputy looked at him pleadingly. "Can't we stop with this bullshit? In seventeen years on this job, I've yet to try one case where everything made perfect sense. As anybody with any experience knows, murderers don't behave rationally. So he took her clothes. Why? I don't give a shit. Maybe some of his blood got on them. Maybe he likes going in drag. They're missing. If they turn up, fine. If they don't, too bad."

Walden asked, "Anything else, Nikki?"

"Ray, you say he dragged the body to his car. What car? According to Deschamps, and the DMV, he has no car."

"That's not quite true," Wise said. "He doesn't own a car, but he's been using one. A Buick Regal, two decades old, registered to George Penn, Deschamps's uncle. It was found this morning near the bar where Deschamps picked up the Downs woman. Lab's going over it now."

Nikki mentally chided herself for not keeping on top of every aspect of the investigation. She should have known about the car. Well, she still had one more card to play. "About the busted file cabinet in Maddie Gray's office," she said. "According to Detective Goodman it's filled with blackmail material."

"Oh, for God's sake," Wise said. "Let's not go off on some wild tangent. Jamal busted open a locked drawer because he thought there was money inside. He found only Maddie's files, which he left in place."

"The killer ignored a box full of jewelry in her bedroom," Nikki said. "Ignored an expensive wristwatch resting on the side of her bath. Ignored a small cash box containing several hundred dollars for office expenses that was on her desk. And he pried open a metal cabinet in the hope there was money inside? Doesn't it seem more logical that the killer was looking for something specific—a folder full of information that Maddie Gray was using to blackmail him?"

"Ray?" Walden asked. He had an amused smile on his face that Nikki found irritating. He was enjoying the Hill-Wise battle a little too much for her taste.

"This is all unnecessary speculation," Wise said. "We don't know who ripped open the cabinet drawer or why. It may not have even been the killer. As for Madeleine Gray being a blackmailer, she made her money from gossip. That's what she did every night on TV, spill the beans on a bunch of celebrities. Naturally, she had a cabinet full of nasty secrets. Where's the blackmail?"

"I was with Detectives Goodman and Morales when they opened her bank boxes filled with cash," Nikki said. "Two hundred thousand dollars. What does that tell you?"

"It sure as hell doesn't tell me we've got the wrong man," Wise said. "Not when our boy was apprehended in the alley just ten feet from his victim with her frigging ring in his pants pocket."

"Why would he risk going back to the body to take her

ring, after leaving all the other jewelry and money at her house?" Nikki asked.

"Because he's an asshole," Wise almost shouted. "Read my lips: Murderers usually don't make sense. It's also possible he didn't see the other stuff."

Nikki was formulating a reply when the phone rang.

Walden scooped it up, listened for a beat, and then crooned a reply that was not quite audible from across the desk. Obviously puzzled, he replaced the receiver. "Dr. Fugitsu's office," he said. "The blood type from under Gray's thumbnail is O-positive, same as Deschamps's."

"All right!" Wise exclaimed.

"The other samples, however, from the fingernails, are AB."

"So she scratched somebody else that morning, or the day before. Maybe somebody she bumped into. We still have Deschamps's type under her thumbnail."

"You're just gonna ignore the other tissue?" Nikki asked.

"Why not? It has no bearing on our case. We've got a type O-pos that does."

"It's the most common type," Nikki said. "The presence of the AB is a problem and we'll need something more conclusive on the O. In four weeks, we'll have the irrefutable DNA results."

"Sure," Wise said, his voice dripping with sarcasm. "We can let Deschamps go home now. He'll just hang around his apartment for several weeks, waiting for us to make sure he killed the Gray woman. Then all we'll have to do is send somebody out to pick him up. Maybe Nikki can go."

She ignored him and concentrated on Walden. "If Madeleine Gray was a blackmailer, Durant is probably not our killer," she said.

"Durant?" Walden asked.

"I'm sorry. Deschamps," she corrected herself. Wise was

staring at her, frowning. She turned back to Walden, determined to move past the gaff. "Couldn't we at least contact some of the people in those files and find out if she's been bleeding them?"

Walden considered it for a few beats, then said, "We'd wind up terrorizing and/or infuriating several extremely important and influential people."

"And," Wise added, "Deschamps's attorney would be very happy to point out to a jury that we were so uncertain of his guilt we initiated a whole new area of investigation."

"I am forced to agree," Walden said. "Deschamps is all yours, Ray. Murder one. Special circumstances. Start the arraignment process." His eyes shifted to Nikki. "Thanks for your input."

She knew it was silly to take the D.A.'s decision as a personal defeat, but she couldn't help herself. Walden must have picked up on her mood, because he added, "If I didn't make it clear before, Ray, as my special assistant, Nikki will be part of your team."

Wise looked as if his boss had just slapped him across the face. "That's not going to work. She doesn't even believe in the case."

"Good. Convince her and you should have no trouble with an impartial jury."

"Jesus, Joe—" Wise began.

"The subject's closed," Walden cut him off. "Keep her fully up to date."

Wise replied with a curt nod. He glared at Nikki as he left the room.

"It's important that we know precisely what they're up to at Major Crimes," Walden said to Nikki. "I suggest you develop some contacts over there. But I caution you: Don't be too candid with them about our progress."

"No?"

"I don't trust their security," Walden said. "Although Lieutenant Corben runs a very effective operation, all it takes is one rotten apple."

"Any particular bad apple in mind?" Nikki asked.

"If I did, I'd let Corben know," he said. "Just use discretion."

"I will," she said.

When she remained seated, he asked, "Something else?"

"This sudden publicity," she said. "I'm not comfortable with it."

"I thought you'd be pleased."

"The article in the paper this morning made it sound like I was in charge of the Gray case."

"We provide journalists with the correct information," he said. "What they do with it . . . But I'll tell Meg to clarify your duties in the future."

"I just want people to get it right that Ray will be the one bringing Jamal Deschamps to trial, not me," she said.

"Point noted," he said.

Wise was waiting for her at his office door. "Would you please come in." It was more an order than a request.

She entered, her wariness increasing when he closed the door. "Let's get this straight at the jump," he said, almost whispering. "I don't know what's going on with you and Walden. Maybe it's because you're black, maybe you're sucking his dick. Christ, maybe he even thinks you can do the job. I don't know and I don't care. All I care about is putting Jamal Deschamps where he belongs. You try to get between me and that, I'll knock you down and kick you out of the way. Am I making myself clear?"

"You were clear the first day I laid eyes on you," she said, seething. "Cellophane."

"Fine. Then I suggest you do two things. First, get Mason

frigging Durant out of your head. That's a closed book neither of us wants opened. Then go on about your business, whatever the hell that is. And I'll get to mine."

"You seem to be forgetting something, Ray," she said. "From this point on, your business is mine."

THIRTEEN

≡ THIRTEEN ≡

Jamal Deschamps hadn't spent much time behind bars. A misunderstanding in a club had led to an overnight in the tank down at the glass house, Parker Center Jail. And there'd been the four days he'd put in at the old Hall of Justice Jail on West Temple Street before Irma Childs calmed down and dropped her assault charges. Still, he felt experienced enough to realize that, as long as you were stuck sitting on your raggedy ass in a jail cell, his setup at the Bauchet Street lockup wasn't so bad. As other high-profile defendants like the Menendez boys and O. J. Simpson had discovered, custody status "keepaway" K-Ten provided all sorts of special amenities, the most notable being that you didn't have to mix with the sort of lowlifes that make up the general jail population.

Jamal was resting on his comfortable bunk, staring at the clean, off-white ceiling and trying not to think too much about the immediate future, when a sheriff's deputy arrived to tell him he had a visitor named Jesse Fallon.

More than a little suspicious, Jamal asked who the fuck this Fallon dude might be.

"Says he's your lawyer," the deputy replied.

"Yeah? Well, that don't make it so."

"Want him to go?"

"No. Let's see what he has to say."

The man who entered his cell was about the same age as his real lawyer, Elmon Burchis, somewhere in his sixties, but other than that he was about as different as he could be. He was big and black, with eyes so pale blue they were sorta spooky. And he was completely at ease, like he'd popped a dozen chill pills at lunch. He shifted a polished, black leather briefcase to his left hand and extended his right. "My name's Jesse Fallon, Mr. Deschamps."

When his offered hand was ignored, he used it to indicate a metal stool that was anchored to the wall. "Mind if I sit?" he asked.

"You got a card with your name on it?"

Fallon plucked a thin oxblood card case from his pocket and removed a small white rectangle from it that he passed to Jamal.

It read "Jesse K. Fallon, Attorney-at-Law." Under that was the name and address of a firm, Jastrum, Park, Wells, that meant nothing to the young man. He slipped the card into his pocket and turned his attention to Fallon. He was intrigued by the lawyer's head. It was a cueball, very round, mainly bald, though a fine frizz of white circled the area above his ears. Some baldies had heads that shined like they'd been polished, but his looked like it had been buffed. It was as dry as dusting powder. Jamal wondered what it would take to make him sweat. Hell of a lot, he figured.

"Park it, if you want," Jamal said, sitting on the edge of his cot. He was curious about Fallon, wanted to hear the big man's pitch. But it was never smart to let the other guy know what was going on in your head. He watched Fallon unbutton the coat of his dark gray suit, caught a glimpse of yellow suspenders and a little extra padding in the gut area.

"They treating you well?" Fallon asked, as though he really wanted to know.

"Room service's a little slow," Jamal said.

"Then we ought to see about getting you out of here." The lawyer placed his briefcase on his knees and snapped open the twin locks.

"That alligator skin?" Jamal asked.

"Actually, it is," Fallon said, mildly surprised.

"Worked a couple months at a tannery," Jamal said. "That much gator must've set you back some serious bones."

"It was a Father's Day present from my daughter."

Well, fuck, Jamal thought. "What's the deal, Mr. Big Coin Brother? You're not my lawyer. Where's Burchis?"

If Fallon was offended by Jamal's tone, he gave no evidence of it. "Mr. Burchis is a very good lawyer for a public defender. Your situation may be a little beyond his capabilities."

"Not beyond yours, huh?"

"Hopefully not."

Jamal didn't particularly like the arrogant old turkey, but he was impressed by him. "I got no money," he said.

"Not a problem," Fallon replied. "Jastrum, Park, Wells can afford to waive a fee every now and then."

Jamal had never heard of anybody doing anything for anybody for nothing. "Why would Jastrum, Whatever want to do that?"

"To keep me happy," Fallon said.

"You mean that much to 'em, how come your name's missing from their lineup?"

"There are other perks besides partnership," Fallon said.

Damn but the guy was an iceman. "So it's gonna make you happy to defend me?"

"Only if we win," Fallon said.

"I didn't kill Maddie Gray."

"That's nice to hear, Mr. Deschamps," Fallon said. "But not quite as important as other things I need to know."

"Like what?"

"Like how your skin got under the dead woman's fingernails."

"No way," Jamal said, leaning forward, tense as a bedspring.

"Good," Fallon said. "Then the traces they found aren't yours and the DNA will set you free."

Jamal frowned and looked down at his hand. He ran a finger over a raised scab on his palm. "Well, this thing did happen when I was trying to, uh, get her ring off."

"What ring is that?" Fallon asked, his eyes losing some of their sparkle.

"When I found her, dead like that. There was this ring on her finger."

"I see. They discovered the ring in your possession?"

Jamal gave an imperceptible nod.

"All right," Fallon said. "You were trying to remove her ring."

"I cut myself on her thumbnail. I mean, she was a long time dead, but I still cut myself."

"On her thumbnail."

"Yeah."

"What about her fingernails?" Fallon asked.

"She got somebody's skin under her fingernails, it don't belong to Jamal Deschamps."

Fallon smiled. "Good answer," he said.

"Truth," Jamal insisted. "What else you need to know?"

"Can't think of a thing right now," Fallon told him, clicking the alligator briefcase shut and getting to his feet. "When I do, I'll be back."

"You know where to find me."

≡ FOURTEEN ≡

That night, Nikki raced home to feed Bird before rushing off to the meeting of the Inglewood Money Mavens. Instead of bounding through the specially hinged panel in the back door as soon as she entered the house, the big dog remained outside, staring at the darkened graveyard down the hill, pretending to ignore her.

Even when she placed his brimming dish on the rear patio, he continued his tombstone vigil. She hunkered down beside him, scratching his neck. "Your food's gonna taste better than any ole bones you could dig up down there," she said.

He turned his big head and looked at her. In the moonlight, it seemed to her that he lifted a disdainful eyebrow. "Okay, so I'm late again," she said. "Worse, I've got to go right out. I'm gonna make it up to you, I swear."

With some reluctance, the dog stood and strolled to his food. Along the way, he paused beside a particularly large mound of his waste matter, staring back at her.

Grumbling, she located the long-handled scooper resting

against the side of the house. Bird waited until she began the cleanup before flopping down to dine.

"You guilt-tripping, smart-ass hound," Nikki said. "This is the thanks I get for not having you neutered."

Bird's eyes went to her for a brief moment. Then, with what might have been a sarcastic chuckle, he returned to his food.

Juanita Janes's apartment was just minutes to the west of Nikki's home, on the top floor of an elegant building in Playa Del Rey. Loreen greeted her at the door with a glass of wine and extended cheek. She was a short, compact, very dark woman. Her face, with its sharp features, active eyes, and long, thin nose, resembled a woodland fox. Her most memorable feature was her dark, lustrous, softly curly hair, a testament to her mother, Rose, who until her death had been a popular hairstylist and owner of the salon that now bore the slightly awkward name of Loreen's The Rose Beauty Palace.

"Juanita's in the kitchen trying to calm Sister Mumphrey down," Loreen said.

"Sister's here?" Nikki asked with some annoyance. She'd never liked the officious woman who'd long ago forgotten that her nickname had no official religious connotation. "When did we vote her into the Mavens?"

"She's not a member," Loreen said, "and won't be until I'm dead and buried. She came with some complaint about Acacia."

"Juanita's daughter? What is she, ten or eleven?"

"Sixteen, honey. And a handful. Sister saw her over at Fox Hills Mall smoking. Weed, Sister says."

"Sister wouldn't know weed if it was growing up her leg," Nikki said.

"Wouldn't surprise me if she had real weeds growin' up

there," Loreen said. "Anyway, she told Acacia to stop smoking and Acacia told her to go fuck herself and so Sister ran over here to carry on in front of Juanita."

"Who's that out there with you, Loreen?" someone called from inside.

"Guess who was the main topic of conversation before Sister showed up?" Loreen whispered to Nikki.

"Probably not Acacia, huh?" Nikki said, entering with Loreen.

A month ago, the women in the room would barely have paused in their chat to wave or embrace her. Now, all conversation ended and almost one by one they nodded their welcome in a strangely formal manner that both embarrassed and annoyed her.

Victoria Allard, a tall, thin woman with the looks and grace of a supermodel, approached and handed her a folded section from the morning's *L.A. Times.* "Wonderful article," she crooned, "and you look so exquisitely dressed in the picture." Since her divorce, Victoria had been making ends meet by selling designer clothes and shoes from her home at well below retail prices.

"Couldn't have done it without you, girl," Nikki said, accepting a glass of wine from one of the other Mavens.

Angie Arnold, a short, voluptuous woman, had been stretching her purple tights bending over the CD player, busily changing Juanita's music selections from Gershwin and Porter to Missy "Misdemeanor" Elliott and Young Bleed. She suddenly spotted the newcomer, straightened, jerked her tiny tank top over her large breasts, and let out a squeal of delight. "Hey, Nikki! Girl," she shouted, "you blowin' up all over the TV."

With that, the formality swiftly drifted away like a bad idea and they were all asking her about the new promotion and what the handsome and eligible Joseph Walden was really like, and, of course, what the inside story was on the Madeleine Gray murder.

She played up the promotion, making it sound almost as significant as had the newspaper article (which called it a blow against both racism and sexism in public office). She played down her connection to the Gray investigation. She also played down the sex appeal of Joseph Walden.

"Man's my boss," she said.

"Bad idea to mess with your boss," Christine Martin, a slightly plump, smartly dressed assistant to an advertising executive, agreed.

"Not if you do it right," Angie countered. She was a dental hygienist whose relationship with her employer had lasted longer than most marriages. "But enough about that. What I want to know, Nikki, is did that brother in jail really off the TV bitch?"

Nikki was almost as annoyed by the word "bitch" as if Madeleine Gray had been a friend of hers. "You know her well enough to call her a bitch, Angie?" she asked.

"Saw her once at a party at the St. James," Angie said. "She was layin' it out for every man in the room, from the host, some political asshole or other, to the guy bussin' drinks. Black, brown, yellow, white. Didn't matter to her. When it came to dick, Maddie was a equal opportunity fuck. Never know it though, all these so-called celebrities sayin' all these nice things about her on the tube, now she's dead. I 'magine she and the brother you got in the slams were bumpin' heavy?"

"I just can't talk about it," Nikki said.

"Oh, come on," Christine Martin pleaded. "Just one tiny little secret?"

Nikki was saved from another negative reply by Sister Mumphrey, all three hundred pounds of her, barreling into the room, proclaiming, "That little girl's got a date with Satan, Juanita. You better do something and do it quick."

Their hostess, elegant as always, in a pale purple gown, looked nonetheless dismayed. "I'll have a talk with her, Sister," she said. "Thanks for your concern."

Nikki and Loreen exchanged glances. Loreen winked and said, "Sister, you want to bless this gathering before you leave?"

The fat woman's head spun toward her. "Well, Loreen Battles, I may not be empowered by the good Lord to bless, but I am a religious woman and proud to say it aloud, no matter how sinful the atmosphere."

"This atmosphere's sinful?" Christine Martin asked angrily.

"I see people drinking spirits," Sister Mumphrey said. "And Evangeline Arnold's top is so small her tits are falling out. And—"

"Sister, I really do want to thank you for coming by," Juanita said, interrupting the uninvited guest's critical flow. She took the woman's balloonlike hand, intending to lead her out. Only Sister wasn't quite ready to leave.

"Money is no substitute for the rewards of heaven," she informed the Mavens. Then she spied Nikki. "Well, Nicolette Hill. I been hearin' all about you, girl."

"Nikki's been on the TV more today," Juanita said, "than I'll be on all week."

"Not from the TV," Sister said. "I don't waste my time watching TV. No, I been hearing about Nicolette from her daddy."

Nikki stared at the fat woman, wondering where in the world she and her father might have gotten together. As if tuned in to her thoughts, Sister said, "Tricia and I have got real friendly thanks to our church work." Tricia was Nikki's stepmother, the main reason she wound up being raised by Grandma Tyrell.

"You and Tricia," Nikki said. "Don't that figure."

"A fine woman. A real Christian. Your daddy's a fine man, too. You ought to visit them more often. They'd love to see you, I'm sure."

"Sister," Nikki said, trying to keep her anger under control, "you don't know anything about it."

"I know some of us feels so high and mighty they forgets their family."

"I think Juanita's daughter got it right, Sister," Nikki said. "You *should* go fuck yourself."

There was a moment of silence as Sister's mouth dropped. Then Loreen let out a boisterous laugh and the whole room joined in.

Except for Sister, of course, who stormed from the apartment.

"I thought she'd never leave," Nikki said.

"If I'd known that's all it took," Loreen said, "I'd have told her to go fuck herself thirty minutes ago."

Dinner was buffet-style.

Nikki was seated on the sofa beside Angie Arnold. Esther Douglas, a real estate agent, occupied an overstuffed chair to their right.

"Imagine that uptight Sister Mumphrey dissin' my tits like that," Angie was saying.

"I think it was your outfit she was dissin'," Nikki said.

"Yeah." Angie grinned. "Not even Sister's gonna find fault with these tits. And they're not even my best asset."

Esther gave her a polite but fleeting smile and turned to Nikki. "Sister seems to have a habit of riling folks," she said.

"Some people are like that."

"You know, when I was reading about you today, I got to wondering: You gonna be running for district attorney one of these days?"

"I don't suppose I'd turn the job down."

"I don't suppose, either. The newspaper said you graduated top of your class. You could have started out with one of the big law firms at a very nice salary. Especially since you'd have helped satisfy two quota categories. Instead, you became a prosecutor. Why would a bright young woman do that, politics not be on your mind?"

Nikki had known Esther for about two years, ever since the initial meeting of the Mavens, and while she had the real estate saleswoman to thank for her home in Ladera Heights, they weren't tight friends. Until that moment, they'd never discussed anything more personal than closing costs and interest rates. Nikki didn't feel like changing that status just because a newspaper article had turned her into a semipublic figure.

"Prosecuting may be a nasty job," she said, trying to keep it light. "But somebody's got to do it."

"C'mon now, girl. I'm bein' serious. Why's prosecutin' people turn you on?" Esther demanded.

Nikki had never been a fan of introspection, mainly because her brief attempts at it had been too painful. Even as a little girl, she'd wanted to pursue a career in law enforcement. Behind the surface reasons—a belief in the justice system, a desire to aid in the war against crime—was a stronger, very personal motivation involving her feelings toward her father, which her innate sense of self-protection warned her not to confront. She surely was not going to poke around inside her psyche just to satisfy the curiosity of some pushy acquaintance.

"You have the opportunity," Esther said, "to become a leader of the African-American community—"

"Don't tell me about my opportunities." Though Nikki unleashed just a small part of her anger, it was enough to quiet the room. The other Mavens had stopped eating and were staring at her.

"The culture needs some strong black female leadership," Esther said.

Nikki teetered on the edge of giving Esther the same suggestion she'd offered Sister Mumphrey. Instead, she said, "You're right. The culture doesn't give a damn for women and even less for black women. So, sure, having black women in positions of power is an important thing. But that's not the role I picked for myself. I just ain't that grand, baby. If I can make this city one killer or rapist or child molester safer, that's good enough for me. Hell, Esther, maybe I just like putting folks in jail."

Before the real estate agent could press her further, she stood up and carried her plate into the kitchen. She stayed there, chatting with Juanita and Victoria Allard, until they were interrupted by the club treasurer, Lois Needham, a tiny woman with a squeaky voice who had been called "Mousie" most of her thirty-five years. She slapped the leather-case notepad she was carrying and said, "C'mon, ladies. Time to talk money."

It was a typical session, beginning with Mousie's report, which, owing to the market's upturn, was good news. This was followed by discussions of weight gain and loss, a new pill for clearer thought, and men, none of which had anything to do with their portfolio. Four of the Mavens had serious suggestions about stocks they'd been watching and these were voted on quickly and efficiently in between more talk about men, problems with offspring, job complaints, and current movies.

The meeting broke up at a little after ten.

"You got an edge to you tonight, girl," Loreen said to Nikki as they left Juanita's building. "What's up?"

"People shaking my tree. Esther telling me how to lead my life."

"She should talk. Missy No-Money-Down."

"Sister Mumphrey feels she has to stick her big nose into my family situation."

"That's Sister's way," Loreen said as they arrived at her aqua BMW. "She's got no life of her own. She'd love to think she'd been on your mind all evening."

"Not her. My father."

"Honey," her friend said, taking her hands, "I got a shooting pain in my heart over what you been through. Never knowing your mama. Having your daddy turn his back on you, like it was some fault of yours she died, instead of God's will. With all that, it made you a stronger woman than you might have been."

"Whatever doesn't drive you crazy or put you under makes you a better person," Nikki said, "that the idea?"

"Yeah."

"I think you been spending too much time under the hair dryer."

"You talking about Phil the hair dryer, or 'Toine the hair dryer?"

Nikki shook her head and smiled. "You're impossible." Then she hugged her friend.

"You gonna be okay?" Loreen asked.

"I'm fine," Nikki said. "Just need a little sleep."

"If sleep doesn't come and you want to talk, call me."

Nikki thanked her and headed away. She'd almost reached her car when Loreen passed by, tapping the BMW's horn and waving. Nikki unlocked her door and slipped behind the wheel. She started the car and drove away, thinking about the last time she'd had a conversation with her father.

It had been just after her grandmother's funeral. He had called her at work to thank her for taking care of the arrangements. She had been surprised when he went on to question her about the man she'd been with at the church. Feeling surprisingly girlish, she'd started to tell him about Tony Black. He'd interrupted her midsentence. "Sorry, but I gotta cut this short. Tricia has to use the phone."

When Blackie died, there had been no appearance at the funeral and no phone call. Just a Hallmark condolence card signed "from William and Patricia Hill."

Nikki was so busy reliving painful memories she didn't notice the sedan that followed her from Playa Del Rey, zooming past as she turned into her drive.

≡ FIFTEEN ≡

In the community of Manhattan Beach, not far from Ladera Heights, there exists a park built around a five-story mountain of sand. Nikki made a practice of climbing its difficult surface at least three days a week.

Her time of choice for the workout was sunrise, when the temperature was tolerable and she didn't have to worry about some novice climber suddenly turning into a gasping and moaning roadblock directly in her path. The morning after the Mavens meeting, for no particular reason, she pushed herself for one more climb than usual and hit the top just as the sun was balanced on the eastern skyline. She was breathing heavily; her leg muscles were burning but she felt good. Alive. *Love those endorphins!*

Bird, who was not allowed on the sand, had long ago settled for using the wooden stairwell to keep pace with his mistress. He rested beside her, panting not from the climb but to cool off his body.

As she did her stretching and bending, Nikki became aware of two young brothers watching her. They had the loose-limbed appearance of athletes and were wearing Nike gear that looked like it had arrived from the factory that morning. The shorter of the two approached her, drawing back as Bird leaped to attention.

"Hi," he said to Nikki, keeping his distance from the dog. "My name is Charles."

She paused in the middle of a stretch. "Sit, Bird," she said. She looked at the young man, saying nothing to him, waiting to hear his pitch. He surprised her by saying, "My friend finds you very attractive."

She looked over at the other young man, who was grinning at her. "Cat got his tongue?" she asked.

"He's sorta shy. Prefers it if I break the ice."

It's a complicated old world, she thought, *and it isn't getting any simpler.* "Better get yourself a new pick, because this ice is definitely not broken," she said. "In fact, it's getting frostier by the minute." She continued her stretches, plainly ignoring him.

He mentioned his friend's name, which was the same as a legendary baseball player. "You've probably heard of his father."

Nikki undid the towel that was tied around her waist and began dabbing at the perspiration on her face. She said nothing.

"He'd like you to have dinner with him tonight," Charles told her.

"Not with him or his father. Tell him he might get better results next time if he did his own asking." Bird was picking up her annoyance. He emitted a rumbling low growl.

Charles glanced at the dog and lost just a bit of his confidence. "Name the place," he said to Nikki. "The new Spago. The Shark Bar."

"You got wax in your ears?" she asked.

Charles waved a dismissive hand and turned away, swaggering toward his friend. "Forget it," he called out. "Dykesville. Probably gets it on with the dawg."

Bird looked at his mistress, waiting for a signal. "Be," she said softly, and the dog leaped toward the walking man, teeth bared. Charles screamed and rushed to escape those fierce teeth, stumbling in the sand and colliding with his friend.

"Bop!" Nikki shouted.

Bird shifted immediately into docility a few feet away from the flailing boys. His owner smiled, not at the discomfort of the two jerks who were then rolling ass over elbow down the face of the dune, but at a memory triggered by the action commands. Who else but a jazz buff like Tony Black would have trained his guard dog to attack on the word "Be" and stop on the word "Bop"? Who else but a jazz buff like Tony would have named his dog Yardbird in the first place?

As the frightened Charles and his shy friend beat a graceless retreat to the parking area below, Nikki welcomed Bird into her arms. "Good dog," she said. "Good Bird." Then she and the Bouvier made their separate descents, unaware of another young man who'd been following Nikki since the night before and was particularly fascinated by the big dog's devotion to his mistress.

≡ SIXTEEN ≡

The majority of Nikki's morning was spent at the Major Crimes section of the LAPD's Robbery-Homicide division, going over the reports of Detectives Goodman and Morales. Lieutenant Foster Corben, the large, rawboned head of Major Crimes, had welcomed her with formal cordiality and assigned one of his detectives, a young white woman named Harriman, to assist her.

This assistance consisted of locating an empty desk and then finding the materials Nikki specified. Detective Harriman was cooperative but distant. That was fine with Nikki. She needed information, not a new best friend.

Just before noon Nikki's cellular chirped. It was a clerk, telling her that Wise had called a meeting. She closed her notebook, capped her pen, and carried the reports and transcripts to Detective Harriman's desk. The detective was on the phone. From the expression on her face and the way she protected the receiver, Nikki suspected it was a personal call. To a lover, perhaps. Or maybe just a snitch.

She waited a beat, wanting to thank Harriman for her

help, but the phone call didn't seem near completion, so she just tapped the detective on the shoulder, mouthed the word "thanks," and turned to go.

That's when she saw the man staring at her.

He was at a desk across the room, tall and handsome with skin the color of dark caramel, wearing a blue-and-white-striped shirt, a solid blue tie, and dark gray silk slacks. He didn't seem to care that he'd been caught staring. He grinned at her.

She responded with a noncommittal smile.

He looked vaguely familiar. An old schoolmate? Somebody she'd dated? Maybe he'd worked one of her cases?

She shrugged it off and started toward the elevator. In her peripheral vision she saw him stand. Was he going to follow her?

He was.

Damn, she thought, *do I know him or not?*

"Miss," he called.

She turned.

"I've got something belongs to you," he said. He reached into his back pocket, withdrew a black leather wallet. He took two dollars from it and held them out.

She stared at the bills in his hand, frowning because she was getting the idea that maybe her leg was being pulled.

"These are yours. And this is for the interest." He added a third dollar.

She looked from the money to him. "You some kind of lunatic?"

"No ma'am. You generously loaned me some money. I'm just paying you back."

"I didn't . . ." She was going to tell him she was certain she'd never loaned him any money. What stopped her was his sudden shift in appearance. His jaw dropped and became slack. His eyelids lowered to half-mast. His right shoulder dipped and a bend of his knees transformed him from an athletic man in his thirties to a shambling drifter of undetermined age.

"Ol' Juppy never fo'gets a face," he said. "Or a debt."

She was stunned by the transformation. The sound of laughter broke the spell. Several of the detectives had been watching the performance. "Damn, Virgil," one of them said, "that's some smooth pick-up technique."

Nikki's face was burning. She turned on her heel and continued on to the elevator.

Virgil ran after her. "Hey, wait a minute. Really," he called, "I didn't mean to take your money. I was undercover and I didn't know who might be watching."

She pressed the elevator button.

"Look, my name's Virgil Sykes," he said. "I know your name, Nicolette."

The elevator door opened. Several people got off, including an attractive African-American woman in black jeans and a Day-Glo T-shirt.

Nikki stepped into the elevator.

"Wait," the man shouted.

"Hi, Virgil, honey," the woman in black jeans said in greeting.

"Bye, Virgil, honey," Nikki said as the elevator doors closed.

She arrived at the meeting in Wise's office to find the head deputy and Detectives Goodman and Morales all looking depressed.

"What's up, Ray?" she asked. "Your subscription to *Hustler* give out?"

Wise was too down to respond in kind. "The results of Deschamps's polygraph have come in," he said. "The news is not good."

"When did we give him a polygraph?" she asked.

"*We* didn't give it," Wise said. "His frigging lawyer requested it."

"Bleed 'em and plead 'em? A polygraph?"

"Mr. Deschamps has new counsel," Wise said. "Jesse Fallon."

Nikki knew the name, of course. Fallon was a legend. "The black Melvin Belli" was how one of her law professors described him. "How in the sweet brown-eyed world did Deschamps get himself an attorney like Jesse Fallon?"

The two detectives looked blank. Wise shrugged. "With all due respect," he said acidly, "you don't suppose it could have been the notoriety of the murder coupled with the color of Deschamps's skin?"

"Fallon's never been interested in notoriety before," she said. "He's made his bones a hundred times over. I heard he was all but retired."

"What difference does it make?" Wise whined. "The old bastard's involved and he's whipping our ass. Let's move on—to the progress our LAPD associates have been making."

More bad news. The detectives had just come from interrogating Dorothea Downs, the woman Deschamps claimed to have slept with the night of the murder. His alibi was firming up.

Wise sighed. "Is the woman a whore?" he asked the detectives.

"Whore?" Morales said. "Naw, she's just a gal who likes the baby's arm every now and then."

"She works for a boutique," Goodman said. "Sells clothes."

"Don't take me literally, detectives. I wasn't asking if she hooked. When she gets on the stand, what will the jury see? Will they see a woman of loose morals who can't be trusted to tell the truth? Or will they see a nice, upstanding female with whom they can identify?"

"She got dyed hair," Morales said. "Orange like a Popsicle."

"Good," Wise said.

He was asking them more about Dorothea Downs when Walden called, requesting his immediate presence. "The detectives are here. Shall I bring them?"

Evidently the answer was no, because when Wise replaced the phone he said, "Gentlemen, that wraps it up for now. Nikki, he wants us."

Nikki thought the two cops looked like they'd been given the day off. She wanted to catch them while they were in that mood, so she followed them into the hall. "Detectives," she called, "could I ask you for a favor?"

They turned to her.

"I went through most of the files today at your office. But I'd like to take a look at your murder books on Madeleine Gray," she said. "At your convenience, of course."

Goodman hesitated before replying. Each homicide detective maintains a murder book that is supposed to contain every bit of information that officer has collected and every event in which he or she has participated. Because of the myriad details that go into it, a murder book can in fact be a series of thick volumes. Often, these books are used by superiors to gauge a detective's effectiveness.

"It's for my eyes only," Nikki said. "The district attorney expects me to provide him with an overview of the case against Jamal Deschamps. It'd help if I could get an idea how the investigation has been progressing. All very informal. I won't be quoting you or anything like that."

Morales shrugged. "I know you think I'm nuthin' but a refried asshole, Nikki, but I'm here for you. Anything you need."

Said without his customary smirk or leer, the sincerity of his reply surprised her and threw her off balance. She felt she should make some gesture to indicate that his friendship was appreciated. But she couldn't shake the belief that any display of warmth would be misinterpreted. So she offered him a tentative smile and turned to Goodman. "What about you, Ed?" she asked.

"Why not? My life's an open murder book."

She thanked them and, spotting Wise heading for Walden's office, moved off in that direction herself.

≡ SEVENTEEN ≡

Goodman was relieved that the D.A. had excluded him and his partner from the meeting with Wise. Walden wasn't a bad guy, but, as Goodman saw it, the strain of dealing with the hue and cry over Maddie Gray's murder was taking its toll on the man. He didn't want to be around when or if the D.A. blew his stack.

Morales evidently had noticed the change in Walden, too. "Big shot's not smiling so much these days," he said as they descended to the parking area. "I never liked the *cabrón*. Right from the start I got him figured as Tom Gleason in blackface."

"That's a little harsh," Goodman said.

"You knew he was Gleason's boy, right?"

"Yeah. Still, he'd have to go some to be as big an asshole as Gleason."

"Asshole and a half. Thanks to him we got at least four stone killers walking the streets today," Morales said as they got into the car. "Crazy Eights."

"I used to hear those stories," Goodman said. "Mainly from Jay Barkovich."

"Sure. Barko and his partner—what was his name, Ruger?—they took every last fuckin' Crazy Eight off the streets. Had 'em in the lockup. Gleason gives 'em a pass, a slap on the wrist, because some minister swears they was good boys at heart. Good boys! I hope that fucker Gleason is rottin' in hell with some of those good boys."

"What's with your hard-on for the Crazies?" Goodman asked.

Morales paused only briefly before turning on the ignition. "It's personal," he said, the finality of his tone ending the discussion.

The two detectives spent most of the afternoon at the scene of a drive-by shooting on the Hollywood Freeway near the Cahuenga Pass. The vic was a male Caucasian, age eighteen, who'd spent some of his childhood in a popular TV series about street life. The bullet had removed the back of his head. He'd been in the slow lane, but it was still a minor miracle that his untended Mercedes-Benz 300SL had avoided collision, merely swerving to the right and nestling against the far side of an exit ramp.

It was a wearying investigation. The freeway, connecting the San Fernando Valley to Hollywood and downtown L.A., was clotted with vehicles nearly every minute of the workday. Surely someone had witnessed the shooting. But had that someone thought to study the killer's car? To write down the license number? Would they be part of that diminishing number of citizens willing to stand up and be counted?

Photos of the traffic were taken periodically by the highway patrol. With luck they might have caught something useful.

By five-thirty, the detectives had not received their golden phone call and nothing had dropped into their laps except a small vial of cocaine found in the 300SL's glove compartment. Goodman didn't mention drugs when he notified the boy's mother, but he might as well have. She seemed to blame him for her son's death, pounding him with her tiny fists. He and Morales finally got her to calm down enough to tell them how to reach the boy's father, who, it turned out, was a barber at one of the Hollywood shops where the term had been replaced by "stylist." The man fell apart completely and had to be sedated.

Another day on the job.

They arrived at the Academy shortly after seven.

Gwen Harriman was drinking with her partner, a Samoan named Manolo who stayed twenty to thirty pounds beyond the LAPD weight limit except for the periods set aside each year for annual physicals. Judging by his size, that time was far off.

By eight, Morales left to have dinner with his family. An hour later, Manolo departed in search of another few pounds of body fat. He'd tried to convince Gwen and Goodman to join him but they'd both previously gone through the expensive and generally unappetizing experience of dining with the big detective who enjoyed talking with his mouth full.

By ten, Goodman was sorry he hadn't eaten earlier. The room was spinning. Gwen was bending his ear about a boyfriend who was not treating her right.

"Get *him* on the horn," Goodman said. "Tell *him* your problems."

"You're more understanding," she said. "Besides, I can't phone him at home."

"Married?"

She nodded, then finished her bourbon. "Let's go to your place."

"Not tonight," Goodman said.

"Then let's have another drink," she said.

So they did.

≡ EIGHTEEN ≡

Nikki's afternoon had been considerably less active than that of the two homicide detectives. For a half hour she sat in Joe Walden's office watching in silent amusement as he chewed the ass off Ray Wise for selling him on the Deschamps indictment. Following that entertaining interlude, she returned to her desk to immerse herself once again in the known facts of the case.

She was rereading Goodman and Morales's initial interview with Deschamps when she became aware of something in her doorway. A brown hand waving a white handkerchief.

"I hope that's clean," she said.

A sheepish Virgil Sykes entered the office. "Pressed it myself this morning," he told her, tucking it back into the top pocket of his suit. "Didn't want you to shoot me before I could apologize."

She thought, somewhat begrudgingly, that he wasn't a bad-looking man when he cleaned himself up. "Who you pretending to be this time, in your nice threads? A Fuller Brush salesman? A defense attorney?"

"Nope. Just a cop who had to give a deposition to one of your associates."

"Which associate?"

"Dimitra Shaw."

"The Sutter case?" she asked. It had been at the top of the media slice-and-dice list before the naked body of Maddie Gray refocused their attention. A three-year-old boy had been beaten to death. His adoptive mother, who was being charged with the crime, had declared that the child battered himself to death in a fit of rage.

"The Sutter, yeah," he said, shaking his head sadly. "Listen, you mind if I park for a second?"

She hesitated, then said, "For a second."

"I'm really sorry about that stunt at the office," he said, taking a stack of books from a chair and placing them on the floor. "Sometimes I can't help being an asshole."

"They have shrinks for problems like that." She wondered if he was being straight this time or just opting for a subtler put-on.

"Anyways, I just wanted to say I'm sorry. I was hoping we could make out like it didn't happen and start out from the jump again."

Her bullshit sensors, hair-triggered by past experiences with gangstas, junkies, murderers, and men in general, were on full alert. "What is it you really want, Mr. Styles?"

"It's Sykes," he said. "Virgil Sykes." He broke into a grin. "You remembered my name. That was a put-down, right? You playing the dozens? What comes next, a 'you so stupid' rank?"

"I don't see you as being stupid," she said.

Their eyes met and held for a moment. She looked away.

"How's the Gray case going?" he asked. "You keeping Goodman and Morales hoppin'?"

"Not me, exactly," she said. "I'm just gathering rosebuds for my boss."

"But you got eyes for doin' more than that."

"You my psychic friend?"

"What else? You want Ray Wise's gig?"

She'd certainly given it a thought. "Why not?"

"Not gonna happen."

"No?" She could feel herself flushing.

"Course not," he said. "It's one thing for Walden to make you his assistant, cause that's what guys have—women assistants. But how's that gonna look, if a black D.A. appoints a black honey as his chief deputy?"

She glared at him, anger spreading through her body like fire. "How's that gonna look?" she repeated incredulously. "Why you smug, jive-a—"

"Gotcha," he said, chuckling.

She shook her head. "You're a bad man," she said, unable to hide her smile.

"Like I'd seriously think it'd be a mistake to replace a bigoted asshole like Wise with an intelligent, dedicated, open-minded prosecutor such as yourself."

"You don't know what kind of prosecutor I am."

"Sure I do," he said. "I checked out some of your work in Compton. The Gandy trial, Mary Loomis—that was a good one, set fire to her old man—the Dawes boys . . ."

"You looked up my trials?" She couldn't believe it.

"I had somebody fax me the salient details."

"Why?"

"Why you think? I'm interested in you." He said it as if it were the most obvious thing in the world. "I figured it'd give us something to talk about at dinner tonight."

"Not tonight," she said.

"But you haven't heard the program."

"It doesn't matter," she said. "I've got other plans."

"Big mistake," he said.

"I'll try to live with it," she said.

He stood. "Well, then, I guess I'll jus' try to live with your rejection."

She watched him walk slowly from her office.

A beat later, he was back. "Damn, woman, you let me walk out of your life, jus' like that?"

"I sorta figured we might be meeting up again," she said.

"Look," he said, "we been going around it today, but I really think something might be brewin' here."

"My fiancé would be happy to hear that," she said.

"Fiancé? Aw, shit. Don't tell me that. The Lord couldn't be that cruel, to put you in my path twice and then have you be private goods."

"No," she said, amused by his terminology. "No fiancé. I'm still *public* goods."

"Well, now," he said, straightening, the smile back on his handsome face. "Then there's the chance we can pursue the idea of gettin' together?"

"You know where to reach me," she said.

"And I will," he said. "You can count on it."

≡ NINETEEN ≡

The deputies came for Jamal at 6 P.M.

When Jesse Fallon had visited earlier in the afternoon, the lawyer had said nothing about him being moved to a new jail. What Fallon had said was that, because of the polygraph, he'd probably be a free man within twenty-four hours. The case against him had all but fallen apart.

Jamal tried to explain this to the deputies. The only one who bothered to listen showed him the computerized removal slip ordering his relocation to Wayside, a facility sixty miles north of the city.

"What's the point, if I'm getting out tomorrow?"

The guard was big and burly, a buzz-cut redneck version of William "The Refrigerator" Perry. His lazy eyes stayed on Jamal for a beat. "I don't know nuthin' about you getting out. I don't know nuthin' about nuthin' except this removal slip. So get your stuff."

They transported him in a yellow bus, along with four other men in prison garb. Each was handcuffed to his respective seat. Two armed guards went along for the ride, sitting behind wire mesh, one at the rear, shotgun on his lap, one at the front, beside the driver but facing back.

In spite of shouted orders from the guards to shut up, two of his fellow prisoners kept up a steady stream of mouth music all the way to the new jail. Judging by their chatter, the little one, with what appeared to be several pink burn splashes on his dark face and neck, was nicknamed PhillyQ. His beefy, slack-jawed, droopy-lidded friend answered to a name that Jamal assumed was Mar-ket, because the guy looked like he was full of groceries. He discovered later it was Mark-It, because he liked to leave his mark on things. With a knife.

They arrived at Wayside shortly after the dinner hour and were quickly logged in and led to the dining hall. They were treated to a meal of chicken and potatoes, heavy on the lumpy white gravy, what Jamal used to call "gran'ma food," along with the usual dessert, "gorilla biscuits," oatmeal cookies so thick it was rumored the kitchen crew used their armpits to mold them.

That image did nothing to improve Jamal's appetite. He moved the food around his plate while idly observing his fellow inmates. He'd been spoiled by the private digs near the courthouse. He didn't like being a member of the general jailhouse population. He was worried about being beaten or raped before Fallon could get there with the golden key. And he was picking up weird vibes from PhillyQ and Mark-It, who were sitting across from him, no longer talking, just staring at him like it was him who cut the cheese.

Feeling definitely creeped out, he stood, picked up his plate, and began to carry it to the dirty-dish counter. Mark-It rose, too, then PhillyQ. The big man suddenly elbowed the little brother, forcing him to drop his plate. It clattered on the floor, followed by the sound of nervous laughter. Then silence.

PhillyQ shoved back against the big man, but Mark-It barely budged. When he returned the shove, PhillyQ went reeling toward Jamal.

Jamal saw something in the little con's hand that caught the light. A metal spoon. *Oh, shit, a shiv!* He took a step backward and bumped against somebody. A glance told him it was a big con he'd never seen before, glaring at him like he was a bug on the floor.

PhillyQ was almost where he wanted to be. He flipped the spoon so that its handle was pointed at Jamal's stomach.

Without hesitation, Jamal kicked out, the toe of his shoe connecting with PhillyQ's family jewels just as the sharpened spoon handle sliced a groove along his inner thigh.

As PhillyQ folded and hit the deck on his side, squealing, Jamal felt a push from the rear, then a hot, stinging sensation deep in his back, beneath his left shoulder blade. The room shifted and the floor rose up to greet him, moving much too fast. He landed hard only a few feet away from the puking PhillyQ.

Everybody in the room seemed to be screaming and yelling, but Jamal was having trouble hearing. Something was wrong with his eyesight as well. Colors were fading. Just before blackness took over he thought he saw beige uniforms moving toward him through the crush of county-jail blue.

≡ Twenty ≡

At eight that night, when Nikki arrived at Loreen's beauty salon, she found it crowded and overflowing with hip-hop, talk, and laughter. The establishment had begun to outgrow its neighborhood strip mall origins back when Rose Battles was still its proprietor. Once Rose's Beauty Palace had been passed on to Loreen, she acquired the store space to the west, knocked down the common wall, and expanded the operation from four to eight chairs, each of which rented to an independent stylist at $650 a month. Nikki had never seen an empty chair in the place.

When she entered, the women filling them looked up from their magazines or paused mid-gossip. *Ain't celebrity grand.*

"Well, hello, missy," her stylist, Baron, said, deserting his customer to study her hair. "We plan on makin' any more TV appearances, we're gonna need a little topside tidyin' up."

"Gee, Mr. Silver Tongue, you sure got a way with a compliment."

"Honey," he said, indicating with a toss of his head the gimlet-eyed woman sitting in his chair, "tonight Mr. Silver Tongue's all complimented out."

"I'll try to make it in Monday, let you do your magic on my topside," she said, glancing around the shop. "Where's the boss lady?"

Baron pantomimed the smoking of a cigarette.

Jocasta, the manicurist, a news junkie who'd been dividing her attention between her customer's cuticles and the television set suspended from the ceiling in a corner of the room, called out to her. "Hey, Nikki, what's with Jamal Deschamps? Court TV says he's innocent."

"Court TV probably knows more about it than I do," Nikki said.

She found Loreen sitting on a white plastic chair behind the building, puffing on a cigarette and staring at a scruffy garbage dump just off the mall's rear access road. "Enjoying the sunset, huh, girlfriend?" Nikki said.

Loreen's foxlike face brightened and she smiled, exhaling a plume of smoke into the still evening air. "Nikki," she said. "Don't tell me it's that late already?"

"Depends on what you call late." She watched Loreen toss away the cigarette and use both hands to push herself from the chair, wincing. "Hip giving you trouble again?"

"It's nothing," Loreen said, hobbling a little as she approached. They hugged.

"I missed lunch," Loreen said. "Had a last-minute press and curl. So I'm hungry enough to max out both our credit cards."

She led the way back through the shop. As they passed a screened-off area where a hair weaver plied her trade, a customer was just leaving. She was a big, flashy woman wearing a glittery tank top and shorts. One look at Nikki and the smile on her face froze, then disappeared. "You bitch," she screamed. "Took away my man."

The shop went silent, except for LL Cool J rapping away and the thrum of the dryers.

"Oh, hell," Loreen said, moving between Nikki and the woman. "Violet, you got your weave done to your satisfaction?"

"Ain't 'bout my weave," Violet said. "It's 'bout that Oreo bitch hidin' behind you."

Nikki stepped away from her friend to face the furious woman. "No reason for me to hide, Violet," she said, surprising herself with the calmness of her voice. "You're angry at the wrong person and you know it."

"Wrong person?" Violet took a step toward her. "You the one sent my man to San Quentin for no reason."

Nikki shifted her stance only slightly and stood her ground. "Girl, they must've tied your weave too tight. Your man shot a Brink's guard. Came near killing him."

"He say he didn't do it," Violet shrieked.

"He also says he never laid hand to you," Nikki said. "That the truth?"

Violet was momentarily silent.

"You're what, about twenty-five, girl?" Nikki went on. "I guess you needed a weave because your nice nappy twenty-five-year-old hair fell out in one clump all by itself. Your truthful man didn't get drunk one night and yank it out by the roots."

Violet's eyes filled with tears. "Don't make you no less a bitch," she said before pivoting on her heel and heading for the cashier. All other eyes in the shop were still on Nikki. She could feel her skin tingling. Loreen moved behind her and said, "You figuring on taking a bow, or can we just go?"

"We can go," Nikki said. "Where'd she get that hair for

the weave, anyhow? Can't be human. Must be a goat somewhere with his ass all naked."

The two friends left the shop staggering with laughter.

They dined on Caribbean food at Mo Bay in Venice. They
covered the usual topics: family problems (Loreen's little
sister was hanging with a guy who looked to her like he was
cracked out), the men that should have been in their lives but
weren't, women they couldn't stand, movies bad and good,
general gossip, their hatred of general gossip.

"Speaking of which," Loreen said, "Jocasta said she
heard it mighta been Satanists who murdered Maddie Gray."

"She didn't get that from Court TV, I hope," Nikki said.
"Satanists! I'll have to pass that along to Joe Wal—"

A pager sounded. Both women grabbed their purses, then
looked at one another and laughed. "Who's got the problem?" Loreen asked.

It was Nikki. The digital number on her pager belonged to
the D.A. He'd added a double "8," which indicated an emergency.

She fished a cellular phone from her purse.

While Nikki listened to what the district attorney had to
say, Loreen sat back in her chair, looking at the other diners
and pretending she wasn't the least bit interested in their
conversation. "Everything all right?" she asked as soon as
Nikki clicked off the phone.

"I've got to drive out to Wayside Park," Nikki said, waving to the waiter for the check.

"What's goin' on there?"

"Some cons stabbed Jamal Deschamps about an hour ago.
It's not clear how much damage they did. Joe wants me to
drive there and find out."

"Save yourself some time and travel," Loreen said.
"Come back to the shop with me. By now Jocasta's got the
whole story."

≡ TWENTY-ONE ≡

At just after ten the next morning, Eddie Goodman sat on the couch in the district attorney's office watching Joe Walden pace while engaged in a telephone conversation with some unidentified party. Morales was at the other end of the couch, slurping a cup of hot coffee. Ray Wise sat stiffly in his chair near the D.A.

The room's other occupant was the attractive but cold deputy D.A., Nikki Hill. Goodman had read in the paper that her old man, William Hill, had retired after putting in twenty-five years as a cop. *Maybe I should look the guy up, find out what you do with your days.*

The morning *L.A. Times* lay scattered on the floor as if Walden had thrown it down in disgust. The headline read "Maddie Murder Suspect Attacked." *What a cluster fuck this is turning into.*

The D.A. hung up the phone and announced to the room, "He's lost some blood, but he's out of danger. Fortunately for us, since, as his lawyer has been informing me hourly, he should not have been in jail in the first place." His tone was definitely accusatory, Goodman thought, aimed primarily at Wise. But he and Morales were not there to be patted on the back.

They'd already had their session with their supervisor, Lieutenant Corben, whose salty comments about their handling of the case were still ringing in his ears. Hoping to forestall more agony, he asked the D.A., "How'd Jamal wind up at Wayside, anyway?"

Walden leaned back in his chair and looked at Nikki. She said, "They claim it was a computer glitch. The removal slip was supposed to be for a prisoner named Desmond."

Walden used his thumb and middle finger to massage his eyes. He looked worked over. Probably had had a rough night, fielding calls from irate, insecure politicians and pit-bull members of the media. Well, Goodman had had a pretty rough night himself.

He tried to put it out of his mind. This was no time to be caught off base, mooning over something that had nothing to do with the Gray murder.

"Any idea why he was cut?" he asked.

"What's the difference?" Wise said. "Can't we get this meeting back on track?"

"Damn it, Ray," Walden said heatedly, "I've had just about enough of your bloody impatience. That's what got us into this jackpot. You and your 'slam dunk' case."

Wise paled and seemed to shrink in his chair.

"The two cons who cut him were third-strike lifers," Nikki replied to Goodman's question. "Maybe Deschamps gave 'em a sideways glance. That's all it would take."

"What do they say?" Goodman asked.

"They say they're innocent. It was two other guys."

"Let me talk with 'em," Morales said.

"You? Why?" Walden looked surprised.

"I know how to get bangers to open up."

"What makes you think they're bangers?" Walden asked. "Nothing in their jack—"

"They're Crazy Eights," Morales said flatly. "Gang names are PhillyQ and Mark-It. Sorta a hobby of mine, keepin' up on the Crazies."

"Well, they're not our immediate problem," Walden said. "And maybe if you'd spend as much time on the job as you do on your hobbies, you and Detective Goodman might have provided us with a better suspect than Deschamps. I'm now in a position where I have to eat shit every time the phone rings. I don't like shit on my menu, gentlemen. I need a suspect who'll go the distance, and I need him fast. Stop dragging your feet, and do your bloody job."

Jesus, Goodman thought, was the miserable night he'd just spent going to be a harbinger of a downward slope his life was taking? He saw Morales's shiny black eyes suddenly dull and his mustache begin to twitch. Before his partner could say something that would dump them even further into the crapper, he addressed Walden himself. "We've been putting in nineteen- and twenty-hour days on this. Not exactly dragging our feet. We've given Mr. Wise evidence suggesting other lines of inquiry."

Walden looked questioningly at his head deputy. "The blackmail theory," Wise said. "We talked about it."

"Right," Walden said without enthusiasm. "Anything else?"

Goodman said, "The bracelet found at the vic's home."

"The one that Ray told me had been given to the Gray woman by Deschamps," Walden said, heavy on the sarcasm.

"According to the inscription," Wise said defensively, "it was a gift from somebody with the initial 'J.' We had a suspect named Jamal. Hell, maybe he did give it to her. The fact she had it doesn't necessarily mean it came from her killer."

"I think it does," Nikki said. "According to Arthur Lydon,

Maddie's assistant, she didn't wear jewelry. He'd never seen the bracelet before. So the killer either gave it to her that night, or it was something she only wore for him."

"Logical," Walden admitted. "So what does that tell us?"

"That the killer's a 'J,'" Nikki said. "And the little lion hanging on the bracelet must have some significance. Leo the lion. Astrological sign. MGM Studios."

"Do we have anything on the bracelet's history?" Walden asked Goodman.

"We know it's fourteen-karat and that it was handcrafted. We'll show it to some local jewelers and see what they can tell us."

The D.A. nodded. "What else have you got?"

"The files in Madeleine Gray's special cabinet drawer," Goodman said.

"If the killer pried the drawer open," Walden said, "we can assume he got what he was after. The celebrities whose files were left behind are probably the only people in L.A. we can be reasonably certain did not kill Madeleine Gray."

"Unless the killer missed what he was searching for," Goodman said.

"All right, detective," Walden said. "You've sold me. Here's how it works. One man gets a look at the files and interviews the involved parties. That same man bears the full responsibility if any of the information they contain is leaked to the press. Guess who that one man is going to be."

"Gonna eat that taco?" Morales asked, barely waiting for Goodman to say no before scooping it off of its cardboard plate. They were having lunch at the Tico Taco on Fairfax, standing up at a wooden counter at the rear of the fast-food hut. "Why don'cha buy a burrito so I can eat that, too," the thick-chested detective said, wiping his fingers daintily on a small white paper napkin with red and green pepper borders.

"Huh, sure," Goodman said, distracted.

"Hey, man, your mind's been on vacation ever since Walden put you on the spot."

"Sorry, amigo," Goodman said. But it was Gwen, not Walden, who was occupying his thoughts.

The night before, he'd wound up at her place with takeout ribs. The cocktail of choice had been tequila shooters. A bunch of them and somehow their interest in the ribs had waned to the point where they were rolling around on the carpet, undoing buttons and belts and such.

He was enjoying himself pretty much for a near senior citizen when the phone rang. He was surprised when she pulled away to answer it, then annoyed when she turned her naked back to him and began to whisper into the receiver in a tone that could only be described as intimate.

He watched in silence from the floor as she replaced the receiver and began to put on her clothes. "Sorry, Ed," she said, not able to meet his gaze. "I've gotta go."

"It's nearly midnight," he said. "Your boyfriend just ditch his wife?"

"You don't know anything about it," she said tersely.

"I guess not," he said, looking for his pants.

She gave him a sad smile. "You were the one who told me to go out and find somebody new, remember?"

"I was just mulling that dumb idea over," he said.

She grabbed her purse and headed for the door. "Why don't you stay here tonight? Sleep a little before getting behind the wheel."

"Kind of you," he said, though he had no intention of staying.

"I'm sorry," she said. "I wouldn't have started us up again if . . ." She let the thought drift away.

"I know," he said, flopping onto the couch, holding his right shoe.

She left, closing the door quietly behind her.

"Ed Goodman, what an asshole thou art," he said to the room.

He put on his shoe and reached for the tequila bottle on the coffee table. His hand hesitated, then picked up the phone instead. He punched the star key, then the six and the nine.

The combination triggered an immediate response—the dialing of the number of the last person to have called Gwen's number. Goodman's mouth felt dry as he listened to one ring. Then two. Then:

"TAA," a male voice said. "This is security."

Damn. A business number. With how many employees? "I'm sorry," Goodman said, improvising, "I didn't want security."

"Switchboard's closed for the night," the man from security informed him. "Try again after eight-thirty tomorrow morning."

"Thanks," Goodman said, replacing the phone.

He tried to shake the wooziness from his head. What the hell was he thinking? Suppose Gwen's lover boy had picked up the phone, what would he have done? Would he have asked the son of a bitch his intentions? Christ, he may not know the guy's name, but he sure as hell knew his intentions: to get his ashes hauled whenever he wanted. Gwen obviously was happy to oblige. He, Goodman, was the odd man out in this triangle.

He stood unsteadily, grabbed his coat, and staggered from the apartment.

"What's it gonna be," Morales asked him as they headed from Tico Taco to their sedan, "jewelry stores or the assholes she was blackmailin'?"

"The assholes," Goodman said as they got into the car.

"Checking out the ways other people tried to screw up their lives might be just what I need."

Morales put the car in gear but didn't step on the gas. He faced Goodman. "You bummin' me out, man. You can't let Walden get you down like this."

"It's not Walden and I'm not down. I'm fine. I'm high on life."

"Yeah," Morales said, nosing the sedan into traffic along Fairfax. "And I'm the fucking king of Spain."

...

≡ TWENTY-TWO ≡

I'll see if he's in," the very elegant, slightly anorexic black woman named Rae said into the telephone. She pressed the hold button and looked across the office at Jimmy Doyle, who was lying down on a brown nubby-weave couch reading the *Chicago Tribune*. On the floor beside the couch were discarded copies of the *Washington Post*, the *New York Times*, *USA Today*, the *L.A. Times*, and *High Society's Celebrity Skin*, all of which she'd picked up that morning for him at Freddy's Georgetown News.

"Jesse Fallon?" she asked.

He dropped the *Trib* and twisted on the couch to grab the phone on the table near his head.

"Yo, Jesse."

"It's official." The lawyer's voice was all business. "Jamal Deschamps is a free man. Or will be as soon as he's able to leave the hospital. I assume this cancels my debt."

"It's marked paid in full," Doyle said. "You do good work, Jesse."

"Even when crucial information is kept from me."

"What information?" Doyle asked.

"The ring. You didn't tell me Deschamps was found with the dead woman's ring in his pocket."

"This is the first I'm hearing about a ring," he told Fallon. "What's your interest in Deschamps, Jimmy?"

"I hate to see an innocent man get railroaded," Doyle said. "Simple as that."

"I hope to God you had nothing to do with the attempt on his life."

"Why would I go to all the trouble of getting you to clear his name," Doyle asked, "if I wanted him dead?"

"I don't suppose I'll ever know the real reason behind anything you do, Jimmy," Fallon said. "And I'm not sure I want to know."

They said their good-byes. Doyle reached back, pushed the plunger on the phone cradle, breaking that connection. Then he swung his body around until he was sitting up, sock feet on the thick carpet. He closed his eyes, summoned up a number, and hit the phone keys, a lot of them.

"L'Homme Magnifique," a bored feminine voice informed him.

"Zorina?"

"Yes. Who's this?"

"The fat fart from D.C."

He could almost hear her smile. "Need another tie?" she asked.

"Oh, yeah," he said. "My guess is I'll be back in L.A. tomorrow. Let's say your place at nine."

"So your 'big deal' is on again, huh?" she said.

"With a little push from this end."

"What is it you do, anyway?" she asked. "Politics? Show business?"

Doyle considered the question for a beat. "I sorta cover the waterfront," he said.

≡ TWENTY-THREE ≡

"Come in," Ray Wise said glumly. He was sitting perpendicular to his desk, slumped back, staring straight ahead at a blank wall. Nikki assumed that he'd spied her with peripheral vision, since he hadn't turned his head when she appeared at his door.

"You left a message you wanted to see me?"

"Sure. Sit down."

He took his time shifting his narrow body on the chair so that he could face her. She decided she preferred him when he was alert and arrogant, as opposed to his present state, which was almost civil and perplexed. "I . . . ," he began. He frowned and tried again. "We're both in the same boat," he said. "The same sinking boat."

Nikki remained silent, waiting for him to make his point.

"Years ago, we faced an even more difficult crisis. We put aside our . . . differences for our common welfare."

"And you hung around here, jollyin' it up with fat-ass Gleason," she said, "while I was bustin' my hump in beautiful downtown Compton."

His lip twitched in annoyance. "The point is, we both survived."

"At different levels of survival, Mr. Head Deputy D.A."

"Of course. You were the one who fucked up."

"Well, which one of us is the fuckup this time, Raymond?"

He slumped back in his chair. "Point made," he said. She thought it was probably the closest he'd come to admitting his fallibility.

"So what do you want from me?" she asked.

"Cooperation."

She mentally poked at the word. "You want to parse that for me a little?"

"I want . . . I would *appreciate* your consulting me before you make your reports to Walden."

"Why should I go to all that trouble?"

"It's as much to your advantage as it is to mine that our reports reflect a uniformity of opinion. It'll make both our jobs easier."

"And if our jive don't jibe?"

He gave her a mirthless smile. "Then I suppose the final decision should be made by the person with seniority."

"That's what I figured," she said, standing.

He waited until she was almost out the door before saying, "There would be a quid pro quo, of course."

She turned, suspicious, but also curious.

"Assuming the LAPD ever arrests anybody else for the Gray murder," he said, "I'll see to it you're a major part of the prosecution team."

"Joe Walden already put that on my plate."

He smiled again. "That's what I mean about experience. You didn't hear him use the word 'major.' He said you'd be part of the team. That could mean anything from flogging the clerks to making runs to In and Out Burger in the middle of the night."

She looked at him.

"I'm offering you a seat at the table," he said.

She tried not to show her surprise. "You don't have that authority."

"Let me amend my statement. I will recommend to Joe that you be my second chair. Considering the confidence he has in you, I don't believe he'll say no. Especially if your reports indicate we're on the same wavelength."

He was leaning forward, the tips of his fingers touching his desk as a form of delicate balance. She could feel his eagerness. He needed her support. She needed the career boost a high-profile trial would provide. Once again she would be getting into bed with the weasel, metaphorically speaking of course, thank the Lord. This time would be a little different. This time it was she who had the D.A.'s ear. This time she knew a good deal more about how the game was played.

"We'll give it a try," she said.

≡ TWENTY-FOUR ≡

Goodman moved along the antique brick walkway from the two-story house to the street. He double-timed it, ignoring the well-tended shrubbery and little islands of exotic, multihued plants. He could feel the eyes of Nita Morgan, the angry lady of the house, boring holes in his back. She'd called him a series of imaginatively obscene names and threatened to sue him, the LAPD, and every other law enforcement entity in Los Angeles, including the highway patrol and the FBI.

Adding to her intimidation quotient was Goodman's memory of her as a terrifying vampire in a popular television series of the sixties. (Madeleine Gray's folder had IDed her as "Batgal.") He kept flashing on her in pale white makeup, hair a mass of black and white strands, inch-long fingernails the same color as the blood coating her vampire fangs.

He shivered, jerked the passenger door open, and lowered his weary bones into the sedan. His neck felt red and hot.

Batgal had been his third visit to a Madeleine Gray "client." The first two had been just as unpleasant and unproductive.

Morales hummed a little tune, smirking.

"Okay, damn it," Goodman said. "Walden was right and you were right. This is not only a waste of time, it is a fucking *embarrassing* waste of time."

"Maddie's killer ain't in those files," Morales said, starting the car.

Goodman had no evidence to the contrary. Nor did he have the heart to rattle the cages of the rest of the people on the list. "Okay," he said. "Screw this. Let's go get the gold bracelet and visit some jewelers."

It was a good suggestion, but they weren't able to act on it. When they opened the box marked "Gray, Madeleine" in the evidence room, and spread out the assortment of items on the table, the gold bracelet was missing.

Goodman checked the evidence logs. There it was, neatly typed. "1 bracelet, gold, w. lion charm & inscription, 'M. We'll always have Paris. Love, J.' " The entry included the date and time the object was logged in. It had not been logged out.

The officer in charge of the evidence room was quick to note that only authorized personnel had access to the boxes. "If something's missing, whoever took it was here on official business," he told them defensively, indicating the visitor sign-in sheets.

Goodman flipped through the top few pages. So many crimes had been committed since the Gray murder that an army of people had trooped through the room. "Looks like a roster of the LAPD and the D.A.'s office," he said glumly. "Useless."

"Hard to believe somebody in law enforcement must not be as honest as you and me, partner."

"At least they left us the ring," Goodman said. He picked the bauble from the box and examined it. "I wonder why?"

"So we got a ring," Morales said. "Big deal."

"Could be. Remember what Arthur Lydon said about Maddie not wearing jewelry. The bracelet is jewelry. This is jewelry. Maybe the killer gave her this *and* the bracelet."

Morales shrugged. "Before we go running around to jewelry stores, let's show this to little Arthur first, huh? Make sure he don't recognize it."

"I've got his number written down somewhere."

Morales groaned. "You really think this ring's gonna open any doors for us?"

"At least it'll keep us in motion," Goodman said as they walked toward the front of the building. "Always better to keep moving."

"We that desperate, huh?"

"We're at a dead end," Goodman said. "We got no suspects. We got Corben and the D.A. shouting in our ear. We seem to have lost, misplaced, or been robbed of our most important piece of evidence. So, yeah, I'd say 'desperate' covered our situation."

≡ TWENTY-FIVE ≡

According to Arthur Lydon's answering machine, he was spending the day working at the house in Laurel Canyon. Goodman and Morales arrived there to find a bored uniformed policeman sitting in the front room listening to a Walkman. He was young and eager and nearly ripped off his ear removing the headset when he saw them.

He recovered quickly enough to explain he'd opened up for Lydon an hour and a half earlier. Though Goodman and Morales were well acquainted with the layout of the house, the young policeman felt he had to act as their guide to Lydon's office.

To his dismay, the little man wasn't there.

They found him in the upstairs office, seated at Madeleine Gray's desk, pecking at the keyboard of her computer. He gave them a nervous smile when they entered.

Goodman scanned the room, pausing at the dented filing cabinet from which the files had been removed. He didn't know what he was looking for. The area had been gone over thoroughly. "You're not supposed to be up here, Mr. Lydon," he said.

"I'm sorry. I didn't know." Lydon closed down the computer and stood. He was wearing a butter-yellow shirt and tight orange jeans. With his spiky hair and big eyes, he reminded Goodman of the little cartoon bird who keeps seeing a puddy-tat.

"I explained to you, Mr. Lydon," the young policeman said, "that you were supposed to limit your activity to your office area."

"I misunderstood," he said, walking past them, heading for the door.

"What sort of work were you doing up here, Mr. Lydon?" Goodman asked.

"Maddie's uncle, Clarence Justus, from Ann Arbor, Michigan, asked me to put her affairs together for him. He's requested that her remains be shipped to Ann Arbor for burial there. The people at syndication are furious. They'd hoped for a big Hollywood thing at Forest Lawn. They're repackaging her old shows for cable."

Goodman had interviewed several of the people at the syndication company. While he considered none of them serious suspects, they seemed to be very callous invidiuals who, like her technical crews, felt it unnecessary to pretend to have liked Maddie Gray. "They can always bury her in effigy," he said.

"I doubt that Mr. Justus would allow it," Lydon replied, not realizing the detective was being facetious. "He's taking a very proprietary stand concerning Maddie and her work."

Justus was, Goodman knew, the dead woman's only known relative. He had been phoning Lieutenant Corben daily, demanding progress reports. He'd made such a pest of himself that Corben had the Ann Arbor PD check the guy out to make sure he hadn't been in the Southern California area on the night of the murder.

"That's why you were up here in the forbidden room, pounding on her computer? Putting things in order for the uncle?"

"Why else?" Lydon turned and made his way down the stairs, followed by his police guard. Goodman watched him go, feeling almost as frustrated as the puddy-tat.

He went to the computer, turned it on. It whined, hummed, and clicked. Little numbers began spinning on the left-hand corner of the monitor. Eventually, a full color photo of Maddie Gray appeared on screen. A recorded voice, presumably Maddie's, said, "Get to work, bitch, the rest of the world is gaining on you."

"It passed me by a long time ago," Goodman mumbled to himself.

"Huh?" Morales asked.

"Nothing."

"Let's show Mr. Sweetie the ring an' vamoose," Morales suggested.

Goodman, who knew less about computers than he did about women, tapped a few keys. Maddie Gray's picture was replaced by a list of numbers from one to twenty. He typed the number nine and the enter key.

A message appeared on the screen: "The drive or network connection that the shortcut '9' refers to is unavailable. Make sure that the disk referred to is properly inserted or that the network server is available and try again."

The message might as well have been written in Farsi.

Goodman turned off the machine and led Morales back down the stairs.

Lydon was at his own desk. The young policeman was on a couch against the wall, evidently determined not to let him out of his sight again.

The little man studied the ring from several angles, then announced, "It's not at all tacky, like that bracelet you showed me. Rather nice, actually. Very pricey, I'd say."

"Ever see it before?" Morales asked.

"No. Should I have?"

"It wasn't Ms. Gray's?" Goodman asked.

"I told you, Maddie didn't wear jewelry. Certainly not on her hands. She had beautiful hands. Big, but beautiful."

Goodman took back the ring and thanked Lydon for his help. He asked the policeman to walk them out.

At the door he told the young cop, "Don't let him leave here with anything he didn't come in with."

"He brought a briefcase. Want me to search it?"

"That's probably a good idea."

"Want me to search him?"

Morales grinned. "Lydon might dig it."

"And he might not. I'd just give him a visual," Goodman told the young cop. "Be on the lookout particularly for a computer disk."

"Will do, detective."

In the car, Morales said, "We're not that far from Big Boss Burger. One Big Boss with the hot sauce comin' up."

He started the engine and was rolling down the canyon road when Goodman shouted, "Stop!"

"What's up?"

Goodman pointed at the home about a hundred yards from the Gray house. It was a ramshackle wooden cottage with a shake roof, wedged in among the rock outcroppings. A dusty Jeep Cherokee was in the drive and a man in his late twenties or early thirties was extricating a large wooden carving of what appeared to be the Madonna from the rear of the vehicle. "The Palmers are back," Goodman said. Stephen and Caitlin Palmer were the only neighbors of

Madeleine Gray's who had not been interviewed. Their place had been shuttered since the murder.

The two detectives were waiting for Stephen Palmer when he returned to the Cherokee for more wooden statuary. He looked younger the closer you got, Goodman decided. Definitely still in his twenties, with curly black hair and a pleasantly bland face. He was wearing khaki pants and shirt and pale yellow desert boots. They flashed their badges. He didn't seem too surprised to find two policemen in his driveway.

"I guess you're here about Maddie?" he said.

"That's right," Goodman said. "Is Mrs. Palmer with you?"

"Inside, unpacking. We just got back from TJ."

The Palmers, it seemed, traveled to Tijuana every so often to stock a shop on Melrose where they sold Mexican artifacts. "Not the kind of junk you can get on Olvera," Palmer was quick to point out. "High-end merchandise."

He led them inside a small but high-ceilinged house filled with rough-hewn furniture, statues of saints, candles, elaborate horned and fanged masks, and one whole wall devoted to Day of the Dead gewgaws. To Goodman's amusement, Morales seemed very uncomfortable in the presence of the artifacts, eyeing the plaster skeletons and devil masks suspiciously, as if he expected them to claim his soul at any minute.

Caitlin Palmer was a willowy brunette wearing a white cotton blouse that had been wilted a bit by the drive, designer blue denims tight enough to have been painted on, and thick, cork-soled clogs held to her feet by rainbow-colored straps. Glasses with extra-large round lenses perched near the end of her handsome aquiline nose. She was at least ten years older than her husband, maybe more.

Her gray eyes focused on Goodman over her glasses as

she said, "It's a horrible thing. We just heard about it yesterday. We'd been in a little village named Tuscana. About forty miles out of Tijuana. Heard of it?"

Goodman looked at Morales, who shrugged.

"They have this marvelous craftsman—"

"Darling, these guys aren't here to talk about arts and crafts," her husband said.

Her expressive eyes flashed, then froze. "No, of course not. You're here about Maddie."

"Did either of you know her very well?"

"As neighbors know one another, I suppose," Caitlin Palmer said. "To say hello. We've never been invited inside her house. Have we, dear?"

Her husband gave a vague shrug.

Goodman was trying to place her accent, the crisp articulation, the almost musical speech pattern. Not quite British or Irish, but somewhere in between. Probably the never-never land of Affectation. "Ever meet any of her friends?" he asked.

"I can't imagine we have. Except for her little fairy, of course."

"Excuse me?"

"She means her assistant. Art Lydon. He's been by the shop."

"I'm sorry, lover," Caitlin Palmer said to her husband. "No offense meant."

"None taken, precious," Stephen Palmer replied through clenched teeth.

Another Hollywood Couple of the Year, Goodman thought. He asked, "What time did you leave for Tijuana?"

Caitlin frowned. "About five P.M.? Wasn't it about five?"

Her husband nodded in agreement.

"Either of you hear or see anything odd before you left?"

"I was too busy getting ready. Stephen, you were out front."

Stephen shrugged. "Nothing . . . out of the ordinary."

"Thank you both for your cooperation," the detective said.

"Come back anytime," Caitlin Palmer said. "You, too," she said to Morales.

Stephen walked them back to their car. Before getting in, Goodman asked him, "What did you mean by 'nothing out of the ordinary'? What was 'ordinary'?"

"Oh, just . . . Maddie had a temper and she liked to shout."

"So you heard her shouting the evening of the murder?"

"Art told me it was her favorite way of talking."

Morales slid across the car's front seat, the better to hear Palmer.

"Was she shouting at Art?" Goodman asked.

"Not Sunday. I don't know who it was. Somebody in a very nice beige Jag convertible. Not the true classic, the, what was it, the XK 140. God, that was a stunningly beautiful car. The smooth lines. The old hood ornament. Not that tacky medallion."

"But it wasn't an XK you saw," Goodman said to put him back on track.

"It was more sixties. An XKE, maybe. Still pretty handsome."

"You saw the car but not the driver?" Morales asked.

"The ragtop was up when it passed, traveling very fast."

"Did you hear what Ms. Gray was shouting?" Goodman asked.

"Just 'fuck you' over and over again."

"No name?"

Palmer thought about it. "Not as I recall."

"And she sounded how? Playful? Mildly angry? Furious?"

"Like she had a real burr up her ass. She'd have to have been furious to wish the other person dead."

"That's what she did?" Goodman asked.

Palmer frowned. "I'm sorry. Yeah. In point of fact, she was shouting 'Fuck you. Die. Fuck you.' But, like I said, she shouted a lot. And whoever it was left while she was still alive and vocal."

"Tha's the beauty 'bout cars like that Jag," Morales said, almost mockingly. "You turn the wheel and they can take you right back where you came from."

Palmer straightened. "Well, it didn't return while we were here," he said brusquely.

He made an abrupt about-face and returned to the cottage. Goodman shooed Morales back to his side of the car and got in.

"How many tan XKE convertibles can there be in Southern California?" he wondered aloud as his partner steered them down the canyon road.

"Don't know," Morales answered. "Not my favorite kinda wheels."

"Let's put somebody on the phone calling dealers and car clubs," Goodman said. "Shouldn't take too long to locate the car."

"Then, amigo, we're gonna have to prove the Jag came back here later. That might take a little longer."

≡ TWENTY-SIX ≡

As a result of a telephone call she'd made several days before, Nikki was having lunch with a young woman named Sue Fells whom she hadn't seen since law school. Sue, who'd been an overweight, bookish grind while a student, had matured into a trim, handsome power player. Most of that transformation had occurred while she was working her way up from a clerk to a junior partner of the firm of Jastrum, Park, Wells.

Sue's hazel eyes surveyed the quiet tearoom that she had chosen for their secret meeting as she said, "You know, Nikki, I wouldn't have taken this risk for another soul."

"I appreciate that," Nikki replied, using her fork to poke at the weird-looking potato mess on her plate. "What do they call this?"

"Shepherd's pie," Sue said. "Supposed to be good here."

"Yeah? Well this one they can give back to the shepherd."

Sue laughed. "Still the same old Nikki," she said.

"Not hardly." She took a sip of tea that was too hot and said, "So give, Sue. Tell me about the great Jesse Fallon."

"I know from experience that our living legend is an insufferable, arrogant asshole who treats his clerks like dog shit."

Nikki grinned. "Don't hold back. Tell me what you really think."

"I owe you big time," Sue said. "You all but dragged me through first-year law. But I would have done this just to get back at Fallon."

"So do it," Nikki said.

"The old man's practically retired these days," Sue said. "Spends more time out of the office than in. Usually, Walter Park has to beg him to take on a client. This time Fallon demanded that Walter let him take on Deschamps pro bono. Must be a friend of the family, something like that."

Nikki hoped that wasn't the case. "What about paperwork?" she asked.

"In Fallon's office, under lock and key," Sue said. "Impossible to get at, especially since he's got a witch of an assistant who watches over him like a mother hen. But," she grinned triumphantly, "even a hen has to waddle away from the nest to eat. So . . ."

She reached down for her purse. From it she withdrew a short stack of papers that she handed across the table. They were photocopies of pages from Fallon's appointment book.

"I don't know if it'll help," Sue said. "I don't even know what you're looking for."

"As I said on the phone," Nikki replied, greedily scanning the pages, "it's nothing that'll impact on your firm in any way." She hoped that was the truth.

"I wouldn't mind if it impacted on Fallon," Sue said, taking a sip of tea.

Joe Walden was on his way out of the office when Nikki returned. "I'm headed for a late lunch with the mayor," he told her. "I don't suppose there's anything new on the Gray case I could serve him for dessert?"

She hesitated, thinking of the xeroxes in her briefcase. But she had no idea what, if anything, they might divulge. She shook her head.

He frowned. "Those Homicide clowns are dragging their feet, I know it. When was the last time you checked with them?"

"I called about an hour ago," she said. "They were in the field. I left word."

"Do better than that," he said. "Their investigation is running like a dry creek. Get their cellular numbers and bug the hell out of 'em. Ride 'em hard. If they give you any trouble, come to me and I'll start kicking ass big time."

Right. Like she was really going to come to her boss and tell him she was incapable of doing her job. She watched him bounce off a desk as he rushed to the elevators. He was just about running on empty. Not enough sleep. Too much on his mind. It had not been the right moment to explain that neither Goodman nor Morales carried a cellular phone. As Carlos had explained, "They tell us we gotta have a name tag for crime scenes. Fifty bucks, but I buy the fucking name tag. They tell us we gotta buy a beeper. Okay, beep beep. I do that. Then they *suggest* we carry a phone. Well, screw the suggestion. They want this *hombre* to fork out the money for a goddamn phone, they gonna have to put it in writing."

Before going to her office, she detoured to the reception area, slid the magnet next to her name from "out" to "in," and picked up her messages—eight pink phone slips. Four were party invitations from people she didn't know. A literary agent she'd never heard of wanted to speak with her about an autobiography. Two journalists wanted to interview her. A local ad agency wondered if she did product endorsements.

"Here's another," said the receptionist, a young black woman who evidently spent most of her free time working on her perfect oxblood nails. "Just came in. Collect call, from Folsom Prison."

Nikki added that pink memo to the others.

"The, uh, party said he'd call back," the receptionist told her.

"Yeah," Nikki said. "He always does."

In her office, she trash-canned the pink memos and spread out the photocopied sheets carefully on her desktop. Sue had apparently been right: judging by the few notations on his calendar, Fallon had not been very active. She easily found the date and time he'd set for his first appointment with Deschamps at the Bauchet Street lockup. The pages for the preceding days had been mainly blank, except for a smattering of incoming calls. On the day before his lockup visit, Fallon had heard from two people—an L. Langham and a J. Doyle.

There had been two more "J. Doyle" calls.

Nikki looked at the phone directories resting in her bookcase. *How many J. Doyles can there be in Southern California?* she wondered, as she dragged the thick volumes back to her desk.

There were nineteen in just the greater L.A. area. J. Doyle might be from Santa Monica or Pasadena or—

Her phone rang.

The receiver was halfway to her ear when she remembered Mace Durant's promise to call again. "This is Nikki Hill," she said warily.

"This is the lucky man gonna have dinner with Nikki Hill tonight," Virgil Sykes said, "or know the reason why."

"Okay," she said.

He was silent for a beat, then said, "Beg pardon?"

"I said 'okay.' Dinner tonight sounds fine."

"Good," he said, apparently thrown off balance by her quick acceptance. "Good," he repeated. "Excellent, in fact. Pick you up at the office . . . ?"

"My place," she said. "It's—"

"Don't make it too easy," he said. "I'm a detective. I'll find out where you live. Eight o'clock okay?"

"Uh huh," she said, wondering what she was getting herself into.

≡ TWENTY-SEVEN ≡

See the mark there," the elderly jeweler instructed Goodman, holding out the ring that Jamal Deschamps had taken from Madeleine Gray's corpse.

The two detectives and the jeweler were in the back room of the latter's unpretentious shop on Fairfax Avenue. Goodman, squinting, saw only a smooth double-tiered inner band of what the jeweler had called an unusual design—a combination of platinum and fourteen-karat gold, with a three-carat blue diamond in a prong setting. Maybe there was one little speck of something on the band, the detective thought. He squinted. "Better lend me your loupe, Alphonse. With my eyes, I can barely make out the ring."

"Wait'll you're my age, Eddie," the jeweler said, searching his bench for a magnifying glass. "Then you'll really have something to grouse about."

"How old are you, Alphonse?" Morales asked, tearing himself away from an Erte sculpture of an obviously female sprite.

"Eighty-eight, my last birthday," Alphonse replied proudly.

"Oh, man," Morales said, "that may be too much life for me."

"Beats the alternative," Alphonse said.

Did it? Goodman wasn't sure, the way things were going. He held the magnifying glass. Yes, there was something on the ring's surface. "What am I looking at, Alphonse?"

"The signature of the artisan who designed and created the ring. The backward 'R,' with a box around it."

Goodman thought he saw it. "Recognize the signature?" he asked.

"Two people use it. Emilio Rodriguez of Taxco, and his son Emilio, Junior, who lives in Santa Barbara. This, I'm fairly certain, is the boy's work. His father wouldn't use platinum. And the setting was just a bit careless."

"You handle their stuff?"

Alphonse shook his head and smiled. "Thanks for the thought. Emilio sells only from the family shop in Taxco. The boy's work is much too upscale for my customers."

"Then where . . . ?"

Alphonse studied the ring and said, "Platinum and gold. Probably Halyard's."

"In Beverly Hills, right?"

"There's a Halyard's in Orange County, too. At Fashion Square. But I'd try Beverly Hills first. You guys wouldn't be working the Gray murder? Is that what this is about?"

Goodman gave him a noncommittal smile and returned the ring to its plastic baggie carrying case.

Alphonse led them back through the store, where his wife was waiting patiently for a young man wearing black trousers, a white shirt, and a yarmulke to make up his mind about a signet ring. Alphonse's wife was half his age, a big, blond Israeli woman who disliked Goodman and made no pretense about it.

That was the way it was. The guys you put away—in

Alphonse's case, for armed bank robbery—might forgive you, but the wives never did.

Leland Petit, the manager of Halyard & Company of Beverly Hills, had taken the day off. His assistant was an arrogant woman of middle age whose angular body made her look vaguely awkward even in an obviously expensive designer dress. With a brusque Teutonic accent and manners to match, she assured them Petit would be at the store in the morning.

"We can't wait," Morales told her. "Why don't you just take a look—"

"I know nothing about this," she interrupted. "This is a matter for Mr. Petit."

"Tell us where he is and we'll find him," Goodman said.

"That I cannot do," she said and started to walk away.

"Hold on, lady," Morales said. She stopped, frowning in annoyance. "We talkin' murder," the detective continued. "We gotta speak to Petit right now."

"Impossible."

"Nothin's impossible in a murder investigation," Morales insisted.

"Fine. Then you go to the island of Catalina and look for him. He's there with a friend hunting wild boar. Where specifically, I have no idea. No telephone. No beeper. Just the two men and two guns. If you find him, be sure to wear a sign, so he will not mistake you for a boar." With that, she left them.

"A real ball buster," Morales grumbled as they exited the store.

Goodman, though his opinion of the woman had improved a little with the boar comment, was forced to admit his partner had a point. "We'd better bring a warrant tomorrow," he said. "Just in case."

≡ TWENTY-EIGHT ≡

Th at's a big hunk o' dog meat you got there," Virgil said, eyeing Bird with caution. The animal had insisted on answering the door with Nikki. Now he positioned himself between his mistress and the tall stranger.

"If we shake hands," Nikki said, "he'll relax a little."

She reached across the dog. Virgil took her hand and kissed it.

The animal did not relax.

"Bouviers are very possessive," she said.

"No shit. He's barin' his teeth."

"Don't worry. Bird's a sweetheart." She ran her hand through the dog's curly hair. "How's about a drink?"

Bird let out a low, rumbling growl.

"Might as well head on out," Virgil said. "Reservation's for eight-thirty."

"Okay. Give me a minute."

She left them and walked swiftly to the bedroom, pausing only to pick up her ratty Bugs Bunny slippers from the kitchen floor. When she'd told Loreen about the date, her

friend had urged her to hide the slippers. "They look like rab-
bits with the mange," Loreen had said. "Turn a man off faster
than a cold shower. I swear, I ever get caught in an alley with
a ugly crack-head rapist, I pray to God I'm wearing your
Bugs Bunny slippers."

Nikki carried the fuzzy footwear to the bedroom and was
about to toss them into the closet when she stopped herself.
The room was a mess, as usual. She'd considered straightening it up, then decided it would be one more reason not to
let this first date turn into a one-night stand.

Just to make sure she'd be sleeping alone, she placed the
slippers on the bed and shined her reading lamp directly on
them.

Satisfied, she rushed to the bathroom, filled her handbag
with breath spray, comb, makeup, and other essentials. She
returned to find Bird and Virgil glaring at one another.

"You just move in here?" Virgil asked.

"Umm," she said. "Haven't had a chance to go furniture
shopping."

"It's a big place," he said. "Great location." Then he yelled
"Aiee," because he had just felt a dog's nose poke between
his legs.

Nikki couldn't help laughing. "He's just sizing you up,"
she said, grabbing the dog's collar and pulling him away
from the detective.

"Oh?" Virgil grinned. "How do I fare?"

Nikki bent down and put her ear to Bird's mouth. "He
says you're about average."

"The dog lies," he said, ushering her to the door.

The drive to the restaurant began on an up note, with Virgil amusingly describing his past misadventures with dogs,
cats, and other household pets. He was in the middle of a
story about a beautiful voodoo priestess and her snake when

Nikki realized his attention was drifting from the freeway to the rearview mirror. She turned and saw nothing but headlights. "Something back there?" she asked.

"Car coming up fast," he said. "Satchel Paige may have been one hell of a ballplayer but he wasn't much at givin' advice. Somebody's gainin' on you, that's exactly when you wanna be . . . Damn!"

She turned her head just as a flat-gray Chevy roared past, missing their car by inches. Nikki thought she saw a young boy grinning at them.

Virgil's face hardened and he pressed down on the gas, taking off after the sedan.

"What the hell are you doing?" she asked in alarm as he shifted lanes so abruptly he nearly cut off a little sports car.

"Punk tried to shake my tree, baby. Now I'm gonna shake his."

The Chevy was pulling away. Nikki saw that its license plate was covered with mud or paint. Virgil pushed the T-Bird, weaving in and out of the freeway traffic, causing other cars to swerve perilously.

"Stop this," Nikki said. "Some little boy disses you, you're gonna risk a smashup?"

He didn't seem to have heard her. Too intent on closing the gap.

He was within a car length of the Chevy when the driver's window rolled down and a beer bottle flew out and exploded against the T-Bird's windshield.

Ducking instinctively, Virgil yelled, "Bastards," as he steadied the wheel, managing to avoid a collision with a truck that Nikki had thought inevitable.

"That's enough, damn it!" Nikki shouted.

The Chevy suddenly cut across two lanes of traffic and left the freeway at Culver City. Virgil followed their lead, apparently mindless of the other vehicles, prompting a chorus of horns and yells and the screech of brakes.

The chase continued down the less crowded Washington Boulevard at a speed approaching ninety mph. Nikki glared at Virgil, a man obviously too obsessed to consider the threat he was posing. She had just about made up her mind to reach over and turn off the ignition key when they heard the siren.

A blue-and-white, bubble blazing red, roared up behind them, cutting them off, forcing the T-Bird to the curb.

In seconds, two uniformed policemen, both white, were out of the prowl car, guns drawn and flanking their vehicle. "Hands on the dash," the one near Virgil ordered.

Nikki placed her hands in front of her. Through the splintered windshield, she saw the Chevy disappearing into the distance.

"On the dash, now," the cop shouted at Virgil, who finally complied. Nikki could feel the fury and frustration coming off of him like a blast of energy.

Through clenched teeth, he said, "I'm a plainclothes officer with the LAPD. My ID is in the top pocket of my shirt. I—"

"Just cool your jets," the cop from Culver City said. He opened Virgil's door and, keeping his gun aimed, reached in and fumbled the brown leather folder from the detective's pocket.

With some reluctance, he holstered his pistol and placed the ID and badge on the dash between Virgil's vibrating hands. "He's a lawman," the cop told his partner.

"Then he oughta know better'n to be flying down Washington like that," the partner said.

"I was in pursuit of a vehicle," Virgil told them, enunciating slowly.

"I didn't see no vehicle 'cept yours, brother. And you was

traveling at eighty-plus. Dumb fucking thing to do along a boulevard where there are kids and old folks. I oughta run you in anyway, but we'll write this off to professional courtesy."

"That's mighty white of you, officer," Virgil said.

The cop glared at him. "You got that right," he said. "You better replace your windshield. It's against the law, driving with it in that condition. The next officers you meet may not be as white as us." He and his partner sauntered back to their bubble car.

Virgil turned to Nikki and said sheepishly, "I handled that pretty well, huh?"

She shook her head sadly.

"I'm sorry. It's stupid to let my temper get the upper hand."

"Those officers were right. You coulda killed somebody. Us included."

"I know," he said. "I had no right taking chances with your life. It won't happen again, Nikki, I promise."

"Maybe you'd better just take me home."

"Please don't say that. I know I just put you through a bad time, but let me try and make up for that."

What in the world's going on in my head? she wondered. *Why am I cutting this lunatic so much slack? Do I really want to know the answer to that question?*

"Okay. Dinner," she said. "Can you drive with the windshield messed up like that?"

"Sure." He took his gun from its holster and knocked out the pieces of broken glass until he had a clear view. "My insurance company's gonna jus' luuuv me," he said.

The restaurant he selected was a new place on La Cienega Boulevard called the Other LA. It reminded Nikki of an upscale roadside tavern in some 1950s movie—wooden floor, heavy dark tables and chairs, and padded leaf-green leather booths with brass studs. The difference was that moss was hanging from the rafters and a huge oak tree seemed to have sprouted up in the center of the room, its leafy top extending toward an open skylight.

Once they were ensconced in their booth, Virgil seemed to relax, but she noticed he'd positioned himself in the corner where the leather met the wall, the better to get a 180-degree view of the room and its inhabitants. *Great. Reckless* and *paranoid.*

Their drinks arrived at their table with astonishing speed, carried by a handsome, very light colored man whom Virgil greeted enthusiastically, asking him to join them. The man's name was Desmond St. Jean and he and his brother, Phillipe, both Creoles from Louisiana, were the owners. He was charming and flirtatious, assuring Nikki she was much more beautiful than her picture in the paper. He suggested that they let him create the menu for them.

Watching him move on to greet his other patrons, Nikki said, "That man's a serious hunk. Somebody should put him in a movie."

"He'll think that's pretty funny. See, him and his brother, we all met makin' the rounds out here, tryin' to get some producer to do just that."

"*You* wanted to be an actor?"

"Sure. And I wound up working undercover. Pretty much the same, except the pay is lousy and the bullets are real. But I can guarantee you, actors—even the superstars—don't eat any better than we will tonight."

The first course, a delicious crawfish bisque, was followed by a seafood jambalaya. She studied Virgil while they ate, trying to get a fix on why she found him appealing. He was handsome, of course. But she'd had handsome. He was . . . different. A man who gave his emotions full rein, moving from laughter to anger, from crude to sensitive, in the blink of an eye. Life with him would never be dull. But wasn't dull what she wanted? Hadn't her time with Tony taught her anything? Was it recklessness that attracted her?

Virgil freshened their glasses with the dry white wine Desmond St. Jean had sent to their table. "I saw your boss on TV today," he said. "You and him any way involved?"

She shook her head. "Strictly business."

"I thought I caught something in his face when he started talking about you."

"He was talking about me on TV?"

"Said you were his eyes and ears on the Madeleine Gray investigation."

"Well, that's nice of him," she said, feeling a little giddy from the drinks and the wine. "And you caught something in his face, huh?"

"The camera picks up funny stuff," Virgil said.

"An actor," she said. "Came all the way out here to be an actor."

"Why else would anybody come to this loony land?"

"I wouldn't know," she said. "I didn't have a choice. I was born here."

"Where abouts?"

"Grew up in South Central."

"Paper said your daddy was on the job for a full twenty-five."

She nodded, keeping her face neutral. "I didn't see much of him. My grandma raised me after my mama died."

"Brothers or sisters?"

"No." Actually, she had a half sister, but she barely knew her. "You?"

"Had an older brother. Passed away."

"I'm sorry."

"We grew up down south. Thibodaux, Louisiana."

"Then you're a Creole like Desmond?" she asked.

"Not exactly. See, the St. Jeans were part of what they call the Creole aristocracy. Their ancestors were opera singers and poets and composers. My daddy was a sharecropper. The thing we have in common, Desmond's family and mine, is that we're too black to suit white folks and too light to suit blacks. That's down South. Out here, we're professionals."

He looked at her. "You're sorta fair yourself," he said. "Got that touch of red. 'Redbone.'"

"You're starting to sound like your alter ego, Juppy."

"Yeah." He grinned at the memory. "I called you 'Red' that day. It fits. You mind the name?"

She always had. But maybe she was changing.

"It kinda goes with those freckles."

"Never liked the freckles." She was definite about that.

"They're sweet."

"Enough about my freckles. I want to hear about you."

"Well, like I say, my daddy farmed land. His daddy was a local judge. A white man. Had himself a legitimate white family but he saw to my grandma, and he seemed to like her well enough. When he died, he left her some money. She passed it on to my brother and me. I took my share and got out of that little tarpaper shack fast as I could. I was sixteen."

"You came out here then?"

"Nope. Got as far as Atlanta. Met a woman who picked me clean. Followed her and her pimp to Chicago where a cop friend of my daddy helped me get some of it back. I stayed on with him and his wife, finished high school, and then came out here to be the next Billy Dee Williams."

"Did you know anybody out here? The St. Jean brothers?"

"I didn't meet them 'til later," he said. "But my bro was out here. Caesar. You gettin' the idea my mama liked Roman history? Anyway, I spent my first year in L.A. sleeping on the couch in Caesar's downtown loft."

"How'd he die?" she asked.

"He was an innocent. Couldn't tell the scumbags from the good guys. Wound up on crack."

He looked down at the tablecloth, lost in some private memory.

Nikki felt her heart opening up to him. "It's getting late," she said.

During the drive to Ladera Heights, they communicated mainly in silence, he glancing her way from time to time, knowing her eyes were on him. "I definitely get the feeling we're starting something here, Red," he said.

She had that same feeling. It scared her.

As they strolled to her front door, they heard Bird inside galumphing across the living room to greet them. Virgil stopped Nikki and drew her to him. When they kissed, she felt like Sleeping Beauty. Sexually speaking, she'd been asleep for so long the intoxication of a new romance was waking up her body.

But as good as she felt, hot from the kiss and pleasantly woozy from drink, she didn't want to give it up just then. Not on the first date with this reckless wildman. That's why she'd left the bunny slippers out, why she hadn't bothered to clean up the bedroom. Of course, she could run in there and fix it up in seconds . . . *No! I don't really know this man. And as good as his body feels next to mine, and it does feel good . . .*

With some reluctance, she pulled away from him.

He stared at her in surprise.

"Time to say good night, Virgil."

"Seemed to me that that kiss was saying 'Come on in, Virgil.'"

"Then I guess I should have saved it for next time."

"Tomorrow night?"

"That'd be—"

She was interrupted by the roar of a souped-up engine. The Chevy they'd been chasing earlier rounded the corner and screeched to halt beside Virgil's T-Bird. Inside the house, the big dog sensed conflict and began to bark.

Virgil ran down the walk, drawing his gun. The driver's widow descended and the boy behind the wheel tossed a beer bottle that broke at the detective's feet. Then the Chevy spun away, leaving rubber streaks along the otherwise spotless street.

By the time Nikki reached Virgil, the car was long gone.

"You were gonna shoot 'em for throwing bottles?" she asked.

Virgil looked at the gun in his hand and smiled, putting it away. "See, Red. You've been a good influence on me. I didn't even pull the trigger once."

"Any of that broken glass catch you?" she asked.

"Naw." He shook his head in wonder. "It just keeps gettin' worse. Kids so crazy, if you don't roll over when they first mess with you, they spend the whole night following you around, tryin' to get even."

"That how you see it?"

He frowned. "Yeah. You got other ideas?"

"They went to a whole lot of trouble. Laid in wait to trail us to the restaurant, then here. Just because you chased them on the freeway?"

"Why else?"

"Maybe they recognized you. Or me."

"Ahhh. I see what you're gettin' at." He smiled. "This is the price I pay for going out with a celebrity who's a figure of controversy."

"You *can* be an idiot," she said. "A sweet idiot." She

kissed his cheek. "Try to stay out of trouble on your way home."

Watching him drive away, she doubted he was taking the incident as lightly as it seemed. She wasn't taking it lightly at all. She gave the street a wary scan, then stepped around the shards of broken bottle and went into the house to calm Bird down. The glass cleanup could wait until morning.

≡ TWENTY-NINE ≡

Jamal Deschamps woke up Friday morning to the smell of coffee. He didn't care for brew, didn't like the taste of it, but the odor was definitely def. He smacked his lips a couple times to break up the sleep dust, then let himself slowly drift to the surface of consciousness. He opened his eyes and saw two dudes parked near his bed, quietly sipping from white cups.

He was propped up. The nurse, a horsey-looking sister with a lot of miles on her, had rigged some kind of pillow thing to take most of the pressure off his back wound. But he could feel the deep cut throbbing away. The sutured slash across his leg was singing a little pain song, too.

Medication time.

"One of you guys reach the buzzer for the nurse?" he asked.

Jesse Fallon, who was nearer the hanging buzzer, gave it a squeeze.

"Nice of you to come visit, Mr. Fallon," Jamal said. "Been here long?"

"Just long enough to enjoy a cup of coffee. Care for one?"

"Nope. I get my breakfast later."

"They treating you well?" Fallon asked.

"It's okay. Who's your shadow?"

The man sitting on Fallon's left was of medium height, just a bit on the skinny side, in his forties, maybe, with the goofiest comb-over Jamal had ever seen on a white guy. It sorta swirled around the man's dome without doing much for the bald center.

"This is Ernest Jolley," Fallon told him. "He's going to be handling your suit against the Los Angeles Police Department, the district attorney's office, and the City of Los Angeles."

"Since when did I decide to sue City Hall?" Jamal asked.

"We'll ask for ten mil. I think we can expect a settlement of upwards of two," Jolley said. He was a very pale man with blunt features and something that might have been a strawberry rash on his right cheek.

Jamal turned to Fallon. "I don't get it."

"Simple business," Fallon said. "In today's market, when someone makes a mistake, they pay for it. Arresting you was a mistake."

"Two million, huh?"

"At the very least."

"How do we split that?" Jamal asked.

Fallon seemed to find the question amusing. "Sixty-forty," he said.

"I suppose I know who gets the forty," Jamal said. "Let's see, forty percent of two million dollars is . . ."

"A good day's work," Fallon assured him.

≡ THIRTY ≡

By ten-fifteen that day, Goodman and Morales were in Halyard & Company Fine Jewelers, standing at the rear of the main showroom with the store's manager, Leland Petit, a rangy fellow with a deep tan who resembled the late actor Rock Hudson during his healthier days. He glanced at the ring that Goodman had just handed him, then returned it, saying, with a surprising amount of sincerity, "I wish I could help you, but it's store policy not to give out information about our customers."

Standing just a few yards away, his officious assistant flashed a triumphant smile.

"Then the ring does belong to one of your customers?" Goodman asked.

Petit grinned good-naturedly. "I don't believe I said precisely that."

Goodman was conscious of Morales shifting his feet impatiently beside him, and he was getting a little annoyed, himself. "We really didn't come here to banter, Mr. Petit," he said. "We're investigating a murder and we feel you have information we need. Now, we can go into your office and have a chat and then be out of your hair in ten or fifteen minutes. Or we can insist you come down to where *we* work."

Petit lost maybe a fraction of his charm and said, "I don't imagine Mr. Halyard would expect me to abide by his policy if it meant breaking the law. So if you are legally empowered to request my assistance . . ."

"We are."

"You have a warrant to peruse our files?"

Goodman sighed and turned to his partner.

The previous evening, when Morales had gone to Ray Wise with a request for a warrant, the head D.D.A. had shined him on. "Don't worry. Halyard's will cooperate." Right. Well, he knew how to salvage the situation. "Hey, Wha's yo' problem, man?" he shouted at Petit, loud enough to be heard by every customer on the store's ground level and possibly on the floor above, too. "You tryin' to interfere in a murder investigation?"

Petit paled under his tan, but he stayed controlled. Facing the room, he calmly addressed his customers, "Just a little misunderstanding."

To the detectives, he said, "Gentlemen, will you follow me?"

As they passed the somewhat shocked assistant manager, Morales puckered his lips and blew her a kiss.

Petit's office was small but elegantly furnished, with a private display counter for special customers.

"You want to look at the ring again, Mr. Petit?" Goodman asked.

"I know the piece. It was commissioned through our store."

"The work of Emilio Rodriguez, Jr., right?" Goodman said, and was immediately annoyed with himself for letting an asshole like Petit push him into showboating.

Not that the store manager was impressed by his knowledge. "Young Emilio created the ring," he said.

"For Madeleine Gray?"

Petit's eyes opened wide in surprise. "That's the murder you're investigating?"

"Not for Madeleine Gray, then," Goodman said. He was definitely losing it, leaping to the wrong conclusion and telling this guy too much.

"Ms. Gray was a customer," Petit said, apparently perplexed. "But that ring . . . I know of no connection . . ."

"Just tell us what you do know about the ring."

Petit looked from Goodman to Morales, who was scratching his balls while studying a silver urn resting on black velvet. "The ring," he said, a bit dazed, "was created for Mr. John Willins. He requested the band be both gold and platinum, symbolizing the recording industry's highest accolades."

"Willins makes records?" Goodman asked.

Petit nodded. "Mr. Willins owns Monitor Records."

"Got an address for him?"

Some snootiness returned to Petit's demeanor. "You've probably seen the building. It occupies a full block on Sunset with a huge monitor beacon at its top."

Shit, Goodman thought. That *Monitor Records*.

"I meant a home address," he said lamely.

"I'll see." Petit sat down at an antique desk that held a small black laptop computer. He touched a few buttons on the machine's keyboard.

"Did this Willins guy say who the ring was for?"

"I assumed for his wife. It was sized for her. He gave it to Madeleine Gray?"

"We don't know that," Goodman said.

Petit shook his head in amazement. "The man's married

to Dyana Cooper and he's buying a ring for Madeleine Gray?"

Dyana Cooper! Jesus. Even Goodman, who hadn't been to a movie in ten years or purchased a cassette in twenty, recognized the name. "We don't know who he bought the ring for," he repeated. The idea of a celebrity of Dyana Cooper's international stature suddenly becoming part of the Gray investigation sent a chill down his spine.

Petit frowned at the computer monitor. "I'm afraid all we have is the billing address, which is his office on Sunset." He stood up, shaking his head. "John Willins and Madeleine Gray," he said, mainly to himself.

"Listen to me, Mr. Petit. We haven't determined the significance of the ring, if any," Goodman said. "So I'd stay off the phone to the *Enquirer* for a while."

Petit straightened, and his handsome face showed just a hint of anger. Goodman thought that was about as much as it ever would show. "Is there anything else I can do for you?" the store manager asked.

"How much for this silver thing?" Morales asked, pointing at the urn.

"Nine thousand dollars," Petit replied.

"Nine thou . . ." Morales' face broke into a wide grin. "You're shittin' me, right?"

Petit solemnly assured the detective that he wasn't shitting him.

Willins was gone for the weekend.

The receptionist, a spectacular blond wearing wraparound eyeglasses with frames that matched her neon lime jumpsuit, referred the two detectives to his personal assistant, a slightly more subdued though no less attractive African-American in an off-white power ensemble. She listened to their request and excused herself for a minute or two, returning with the news that Mr. Willins would be tied up until two, but would be expecting them at that time at his home in the Pacific Palisades. She even offered to draw them a map to help them find the place.

"Map? Doan need no stinking map," Morales said, imitating one of his favorite movie characters.

"Ignore him," Goodman said. "We'll take all the help we can get."

≡ THIRTY-ONE ≡

So you seeing this Virgil again tonight, huh?" Loreen asked during their daily phone call. "Big Friday night date."

"Uh huh."

"Go for it, girl. Do not stop and think. You do entirely too much stopping and thinking."

A clerk appeared at the door to Nikki's office, waving a pink message slip. Detective Goodman wanted her to call him immediately. "Gotta run," Nikki said to Loreen. "You sure you don't mind dropping by the house tonight to feed Bird for me?"

"Anything in the name of love," Loreen said. "I'm expecting a full report later about how things go. You know how I live for these secondhand turn-ons."

When Nikki entered the Major Crimes bullpen at Parker Center, Virgil was the first person she saw. The outfit he was wearing was a far cry from his date attire—funky, baggy Levis and a sweat-stained black T-shirt. He was at the rear of the busy room, studying game-plan squiggles on a blackboard with a white detective with a mop of red hair who, judging by his similarly grimy duds, was probably his partner.

"Over here, Nikki," Morales called from somewhere to her left. Reluctantly, she turned to him and Goodman. They had their sport coats on and looked anxious to be going.

"I got here as fast as I could," she said, joining them.

"No problem," Goodman said.

"I appreciate your asking me along," she said as they started for the door.

"Glad to have you."

"Is Dyana Cooper gonna be there?" she asked.

"That'll be up to Willins," Goodman said. "He knows we're coming."

At the door Nikki turned just as Virgil left the blackboard. Their eyes met. Then she heard Morales clear this throat. Unexpectedly, he'd been waiting for her to exit. He'd missed their eye play the way Michael Jordan misses a free throw.

"He's too young for you, Nikki," he said as they walked away down the hall. "An' besides, he ain't a nice guy like we are."

"Oh?" she said, expecting him to elaborate.

Morales had said all he wanted to on the subject.

≡ THIRTY-TWO ≡

Goodman felt his heart beating faster as their sedan stopped beside the gatehouse at 203 Bonham Road in the Pacific Palisades. The duty guard was expecting them. He glanced at Morales's ID and waved them through. "The guy in blue'll show you where to park," he said.

A black man wearing powder-blue sweats and a communications headset appeared from behind the mansion, double-timing toward them. Goodman saw the heavy object outlined under the sweat jacket at the same time Morales observed, "Guy's packin'."

Arriving at their car, the man said, "We'd appreciate your parking in the lot, detectives. We like to keep this area free, in case of emergency."

"You expectin' an emergency?" Morales asked.

The man smiled. "Earthquake, flood, fire. Riot. This *is* Southern California, sir."

Morales followed his instructions, parking beside a Lexus painted a deep purple color that Goodman didn't think he'd ever seen before on a car.

The man in blue was waiting for them on the path. "This way, please."

He led them to the mansion's front door, which he opened with his left hand, continuing to face them. Not being suspicious, Goodman thought, merely prudent. A pro.

Inside, just past the door, a young Latina in a maid's uniform waited with a look of infinite patience on her placid, pretty face. *"Señorita. Señores. Por favor."*

They followed her through the tastefully decorated home to a bright, comfortable room with plaster walls and lots of windows. Dyana Cooper was seated on a couch, a small woman, buffed to an almost muscular finish. Her eyes, too emerald green to be natural, shifted from Morales to Goodman, and finally to Nikki, where they seemed to soften. Goodman decided he'd been wise to invite her.

A tall black man in a subdued Hawaiian sport shirt and tan silk slacks stood just to the left of the couch. Goodman sensed he was keeping his distance because he wasn't clear on whether or not to shake hands with the police. "I'm John Willins," he said. "This is my wife, Dyana. The gentleman by the sideboard is a friend of ours, James Doyle."

As Goodman turned to the plump man who saluted them with a glass of brown liquid, he felt a strange sense of déjà vu with a decidedly negative twist. He filed it away and performed the introductions for his group. "Deputy District Attorney Nikki Hill, Detective Carlos Morales, and I'm Detective Ed Goodman." He thought his name may have registered with the plump man.

"Sit," Willins said. "Serena can bring you tea or a soft drink. Or . . . whatever."

Celebrities were always difficult to deal with. The wealth and power generated by the entertainment industry had long ago turned Southern California into something of a monarchy with show business luminaries elevated to a royal status. Goodman had done his jester's dance down hallowed halls in the past, and he did so once again. "Mr. Willins, could we speak with you alone?"

Willins looked genuinely surprised by the request. Then his eyes went not to his wife, but to Doyle. The plump man barely moved his head in a negative gesture, but Goodman caught it.

So did Nikki, apparently.

"Are you a lawyer, by any chance, Mr. Doyle?" she asked.

"Not by any chance," Doyle said, adding, "though I have nothing but respect for the law and its minions and interpreters. Should Mr. Willins have a lawyer present?"

"I wouldn't think so," Nikki said.

"Since our questions are specifically for Mr. Willins," Goodman said, "perhaps you and Mrs. Wi . . . Ms. Cooper might find them a bit on the boring side."

"I'm interested in anything that has to do with my husband," Dyana Cooper said.

Hell, Goodman thought. *However this turns out—in criminal court or divorce court or both—they can't say he didn't provide the opportunity for discretion.* "Maybe I will have some tea," he said.

They all sat down.

While Serena provided them with glasses of the amber liquid, Willins asked, "What's this all about, detective?"

"We've come into possession of an object we think may belong to you."

Willins raised his eyebrows. "You have it here?"

Goodman dug into his shirt pocket. He noticed that Nikki was staring at Doyle, studying him. Morales was gulping his iced tea, lost in the José Jimenez act he did so well it was impossible to tell when he was paying attention or when he wasn't.

Goodman handed his host the baggie with the ring. Curiosity rarely got the better of him, but his skin was crawling, he was so anxious to see Willins's reaction. Would he play dumb? Would he break down and confess?

What he did, after shaking the piece of jewelry onto his large palm, was grin. "It's your ring," he informed his wife.

"It sure is," Dyana Cooper said, apparently delighted. She slipped it onto her finger.

Goodman turned to Doyle, who was watching the couple. Was the plump man bored? Vaguely interested? Bemused?

"You recognize the ring then, Ms. Cooper?" Nikki asked, for the record.

"Oh, yes. But please call me Dyana." She had her hand in front of her face, studying the effects of the gold and platinum ring against her brown skin. "I've been looking all over . . . wherever did you find it?"

"You lost it when?" Nikki asked.

Dyana's fine brow rumpled in thought. "Sometime last weekend is when I noticed it was gone. I don't wear it every day. I looked for it in my jewelry box and it wasn't there."

"It's pretty valuable, isn't it?" Nikki asked.

Dyana shrugged. "I imagine it is."

"Must be insured, huh?" Nikki wondered.

Dyana looked at her husband, who nodded.

"Then I suppose," Nikki said, "that you've repor—"

"I guess when you have as much jewelry as Dyana," Doyle interrupted, "it's hard to realize that a piece may really be missing and not just misplaced."

Goodman observed Doyle while he asked Dyana Cooper, "Then the insurance company hasn't been notified that the ring was missing?"

"I wasn't sure it *was* missing," Dyana said.

Goodman turned to face the couple. "Did either of you know Madeleine Gray?"

"We both did," Willins said. "Most people in our business did. A terrible thing."

Morales began making sucking noises with the ice in his empty glass and Dyana got the message. She summoned Serena, who did her thing with the tea pitcher.

"Any idea how she might have come into possession of your ring?" Goodman asked.

"*Maddie* had the ring?" Willins asked. "When was it you saw her, honey?"

"Last week," Dyana said. "We were at the Ivy. We dined separately but we met while waiting for our cars. Hers came first and she talked me into going with her to look at gloves at Neiman's.

"Oh, my God," she said, her right hand going to her forehead while her face expressed a mixture of surprise and wonder. "That must have been how it happened. On the drive back from the store, I removed the ring to try on the gloves I'd just . . . And you found it at her home?"

"I guess she was holdin' it for you," Morales said. "Probably waitin' to surprise you with it, next time you two met up in a restaurant."

So he'd been paying attention after all.

"Well, it's wonderful to get it back," Dyana said. "I just wish Maddie were here today, returning it."

"I'm afraid we'll have to hang on to it for a while," Goodman said.

"Why? It's mine."

"It's also evidence."

"I don't understand. Evidence of what?"

"You'll have to take our word for it."

Reluctantly, she slipped the ring from her finger and held it out to him.

He opened the baggie for her to drop the ring in. Pocketing the item, he asked Willins when he'd last seen Madeleine Gray.

The big man shrugged. "Oh, Lord, I don't really know. I remember exchanging a few words with her at the Grammys. Five months ago. Six months."

"No more recently than that?"

Willins shook his head. "I don't believe so."

"Not the night she was murdered?"

"That night I was right here." He looked at his wife. "I worked hard for a lot of years to get my company to the point where I could spend my evenings with my family."

Goodman stood. "We've taken up enough of your time," he said. "Thank you all for your cooperation."

Willins walked them to the front door.

Morales, who was bringing up the rear, paused to glance out of a window that faced the ocean. "Partner, look at that set of wheels. Beauty, no?"

Goodman, Nikki, and Willins all moved to the window.

At the rear of the house several vehicles were parked, among them a Rolls Silver Wraith, a dark blue Range Rover. And a beige Jaguar soft-top.

"Ah, the Rolls," Willins said. "It is a beauty."

"I was talkin' 'bout the Jag."

"The XKE. I bought it when I got my first job in the music industry," Willins said wistfully. "Took me six years to pay it off and I suppose I've spent more than twice the original cost keeping it working."

"Looks like it's in great shape," Goodman said.

"Come on, I'll show it to you," Willins said.

"We're kinda in a rush right now," Goodman said. "Another time, maybe."

As their car moved past the gate and headed out of the Palisades, Goodman asked Nikki for a court order to have the Jaguar impounded. "ASAP," he said, "before Willins decides to get it painted a different color."

"I don't think Dyana Cooper was lying about the ring being hers," Nikki said.

"She's an actress," Morales said. "They can make you believe anything."

"Actresses are still women."

Goodman shrugged. "Might be a marriage of convenience. She finds it convenient for him to stay out of jail. Who knows?"

"Nice alibi the guy's got," Morales said. "He was home. I don't guess the wife or people on his payroll would lie just 'cause he wanted 'em to. And who's this Doyle? I don't trust fat men who don't blink."

"I think he got Jesse Fallon to free up Deschamps," Nikki said. She told them about Fallon's appointment calendar.

"I don't understand," Goodman said. "If he's playing on Willins's team, and he knows Willins is our boy, wouldn't he want Deschamps to stay our number one suspect?"

"Maybe Willins didn't want to see an innocent man pay for his crime," Nikki said.

Morales rolled his eyes. "More likely this guy ain't the same guy phoned Fallon. All them Paddy names sound alike."

"Here's a thought," Goodman said. "Maybe Doyle wanted Deschamps off the spot so that Willins would be more in need of his services, whatever they are."

"Tha's cold," Morales said. "You know this guy, Eddie?"

"He does seem sorta familiar. But I can't quite place him."

"He kept starin' at you, like he's got some kinda hard-on for you."

"I'm not flattered," Goodman said.

* * *

At four-twenty that afternoon, the detectives, along with two uniformed policemen and a forensic expert, seized the Jaguar.

They had little opposition.

The gatekeeper was respectful of the badge. The armed guard in the blue sweats was a bit more truculent, but even he understood the power of a court order. Willins and Doyle were not there at the time, but Dyana Cooper was.

In response to Goodman's request, conveyed via the blue sweatsuit, she provided them with the keys to the car. She remained inside her home, but as they were carefully preparing the Jag for the trip downtown, Goodman chanced to look at the house and saw her standing at a window, watching. She seemed only mildly curious, if curious at all. Maybe the show of disinterest was another example of her acting skill. Or maybe she had something else on her mind.

≡ THIRTY-THREE ≡

Tell me why I'm not going to regret this forever, Ray," Joe Walden said.

Wise cleared his throat. "I . . ." he began, faltered, and nodded toward Nikki, who was sitting beside him in the conference room ". . . that is, *we* both feel Detectives Goodman and Morales had cause to seize the car."

Nikki chanced a quick look at her watch. Seven-fifty. She'd left a message for Virgil with the receptionist, saying that she'd been called into a last-minute meeting and for him to wait in her office. But their date had been for six-thirty and she doubted—

"What do you think, Nikki?" Walden was staring at her.

Her mind flip-flopped, but she replied smoothly, "Like Ray said, we're both in sync on this one."

The big man slumped in his chair. "Christ, I guess we've bottomed out anyway. One more newsworthy fuckup won't matter."

She could understand the D.A.'s depression. The rush to arraign Jamal Deschamps was a mistake that had assumed monumental proportions. Just that morning, the announcement of Deschamps' ten-million-dollar lawsuit against the city and county had pushed all other events, including a nuclear bomb test in southern Asia, far into the TV news background.

Nikki and Wise had expected their midday report on the John Willins connection to lift the D.A.'s spirits. It had had just the opposite effect. After a moment of apparently stunned silence, he'd exclaimed, "My God. John Willins? We're on fifty committees together. The man's a true civic leader. He's done as much to keep South Central from disappearing into rubble as any other humanitarian in this city. Dear God, don't tell me we're going to be trying John Willins for the murder of a white woman?"

Wise and Nikki had exchanged glances and remained silent.

"All right," Walden had said, after taking a deep breath and letting it out slowly. "We're going to stay in control of this one. I'll tell Corben at Major Crimes the same thing I'm telling you: Anyone leaking Willins's name to the press won't just wind up out on their ass. I'll see to it personally they never work in this state again. Understand?"

They'd nodded their complete understanding.

Later, when Goodman informed her that the Willinses' Jaguar had been seized, Nikki, in the new spirit of cooperation, had brought the news directly to Wise. Together they'd carried it to the district attorney, prompting the late-hour meeting.

"We have no hard evidence against John," he said.

"Except the ring."

Walden shook his head and looked rueful. "Perfect," he said. "This damned lawsuit of Deschamps's. I was hoping to diffuse it a little by disclosing the information that one of the main reasons the media's new hero was arrested was that he'd stolen a ring from the dead woman's finger. Now I have to continue to keep the ring from the press."

"Until Willins is arrested," Wise said.

Walden considered that. Finally, he nodded. "Right. Then Mr. Deschamps's five minutes of fame will have ended." He scowled. "But, unfortunately, the discomfort he has caused us will seem like happy days compared to what we'll be going through trying Willins for murder."

"The bright side," Nikki said, "is that we won't be trying him unless we have a pretty good case against him."

He gave her a thin smile. "Pretty good?" he said. "My dear Nikki, before I agree to bring John Willins to trial, I will have to have a case so airtight, we could float it clear acros the Pacific without taking on a drop."

She hoped Virgil would be waiting at her office, but the room was empty.

Disappointed, she sat down at her desk, then saw the folded piece of paper stuck between the rows of her computer keyboard.

"Got tired of staring at your messy office," the note read. "Going to Baby Doe's for a drink. Or two. Four's my limit, so come soon. V."

She began filling her briefcase. Then stopped. She wasn't going to be doing any homework that night and she knew it.

The phone rang. She grabbed it merrily and said, "I'll be right there."

The voice on the other end said, "I have a collect call for Nikki Hill from Folsom Prison. Prisoner J43205."

The end of a perfect day. "Yeah. Go ahead," she said.

"Hi, Nikki." Mace Durant's deep, depressing voice filled her ear. "Tried to get you yesterday, but they said you were out."

"I was."

"Funny thing, hearing about somebody being 'out.' It's a idea you sorta lose track of when you're spending your whole life 'in.'"

"You working on some kind of stand-up comedy routine, Mace?"

"Not exactly, Nikki. Nothing funny about bein' in the joint."

"What do you want?"

"Hear they gonna arrest somebody for the Maddie Gray murder."

She frowned. "Who might that be?" she asked.

"Name don't mean nothing to me. Guy who makes records."

Some secret! "Who told you that?"

"I hear this stuff aroun'. All we got to do in here is talk, listen, 'n' try to survive."

"You're pretty good at all of that, Mace."

"Been at it awhile, thanks to you."

"Me? I didn't tell you to shoot anybody."

"The reason I called: The ole dude runs the liberry went a little soft in the head and they lookin' for somebody else to take over. A word from you wouldn't hurt."

"Can you read, Mace?"

"Don't dis me, Nikki. I been to school. I can take care of the liberry jus' fine. You gonna he'p me?"

"I don't know," she said. "I'll have to think about it."

"Sure would be nice sittin' in the liberry all day. Not worrying about some white boy stickin' me with no shiv soon's I turn my back."

"Hey, you hear anything about the stabbing of Jamal Deschamps?"

"Gang thing."

"That's your answer for everything."

"Gangs are into everything."

"Deschamps in a gang?"

"I don' know about that, Nikki. More likely he pissed

some gangsta off. The job got handed aroun'. Want me to see what I can find out?"

"No," she said. "You stay out of it."

He chuckled. A moist, unhealthy sound ending in a coughing fit. "Worried about ole Mace, huh?"

"Just don't want you getting messed up on my account," she said.

"Now who's bein' the comedian?" Mace asked.

When Nikki finally arrived at Baby Doe's the place was packed with singles revving up for the weekend. Virgil was at the crowded bar talking to an attractive, well-dressed woman who was pressing her thigh against his. Her sister deputy D.A., Dimitra Shaw.

Nikki was still several feet away when Virgil turned to her, grinning. "Hey, Red."

She wondered if he had some sixth sense. "Eyes in the back of his head," Grandma Tyrell would have called it. Then she realized he'd seen her reflection in the bar mirror.

He rose from his stool, taking her hand and pressing it to his lips, at the same time drawing her closer.

"Dimitra keeping you company?" she asked sweetly.

"She walked in here," he said, "I thought it was you for a minute."

The resemblance had been noted before. Initially, Nikki hadn't given it much thought. They were both light-skinned, and lots of black women used her brand of makeup and went to Loreen Battles's beauty parlor. But as time went on, Dimitra had started to shop from Victoria Allard, sometimes purchasing the exact blouse or skirt Nikki wore. Their lunches together, which at first had been occasional, turned into almost daily affairs, during which the younger woman would ask Nikki's advice about everything—from cases she was trying to men she was seeing.

The situation finally came to a head when Dimitra dropped by Nikki's apartment one evening to tell her the great news: she'd just moved in down the block. Though considerably irritated, Nikki had invited her in, poured her a glass of wine, and calmly explained the facts of her life. "I'm a private person," she'd said. "I have my agenda pretty well figured out. I just don't have the inclination or the temperament or the time to put up with a homegirl who's always in my business. You'd better start tending to your own life instead of worrying about mine."

She'd expected Dimitra to react with either tears or anger. Instead, the young woman had reached out a hand, grasped her arm, and said, "Thank you. That's exactly the kind of advice I needed to hear."

They exchanged hellos after that. On occasion, they had longer work-related conversations. The intensity of Dimitra's identification with Nikki seemed to have abated, but it didn't disappear.

"Poor Virgil looked like you'd left him high and dry," Dimitra was saying.

"Lucky thing you were around to wet him up a little."

"Wet and wild, that's the way to be," Dimitra said.

"Maybe we should go have dinner," Virgil said, a shade anxiously.

Nikki looked at him with raised eyebrows. "Dimitra joining us?"

He seemed at a loss for words.

"I, uh, got plans for later," Dimitra said. "You kids go along now and have fun. Don't do anything I wouldn't."

As they worked their way through the crowd, Virgil said, "It's amazing how much you women look alike. Almost could be sisters."

"Almost, but not quite," Nikki said.

≡ THIRTY-FOUR ≡

I ain't big for overtime," Morales complained, wandering impatiently around the crime lab. Goodman was seated on a chair, trying to ignore his partner's complaints while relaxing his whole body, the way his doctor had instructed. "Tonight I'll wind up eatin' dinner at ten, eleven o'clock," Morales continued, "an' the food is jus' gonna sit on my stomach in bed."

Goodman was getting pretty good at perfecting his total relaxation technique.

"Can you give that a rest, amigo. You freakin' me out. All that groanin'."

Reluctantly, Goodman opened his eyes. "It's humming, not groaning," he explained for the tenth or twelfth time. "It clears the head and makes meditation easier."

"Yeah, well, save it for your apartment, huh? What the fuck's keepin' these guys?"

As if in reply, a lab technician entered the waiting area. He was a pale young man with a crew cut and a cheeriness that Goodman found a little grating. He ushered them into a workroom with white Formica counters on which rested an assortment of odd-looking machinery. Early in his career, Goodman had made the mistake of inquiring about a gadget for measuring the whorls in fingerprints only to emerge hours later on the cusp of an anxiety attack but no wiser in the ways of forensic testing. Since then he'd been happy to simply take the words of experts. No detailed explanations necessary, thank you.

The young tech gestured to a counter where two plaster casts rested side by side. "The one on the left is a moulage made from a tire track in front of the Laurel Canyon home," he said. "The radial has plenty of tread. It left a neato impression on that gravel drive. Naturally, we've got photos of the whole drive. I could lay 'em out and show you the exact path the tire took, from the point where it left the road to turn in to the house."

"This'll be fine," Goodman said. "The other cast comes from a tire on Willins's car?"

"Yep. A perfect match."

"No chance we could be talking a different car here?" Morales asked. "Say another Jag XKE with the same brand of radials?"

"No, no, no," the tech replied. "The beauty part is right here." He pointed to a raised spot along the mold. "That's a little chunk that got taken out of the rear right tire of the Jaguar that was brought in. The car hopped a curb, hit a pothole, something. It's unmistakably the tire that made these tracks. Neato, huh?"

"Definitely neato," Goodman said.

As he and Morales walked out of the lab, he said, "Maybe we ought to check with Serology." Samples of something that may have been blood had been taken from the Jaguar's steering wheel and leather armrest.

"They said they wouldn't have nothing till Monday morning. Let's give it a rest, huh?"

"Yeah," Goodman said. "We can all use a rest."

On the twenty-minute drive to his apartment, Goodman heard two repeats of a news item coming from an unnamed source at the LAPD: one of the city's most respected businessmen would be arrested shortly in connection with the Madeleine Gray murder.

He was still ruminating on the identity of "the unnamed source at the LAPD" while fiddling with the key in his apartment lock. Before he could get the door open his neighbor from across the hall, Dennis Margolis, called out to him. He stood in his doorway in faded pajamas and ratty robe, a lonely, balding man with a perpetually worried face that suggested the rigors of everyday life were a bit more than he could cope with.

"Hi, Dennis," he said. "What's up?"

"I just told them the truth, Ed," he said.

"Told who, Dennis?"

"They came to my door. I think they talked to the whole building. I'm sorry to hear you're in some kind of scrape."

"Whoa, partner. Let's take this one step at a time. Who came to your door?"

"Two men."

Goodman frowned. "Description?"

"Ordinary. Guys in suits. Maybe a little rough looking. But I guess if you're in law enforcement, it's a good thing if you look a little rough."

"These guys were in law enforcement?"

Dennis hesitated. "They showed me badges."

Goodman knew that on a scale of easy accessibility, badges ranked somewhere between handguns and toilet paper. "What did they want, these lawmen?" he asked.

"They said you were in deep shit and I would be in deep shit, too, if I held back anything I knew about you."

"So they asked you questions?"

Dennis nodded. "I'm not a terribly good liar," he said apologetically.

"What was there to lie about?"

"Your gun going off that time. At that party."

Goodman had thrown a party to celebrate his last wife's remarriage. That must've been five or six years back. He'd invited most of the tenants and several cops and some women friends. The booze had flowed and everybody had gone a little goofy. One of the tenants had found his gun in a closet and tried a little target practice in the bedroom, blasting out a section of wall.

"They knew about the gun?" Goodman asked incredulously.

"I think that Yokum guy in 4D told them about it. All I said was that it happened. They also asked me about some woman named Jastrup I'd never heard of."

Seven years before, the Jastrup sisters had moved into the building. They were beautiful, young, and fun. And they were call girls. When their madam was arrested, as madams inevitably are, even in Los Angeles, they'd come to Goodman for help.

By calling in a favor or two he'd kept them clear of the roundup of the madam's other employees. Instead of a simple note of thanks, Edie Jastrup offered him a gift he'd been unable to refuse—a fun-filled weekend as her guest at the Four Seasons Hotel in Palm Springs. Cupid amuses himself in perverse ways: at the end of the no-strings-attached holiday, Goodman asked her to leave the life and move in with him. She did.

They were together for the better part of a year, when, for some reason he never understood, she let her sister talk her into a fall from grace. Their idyll came to an abrupt close on a typically bright and sunny morning when she returned from an all-nighter with a Hollywood bad boy, still jazzed from champagne and crank.

Edie Jastrup. So long ago and with him still. As were they all.

"Hope I didn't make any trouble for you, Ed?" his neighbor asked.

A gun going off at a party. Edie. A long time back. "Nothing for either of us to worry about, Dennis. Thanks for letting me know what's going on."

He entered his apartment, conscious of Dennis standing there, looking after him.

Damn it, life was getting complicated.

In the living room, the blinking red indicator on his answering machine was like a beacon in the darkness. He flopped onto the couch and leaned toward the machine to press the playback button.

The voice was one he didn't recognize. Male. Hoarse. Threatening. "We got your number, asshole. Drunk. Crooked cop. Pimp. You're done."

He wasn't bothered by what the caller had said. It was bullshit, more or less. What bothered him was that the guy had his unlisted number.

Grumbling, he went to his kitchenette and poured a shot of tequila. He tossed it back and returned to the phone. He punched the star-six-nine combination and discovered the anonymous call had been placed from a Hollywood pay phone. Then he dialed a new set of numbers. After five rings Gwen Harriman's recorded voice informed him she was not there, but would return his call as soon as possible if he left his name and number.

He didn't.

≡ THIRTY-FIVE ≡

Nikki was surprised to discover that Virgil lived in Hollywood, on one of those tree-lined streets south of Sunset devoted to upscale apartment buildings and condos. He occupied the upper half of a duplex, one of four similar buildings surrounding a lovingly landscaped brick patio. Standing at the top of the stone stairwell leading to his apartment, waiting for him to unlock the door, she looked down at the pond in the center of the softly lit patio and asked, "Koi, too?"

"Pretty damn elegant, ain't it?" he said, holding the door for her to enter.

"My thought exactly," she said.

The building, she figured, was about forty or fifty years old. His furnishings were very contemporary—dark leather and light-colored wood, a thick, pale carpet on the floor. One wall was given over to books and electronic gear. African artifacts—sculptures, snake carvings, textiles—were scattered about.

Among the wall masks was a strange heart-shaped face

with narrow slit eyes and stylized, jagged hair that reminded Nikki of Bart Simpson's. "That's a Fang mask," he said from the kitchenette. "In Gabon, it's used in a ritual where men are initiated into the ngil society. The ngils are the Fang cops."

He returned with a snifter of brandy. "Excuse me a minute," he said, handing her the snifter, "while I drop this coat and tie. Look around. Make yourself comfortable."

She studied the masks a few seconds longer, then moved on to browse through his books. African and American history. Biographies. True crime. No fiction. His music tastes were less restricted. Hip-hop. Pop. Jazz. Some classical. She turned on his CD player and the voice of Luther Vandross came from speakers cunningly hidden around the room.

Damn but the man keeps it clean and neat in here! she thought as she sat on the sofa. She hoped he wasn't a compulsive neatness freak. She kicked off her shoes and tucked her legs under her, sipping the smoky-warm brandy.

"I imagine you're wondering how I can afford to live here?" he asked, reentering the room, his shirtsleeves rolled and collar open.

"The question crossed my mind."

He explained, pouring himself a snifter, that soon after he'd made detective, he'd been assigned to a murder in the complex. "Somebody had carved up this Limey screenwriter like a Christmas turkey. The other residents were shakin' in their Guccis. So, when yours truly put the arm on the twisted little knife artist, the landlord thought it might be a good idea to have a cop on the premises."

"And he just happened to have a vacancy," she said.

He grinned, taking a seat beside her on the sofa. "Yep, this is where the murder took place. In that bedroom."

"Romantic," she said.

"I wouldn't have mentioned it to a civilian."

"Was Dimitra impressed?"

"Dimitra? What made you think Dimitra's been here?"

"Maybe because when I got to the bar tonight, she had her knee in your crotch."

"Is that what that was? Her knee?" His smile was so damned charming it undermined her jealous pose.

The smile left his face as he looked at her, and the intensity of his inspection began to excite her. He must have sensed it because he took the snifter from her hand and placed it and his own on the coffee table. Then he pulled her to him, held her tight, pressed his lips against hers. The feeling of letting go was incredible.

Somewhere nearby, Luther Vandross was singing about not wanting to be a fool for love. Then she and Virgil were in the dimly lit bedroom and Luther's blues were no longer a part of her mural. Nor was Dimitra Shaw. Nor Madeleine Gray. Nor even the poor screenwriter who'd bled to death in that very place, probably a victim of love's folly. All of that was for some other time.

She was in the now of it.

She stood before him, looking into his eyes as his fingers slowly worked on the buttons of her blouse. The garment seemed to float from her body.

He found the zipper on her skirt easily and it too made its way to the carpet.

"Damn it, Red, you're fine," he said.

His hand went to his shirt, but she stopped it. "My turn," she said.

She unbuttoned the shirt. As he shrugged it from his shoulders, she reached out and ran her hand over his bare chest, smiling at the smooth, hard wonder of his body. Smiling more as his breathing grew heavier.

Her hand was at his belt, freeing its clasp. He stayed still as she undid the top button of his pants. At an almost sadistic pace, she slowly pulled down the zipper, lightly brushing him with her knuckles.

Then she took his right hand and placed it at the tab at the front of her black bra. It parted and his hand moved of its own volition, circling her right breast slowly and lightly with his fingers, narrowing the circle to the tip of her erect nipple.

She closed her eyes and felt his breath on her left breast, then the touch of his lips there. Her knees felt weak, but he was ready for that. He was ready for everything.

One of his arms found the bend in her legs; the other circled her back. He lifted her tenderly and carried her the few feet to his bed. He placed her at its center, atop a soft down duvet.

He lay beside her, kissing her forehead, her eyelids, her nose, her lips. Her mouth eagerly accepted his tongue, toyed with it, caressed it with her own. His hands moved over her body, lovingly studying its contours. Wherever he touched, her skin tingled.

His tongue withdrew and tasted the corners of her mouth. Then he slid down the bed, lips pressed against her stomach, tongue busy. She closed her eyes as she felt her silk panties being drawn down her legs.

Oh, please, she thought. *Let this be the start and not the end.* Then the ecstasy was so intense it didn't matter much what it was, beginning, end, or anything in between.

She did not have to tell him when she wanted him to enter her.

He paused to find a condom in a bedside table drawer. She waited for him to break the seal, then said, "Let me."

He moaned as she unrolled the condom over his erection.

He started to lean forward, but she pressed her hands on his chest. "Let me," she said again, and when he answered, "Yes," she straddled him, placing him inside her.

She began rocking, slowly at first. Then her movement became feverish, demanding.

Like a dancer adjusting his style to his new partner's, Virgil's body matched hers in intensity, meeting her thrusts with perfectly timed thrusts of his own.

How can he know so much? she wondered. *How can a man with a backbone move like that?*

And then she shivered and that wonderful, all-encompassing warmth spread through her, making all questions moot.

≡ THIRTY-SIX ≡

I can tell you this for a fact," Lieutenant Foster Corben said to Goodman on Monday morning. "No one from the LAPD, not Internal Affairs, not the chief, nobody from around here is talking to your neighbors."

Corben was as burly as a middle-aged former linebacker. He had dun-colored hair, small active brown eyes, and a razor cut of a mouth over a jutting chin. He sat at his desk, big head cocked to one side, mouth half-open, studying his detective.

"Thanks for checking it out," Goodman said.

"Any idea who these guys might be?" Corben asked. "What they're after?"

"My guess is they're people working for Willins," he said. "What they're after is background info that'll make me look like a donkey in court."

Corben frowned. "You're not getting paranoid on me, are you, Goodman?"

"Oh, I'm paranoid, lieutenant. But that doesn't mean they're not out to get me."

"When they do, we'll talk about it," Corben said, dismissing him.

An hour later, Goodman was back in the lieutenant's office. Morales was with him. According to a report from Serology, a blood trace scraped from the steering wheel of the Willins Jaguar was a match for Madeleine Gray's type, O-negative.

"They also found another trace on the door handle," Corben added. "Type AB."

Goodman frowned. "The company carrying Willins's life insurance claims he's an O-positive kinda guy."

"Yeah," Corben said. "So they're saying over at the D.A.'s. Seems AB is what they found under Maddie's fingernails, too. They're thinking maybe a slight mistake has been made. Ah, judging by that expression on your face, Goodman—sorta like you been slapped in the puss with a flounder—you know somebody who might be AB."

Goodman nodded. "The wife," he said. Why hadn't he even considered that possibility?

"Hell, the first I saw of the Jag," Morales said, "it looked like a lady car to me."

"You gentlemen are invited to a meeting over at the D.A.'s to discuss the new developments," Corben said.

"When?" Goodman asked.

"As soon as you get there."

≡ THIRTY-SEVEN ≡

Nikki had begun the week feeling great, but her romantic glow was dimmed somewhat by the report from Serology.

She and Wise spent the morning feverishly putting together a case against Dyana Cooper. And they weren't entirely satisfied with the results. Sitting in the district attorney's office, watching Detectives Goodman and Morales file in gloomily, she realized that no one seemed very pleased by their prospects.

"All right, folks," Walden said, when the detectives had taken their seats. "Serology has dealt us a new hand. Let's review the bidding, Ray. What've we got?"

"One: vic's blood type on the Jaguar," Wise said. "Two: Dyana Cooper's blood type found under the vic's fingernails."

"Three: Cooper's blood type and fingerprints found on probable death weapon in vic's home," Nikki added, just as she and Wise had planned, to demonstrate their solidarity. "Four: cast-iron witness to the Jaguar being in vicinity of vic's home the evening of the murder."

"Tell me about motive," Walden said.

"Jealousy or a reaction to blackmail," Wise said. "Or a combination of both."

"Take 'em in order," Walden said.

"All right. Jealousy," Wise said. "Husband is screwing Maddie."

"Proof?" Walden looked around the room.

"There's the ring, evidence piece number five," Wise said.

"The ring Willins supposedly bought for his wife?" Walden asked.

"The ring that wound up on Maddie Gray's finger," Nikki said.

"You don't believe Dyana's story about leaving it in Madeleine Gray's car?"

"Gray was wearing it when she died," Nikki said. "You find a friend's ring, you give it back. You don't start wearing it."

"Gray was a blackmailer," Goodman said. "Maybe the ring was part of a payoff Dyana Cooper was making."

"Let's stay with jealousy," Walden said. "How does the ring play into that?"

"Willins and his wife have a beef," Wise speculated. "He gets so pissed off, he takes her ring and gives it to his mistress."

"Possible," Walden admitted. "But we still don't have any evidence to support a romance between Willins and Maddie."

"We'll go talk to the *maricón* who worked for Maddie," Morales said. "And we can check out her competition. Those fuckers are in the gossip business and they didn't like her, you can bet. They'll know exactly who was slippin' her the sausage."

Walden winced at the detective's metaphor but agreed with his suggestion.

"Why do you suppose the ring was still on Maddie's finger?" Nikki asked. "I mean, the body was left in the alley, naked, with a ring on her finger. Why leave the ring?"

"Maybe Cooper just overlooked it," Wise said.

"An expensive, one-of-a-kind ring that'd lead right back to her? Might as well leave a calling card."

"As you and I agreed, Nikki," Wise said, "it's unlikely the death was premeditated. Cooper wasn't planning on killing anybody. Once that happened, she panicked. Forgot about the ring."

"She panicked, but she dragged a naked body out to her car . . ." Nikki turned to Goodman. "Have they found any blood or hair in the Jag?"

"Not as of a half hour ago," Goodman said. "But about the ring. The jeweler told us it was Dyana Cooper's size. Gray was more zaftig. The ring was tight on her. So tight, Deschamps had to break her finger to remove it. Maybe Cooper couldn't get it off and didn't have the heart to use a knife."

That seemed to be an acceptable explanation. Morales, who'd been slumped in his chair, seemingly bored by the discussion, straightened suddenly. *"Tortilleras!"* he exclaimed.

"Say what?" Walden asked.

"Tortilleras! Lesbos! Maddie and Dyana were bumpin' the fuzz," Morales explained enthusiastically. "Maddie throws her over. Or they get in some catfight. Whatever. If they're lovers, then everything fits."

They considered that possibility for a few silent moments. Wise nodded, warming to the idea. "Gray's autopsy finding: evidence of sexual activity without the presence of sperm," he said. "It plays. She gave Maddie the ring. They got in a fight. Maddie dies and Dyana can't get the ring off her finger."

"If Cooper is a lesbian or bisexual," Walden cautioned, "it's not a preference she developed overnight. Celebrities live in goldfish bowls; somebody should have some thoughts on the subject. When you gentlemen chat up the gossip crowd, you might want to put that on your discussion list."

"You don't want us to ignore the blackmail angle?" Goodman asked.

"Absolutely not," Walden said. "I assume you're going over Cooper's background with a fine-tooth comb?"

"Any skeletons in her closet, we'll find 'em."

"The only thing in her closet is her," Morales insisted. "Maybe Maddie tried to sell her some videos of their sessions."

"You want us to bring Cooper in?" Goodman asked. "For questioning, at least?"

Walden considered it, then replied, "With the press hanging around, if you bring Dyana Cooper in for questioning, you might as well accuse her of the crime. I don't think we're there yet. We still don't have a definite on the murder weapon. Our witness who places the Jaguar at the Gray home in the evening also saw Gray alive after Cooper drove away. That may negate the tire prints. Cooper can say that the blood was spilled before she left."

He turned to Nikki. "You were on the money about Deschamps. What do you think about Cooper?"

She glanced at Wise, who nodded imperceptibly. "Ray and I have been picking this apart for the last couple of hours. We just don't have enough to make a case."

"All right," Walden said. "Detectives, it's up to you. Nail it down for us."

≡ THIRTY-EIGHT ≡

The golden phone call came in four days later.

It came from a patrolman named Fuller who suggested Goodman visit the home of a family named Rosten at an address just up Laurel Canyon from Madeleine Gray's.

When Goodman and Morales arrived, Fuller was having coffee with Mrs. Kenneth Rosten, whom he referred to as Lu-Anne, and her teenage daughter, Missy. Looking at the mother and daughter was like seeing the same person at two stages of life. Both were small, nervous, and had features that were sort of . . . well, "rodentlike" was what Goodman wrote in his notes. There was also something disturbingly sensual about them, almost feral, which he didn't write down.

Dull brown hair on mom, with a few strands of gray. Bright orange hair on daughter. Mom in her short skirt and loose blouse. Missy in her ripped Levis and skimpy blouse with tears to provide a peek-a-boo view of her bra and tummy. A stud was stuck into her left nostril.

"You mind telling us what you told Officer Fuller?" Goodman asked the girl.

"Teddy and I were driving home from Weezie's and we saw this car at Maddie Gray's place."

"Teddy would be . . . ?" Goodman asked.

She slumped back in her chair and began rubbing her stomach, running her fingers in and out of the holes in her blouse. "Teddy Maxwell. My beauhunk."

He assumed that meant boyfriend. "And Weezie's?"

She rolled her eyes.

"Tha's a club the kids go to," Morales said. "Over on Vine. Snake pit."

"Okay," Goodman said, wondering how Morales, whose kids were too young, knew where teenagers hung out. "So you and your 'beauhunk' were driving here and you saw a car at Gray's."

"A Jag. One of those real intense Jags. Not all boxy like today."

"When was this?"

She looked at Fuller. "Like I told him, the night of the murder, at just a little before ten. Because, like, I'm fifteen now, I've still got a ten o'clock curfew Sunday nights."

Goodman looked at Mrs. Rosten—LuAnne—who wet her lips with her tongue before nodding in agreement. "She was home by ten."

"Tell me a little bit more about the car, Missy."

"Soft top. Light brown. Tan. Top was up. An XE."

That was almost right. "How do you know it was an XE?"

"Teddy told me. He knows cars. His dad sells 'em."

So, they moved on to Teddy Maxwell.

Thanks to a maid at the Maxwell home, they found him with two of his buddies at a gun club on Manchester, having a fine time blasting targets to smithereens with Hämmerli 280s, high-end, high-tech handguns.

The boys, with their buzz cuts, white cotton shirts, and chinos, struck Goodman as throwbacks to the 1950s, except for the weapons in their fists. They seemed not at all intimidated by the two detectives. One asked to see their guns, a request that was denied.

Goodman, who didn't like the idea of gun clubs in the first place, and who really didn't like the idea of seventeen-year-old boys waving weapons around, not to mention the noise, made the interrogation short and sweet.

What he got from Teddy Maxwell was that the car he and Missy Rosten had observed at ten to ten on the night of the murder had been an XKE. Just like the one that they'd seen at the Willins home.

≡ THIRTY-NINE ≡

Sorry to interfere with your plans for the evening," Joe
Walden said to the four people in his office, "but in approximately"—he consulted his watch, which read 8:03—
"twenty minutes, Dyana Cooper will be arrested for the
murder of Madeleine Gray."

Nikki was seated on the couch, sharing it with a seemingly bemused police lieutenant named Rockland who was
in charge of media relations for the LAPD. Wise was occupying the soft leather chair to the left of Walden's desk. To
the right sat Meg Fisher, a stylish if slightly jaded-looking
woman in her fifties who supervised public relations for the
office and who frequently was mentioned in the press under
the sobriquet "spokesperson for the district attorney."

"Assuming all goes according to plan," Walden continued, "Ms. Cooper will be escorted to Interrogation at Robbery-Homicide. From there, she will be taken directly to
the jail at Parker Center for booking. She will then be
transferred to Sybil Brand."

"No bail?" Rockland asked.

"That's the way the warrant reads," Walden said.

"Arraignment will be when?" Again from Rockland.

"Monday morning, bright and early, before Judge Rule."

"Pays to have a friend in court," Rockland said. "Well, we'll want to make the ten o'clock news with the announcement of the arrest, so I'd better start my calls. I'm pretty sure Chief Ahern will want to break the news himself."

"Better him than me," Walden said.

Rockland frowned. "Meaning what?"

"Everybody loves Dyana Cooper. In a situation like this, people may decide to blame the messenger."

"She's a murderer, right? The arrest is righteous?"

"Legally? Most definitely," Walden replied. "But the public may have other ideas."

"I'll pass along your concerns to Chief Ahern." Rockland made his exit.

The room was quiet for about as long as it should have taken the lieutenant to reach the outer limits of the offices. Then Meg Fisher said to Walden, "You naughty man. Even if Dyana Cooper resembled the late Mother Teresa, it would still be the kind of CNN moment any public official prays for. In fact, while Lieutenant Rockland is busy getting his ducks in order, I should probably make a few calls myself. Starting with CNN. I'm off to my spider's web, to spin, spin, spin."

"I thought she'd never leave," Wise said sourly when the PR woman had gone.

"You're not fond of Meg?" Walden asked.

"I didn't like her when she covered the crime beat for the *Herald-Examiner.* I didn't like her when she read the news on Channel Five. Why should I like her now?"

"Because she's on our team."

"Reporters are reporters, Joe, and sooner or later they'll piss on the carpet."

"Meg is the best, Ray. It's easy to find somebody to clean carpets."

Nikki, who'd lost much, if not all, of her patience in the last ten or fifteen minutes, said, "If that's it, Joe, I'm going to try to grab a bite before going over to Parker Center."

"Anything breaks," Walden said, "phone me immediately, regardless of the time. Otherwise, I'll see you tomorrow afternoon at the two P.M. strategy meeting."

At that meeting areas of responsibility would be carved out and the lead prosecutors would be announced.

"I'll be there," Nikki told him.

≡ FORTY ≡

At approximately eight-thirty P.M. that night, Goodman and Morales and two uniformed officers arrived at the Willins mansion in the Palisades with a warrant for the arrest of Dyana Cooper Willins. What they carried specifically was a Ramey warrant that would allow them to go into the home to arrest her, even if permission to enter was withheld. They needn't have bothered. Neither she, nor her husband, nor their security guards offered any resistance.

Goodman was pleased that they allowed it to progress so uneventfully. As a sign of his gratitude, he exercised his option to bring in his prisoner without the use of handcuffs or shackles of any kind.

≡ FORTY-ONE ≡

Nikki arrived at Parker Center at a little after nine P.M.

She'd not quite finished her second cup of coffee when Jesse Fallon joined her, looking as kindly and avuncular as Santa Claus. Nikki thought she might have been taken in by his benign appearance if she hadn't known of his effectiveness in freeing Jamal Deschamps or heard Sue Fells's vituperative opinion of him. He introduced himself, unnecessarily adding that he was representing Dyana Cooper.

"Some coincidence," she said, "you representing Jamal Deschamps and Ms. Cooper." When he replied with an enigmatic smile, she added, "You're also a friend of a Mr. James Doyle, aren't you?"

To her gratification, he seemed momentarily at a loss. He rebounded quickly, however. "I know the name, but I would not classify Mr. Doyle as a friend." Before she could press him further on the subject, he shifted gears and said, "I do wish Ms. Cooper's arrest could have been handled with more civility."

"Beg pardon?"

"You didn't have to humiliate my client by sending police to her home," he said. "She would have surrendered herself gladly had she known you wanted her."

Nikki smiled. "Counselor, this is a murder case. We don't usually provide special treatment for murderers."

"Ms. Hill, you know as well as I that Dyana is not a murderer."

"Maybe you should save that oratorical jive for a jury, Mr. Fallon."

"I don't try cases, Ms. Hill." His pale blue eyes radiated such intelligence and perception that she felt he might be reading her mind. "Those vigorous tasks I leave to younger, more aggressive and ambitious attorneys, such as yourself. My role in life is to try and keep people from making serious mistakes. You know what I mean, don't you? The kind of silly missteps that can destroy a career."

The man was definitely on the spooky side.

Before he could jump into her head completely, she moved away from him to an empty desk. She remained there, consulting her notes until the detectives arrived with a remarkably composed Dyana Cooper.

Goodman invited Nikki into the room to observe the interrogation. She carried her own metal chair, which she placed in a corner, removed from the scene of the action. She sat there quietly, watching the two detectives do their job and Fallon do his.

"Did you murder Madeleine Gray, Ms. Cooper?" Goodman asked casually.

"No, I did not."

"When was the last time you saw her?"

"The evening of her death."

"At her home?"

"Office. Home. Yes."

"You were there because . . . ?"

"We'd met at a restaurant—"

"The Ivy, right? When we visited your home, I remember your telling us about that," Goodman continued. "You said you went with her to buy gloves."

"Yes. I told you that."

"But it wasn't true," Goodman said.

"No."

"We know that because we talked with the parking guy at the Ivy. That's a problem with being famous, Ms. Cooper. People remember every little thing you do."

"That's one of the problems," she said.

"What are some of the others?"

"When Ms. Cooper writes her autobiography, detective," Fallon said, "we'll send you an inscribed copy."

"According to the carhop, all you did was whisper a few words with Madeleine Gray. Why'd you tell us you drove away with her?"

"I . . . it seemed a simple way of explaining how she got my ring."

"Okay," Goodman conceded. "Why don't we move on to why you happened to be at Madeleine Gray's home that night."

"That evening," Jesse Fallon corrected.

"Yes, that evening," Goodman said.

"Well, I bumped into Maddie at the restaurant and she said a studio publicist had asked her to interview me about my new film, *Whirligig*. She suggested we meet at her place to go over a few of the topics we'd be discussing."

"Sort of a rehearsal?"

"Maddie preferred an informal run-through. It seemed like a good idea. Especially since we really didn't know each other all that well."

"How *would* you describe your relationship?" Goodman asked.

"We exchanged hellos a few hundred times. I'd go on her show if I had something to promote. I suppose we were acquaintances."

"That true of your husband, too?"

"I think so. But you'll have to ask John about that."

"So you went to her place in the Canyon."

"Yes."

"Anyone else there?"

"Just Maddie and me. Which I thought was a little unusual. I was expecting a secretary to take notes, possibly an audio guy to tape our conversation. But it *was* a Sunday."

"In the past, these kinds of assistants were present?"

"Yes. This was quite different. Maddie had been drinking and she wanted me to drink with her. When I refused, she got upset. Started screaming at me that I thought I was too good to drink with her. Nonsense like that."

"Any idea what was on her mind?"

"I never found out."

"Meaning . . . ?"

"I left."

"Not even a guess as to what was bugging her? Why she was drinking that day?"

"No idea. As I said, I didn't know her on a personal level."

"She mention anything to you about money?" Goodman asked.

Nikki noticed that Dyana Cooper hesitated, her eyes shifting to Jesse Fallon. If a signal passed between them, Nikki missed it.

"I'm not sure what you mean," Dyana Cooper said to Goodman.

"You unnerstan' money, huh?" Morales asked, entering the discussion. "Cash."

Dyana Cooper's mouth twitched, possibly in annoyance.

"There was no reason for Maddie and I to discuss money. I wasn't being paid to do the interview."

"What about you paying her to keep her mouth shut?" Morales asked.

"Oh, my," Fallon said, "where do you people get your fanciful imaginations? If you have no more earthbound questions to put to my client, I suggest we call it a night."

Goodman ignored the suggestion. "Wasn't Madeleine Gray blackmailing you, Ms. Cooper?"

"No. Of course not."

"Was she blackmailing your husband?"

Again Dyana Cooper turned toward Fallon, who replied, "If you would like to pose that question to Mr. Willins, I will try to arrange it."

"I'd appreciate that, Mr. Fallon."

"Are we finished here?"

"Not really," Goodman said. "Ms. Cooper, how did your ring come to be in Madeleine Gray's possession?"

"When she started getting abusive, I stood to leave and she pushed me back onto the chair. That's when she saw the ring on my finger. She grabbed my wrist and pulled my hand close to her face so that she could get a better look at it. Then she . . . yanked it off my finger."

"You just sat there and let her take your ring?"

"It was so unexpected. I didn't really comprehend what she was doing until she had it. Then she tried it on and couldn't get it off."

"So you struggled over the ring?"

"Yes. But it wouldn't come off. Maddie went crazy. Yelling. Screaming. She scratched me." Dyana held out an arm and drew back the sleeve of her blouse to disclose three inch-long parallel healing scratches along her right wrist.

"We'll need to photograph that," Goodman said. "And we'd like blood samples."

Dyana consulted her lawyer, who shook his gray head. "I don't think so."

"You don't need permission, detective," Nikki said. "This isn't testimonial or communicative evidence. The right against self-incrimination doesn't apply here."

"No, Ms. Hill," Fallon said. "What we have here is a simple Fourth Amendment unreasonable search and seizure issue."

Nikki shrugged. "All right, so I'll get a search warrant for the blood," she said. "Or get a court order at the arraignment."

"Just want to keep everyone honest," Fallon said. "Now may I arrange bail for my client?"

"We're not finished here," Goodman said. "Ms. Cooper, what happened after Madeleine Gray scratched you? What did you do?"

Dyana looked at her lawyer. This time, Nikki saw him nod. Dyana said, "I . . . I panicked a little, I'm afraid. I hit her."

"Hit her?" Goodman asked. "With your hand?"

"No. With some sort of sculpture that was on the table."

"Could you describe the sculpture?"

"Round and smooth. Globular."

"How many times did you hit her?"

"Just once," Dyana said. "Then I dropped the object and ran out of the house."

"You sure you didn't hit her a couple more times?"

"Ms. Cooper answered the question, detective."

"So you hit her . . . once . . . and ran. Was she hurt?"

"She . . . There was a little blood on her forehead. But she didn't seem hurt. She chased me along the drive out to the road, cursing the whole time. It was a nightmare. I got into my car and drove away."

"Your car being the beige Jaguar we impounded?"

"Yes."

"That was the last you saw of Madeleine Gray?"

Dyana nodded.

"Could you answer 'yes' or 'no' for the tape recorder?"

"Yes."

"What did you do then?"

Dyana frowned. "I'm sorry. What?"

"After this unpleasant episode with Madeleine Gray, what did you do? How'd you spend the rest of the evening?"

"I . . . I drove home. Put something on my scratches and did some relaxation exercises."

Morales leaned forward and grinned at Goodman. "Some what?" he asked.

"Relaxation exercises. To calm down."

Still looking at Goodman, Morales said, "I bet your hummin' sounds a lot better than some I hear."

Dyana Cooper looked perplexed.

"So you was pretty relaxed after that?" Morales went on.

"Reasonably. Considering what I'd been through."

"Was yo' husban' relaxed, too, when you tole him about it?"

The question prompted another silent communication between client and lawyer.

"No. He was . . . upset," Dyana said.

"*He* start hummin'?"

Dyana's eyes flashed. "No. He tried calling Maddie. No one answered."

"So you two jus' sat aroun' tellin' each other what a bad girl Maddie was?"

"Where's this leading, detective?" Fallon asked.

Morales regarded him sleepily. "Jus' tryin' to find out how your client spent the rest of the evenin'."

"Then ask that. It's getting past all our bedtimes."

"Aw'right. Ma'am, how'd you and your ole man spen' the rest of the evenin'?"

"We had dinner at home. I put our little boy to bed. We watched a video and went to bed ourselves."

Morales wiggled his eyebrows and Nikki expected him to make some comment about the Willinses' bedtime activity. He fooled her. "So you're tellin' us that you were at your home that night between the hours of, say, six P.M. and six A.M. the next morning?"

"That's what I'm telling you."

"Then how can you explain your car being observed at Madeleine Gray's home that night?" Goodman asked.

Dyana Cooper looked genuinely puzzled, but she was an actress. "There's nothing to explain," she said. "It could not have been my Jaguar."

"Certainly that must wrap it up, detectives," Fallon said. "Shall we call it a night?"

Goodman studied the woman, who stared back at him, unblinking. "Okay," he said. "We'll be transferring Ms. Cooper to Sybil Brand." The Sybil Brand Institute was the county jail for women.

Fallon seemed surprised. "Why not work out the bail details here?" he asked.

"Nothing to work out, counselor," Nikki said. "Ms. Cooper is here on a no-bail warrant."

The elderly lawyer sighed, again the patient parent addressing an unreasonable child. "Why are you doing this? You know she's no flight risk."

"You can hash this out with a judge on Monday morning," Nikki said. "But your client will be a guest of the county this weekend."

The look Fallon gave her was almost wistful. "Life would be so simple if only people would cooperate," he said.

"Who wants a simple life?" Nikki asked.

≡ FORTY-TWO ≡

"Hey, you behave yourself," Nikki instructed the big dog as they both went to answer the door buzzer just before midnight. "This man's special."

She assumed Bird had already figured that out. He'd watched with mild curiosity as she spent the last hour cleaning up the house, preparing for Virgil's arrival. Putting fresh linen on the bed, she thought she saw the dog rolling his eyes.

If he really understood her feelings for the detective, he chose to ignore them. As soon as Virgil entered the house and took Nikki in his arms, the dog burrowed his way between them.

"You wanna go to your room?" Nikki asked him sternly.

Bird ducked his head and backed away, allowing them the pleasure of a full-body press.

"Think he'll ever get used to me?" Virgil said.

"Sooner than I will, maybe," Nikki said.

She walked into the kitchen, turned down the lights, and turned on the stereo. Aaron Neville was telling it like it was as she led Virgil past the sliding door to the rear patio. There she'd set up two deck chairs and a metal table that she'd bought at an all-night furniture barn on her way home from the office. A thick Mexican candle shared the table with a bottle of good cognac and two snifters, also recent purchases.

Bird watched them suspiciously as they sat down.

"Nice out here," Virgil said, looking at the flickering lights of Westchester and Venice, and in the far distance, Santa Monica.

"How was the action at Baby Doe's tonight?" Nikki asked, pouring a few inches of cognac into their glasses.

"Askin' the wrong man," he said. "I was at home, just me and the tube."

She cocked a skeptical eyebrow.

He clicked his glass against hers, then sampled the cognac. "Umm-umm, tasty," he said. "My hometown music, too." The Nevilles were singing "Fire on the Bayou."

"So you were watching television all by yourself on a Friday night?"

"Watchin' the election."

"What election?"

"New Miss Universe. Miss Venezuela got my vote, but . . ." He was staring down the hillside. "Are those tombstones down there?"

"It's a little cemetery," she said. "Bother you?"

"No. I sorta like it. Kinky," he said. "Anyway, they threw the contest to Miss Bolivia, who was on the skinny side. Poor Miss Italy—there is nothing skinny about that woman—was right in the middle of her 'This is such a great opportunity' speech when they broke in with the news that Dyana Cooper had been arrested. They quoted an unidentified 'spokesperson for the D.A.' Wasn't you, was it?"

She shook her head. "Nope, I had other fish to fry."

"You there when Goodman and Morales put it to her?" he asked.

"Uh huh." Before he could push her about that, she asked, "Was there an official announcement?"

"Oh, yeah. The little man was all over the tube at ten," he said. The little man was Chief of Police Philip Ahern, a diminutive, wiry specimen who, with his pinched face and combed-over hair, usually resembled a stern schoolmaster at the end of his patience.

"How'd it go?" Nikki asked.

Virgil chuckled. "Well, some reporter from the *Times* asked him if the LAPD was on riot alert and Ahern looked like he ate a bug. 'Who do you suppose will riot?' he asked the guy. 'Shareholders at Monitor Records? Members of the Motion Picture Academy?'

"So some woman from Channel Two informs the chief that Dyana Cooper is an icon for all us Af-ri-can-A-mer-i-cans. And Ahern says he likes Dyana's movies as much as the next guy, but that doesn't mean she can operate under a different set of laws than the rest of us."

"That's okay, isn't it?" Nikki asked.

"I suppose. It might have sounded better coming from a black officer."

"Or my boss, maybe," she said.

"Yeah. Even him. Anyway, the little man ended up with the comment that as hard as it may be for folks to believe, not all murders are racially motivated. Then somebody wanted to know, if race wasn't an issue, why does the LAPD keep arresting black people for the crime."

"Ouch."

"It ended the chief's big moment on a definite downer," he said.

"They'll probably be repeating his ordeal on *Headline News*."

"You're going to watch TV now?" Virgil asked, his fingers tracing a circular pattern on her knee.

"Guess not," she said, glad she'd had time to throw those Bugs Bunny slippers out with the garbage.

At a little after eight the next morning, she was sitting at the kitchen counter, reading the paper, when the district attorney called. "I thought you told me Dyana Cooper was, in your words, 'tucked away at Brand,'" he said heatedly.

"She is."

"Really? Then who am I looking at on Channels Two, Three, Four, Seven, and for all I know, every bloody channel on the dial, including cable and the Internet? Find out and get back to me."

With a sinking feeling, Nikki exchanged the phone for her remote control clicker. In seconds she was watching Dyana Cooper, live and among polite society, on the lawn of her estate. At least twenty media representatives were seated on folding chairs, facing her.

"What's up, Red?" Virgil asked, entering the kitchen, wearing his slacks and dress shirt from the night before. Bird, who refused to let the detective out of his sight, followed at his heels.

"Dyana Cooper's got something she wants to tell the world," Nikki said.

When he sat down beside her, she could smell her rose soap fragrance on his body, mixing with the pungent coffee aroma in the cup he'd just filled. "She's out already?" he asked.

"Justice is swift," Nikki said. "Screwed-up. But swift."

The video camera shifted and they could see John Willins sitting behind his wife, wearing a solemn expression, a sincere dark suit, and with their little boy squirming on his lap.

"Man looks like a ventriloquist with his dummy," Virgil said.

". . . Police Chief Ahern graciously says he likes my work on film," Dyana was saying. "I'm sorry, but I don't like *his* work. Last night he told the world I am a murderer. We're supposed to be living in a country where a person is innocent until proven guilty. Chief Ahern doesn't seem to understand this point of law. Fact is, he and the district attorney are so desperate to respond to the public demand for action they will do anything or say anything to get the pressure off them and onto someone else."

"Does that include manufacturing evidence?" a young man with glasses asked.

"Tell me it hasn't happened here before," Dyana Cooper replied. "Don't forget, only a few days ago, they were claiming Jamal Deschamps committed the crime, in spite of a mountain of evidence to the contrary."

"This is really gonna make your boss's day," Virgil said.

An intense middle-aged female reporter from Channel Eight asked, "What do you think their purpose is in dragging you into their investigation?"

"I was unlucky enough to have seen Maddie on the day she died. That's about it."

"Surely there must be more?" asked a plump black man from Channel Twelve.

"If so, they haven't told me about it," Dyana said. "I don't know what it could possibly be."

"How about blood? Skin tissue?" Nikki asked. "Fingerprints?"

"Why exactly did you call this conference, Ms. Cooper?" a wiry, longhaired young man asked. "It's pretty unorthodox. What do you hope to achieve?"

To Nikki's surprise, a black woman moved quickly behind Dyana's chair, resting her hands protectively on the performer's shoulders. The woman's name appeared suddenly at the bottom of the screen. An unnecessary ID, Nikki thought. Just about the entire viewing audience would recognize the trademark Mohawk hair, large hoop earrings, the brightly colored African dress, and the fiercely determined voice of Anna Marie Dayne. The respected attorney had waged a number of very public and very successful battles against automobile manufacturers and tobacco companies. Her crowning glory, however, had been the freeing of a young black man accused of murdering two FBI agents. She'd convinced the jury that her client had been acting in self-defense. The fact that the jury had been mainly white added to her legend. In less than six years, Dayne had defended three other African-Americans in similarly desperate legal straits and had emerged victorious each time.

"This is perfect," Nikki said. "It's not enough for us to have to convince a jury that one of the most beloved performers in the world committed a brutal murder, but we'll also have to go up against the Joan of Arc of the legal profession."

"Sister is something, all right," Virgil said. "That's some 'do she's got."

"Our purpose here today," Anna Marie Dayne announced, "is to put District Attorney Joseph Walden on notice. Should he heedlessly decide to bring Dyana to trial, we will make sure that every aspect of the process is open to public scrutiny.

"This morning we have informed you of the underhanded attempt to keep Ms. Cooper incarcerated by denying her the privilege of bail. This illogical and mean-spirited act would have placed her in the same perilous situation as that of the equally innocent Jamal Deschamps. Dyana was luckier than Mr. Deschamps: her blood was not spilled within prison walls. Although her reputation and standing in the community have been tarnished, her pride as an African-American who has risen to the top of a profession not overly receptive to members of her race remains gloriously intact."

"Sister *is* something, all right," Nikki said. "She makes denial of bail sound like a miscarriage of justice, reminds everybody about the screwup with Deschamps, and ties the whole thing in a ribbon of racial pride. All in less than two minutes."

On the small screen the reporters lobbed a few puffballs at the actress and her attorney. Dyana closed the show by thanking them for being so generous in spending their Saturday morning with her.

"Right," Nikki said. "Like their news directors and editors gave 'em a choice."

She watched Virgil take his cup to the sink and run water over it. Tucking in his shirt, he returned to her side. On the TV, an announcer was suggesting everyone stay tuned for an analysis of the conference.

"Guess this means our do-nothing morning ain't gonna happen," Virgil said.

"Guess not," Nikki said, thinking how lucky it was that he was a detective and understood how the job worked.

He bent down to kiss her on the lips. Bird growled.

"I'll let myself out," Virgil said. Then, with Bird dogging the detective to the door to make sure he left the premises, she turned to the TV, where several talking heads were starting to pick apart the Cooper news conference.

None of the "experts" could agree on what Anna Marie Dayne and Dyana Cooper had hoped to achieve by the conference. Those sympathetic to the district attorney's office saw it as a desperate attempt to hide facts with emotion, though, of course, they had no idea what the facts in the case really were. The others—defense attorneys in the main—applauded Dayne for her audacity in seizing control of the situation even before the district attorney had a chance to arraign her client.

Tiring of their uninformed rhetoric, Nikki clicked off the machine. A memory of the pleasantries of the night before flitted through her mind before being lost to the tasks of the day.

She refilled Bird's water bowl, then returned to the kitchen counter. Her coffee had turned cold as ice, but she took a sip anyway. She picked up the phone.

She made several calls. The last was to the district attorney.

"How'd she get out?" he asked.

"The desk officer at Sybil Brand said a young lawyer from Jastrum, Park, Wells showed up with an order from Judge Debruccio and a million dollars in cash."

"Debruccio? That figures. Why the hell weren't we notified she was out?"

"To quote the duty cop, 'We don't usually wake up D.A.s in the middle of the night every time somebody posts bail.' "

"Give me his name. I want to thank him personally for his cooperation."

Nikki identified the officer, then asked, "What'd you think of the Dyana and Anna Marie Show?"

"I'd rather have watched Urkel do his dance," he replied.

≡ FORTY-THREE ≡

Eddie Goodman spotted Lieutenant Corben's midnight-blue Chrysler as it turned the corner, heading his way. The blazing noon sun lasered through the haze, frying the back of his neck.

The Chrysler pulled in at the curb, and the passenger door opened, tendrils of cool air greeting him and beckoning him into the car's icy interior. Corben was wearing a yellow T-shirt with "Lake Arrowhead" sewn on a pocket over his heart. Goodman had never seen the lieutenant in anything but a shirt and tie.

Without a word of welcome, Corben started up the sedan and pulled away. "What's up?" Goodman asked. "This about Dyana Cooper getting sprung?"

"You know an old broad named Nita Morgan?" Corben asked.

Goodman winced. Nita Morgan. Batgal. "Yeah," he said. "She was one of Madeleine Gray's blackmail victims."

"She says she's one of *your* blackmail victims."

"The woman's a kook. Played a vampire on TV and I think it went to her head."

"Well, she's your nightmare now, pal. She's bringing charges against you."

"Jesus, maybe it *was* IAD guys at my place."

"It hasn't gone to IAD yet. I just got the call this morning. I don't know who the hell was at your place."

"What's happening to me, chief?"

"Fucked if I know. When was it you talked to the Morgan woman?"

"Couple days ago. I can look at my book for the exact day and time."

"You didn't phone her last night?"

"Last night I was kinda busy with Dyana Cooper."

"Around nine-thirty?"

"In interrogation room three."

Corben seemed to relax.

"She says that's when I phoned her?"

Corben nodded. "Something about ten grand to keep her name out o' the 'bloids."

"Does that sound like me?"

"Hell, Goodman, I don't know how you spend your off hours."

"Thanks for the vote of confidence."

"Here I am, on a Saturday afternoon, putting you wise," Corben said, "when I could be in Studio City porking my girlfriend and/or watching the ball game. I'd say that's an indication I'm in your corner."

"What should I do?"

"Right now? Nothing. If you were in the box with Cooper and her lawyer at the time the Morgan broad says you were calling her, I imagine that's all IAD'll wanna know."

"But somebody's out there, using my name to blackmail people."

"Not using your name, exactly. Morgan says the caller didn't identify himself. She's sure it was you, because you'd been to see her about her nasty little secret."

"I bet Morgan's not the only one on Maddie's payoff list who's been getting calls."

"The only one we know about," Corben said.

"Maybe I should try phoning some of the other—"

"Christ, Goodman, where's your sense? The last thing you should be doing is phoning anybody. At least until we got this complaint cleared away."

"You're right, lieutenant," Goodman said. "But if blackmail victims have been approached, somebody must have a copy of Maddie Gray's special files."

"Why does that thrill you?"

"Right now we've got two possible motives for Gray's murder. Jealousy and blackmail. I've always liked the blackmail angle. Way I see it, after Cooper killed Gray, she broke into the cabinet and took her file. That's why it's missing from our set. The new blackmailer may have a complete set of files, including hers."

Corben had made a long but complete circle and was now steering his sedan toward the curb in front of Goodman's apartment. "Any ideas on how to find the new blackmailer?" he asked.

"Got a pretty good hunch."

"Fine, then you got your things to do and I got mine."

As Goodman opened the car door to the afternoon heat, Corben added, "You go on a hunt for this blackmailer, take Morales along."

"I may not be able to get hold of him."

"Then somebody else on our team. Until we get this other matter cleared up on Monday, I don't want you out there among 'em by yourself. If somebody's fucking with you, let's keep the odds at two to one in your favor."

What Corben said made sense. But if Goodman was going to have to spend his Saturday afternoon with another cop, he could do better than Morales.

Unfortunately, Gwen Harriman didn't seem to be near her phone. And Morales answered his on the first ring.

≡ FORTY-FOUR ≡

Gangbangers," Morales said with disgust as their car started up Laurel Canyon toward Maddie Gray's house.

Goodman looked back at the vehicle that had just passed, a nondescript black 1963 Chevrolet. "How do you know?" he asked.

"Bunch of black kids drivin' in a Chevy and they all got shaved heads, orange shirts, and an attitude. What d'ya think, amigo? A basketball team?"

Actually, Goodman had barely noticed the Chevy. His thoughts had been elsewhere. Arthur Lydon, the late Madeleine Gray's assistant, was the most likely candidate to have stepped into the blackmail breach left by his employer's death.

When no one answered the buzzer at Lydon's hillside apartment, the only other place Goodman could think of to look for him was the Gray home.

"This a wile goose chase, amigo. Le's go back and roust those bangers."

"Even if they are bangers, which I doubt, they're not our concern."

"Concern? It's our day off," Morales grumbled as he parked in front of the multitiered house. "We'd get more accomplished checking out those bangers than lookin' for the li'l man who isn't here."

"If *he* isn't, somebody is," Goodman said. "The front door's open."

Morales scanned the area. "No car. Prob'ly vamoosed."

"Maybe," Goodman said.

They left the sedan cautiously and headed for the open door. Someone had pried the police lock from the jamb. They automatically drew their guns.

Instead of entering the house, they split off. Morales circled to the right. Goodman took the left, pausing at the first window to peek past the curtains into the sitting room. No sign of life. Likewise the room directly behind. The kitchen seemed empty, too. That was as far as Goodman could go: the house had been constructed to fit snugly in a pocket of the canyon wall.

The detective retraced his steps and found his partner waiting for him. Morales shrugged, then walked to the front door. He entered, quickly and silently. Goodman moved a bit more slowly, but just as noiselessly. It took them nearly fifteen minutes to convince themselves that the house was unoccupied. By then, sweaty and on edge, they made another tour of the place, hoping to discover some reason for the break-in.

Morales found it in Arthur Lydon's office. He called his partner.

"Why would the little *maricón* pry open his own desk?" he asked.

Goodman looked at the mess behind the desk. The contents of the drawers had been dumped on the floor. "If not him, who? Burglars?" he asked.

"Leaving all the TVs and stereos?"

With a grunt, Goodman hunkered down to get a closer look at a leather folder resting on top of a pile of papers. He used his pen to flip the top of the folder back.

"Wha'chu got?"

"Lydon's checkbook. Last check was ripped out. Not nice and neat like the rest."

"Somebody broke in here jus' to steal a blank check from Mr. Sweetie?"

Goodman looked at the next unused checks. "His address is on the checks," he said, standing up. "I think they broke in looking for him. And now they know where he lives. We'd better hop back to his place."

"We was jus' there and we know he ain't home."

"Let's make sure."

Lydon resided near the Hollywood Bowl, in an art deco trilevel apartment building halfway up a scrub-and-rock hill, accessible from the street level via a separate stone tower that housed an elevator. The detectives rode it to the top. When they emerged from the tower they were standing on an exposed stone platform that led directly to a third-floor balcony running the length of the building. An equally exposed stairwell led down to the other floors, each of which had its own walkway/balcony.

Lydon's apartment was at the far corner of the bottom floor.

Heading there for the second time that afternoon, Goodman and Morales ignored the cityscape as they moved down the stairs and along the walkway, shooing pigeons from their path. The birds seemed to have taken over the building.

Their defecation, dry and fresh, mottled the walkway. "Flying rats," Morales said disgustedly.

As they approached Lydon's apartment, he said, "Looks like we got lucky." The card they'd stuck in the little man's front door was resting on the cement walkway.

Morales pushed the door buzzer.

No reply.

Pigeons flapped their wings in the sunlight, soaring from the roof of the building down the hillside. The detectives ignored them, concentrating on the quiet apartment.

Morales knocked on the door. "Hey, Mr. Lydon."

The door to Goodman's right opened. The young woman who stepped through it was dressed in starlet housecleaning chic—blond tendrils escaping a tied kerchief, scrubbed face, astonishing body barely covered by a stained muscle shirt and short shorts, two-hundred-dollar running shoes on sockless feet. She was carrying a pillowcase filled with what Goodman assumed was laundry. His imagination went a step further, conjuring up an image of rumpled little items from the Victoria's Secret catalog.

She glanced at him, then Morales, and, registering no emotion at all, started away.

"Miss?"

She turned, wary now.

"Would you know if Mr. Lydon has been home recently?" Goodman asked.

Her large, empty blue eyes seemed puzzled. "Isn't he there now?"

"Doesn't seem to be."

"He was in the laundry room a half hour ago, tying up every one of the machines."

"You're heading there now?" Goodman asked, startled by

the arrival of a pigeon on the walkway rail right next to where his hand rested.

"Uh huh." He saw her eyes shift to the pigeon, then follow it as the bird flew off. She stepped closer to the railing and continued to watch its progress. "I still have . . ."

She paused.

Goodman, who'd been a little lost in those blue eyes, saw them widen. Then the generous mouth opened, ready to scream. But no sound came. He couldn't tell what was happening to the woman. Some sort of seizure?

Her bundle of dirty clothes slipped from her fingers and she began to sway. Goodman grabbed her before her knees gave out. She was no wisp of a girl and her inert weight dragged him down with her, pinning him to the cement walk. He looked up at Morales for help, but his partner was running past them, ignoring them completely.

"What the hell . . ." Goodman rolled the woman off of his legs. She was breathing easily, but she was out. He lifted her head and placed her stuffed pillowcase under it. Then he straightened out her limbs.

He stood up and leaned over the balcony railing in time to see Morales stumbling down the hillside toward . . .

Holy God!

In all his years on the force he'd never seen anything quite like it. Definitely not in the bright Southern California sunshine. A body—certainly Arthur Lydon's—was lying on its back a hundred yards or so down the hill. Blood covered everything—clothes, face, hands, spiky hair. It still looked red enough to be fresh. Even worse, entrails spilled from a gaping wound in the man's stomach like glistening worms. The birds—the pigeons—were engaged in an afternoon meal the horror of which was light-years beyond anything Alfred Hitchcock could have imagined.

Then Morales was there flapping his arms and scattering some of the birds. He looked up at his gawking partner. "Need some help here, amigo," he shouted, "before these fucking flying rats eat up all our evidence."

≡ FORTY-FIVE ≡

Nikki realized that the only difference between arriving at the Criminal Courts Building on that particular Saturday afternoon and on a regular weekday morning was that you didn't have to wait as long for an elevator. Most of the CCB's nine-to-fivers were out enjoying another weekend in paradise, but, thanks to the forthcoming Dyana Cooper trial, the eighteenth floor where Joe Walden held sway was fully staffed.

The prosecutor navigated her way past the guard from county security, a sister with an unyielding attitude, then circled the glass panel desk behind which Jewel, the nicest of three alternating receptionists, pressed a buzzer that unlocked a wooden door on the right. Beyond it was a waiting area that took on an appearance quite apart from the industrial grimness of the rest of the eighteenth floor. Clean and brightly painted, dull floor tiles replaced by a thick new beige carpet, it reminded Nikki of what a real law office should look like.

At one end of the room, two secretaries occupied twin

desks. At the other sat a D.A.'s investigator, his jacket open, exposing a gun in a worn leather shoulder holster. The secretary whose name Nikki thought might be Jeri indicated the closed door to the conference room. "Please go in, Ms. Hill," she said. "They're expecting you."

"They" were fourteen casually dressed coworkers and the D.A., gathered at the enormous conference table, several of them dwarfed by their high-backed, blue-gray leather chairs. Nikki was amused to note that the pecking order was being followed: Walden was at the head. On his left was Ray Wise. Past Wise, the lower-echelon D.A.s and clerks who comprised the special prosecution team sat in order of their seniority. One of the lessons learned from the O. J. Simpson murder case was the impracticality of assembling a team in increments to meet the needs of an ongoing trial. It was much more efficient to keep a full team in place, ready to handle high-profile prosecutions as a functioning unit.

"Hi, folks," Nikki said. "Sorry I'm late."

"We're just starting," Joe Walden said. There were two empty chairs to his right. He indicated that she should take the one nearest him, a gesture that buoyed her confidence.

"Need some coffee? Water?" he asked.

"I'm fine," she said, getting out her pen and opening her notebook.

"We're still waiting for—" Walden said. "Ah, here she is."

Dimitra Shaw entered the conference room and moved to the empty chair beside Nikki. She was immaculately dressed in a smartly cut Italian suit not unlike one that Nikki would have been wearing herself if it had been a workday and not the weekend. She nodded to the crowd. "Afternoon. Joe, Ray. Nikki."

Nikki smiled back through clenched teeth, wondering what the hell Dimitra was doing there. She was not a member of the special team. At least she hadn't been. Nikki looked across the table at Ray questioningly, but he avoided her eyes. Not a good sign.

"Let's get rolling," Walden said. "We've got a lot to cover. Ray, why don't you present your murder time line."

Wise's face contorted into a fleeting grimace and he began. "According to Mrs. Willins, at approximately five P.M. on the evening of the murder, she arrives at Gray's home in her beige 1970 Jaguar XKE Series III." Walden wanted them to use Dyana Cooper's married name in the hope of separating the murderer from the movie star. Nikki thought it was a dumb idea, but if it made Joe happy . . . "An argument ensues. They fight. Willins hits Gray with a sculpture, draws blood. Gray scratches Willins. Of course, all we have is Willins's word for it that the fight took place at this time and not later that night between the hours of eight and eleven P.M., when Dr. Fugitsu tells us Gray was murdered.

"Willins lied to Detectives Goodman and Morales during their first interview at her home and again later at Parker Center when she told them she didn't leave her house that night. Witnesses have definitely placed her car at Gray's at the approximate time of the murder. A probable scenario is that she drove back there, passions erupted again, and Willins brutalized and murdered Madeleine Gray, rolled her body into a rug, and carried that to her car. She then drove the body to the Dumpster in South Central."

Walden opened the floor to questions.

Was there anything to the speculation on the news that the Gray home was not the scene of the crime? "We're ninety-eight percent certain the murder took place there," Wise replied. "We've found signs of a fight. Blood. We know with certainty that Mrs. Willins removed the rug from the premises. Threads matching those on the floor were found in her sports car, along with a strand of the vic's hair. That's confidential, by the way."

"Everything said here is," Walden added sternly.

Could Dyana Cooper have murdered Maddie and disposed of the body without help? "Mrs. Willins is in excellent physical condition," Wise said. "The LAPD is, of course, investigating the possibility of an accomplice. But the assumption is that she acted alone."

Could a celebrity as well known as the suspect have driven a fancy sports car to South Central and dumped the body without being seen? "We'd love for some witness to come forth," Wise said. "So far we've been unable to find anyone who saw Dyana Willins, or anybody else for that matter, placing the body in the Dumpster. We're assuming she used the Jag, although she might have transferred the body to some other, less ostentatious vehicle. If so, we haven't found that vehicle. It isn't any of those at the Willins estate. The police have checked."

On TV that morning, Mrs. Willins had claimed she had no motive. Was this true? Wise was starting to reply when he was interrupted by the harsh sound of a buzzer. Obviously piqued, the district attorney picked up the phone in front of him. "Jeri, you know I said . . . Oh, okay, put him on." The room was quiet while Walden responded to the call with mumbles and grunts. Finally, he said, "I really can't comment on that right now. Sorry."

He didn't seem to notice them staring at him expectantly as he replaced the receiver. He lifted the phone again, punched a button and said, "Get me Lieutenant Corben, wherever the hell he is."

He turned to the others. "That was a reporter. Arthur Lydon, Madeleine Gray's assistant, has been murdered at his apartment." He wrinkled his nose. "Not just murdered. Eviscerated. The police discovered the body nearly an hour ago.

They apparently assumed I wouldn't be interested. I have to get my information from the media."

"Some cooperation," Wise said.

"If the police won't come to us, we'll have to go to them," Walden said. "At least Nikki will. Right now."

As eager as Nikki was to get in on the action at the crime scene, she couldn't believe that Walden felt her presence at the trial meeting wasn't necessary. "Ray can fill me in on whatever I miss here," she said as she put away her notes.

"I'll catch you up," Dimitra said.

"Good idea," the D.A. said. "Talk to Dimitra." Stiffening a bit, he added, "She and Ray will be leading the prosecution team."

Nikki prided herself on her ability to roll with the punches. But this one was a knockout blow. Her shock must have been obvious to everyone in the room.

Walden lowered his eyes and began straightening papers on the table.

"I'll be down here working with Ray the rest of the day," Dimitra said sweetly. "Stop by or give me a call."

"Sure. I'll do that," Nikki said, almost choking in her anger. As she turned to leave, she glanced at Ray. He too had developed an overwhelming interest in his papers.

Murder by evisceration, Nikki thought. *Good! Maybe I'll pick up some pointers.*

≡ FORTY-SIX ≡

The police were moving in a phalanx across the hillside beneath Arthur Lydon's apartment building. Nikki assumed they were doing a ground search, but they might have been practicing a choreographic ensemble piece for the Rose Bowl halftime.

The uniformed policeman who stopped her when she attempted to move past the gathering crowd frowned at her ID but allowed her access. As she got on the elevator, two female cops were getting off. One was saying to the other, "Talk about your lousy tummy tucks." They both laughed. Nikki felt a chill as she pressed the up button.

She was starting down the stairwell toward Lydon's apartment when she heard, "Hey, Red."

Virgil was on the second-level open walkway. He and his partner were standing with three young women. Virgil waved, said something to the others, and headed her way.

"What you doing here, honey?" he asked.

"I was going to ask you the same thing," she said.

"Corben's got us all on this one. But I'm through now. Let's go take a drive."

"I just got here."

"Yeah, I know." He lowered his voice. "Nothing here I can't tell you about somewhere else."

She looked down the hillside, where uniformed police were continuing their slow sweep of the scrub. The body had been covered with yellow plastic. "Okay," she said.

He turned and waved to his partner. "Later, Roy," the partner called back.

"What's with the 'Roy'?" she asked as he led her to the elevator.

"Cop stuff," he said.

Looking past his shoulder she did another quick scan of the area. "I don't see Goodman or Morales."

"They're not here," he said as they got into the empty elevator. "I'll fill you in."

"You're acting a little weird, Virgil."

"Not weird," he said as they began their descent. "Just cautious. The word is out. 'Cooperation with the district attorney's office is to be suspended until further notice.'"

"Why?"

"You guys leaked the news about Dyana's arrest. Got to expect some reciprocity."

"Because of some publicity bullshit you guys are willing to risk blowing this case?"

"Hold it, counselor. You're playing to the wrong jury."

"Sounds to me like you approve of the order."

"If I did, going off with you now might seem like a real romantic gesture."

"You're a devious man," she said as they left the elevator.

"Me?"

"King of the crooked answer."

"Untrue. Ask me anything."

"Where are Goodman and Morales?"

"I imagine they're in enemy country," he said.

At that moment, the two detectives were in front of the Willins mansion, where their request to speak with Dyana Cooper was being denied by her lawyer, Anna Marie Dayne. "My client is with her husband and child. She is unavailable."

"Well, you see," Goodman said, "there's been a . . . development."

"The murder of Arthur Lydon?"

"Yes."

"It's been on the news," Dayne said. "It has *nothing* to do with Ms. Cooper."

"A woman resembling Ms. Cooper was seen leaving the crime scene."

The lawyer's stance became a shade less combative. "*That* wasn't on the news."

"Not yet, anyway," Goodman said.

"You're not going to bother her with this. She hasn't left my sight all day. Not since our press conference this morning."

"We'd sorta like to hear that from Ms. Cooper. For the record."

"You'll have to take my word for it," Dayne said. She turned to the security guard who stood behind them. "These gentlemen will be leaving now."

"We'll get our answers from Ms. Cooper, one way or another," Goodman said. "That's our job."

"Your job," Dayne said, "is to find criminals and arrest them. I'm helping you with that by saving you time and effort."

With that, she turned on her heel and went back into the building.

"Detectives?" The security guard gestured toward the road.

As they got into their sedan, Goodman said, "I'm not looking forward to meeting that lady in the courtroom."

"She's pretty fierce with that Indian hair," Morales said. "Nice ass on her, though."

≡ FORTY-SEVEN ≡

It was nearly four-thirty when Nikki returned to the eighteenth floor of the Criminal Courts Building to give the district attorney her report on the Lydon murder. Ordinarily, she would have phoned it in, but she'd decided to push the Dimitra Shaw issue.

She relayed the information Virgil had provided, including the eyewitness's account of a woman resembling Dyana Cooper leaving the building around the time of the murder. She ended with the news that Chief Ahern had instructed the Homicide-Robbery officers to keep the D.A.'s office out of the loop.

"Petty bullshit," Walden said. "But you seem to have gotten around it."

"About the Cooper trial," she said. "You must know I was expecting to be the second chair."

"Yes. I'll tell you what I told Ray when he recommended you. You're more useful in your present capacity as my special assistant."

So Wise had actually lived up to his end of their bargain.

Too bad. She would have preferred his being the one who pulled the chair out from under her. She couldn't hate Joe, who'd rescued her from Compton and lifted her out of the deputy pool.

"You'll still be plugged in to every aspect of the trial," he said.

"If that's what you want," she said.

She wasn't about to ask Dimitra to fill her in on the rest of the morning's meeting. Instead, she dropped in on Wise.

The prosecutor was bent over his desk, scribbling something on a yellow pad. He looked up at her and said, "Please, I don't want to talk about it. I did the best—"

"I know. I just wanted to thank you for trying."

"Well, we both knew it would be Joe's ultimate decision." He refocused on his notepad, obviously uncomfortable with the situation.

She was halfway to the door when he called her name. "You know why Joe picked her, don't you?"

"He thought she could do a better job."

He gave her another of his patented disapproving looks. "Still a Girl Scout, aren't you?" He lowered his voice. "Joe's fucking her."

The news shocked her. Maybe she *was* a Girl Scout. "Who told you that?"

"It's common knowledge."

Was it true or was this just another of Wise's sour takes on the way things worked? In either case, she understood his telling her was a sign of friendship, sort of.

"Thanks," she said.

"For what?" he grumbled, his attention back on his yellow pad.

≡ FORTY-EIGHT ≡

Jamal Deschamps had a tough decision to make.

At the suggestion of both his doctors and his lawyers, he'd been taking it easy. Hanging out in the hotel room that Mr. Ernest Comb-over Jolley, had booked for him. Not over-doing the pain pills, but popping one every now and then to stay mellow. Catching up on his tube time.

That Saturday afternoon, he'd been watching an eight-ball championship from Vegas, sipping a brew and nibbling on nachos with melted cheese from room service, when the scene on the monitor shifted abruptly. One second Little Lou Lazarro was attempting a double bank shot, the next some dude in a body bag was being carted away from an L.A. hill-side.

Jamal shook his head, trying to lose a little of the woozy glow from that last Percodan. *What the hell is that fly girl with the mike saying?*

The reporter was passing along the information that Madeleine Gray's "personal assistant" had been murdered.

She added, with a wince, that Arthur Lydon had been mutilated by a large knife, "possibly a machete."

The word slipped past the medication, reminding Jamal of something he'd forgotten, something that the cops might like to know. *Screw the blue,* he thought. *They fucked me over. Let 'em suss this one out for themselves.*

As the evening wore on and the effects of the Percodan and beer wore off, his conscience began to nibble away at the edges of his attitude. According to the incessant newsbreaks, the cops were looking for a woman in connection with Lydon's murder. The woman's description matched that of actress and recording star Dyana Cooper, whom the police suspected also murdered Madeleine Gray.

Cops won't be happy until they put this one on the sister's scorecard, too. Like she'd take a machete to somebody.

What he knew, or thought he knew, might get the LAPD to lighten up on Dyana. But he was free and clear of it now. He didn't want to do anything that might mess up the lawsuit. Or put him in the way of that fucking machete. *Sister's already on the hook for one murder,* Jamal told himself. *One more won't change matters much.*

Still, he couldn't let go of it.

He phoned the law office of Jastrum, Park, Wells.

The guy on weekend duty seemed annoyed that somebody had disturbed him. *Fucker's probably busy with his nose in some law book.*

"I need to talk to Fallon," Jamal told him.

"Mr. Fallon will be in the office on Monday morning."

"I need to talk to him now. Tell him it's Jamal Deschamps needs to talk to him."

The man wasn't too impressed by the name. "I'll leave word for him."

Later that night, Ernest Jolley returned his call.

"Your name Fallon?" Jamal demanded.

"Mr. Fallon isn't available," Jolley said with a patience that underscored his effectiveness as a mediator. "What do you need?"

"Advice."

"About what?"

"I got something I want to talk over with the cops."

"That's probably not a good idea, Jamal."

"This is important." Jamal didn't want to get too specific, since he didn't trust Mr. Comb-over any more than he admired his hairstyle. "Something I feel I have to do."

"At this stage of our negotiation, my suggestion would be to stay as far away from the LAPD as you can. Unless you want to blow the deal. That what you want, Jamal?"

Shit, Jamal thought as he hung up the phone. *Sorry, sweet Dyana. I love your music, but not two mil worth.*

≡ FORTY-NINE ≡

At the Sunday service at Faithful Central Baptist Missionary, Nikki was having a hard time concentrating on the Doctor Reverend R. L. Johnson's sermon. Loreen sat to her left, Victoria Allard, the amateur clothier, to her right, both of them apparently hanging on Reverend Johnson's every word. Nikki's attention had been drifting—from the unpleasant thought that Joe Walden had probably pushed her aside in favor of his lover to her conflicted feelings over the speed with which her affair with Virgil was progressing. Adding to her general sense of unease was the presence, across the aisle, of her father, William Hill, sitting with his aging baby-doll wife, Patricia, and their tall, awkward daughter, Emily.

Nikki studied the girl. Could someone she barely knew actually be her half sister? The girl was what, eighteen? Damn, they hadn't said ten words . . . She paused at the sound of Dyana Cooper's name.

". . . this wonderful woman," Reverend Johnson was saying, "is experiencing for herself the kind of woes the good

Lord uses to test the best of his children. May she have the strength to withstand this persecution."

Persecution? Was the Reverend, a man she'd always considered to be intelligent and just, staring directly at *her?* She flushed and felt self-conscious. And angry.

Loreen picked up on her tension. She leaned close and whispered, "Chill, girlfriend. Even the Rev can go off track now and then."

The Reverend wasn't alone.

After the service, Nikki noticed that several people she'd known since grade school seemed to be avoiding her. She fielded hostile glances from faces she didn't think she'd ever seen before. Worst of all, Sister Mumphrey descended on her. "You heard the Reverend. What in the world is the matter with you people, Nicolette?"

"What people is that, Sister?" Nikki replied, fighting to remain calm. From the corner of her eye she saw Patricia Hill, nose in the air, hurrying her daughter past them.

"Law people," Sister was saying. "Police people."

"I'm not exactly a po—"

"Supposed to be defending us from the evil in the world. Instead you spend your time making life difficult for good folks like Dyana Cooper. A minister's daughter."

Nikki's father was only a few feet away. Tall, graying a little, but as straight-backed and full of pride as always. Staring at her now with a look of . . . what? Disappointment? *The son of a bitch. What the devil does he want from me?*

"African-American woman like yourself," Sister went on, "in a position of power. You oughta be doing good in this world, 'stead of trying to bring down the righteous. I'm gonna light a candle for you."

Other churchgoers were starting to gather, curious about the confrontation. Nikki, hemmed in by the big woman, surrounded by her huge breasts, felt the stirrings of panic. Then she heard Loreen whisper, "Sister, would you light a candle for *me?*"

Sister Mumphrey eyed her suspiciously. "I suppose I could."

"Excellent," Loreen said. "And when you got it burning real good . . . you think you could shove it up your big, fat, sanctimonious ass?"

Sister staggered back, shocked, and Nikki, giggling, seized the opportunity to squeeze past her.

"Put me down for one of those candles, too, Sister," Victoria said.

The three friends linked arms and strolled from the church, giddy as schoolgirls.

≡ FIFTY ≡

D o you understand the charges against you, madam?" the supervising criminal court judge, Peter Deal, asked Dyana Cooper Willins.

Sitting in the crowded courtroom on Monday morning, Nikki watched as the singer-actress managed to look both composed and vulnerable, replying, "Yes, your honor." Anna Marie Dayne was at her side, wearing her trademark hoop earrings and a dress a shade more subdued than at the press conference.

"How do you plead?" Judge Deal asked.

"Not guilty," Dyana Cooper Willins stated simply and convincingly. The one thing she certainly was not guilty of, Nikki thought, was bad acting. The woman had style and class and strength. Maybe keeping a low profile in this prosecution wasn't such a bad thing after all.

Over the next few weeks, that proved to be even more the case. Thanks to the blood samples, fingerprints, and the eyewitness accounts of the presence of the accused's automobile at the crime scene at the approximate time of the murder, Judge Samuel Fried at the preliminary hearing found "sufficient cause to believe this defendant guilty."

After that, the prosecution lost just about every other round.

Instead of the venue requested by Wise, the Van Nuys Branch Court, with its relatively conservative, law-and-order jury pool, the trial would be held at the Criminal Courts Building, the same downtown location where the Simpson case had unfolded. Wise's argument had been that the Gray home, which the prosecution believed to be the murder scene, was in a district served by the Van Nuys Branch Court. Anna Marie Dayne countered by contesting the claim that the Gray home was the scene of the crime. On the other hand, there was no disagreement as to where Madeleine Gray's corpse had been discovered.

Another blow to the prosecution was Fried's selection of Rose Vetters as the judge who would preside over the trial. Vetters, a somewhat eccentric woman in her fifties who wore her pinkish hair in a towering cotton-candy style, had spent years in the district attorney's office before moving on to the bench. Like some others who have made that segue, she was known to demonstrate her "fairness" by favoring the defense.

Finally, Judge Fried, over Wise's almost apoplectic objections, allowed the one-million-dollar bail to remain in effect. He did, however, impose a ban on television in the courtroom and public discussion of the case. There would be no more Cooper press conferences.

Of course, there had been no need for spoken communication when Anna Marie Dayne and her client were greeted by the media upon leaving the CCB. Their victorious smiles were worth several thousand words.

≡ Fifty-one ≡

Jimmy Doyle was in hog heaven.

He was comfortably ensconced in a splendid villa in the Hollywood Hills above Sunset Boulevard that was rumored to have been one of the locations where a late president of the United States had held secret assignations with a sexy movie star. Assistants and secretaries had been hired. Phone lines and computer terminals had been installed, one of the former connecting directly to the Century City office suite that was being used by his handpicked defense attorney, Anna Marie Dayne.

He had tested that line earlier to suggest that Dayne evoke her client's right to a speedy trial, which meant that the courtroom battle would begin no more than sixty days after the arraignment. The logic behind the suggestion was that the prosecution would be hard pressed to put their case together that quickly, while the defense, with a nearly unlimited budget, could hire all the legal and administrative expertise necessary.

Another direct connection led to an unidentified office in

downtown L.A. where five of the country's most experienced spin doctors were providing television and the press with the best-processed news money could buy.

Doyle was in the office he'd established on the villa's second level testing a special lumbar-friendly chair when a secretary informed him that Mr. Sandoval had arrived.

Peter Sandoval was a veteran private investigator with a colorful history that went way back to an association with the late Howard Hughes. There had not been a major celebrity scandal on the West Coast in the past several decades in which Sandoval had not been involved in some capacity. His energy was as infinite as his scruples were limited.

Moving to French doors that opened on a balcony overlooking the city, he said, "I remember this place. You know who used to fuck right in this room?"

"Not only do I know it," Doyle told him, "the provenance probably upped the rent by five grand a month. What have you got for me?"

Sandoval pulled a notebook from his coat. "You'll love this one, Jimmy," he said. "The prosecutor, Dimitra Shaw? She cut off auntie's life support."

"Come again?"

"Her mother was a crack whore and she was raised by her aunt and uncle. This was in Frisco. The old codger croaks when Shaw's still a kid, but the aunt hangs in till she's in her teens, then comes down with intestinal cancer. Too far gone for the knife. In terrible pain. So Shaw gets a nurse to look the other way while she pulls the plug."

"And which part of this story am I supposed to love?" Doyle asked.

"The part about auntie's life insurance. Fifty gee. Peanuts by today's standards, but enough, with the house and a few other things, for Shaw to go to law school."

"No one checked it out?"

"Nope. Written up as death by natural causes. The 'natural' death took place in the middle of the night. There was just one nurse at the desk, Shaw's friend."

"Nurse get any of the loot?" Doyle asked.

"Nothing in her bank records of the time to even hint at it."

"How'd you find out about the euthanasia?" Doyle asked.

"You have to know who to ask," Sandoval replied coyly.

"If I decide to use this, you're gonna have to do better than that."

"Relax, Jimmy. A member of the cleanup crew was there for the whole show."

"Signed statement?"

Sandoval unzipped his briefcase and withdrew a sheet of paper, signed and notarized. "Cost us four large," he said.

"Wisely spent," Doyle said, reading the paper.

"Rumor floating around that Shaw's the D.A.'s current honey."

Doyle thought about that. "What have you got on *him?*"

"Not much. Born in Southern California, some little burg a couple hundred miles inland. Folks died when he was in his teens. Moved in with relatives. Yadda-yadda-yadda. College. Law school. Joined a firm. Then Tom Gleason took him under his wing."

"Good old Tom," Doyle said. "The people's friend. Why do you suppose he decided to act as mentor for Walden?"

"Tom did a lot for the black community."

"Sure he did," Doyle said. "It's a big community, and since the sixties, they've been known to vote. Anything more on Walden?"

"Your average unmarried nonhomo. Seems like a pretty straight shooter."

"What's that mean? I seem like a straight shooter, too."

"I get your point," Sandoval said. "We'll dig a little deeper. See if we can find some broad to slap him with a Clarence Thomas."

"Now you're thinking," Doyle said. "What about the other prosecutor, Wise?"

"So far, all we know is he's a first-class prick."

"Show me a lawyer who isn't."

"About the dude who saw the Jag leaving the Gray home, Stephen Palmer?"

"Forget him," Doyle said. "Dyana's copped to being there in the afternoon."

"I like to be thorough," Sandoval said. "You might find this amusing. The guy's married, but he smokes the skin cigar. Guess who used to be his bung-buddy?"

"Liberace?"

"Your references are a little moldy," Sandoval chided. "No. Not Lee. But just as deceased. That blackmailing little fuck, Arthur Lydon."

Doyle frowned. "I've been meaning to ask: you clear on that one?"

Sandoval put up both hands in protest. "Me use a machete? All that blood. Gimme some credit. I just black-bagged his apartment. You said you'd take care of Lydon."

"I meant I was gonna pay him off," Doyle said. "Wonder who hacked him?"

"That kind of close work suggests a certain, ah, personal animosity," Sandoval said. "My guess would be one of his victims. Like the client. You ask her about it?"

Doyle shook his head. "Some things you're better off not knowing. You don't suppose this Palmer guy is gonna try to hit us up now, do you?"

Sandoval shrugged. "Only time will tell. But even if his little pal trusted him with the key to the vault, the guy's gotta realize the mortality rate on that racket."

"Screw him," Doyle said. "What about the witness who counts?"

"Young Theodore Maxwell?" He reached into his brief-case and withdrew a videocassette and a glossy photograph.

Doyle took the photo. It was very dark and grainy. "What the hell's this?" he asked. "I can't see what the kid's doing."

"It's a bad transfer. The video is clearer. Young Theodore on his first visit to a jab-joint. Sampling a little heroin. Kids today, huh?"

Doyle looked at Sandoval. "You are the best."

"This is my town, Jimmy. I just let other people use it." He handed Doyle the tape. "I figure we can play it nice and give the kid the option of changing his story about the Jaguar. Or we can play it nasty and let the lawyer surprise him by asking him during cross-examination if he does drugs. Either way, his word won't mean shit."

"I vote nice. No sense ruining the kid's life if we don't have to. Drugs! You know, Pete, every day I give the good Lord a little thank-you that I've been spared fatherhood."

"It's got its up and downs," Sandoval said. "My daughter gave me nothing but shit for the first twenty years of her life. Now she's got a big job with the phone company. We get along fine and I got access to any unlisted number I want. For just fifty bucks."

"Family values," Doyle said. "How you doin' on my cop friends?"

"Did you know Goodman was one of the dicks looking into the Lobrano suicide?"

"It took me a while, but I placed the face. He missed the boat on that one."

Sandoval grinned. "They all missed the boat on that one. Otherwise we might not be here today, plotting more evil."

"So tell me about Goodman. Tell me he keeps a white sheet in his closet."

"Wrong closet," Sandoval said. "I think the guy may even be kosher. I pulled his chart. Married a few times, but no record of abuse or anything like that. Just incompatibility. Kind of an off-duty wild man, though. Shooting off guns at parties."

"No kidding? I wouldn't have guessed it. Plug anybody?"

"Naw. Good record as a cop, but at least one fall from grace. There were these sisters, the Jastrups, lived in his building. Hookers working for old Madame Sonya."

"Sonya," Doyle said, smiling at a private memory.

"Yeah, well, when they pulled in Sonya and her operation, Goodman somehow kept the Jastrup girls out of it. Then he took up with Edie Jastrup for about a year."

"How long ago was it they closed down Sonya?" Doyle asked.

"Seven years."

Doyle looked disappointed. "So seven years ago he helped out a hooker. That's not exactly the mighty club I was looking for. He been shooting his gun lately?"

"Not that I've found. He's been taking it real easy."

"Maybe he's on Prozac," Doyle said.

"That wasn't on his medical sheet, but I'll check."

"I was just kidding," Doyle said. "What about the Mexican?"

"Morales? Now there's a real class act. Used to stick perps headfirst into toilets, until one almost drowned and he was suspended. Sadist. Bully. Loudmouth. Asshole. Those were some of the nice things I heard about him. After his last partner got smoked in some dive, it looked like he was gonna have to go solo, he was so disliked. Then Goodman agreed to put up with his crap."

"Why'd *Goodman* need a new partner?" Doyle asked.

"The guy he rode with, Aaron Ferran, ate his gun."

"Why?"

Sandoval shrugged. "Too old. Too lonely. Seen too much of this shitty world."

"Sounds like you could be describing Goodman, too," Doyle said. "Check out the Ferran thing. Maybe he was dirty and his conscience did him in. That'd give us some mud to rub on Goodman. Be off with you, now. I got things to attend to."

"When do I get to meet the lady?" Sandoval asked.

"Dyana?"

"Naw. Showbiz twists I can see any hour of the day. Anna Marie Dayne. When do I get to meet her?"

"Never, if I can help it," Doyle told him.

"Why?" Sandoval looked more surprised than hurt.

Doyle cocked his head to one side. "Because she operates on a different level, boyo. The suckers and mugs of the world are, in her eyes, the poor and oppressed. She believes in honor and integrity and all that other horseshit. I'm afraid it might confuse her to discover we had a scumbag like you on our team."

Sandoval wasn't offended. "What about *you* being on her team?" he asked.

"Me? Every time you pick up a copy of the *L.A. Times,* you don't see a picture of me pattin' some celebrity child molester on the back or posin' with some cop who's just caved in a black guy's dome for going five miles over the speed limit. I keep a profile so low not even *Hard Copy* could stumble over it.

"The secret of my success is this, old son: I'm a stealth scumbag."

≡ FIFTY-TWO ≡

Goodman drove the unmarked sedan down Melrose Avenue, checking the too-cute names of the boutiques and restaurants. Morales sat beside him, sipping coffee from a Winchell's cup and staring at the morning paper. "You looking good, amigo," he said, chuckling. Goodman's photo, accompanying an article about the Lydon murder, shared the front page with a photo of Dyana Cooper and her attorney leaving the courthouse.

"Given the choice of me or you," Goodman told his partner, "it's no wonder whose picture they picked."

"I guess I'm a little too ethnic for the *Times*."

"Too ugly," Goodman said. "Here we go."

There was no place to park in front of Todo Viejo, the shop where the Palmers sold their Mexican artifacts and antiques, so he parked in the bus stop area at the end of the block.

Palmer was at the rear of the shop chatting with a plump woman in black slacks and shirt whose shaggy hair had been dyed the color of Mercurochrome. They were both seated at a nice polished wood table that Goodman though... cedar. The young man held up a just-one-minute fi... continued to listen as the woman explained, in a voice ... enough to etch glass, that since her dog, Ramón, was a Chi-huahua, it was only logical that he have a Mexican dog-house. Palmer said he knew an excellent craftsman in Hermosillo who could create one to her specifications.

There were about ten or twenty other things the detectives could be doing, but Goodman figured he'd let Palmer finish up with the doghouse customer if it didn't take too long. He joined Morales, who was scowling at a display of skeleton figurines. One was in swim trunks on water skis. Another, wearing a policeman's uniform, was pointing a gun at a skeleton with a handkerchief tied around its face, holding a little bag with a dollar sign on it.

"Day of the Dead," Morales said. "*Dia de los Muertos.* Hell, that's every day."

His tone was so bitter, Goodman asked, "What's eating you?"

"Nothing," his partner replied sullenly. Then he added, "My mother believed in all this crap. Not the fucking water-skiers; tha's some kind of Americano rip. But the skeletons. The family picnic. Sweet bread with the little plastic toy baked in. You bite down on the toy it's supposed to be good luck, unless you break yo' damn tooth."

He waved his hand angrily as if to dismiss all the little statues. "Le's wrap this up."

The woman with the bright red hair was still describing, in minute detail, exactly what she wanted. "It should have a sort of pastel Santa Fe exterior. Tile roof of course."

Morales looked at his partner, perplexed. Goodman whispered, "Doghouse."

"Doghouse?" Morales replied, definitely not whispering. "Fuck that." He moved to the desk and faced the woman.

"Sorry, lady, but we here on police business to talk with Mr. Palmer. You gonna have to cut this short."

She looked him up and down. "I pay your salary," she said. "You can wait until I've finished."

Palmer stood up. "I think I've got the gist of it, Frieda," he said to the woman as he circled the desk and stood beside her. "I could drop by your home this afternoon, check out the location, take some measurements, and get my guy working on this immediately."

Frieda was clearly annoyed at being rushed, but Palmer had left her with no alternative but to leave. She made up for it by telling him, "Don't come before three. I can give you fifteen minutes then and no more. And I may ask you to take back that pot you sold me last month. I'm not sure the glaze is exactly what I want."

"I'll look at it. I appreciate your coming in, Frieda. See you at three."

Frieda took her time leaving the store. When she'd gone, Palmer said, "Sorry about that."

"You might want to lock up," Goodman said. "That way, we won't be disturbed."

Palmer frowned, obviously curious. He closed the front door, locked it, and hung the little cardboard "Back in an hour" card. He returned, pulled over another chair for Morales, and then retreated behind the desk. "What's this all about?"

"What exactly was your relationship with Arthur Lydon, Mr. Palmer?" Goodman asked.

"Relationship? I suppose 'friends' would cover it. I was shocked to hear about the murder. Is it connected to Maddie's death?"

"We don't know," Goodman said. "Could you explain your concept of 'friends'?"

Palmer scowled. "I don't understand. Are you accusing me of something?"

"You guilty of something?" Morales asked.

Palmer glared at him but elected not to even try to respond to the loaded question.

"We just want to know if you were close friends," Goodman said.

"I wouldn't say that. Not close. In point of fact, we had lunch together every so often. Talked about common interests."

Morales snickered. Goodman reached into his inside pocket and withdrew a snapshot. He held it out so that Palmer could see it.

It was a picture of him and Lydon in Madeleine Gray's black-sand pool, naked, doing their version of an arms-locked showgirl kick in front of the fake waterfall.

The shop owner raised his hand, but Goodman cautioned him not to touch the picture. "That's you and the deceased, am I right?"

Palmer nodded.

"You guys forget your swimsuits?" Morales asked.

Palmer didn't answer.

"Just friends, though," Morales said. "When was the picture taken?"

"Two years ago."

"Who took it? Your wife?"

Palmer mumbled something.

"Huh? What's that?"

"Maddie took the picture," Palmer said.

"She wearin' her swimsuit at the time?"

Again, no reply.

Goodman took another photo from his pocket. Palmer blinked when he saw it.

"That's you and Madeleine Gray, correct?" Goodman asked.

"Y-yes."

"Way to go, Mr. Palmer," Morales said. "In the short strokes, looks like."

"I—I didn't know—there was a picture . . ."

Goodman replaced that photo with a third snapshot. In this one, Palmer and Lydon were having sex in the sunshine. The store owner's eyes were blinking rapidly in disbelief. "How could they have taken these without my knowledge?"

"You looked pretty busy," Morales said.

Palmer continued to be captivated by the picture of himself and Arthur Lydon.

"We didn't come here to embarrass you, Mr. Palmer," Goodman said. "It's obvious from these photos that you were intimate with both victims." He paused to put the final photo away, then stared hard into Palmer's now watery eyes. "Were you in business with them?"

"This is my business. Mine and my wife's. Maddie and Art had nothing to do with it."

"And you've never seen these pictures before. Or had them described to you?"

"No. I knew Maddie took the shot by the waterfall, because we posed for it. I thought she put the camera away after that."

"Was this something you did all the time?" Morales asked.

"Of course not. I had lunch over there a few times and maybe we passed around a joint or a Thai stick. Maddie was always fun at lunch. Later, she'd get drunk and moody, but at lunch she was fine. I mean, always perverse, but fun." He paused, then asked, "Is this just between us?"

Goodman looked at Morales, then back at Palmer. "I don't know how to answer that," he said. "Suppose for the sake of argument in the next five minutes you confess to a serious crime. Then it isn't just between us anymore."

"I haven't committed any serious crime."

"Then there's nothing to worry about."

Palmer nodded. "I'd like to explain how this happened. You have to understand, Art was a fag. Maddie knew he and I had gotten it on a few times and she assumed I was gay, too. So she'd walk around naked in front of us, fondling herself—she did have a beautiful body—and joke about trying to bring us over to her team. Art knew I was bi, so while she was enjoying her little joke, he and I had our own going. It was like Tony Curtis telling Marilyn Monroe he was bored with women in that movie.

"Anyway, that day, the three of us got totally ripped at lunch. Art and I stripped down. Maddie was already naked. We got into the pool and she was really coming on to me. Tongue in my ear. Groping me. I couldn't hide the fact that it was working, so I figured, what the hell. I pretended she'd changed my luck. I never dreamed Art was taking pictures of us."

"How many more times did you get together?" Goodman asked.

"The three of us, like that? Once or twice, maybe."

"What about you and Maddie without Art?" Morales asked.

Palmer blinked. "You have to understand. In point of fact, my wife and I—Oh, hell, Caitlin is an ice queen and Maddie was like a fever dream. Straights believe gays spend every waking minute thinking about sex. That's how Maddie was. She wanted it anytime, any way."

"So you two had a relationship?"

"It wasn't really a relationship. We just fucked well together."

"That was okay with Lydon?"

"Of course. Look. We weren't conventional people. There was no pressure. No jealousy. Just sex."

"I don't know, Mr. Palmer," Goodman said. "I've always found it's a real bear to keep just one lover happy."

"As I said, we weren't conventional."

"When was the last time you and Madeleine Gray made love?"

"A year ago, about."

"That long ago?"

"In point of fact, Maddie got busy and wasn't available."

"What do you mean, she got busy?"

"She . . . Oh, hell, she shined me on. Said she had too much going on in her life."

Goodman nodded sympathetically. "She was seeing somebody else," he said.

Palmer nodded.

"Any idea who?"

"Art said it was some black guy."

Morales's eyes widened a bit. "Sure it was a *guy?*"

"Oh, yes. Maddie was into men. You must've discovered that by now."

Their investigation had turned up a number of lovers in Madeleine Gray's past, none of them recent, none considered a likely suspect. They were all men, but Morales persisted in hanging on to his lesbian theory. "Did Lydon give you the *guy*'s name by any chance?" he asked Palmer with heavy sarcasm.

"No. He didn't know or he would have told me. You can bet he tried to find out."

"How'd he know the guy was black?" Goodman asked.

"Maddie told him." He smiled ruefully. "You see, for all her worldliness, she'd never made it with a black guy before. Art said she went on and on about how much she'd been missing, how she didn't know what fucking was before this guy came along."

"How'd that make you feel?"

"How do you think? You get over it."

"Some do," Goodman said. "Some don't."

"I did. I can't say I didn't miss her, though."

"What about you and Lydon? When did you see him last?"

"I had coffee with him just a few days before he died. We hadn't had sex for a year and a half or longer."

"What happened there?"

"A mutual friend died of AIDS and both Art and I swore off gay sex. I think he may have backslid—oops, I made a joke. I haven't, because I can get off on women, too."

"Did either Madeleine or Lydon ever give you something to keep for them?" Goodman asked. "Maybe a computer disk? Or a locker key?"

"No."

The detective stood up. "Thanks for your cooperation, Mr. Palmer," he said.

Morales got to his feet slowly. "So women are better?" he asked Palmer.

"For me. It's something we each should try and find out for ourselves."

"Yeah, right," Morales said.

Goodman sat behind the wheel of the unmarked sedan and scribbled as much as he could remember about the interview on his pad. He'd purposely not taken notes in the shop, because he'd wanted to make the meeting seem as off-the-record as possible. Palmer had responded by providing them with an assortment of informative bits and pieces. He'd also proven once again what Goodman's years as a detective had already told him—that people went icebergs one better, showing even less than 10 percent on the surface.

So Maddie Gray had been seeing a black guy for about a year. He'd probably been the one who gave her the trinket that was now missing, the bracelet with the tiny golden figurine. *Damn.* He'd convinced himself the murders were the result of blackmail. Now he was back to jealousy. He made a mental note to check the date of John Willins's birth, just to see if his astrological sign might be the lion.

He turned to Morales. "What's your gut tell you about Palmer? Believable?"

Morales shrugged. "I don't know, amigo. Soon as the guy says he's not gay, I figure he's a lyin' sonofabitch. In point of fucking fact."

"What about the snapshot of him and Maddie going at it?"

"You know the old song about the woman so fine she gives eyesight to the blind? Maddie Gray paradin' around her pool in her birthday suit musta been finer than that."

≡ FIFTY-THREE ≡

The two petite Hispanic women were just part of the crowd of reporters, gawkers, and protesters baking in the midday sun in front of the Criminal Courts Building. They wore identical sweaters—bright yellow with red lettering that read "Alien Power." Returning from lunch, Nikki passed them by, wondering what their grievance, real or imagined, was. In less than thirty seconds, she found out.

On several morning newscasts, a former housekeeper of Ray Wise had accused him of forcing her, a formerly illegal alien, to work for starvation wages. As he limped toward the front doors of the CCB, the two women descended on him, flailing at him with their tiny fists and shouting at him in their native tongue. Blood spurted from his nose.

Far from trying to assist in any way, the crowd seemed to delight in this spectacle. Video cameras clicked on. "Go, aliens," someone cried, and the crowd took it up like a chant. Nikki rushed to grab an arm of one of the attackers, spinning her away from Wise, who struggled free from the other to hop into the lobby.

Nikki followed him in. A guard rushed past them, heading for the two women, who were running away through the crowd. Wise was dabbing at his bleeding nose with a handkerchief. "Those morons wanted them to kill me," he shrieked. "What a world!"

Nikki, who hadn't really expected any thanks for her help, said, "Next time, try being nicer to your housekeepers."

"The woman's a liar," he almost shouted, as they waited for the always overcrowded elevators. "I paid her better than minimum wage."

"Great," Nikki whispered, "but this isn't the best place to be making a speech."

"Caught the bitch wearing my mother's wedding ring. Was I supposed to give her a raise?"

"Ray," Nikki said sternly. "Everything you say now is gonna be on TV tonight."

He nodded and cleared his throat nervously. He dabbed at his nose again, studied the blood on his handkerchief, and said, "Joe's going to have to get me a bodyguard. We all are going to need bodyguards before this is over."

Wise was even more dejected when he appeared at her office door an hour later. "They ought to flush this day down the crapper," he said.

"You're not still stewing about those housekeepers from hell?" she asked.

He shook his head. "I just got a call from Teddy Maxwell's father. The little bastard is recanting. Says he's no longer sure what kind of car he saw at Gray's."

"Let's go pay him a visit," she said.

"Maxwell refuses to let us see the kid. We could force it, but I think we'd be walking the dog."

"Let's bounce it off Joe," she said. "Assumin' he's not too busy fornicating with your second chair."

Walden was in his office with Meg Fisher. He was in a fury. Both of his secretaries were busy fielding phone calls. With every incoming ring, his ire went up another notch. "I understand from Court TV that we've lost another witness," he told them.

"Teddy Maxwell?" Nikki asked.

"Oh, then you know. I don't suppose you felt I'd be interested in these little petty details or that the damned phone would be ringing off the hook for my reaction."

"That's why we're here, Joe," Wise said. "I just heard from the boy's father five minutes ago."

"They must have notified the media before they called us," Meg said.

"Aren't you supposed to keep us a step ahead of the news vultures, Meg? Isn't that what we're paying you for?"

"I thought it was because I remain so cool under fire," Meg said flatly.

Joe turned to Wise. "So how did you fuck this one up, Ray? Pushing the boy too hard? Misinterpreting things he said?"

"He identified the Jag," Wise said. "First to the detectives. Then to me. No pushing. No misinterpretation."

Walden sighed, then seemed to shrink within his large body. "Okay. I'm sorry, folks. I better lay off the caffeine and get more sleep."

Better lay off *something*, Nikki thought.

≡ FIFTY-FOUR ≡

Goodman stood at the open door to Nikki Hill's empty office. Maybe it was just as well she wasn't there, he thought. He could come back some other time. As he turned to head toward the elevators, she appeared, walking fast, a scowl on her face.

"Nikki?"

She stopped, turned to him. Then, as recognition dawned, she smiled. "Detective Goodman. I'm sorry. My mind was on something else."

"I just dropped off some new evidence with George Emerson," he said. Emerson was the deputy D.A. assigned to the Arthur Lydon murder. It would be his case unless or until Walden decided to link that death officially to the case against Dyana Cooper.

"It's good seeing you, detective," Nikki said. "I think Ray wants to schedule some times this week for you and Carlos to go over your testimonies."

"Sure," he said. "Guess you're pretty busy, huh?"

Her brown eyes studied him for a few seconds. "You got a problem?" she asked.

"Uh huh."

"Come on," she said, leading him to her office.

She shut the door after them and gestured to a chair. "What's goin' on?"

"Your boss was right," he said.

"Yeah?" she said, as if that might be a surprise. "Right about what?"

"Remember that meeting when he said talking to Madeleine Gray's blackmail victims wasn't such a good idea? It wasn't. This one lady, an old TV actress named Nita Morgan, is accusing me of blackmail."

He didn't like the way the warmth went out of her eyes. "What would make her do that?" she asked.

"Not long after I went to see her, she got this phone call from somebody asking her for money. Morgan says the caller didn't identify himself, but it was a man and it sounded like me."

"I assume it wasn't you."

"No, ma'am. My guess is it was Arthur Lydon. I think he had a copy of Madeleine Gray's blackmail files and he tried to use 'em and that's what got him killed."

"The files weren't among his effects."

"No, ma'am. I imagine whoever killed him got 'em."

"You mention all this to George Emerson?"

"I, ah, did tell him that one of Maddie's victims had been contacted by a new blackmailer and that I thought it was Lydon."

"You neglected to mention the charge against you." When Goodman sheepishly acknowledged that, she asked for Emerson's take on the blackmail angle.

"He asked for proof, which I don't have," Goodman said.

"He strikes me as the kinda guy who, given the choice of walking or sitting, keeps his chair pretty warm."

She smiled. That was Emerson to a T. "What do you want from me, detective?"

"My boss, Lieutenant Corben, has ordered me to stay clear of Nita Morgan. So I can't very well question her about her story. I was hoping you might."

"Why me?"

Goodman took a deep breath. "The way I see it," he said, "by the time Dyana Cooper's lady lawyer finishes with me and this blackmail claim, I'm going to make Mark Fuhrman look like Policeman of the Year."

"As of this morning there was no Nita Morgan on the list of defense witnesses."

Goodman was surprised. "I just assumed . . . It doesn't mean they won't add her."

"True," Nikki said. "I still have to ask: Why come to me? Why not Ray Wise or Dimitra Shaw?"

"If we may speak frankly," Goodman said, "this is my life and my career and I don't feel like entrusting it to an asshole like Wise. Or to somebody I don't know."

"Gee. You sure know how to flatter a girl."

Oh, Christ, he thought, *I'm playing this all wrong.* "It's not just that. From what I can see, you care about your work. You don't just phone it in."

He thought she softened slightly. "Speaking of phones, I suppose you had access to Nita Morgan's number?"

He nodded. "Unfortunately. But the timing is off," he said. "When she made her initial complaint, she said the blackmailer called her at the same time I was interrogating Dyana Cooper. You were there. You know I didn't leave the box. Today, Morgan changed her mind about the time of the call. Said it was later. I got no alibi for later."

For what seemed like an eternity but was probably a

minute or two, Nikki stared at him, saying nothing. It made him uncomfortable, but he knew the game and stared back, a man with a clear conscience.

"Okay," she said, glancing at her watch, "I'll go see Ms. Morgan."

Goodman felt greatly relieved. "I really appreciate this."

"I'm not going to rambo an old woman," she cautioned. "All I'll do is listen to her story and see if I can shake it a little."

"That's all I ask," Goodman said. "Except, could we keep this just between us for a while?"

"Ray's gonna have to know about it when he goes over your courtroom testimony," she said. "Until then, all you'll have to worry about is Nita Morgan or the defense leaking the story to the press."

Goodman avoided the reporters and cameras by leaving the CCB from a rear exit. He circled the block and was headed toward his office when he spotted Gwen Harriman at the corner, having an animated conversation with a man who seemed vaguely familiar. A big, solid man, with a square jaw, wearing a cocoa-brown suit.

The big man said something that turned Gwen's face into a mask of anger. He grabbed her arms and began to shake her.

Goodman started toward them, then paused. Ten years ago, hell, five years ago, when his own personal brand of male chauvinism was still in full bloom, he'd have thought nothing of giving his instincts full rein. Now he considered the possibility that Gwen might not want to be "rescued." What he was witnessing might be a lover's quarrel.

As he pondered his next move, Gwen made hers, kneeing the big man in the groin. With a howl, he folded, releasing her.

Gwen hissed something at him, turned, and stormed away.

Goodman watched the man gradually straighten. He wiggled the upper part of his body, as if trying to reclaim some semblance of dignity, and followed Gwen.

Goodman followed him.

The man seemed in no hurry as he crossed the street and entered Parker Center.

Goodman pushed through the heavy doors just as the man was stepping into an elevator. Going down.

By the time Goodman got to the subterranean parking level, the man was nowhere to be seen.

He waited for a minute or two, checking cars as they headed for the exit. Then, more than a little annoyed and confused, he got back on the elevator and headed up.

Gwen was at her desk, phone to her ear. He waved to her. She gave him a wink. With a sigh, he sat down at his desk and wondered what the hell was going on.

≡ FIFTY-FIVE ≡

As if the members of the prosecution team needed a reminder, Ray Wise tacked a countdown calendar to his office door. It consisted of a stack of pages, approximately six by six inches, on which three-and-a-half-inch-high numerals marked the number of "Days Left Until Trial." Wise would tear off a sheet when he arrived at work in the morning. By then, one of several office humorists usually had altered the previous day's sheet to read something like "20 Days Left Until ~~Trial~~ Anna Marie Kicks Our Ass" or "19 Days Left Until ~~Trial~~ Wise's Housekeeper Kicks His Ass."

On the morning the calendar read "16 Days Left Until ~~Trial~~ the Battle of the Bitches," an indication of how the staff felt about Dimitra Shaw, Meg Fisher gathered the key members of the team in the small conference room to look at a videotape presentation she'd assembled. Dressed in a smartly cut business suit appropriate to a public relations maven whom fate had suddenly awarded instant access to all media, Fisher dimmed the lights and started the video machine.

The assembly watched the monitor as a montage of newspaper and magazine pieces appeared, all, even the most conservative, favoring Dyana Cooper. There were stories about the Willinses' happy marriage, photos of Dyana Cooper in church, visiting children's hospitals, attending the Special Olympics, welcoming orphans to a luncheon she'd arranged at the Beverly Hills Hard Rock Café.

This was followed by a compilation of pro-Cooper television news bites topped off by a report from a usually scurrilous tabloid show that a group of Catholic African-Americans in Michigan were seriously campaigning for Cooper, a living non-Catholic, to be considered a candidate for sainthood.

Suddenly, Dyana Cooper was replaced by a plump, hard-eyed white woman. This was, according to the screen caption, "Adele Kellman, former wife of Prosecutor Raymond Wise." She was telling the world that she was awarded custody of their child because "Ray didn't have any interest in either our daughter or me."

She was followed by Wise's ex-housekeeper, the new darling of the press, who described in loving detail his disdain for people of color—"black, tan, yellow, all the same to him, all bad."

Fisher turned off the TV. "I didn't mean to single you out, Ray," she said. "We've all had our hits and there will be more to come. Some excellent spin doctors are trying to make this whole office look slightly to the right of Saddam Hussein. We must remember the cardinal rule: Truth is nice, but public perception is everything. . . ."

It wasn't Nikki's cardinal rule. In fact, she was offended by it. She looked across the table at Dimitra and was surprised to see that she wasn't smiling either. Maybe they were more alike than Nikki had thought.

"This office is in dire need of a quick-fix image overhaul," Fisher was saying. "Now is the time to engage in public services that offer positive photo ops. Visits to hospitals, attendance at civic affairs, speaking before groups like MADD or battered wives, upbeat appearances on talk radio and TV. I have some ideas I'll be bouncing off of you within the next few days.

"And, Joe, I've taken the liberty of checking a few upcoming events that I'd like to discuss with you right after this meeting."

Walden took that as his cue to call a halt to the proceedings.

As Nikki was leaving, she passed by Dimitra, who was still seated, staring off into space. "You okay, Dee?" she asked.

Dimitra didn't respond.

Pressure of the job? Nikki wondered. *Pressure of sleeping with the boss?* In either case, none of her affair. She shrugged and headed out.

At twenty minutes before five that evening she was called back to Walden's office. Waiting for her were the district attorney, Wise, and Dimitra.

"Shut the door, will you, Nikki?" Walden requested. "Then take a chair."

When she'd carried out these simple requests, Walden said, "We suddenly have an opening at the prosecution table. Ray has convinced me you should fill it."

Nikki looked at Dimitra, who said, "I'm going on leave from the office."

"Why?" Nikki asked.

"My doctor says I've got to take it easy for a while," Dimitra said. "Nothing serious. But if I stayed on, I wouldn't be able to contribute a hundred percent."

Walden patted the woman's arm in a gesture that seemed

to Nikki to be more than a little patronizing. "She'll be back with us soon," he said.

"Badder than ever," Dimitra said.

"Well, Nikki," the D.A. asked. "You still want the job?"

"Oh, yeah," she said.

Dimitra stood up. "I got things to take care of," she said.

Walden nodded. "If you see Meg out there, ask her to come in."

"We need to have a talk," Dimitra whispered to Nikki on her way out.

Meg Fisher bustled in, carrying the news that the National Association of African-American Leadership would be presenting Walden with its top honor, the Mabwana Amali Cup, when its annual meeting took place in Los Angeles the following month. "Their PR director, an extremely cooperative fellow," Fisher said, "tells me that *mabwana amali* is Swahili for 'man of action.' The dinner will be black tie at that ballroom at the top of the Hotel Balmoral. Our end of it is five tables at two thousand dollars each, and worth every penny."

"I thought we wanted the NAACP," Walden said.

"They passed," Fisher said. "But Af-Am Leaders carries a lot of weight, too."

The answer seemed to satisfy Walden, who moved on to Nikki's appointment.

"We have a bio, but we'll need a more comprehensive one," Meg said. "And, Nikki, if you could ask any celebrities you know for a few quotes."

Annoyed by this petty bullshit, Nikki said, "The only celebrity I've been talkin' to lately is Dyana Cooper."

Meg gave her a flinty smile. "Then we'll stick to just the bio," she said.

*   *   *

Nikki spent as little time as she could with Meg, then devoted most of the afternoon and some of the evening to discussing the trial with Wise and Dimitra. They explained that they had decided to focus on the jealousy motive. It was basic enough for any juror to grasp immediately and it didn't require a ton of proof.

It did require some, Nikki reminded them.

Wise told her that a number of the investigators from their office were working on the John Willins–Maddie Gray connection. "According to the gossip scum they talked to, something definitely was going on. Goodman and Morales have discovered that Maddie was seeing a black man."

Dimitra added that the investigators were taking another pass at Maddie's neighbors and associates and were checking hotels and hideaways. They were presently awaiting copies of Willins's credit card purchases.

Nikki finally returned to her office at seven-thirty with a nearly filled notepad. She spent another hour sorting out the material well enough to proceed in earnest the following morning.

She was sitting at her desk, wondering if Virgil had already had dinner, when her phone rang. A long-distance operator asked the familiar question. This was followed by Mason Durant's deep, depressing baritone.

"Hi, Nikki, thought you might be workin' late. Jus' heard on the news you're gonna be prosecuting Dyana Cooper."

So all that time spent with Meg working out a biography and press release hadn't been a waste.

"Looks that way," she said.

"The brothers in here think she's being set up by the D.A."

"Since the brothers are in there, Mace, I wouldn't say that thinking was something they did very well. If we were going to set somebody up, my guess is it wouldn't be America's sweetheart. It would be one of the usual suspects."

"What they say is you folks are so desperate, you'll prosecute anybody you can get into court. 'Cept the guilty party, of course."

"Goodnight, Mace," she said.

"Wait. You know about this dude, Lee-O?"

"No. Should I?"

"Real bad mother. Very powerful. Mixed up in the Maddie Gray murder."

"Who told you that?" she asked. "The thinkers?"

Mace coughed from deep in his chest. "Keeps gettin' worse," he wheezed.

"You taking something for it?"

"What? Some magic sauce gonna polish up my lungs? Listen, Nikki, you decide you wanna know more about Lee-O, gimme a call. Maybe we can make some kind of deal. I help you out on this; you help me get out of here while I still got some breath."

"I'll keep your offer in mind," she lied, hanging up the phone. Something about "Lee-O" struck a familiar chord. Considering the source, she wasn't going to think too hard on it.

≡ FIFTY-SIX ≡

Two days later, as Eddie Goodman headed to work on a bright, minimally smoggy morning, he pondered the way his life was shifting. On the job, things seemed to be falling into place. The Gray investigation was pretty much complete. The Arthur Lydon case was going nowhere, but since the D.A. had chosen not to attempt to introduce it into the Will-ins trial, there was only the usual pressure to get it off the books. The annoying blackmail charge was looking less and less serious. Especially since Nikki Hill, the new Dyana Cooper prosecutor whose picture had been in every news-paper and on every channel, was in his corner.

That left his personal life, which was in the crapper. Mainly because he refused to accept the fact that Gwen Harriman was in love with somebody else. The hell of it was, he wasn't totally convinced he was in love with *her.* The only thing he knew for sure was that he cared for her and that he felt she was screwing up her life. His experi-ence with romance and marriage had taught him that women didn't like men to try and help them when they didn't want to be helped. He would have to put his concern and curiosity on hold, hoping that one of these days she'd decide to tell him what was going on with her and the asshole she was so fond of she'd kicked him in the balls.

He strolled into the bullpen, expecting to find her at her desk on her second cup of coffee. She was there, all right. So was the big galoot, resting his broad butt on her desk and chatting her up.

Balls all healed, I presume.

Goodman strolled over to the desk sergeant who controlled the traffic into Major Crimes and asked, "Who's the flattop with Gwen?"

The sergeant, a grizzled specimen on the cusp of retirement, squinted across the bullpen. "Lattimer," the sergeant said. "Vice jagoff. Been in a couple times lately."

"To see Gwen?" Goodman asked.

"Naw," the sergeant said. "To put my sorry ass to work looking stuff up for him."

"What sort of stuff?"

The sergeant spun around, punched a few buttons on his computer. He looked at the screen, then brightened. "Yeah. Right," he said. "He asked me to see if this officer worked any of our cases. There was only one. Martinez. Rudy Martinez."

"That the officer's name?" Goodman asked.

"Naw," the sergeant snorted. He seemed surprised at the detective's ignorance. "You don't remember the Martinez case? Rudy Martinez, son of the actor Nestor Martinez? Got involved in some kind of weapons sale and wound up with more bullets in him than Mussolini?"

Goodman nodded, vaguely recalling the murder.

"It was the only one of our cases the computer spit out that had William Hill connected to it."

"William Hill? That's the name of the officer Lattimer asked about?"

"Yep. On the beat his whole career. Retired now, I guess."

Goodman watched the vice cop Lattimer give Gwen a smirky farewell wink. He couldn't read her expression as she watched the asshole depart. She brightened when she spotted Goodman. He jerked his thumb in the direction of the departing Lattimer, raising his eyebrows questioningly. She shook her head as if to say, "It's nothing."

It didn't seem like nothing to Goodman.

≡ FIFTY-SEVEN ≡

It was only nine-fifteen in the morning, but Nikki's desk was covered with transcribed interviews, reports, case studies, and a stack of messages. She picked the one from her bank. Something about an overdrawn account due to a $12,500 withdrawal.

"I didn't withdraw any twelve thousand dollars," she informed a clerk in a deceptively calm voice.

"Twelve thousand, five hundred," the clerk corrected her. "On Tuesday of last week. I'm looking at your account, Ms. Hill. It shows very clearly that you made an on-line withdrawal—"

"Hold it! What kind of withdrawal?"

"On-line, using your computer."

"I wouldn't know how to make a computer withdrawal if you put a gun to my head."

"Just a minute, Ms. Hill."

A woman identifying herself as the branch manager, Mrs. Hellman, took over the call. Her voice was soft and genteel and annoyingly passive as she repeated what her assistant had already informed Nikki.

"As I just told your assistant," Nikki said, "I made no such withdrawal."

"Yes, it is a bit odd. I see that the withdrawal order entered the system only today, yet, for some reason, was predated. Most confusing. But we were following your requ—"

"What happened to the money?" Nikki interrupted.

"Hmmm. It appears you used the funds to open a second account in your name."

Nikki tried to remain calm, but it was an uphill fight. "I didn't use the funds, Mrs. Hellman. This is the first I've heard of the funds. You've obviously made a mistake."

"Our system doesn't make mistakes, Ms. Hill."

"Okay. Close the new account. Take the twelve thousand, five hundred dollars and apply it to my old account. That should solve all our problems."

"We can do that, Ms. Hill," Mrs. Hellman said. "There will be bank charges, of course. And interest on the funds your automatic overdraw protection borrowed from your credit card account."

Nikki counted to ten. "Don't I need some sort of software to bank by computer?"

"Of course."

"Why don't you check my file to see if I ever requested that software, Mrs. Hellman? Then, should you even dream of charging me so much as a plugged nickel because of some screwup in your system, it will be my happy duty to discuss this whole matter with you in front of a judge. I can assure you, I won't be the one paying for the use of the court."

She slammed down the phone.

Almost immediately, it rang.

She grabbed the receiver. "What now?" she asked roughly.

Momentary silence greeted her on the other end. Then Dimitra Shaw's voice asked, "Nikki? You okay?"

"Oh. Dimitra. Just letting off some steam. A screwup at my bank."

"That's how it starts," Dimitra said. "Bank screwup. Dead battery in the car. Phone doesn't work. Little things."

"What are you talking about?"

"Dyana Cooper's people. They just don't let up," Dimitra said. "But that's not life-threatening . . . Look, we gotta meet."

"You in your office?"

"No way. I'm outta there. Can you make it to Jonah's in about fifteen minutes?" Jonah's was a coffee shop four blocks away from the CCB.

"You know how busy it is around here?" Nikki asked.

"This is important, sister. Serious shit. I'm scared and I don't know what to do."

"Jonah's, huh," Nikki said.

The phone rang again before she could get away.

This time it was Detective Goodman with a question about her father.

"My father?" she said, feeling her face flush with heat. "I don't know anything about my father. Or his business, past or present."

The detective was yakking on about some murder vic named Martinez.

"I'm late for a meeting," she said impatiently. "Isn't this something that can wait?"

"I suppose it'll have to," Goodman told her.

As usual, the elevator took an eternity to arrive. By the

time she cleared the building, the fifteen minutes were already up.

Nikki was nearly a block away when she saw the crowd gathering in front of Jonah's. They were looking down at something in the gutter with grim fascination. A siren sounded in the distance, coming closer.

Nikki started running. Then she was pushing past the street gawkers.

The crushed body of Dimitra Shaw was draped over the curb, battered head resting in a pool of blood on the sidewalk, legs in the gutter.

"Oh, my God." Nikki heard the words without realizing she'd said them. She stared down at the lifeless body and her heart seemed to skip a beat in her chest. Her eyes filled with tears.

"Ambulance comin'," an elderly man called out.

"Too late for an ambulance," a young girl said. "She dead."

"What . . . happened?" Nikki asked.

"She was jayin' 'cross the street," the girl said, "an' this car swerved, whomped her an' kep' on goin'."

"What kind of car?" A red wave of anger coursed through Nikki's body, but she couldn't pinpoint its source. Frustration. Guilt.

The girl recognized her. "You the one on the TV? The D.A.?"

"Tell me about the car," Nikki demanded, grabbing the girl's arm.

The girl looked frightened. She jerked free and backed away. "Don't know 'bout any car," she said.

The sound of the ambulance was louder now, almost filling Nikki's head. "Don't you lie to me . . ." But the girl was running away.

Nikki turned to the others and shouted, "Who saw the car that did this?"

They looked at her, dumbly.

"Damn it. Somebody must've seen the car."

She was out of control, weeping and screaming at them. She might as well have ordered them to disperse. By the time the ambulance roared up, she was alone, kneeling in the street beside Dimitra's body.

A paramedic helped her to her feet. "You okay, miss?" he asked.

She ignored the question. She was too busy watching his partner confirm the fact that Dimitra was dead. "Pricks who did this musta been really travelin'," he said. "Knocked her right out of her shoes."

Nikki looked at the leather pumps lying in the street. Her heart broke when she realized they were the same brand and style as the ones she was wearing.

≡ FIFTY-EIGHT ≡

Goodman was at his desk, wondering why Nikki Hill
had gotten so pissed off at the mention of her father, when
his partner flopped down in the chair across from him.

"Alarm didn't go off?" Goodman said.

"Bastards tried to snatch Estella's car," Morales mumbled. Estella was his wife.

"What?"

"Repo guys. Said I was behind in the payments. Bullshit.
Had to dig out my stinkin' canceled checks. Estella screaming in my ear the whole time."

"Get it straightened out?"

Morales nodded. "Yeah. After forty minutes. Computer
mix-up. But no apol—"

He was stopped by Corben shouting their names.

The lieutenant was not in a good mood. "You gents seem
to have missed a beat in the Gray case. But not to worry, the
D.A.'s investigators picked up the slack."

Corben paused, letting them stand there, waiting. Then he

asked, "Ever hear of a place in the desert called the Sanctum?"

Morales didn't bother to reply. Goodman said, "Some kinda spa."

"Very good, detective," Corben said. "Celebrities go there when they want to get away from it all. 'It all' meaning their spouses, primarily. Place's got private cabanas. The staff is paid enough they keep their lips zipped. Anybody caught within five miles with a camera gets the shit beat out of 'em."

Goodman sighed. This was going to be grim.

"So, these D.A.'s men, they find out John Willins goes to the Sanctum. Not a lot, but every so often. Any idea who the lucky gal was who accompanied Mr. Willins?"

"Madeleine Gray," Goodman said gloomily.

"Madeleine Gray," Corben repeated, his face reddening. "What I want to know is why you guys, who are supposed to know what the fuck you're doing, let two putzes from the D.A.'s office get the drop on you like this? It makes us look like ama-chures."

Goodman had gotten into the habit of checking out his volatile partner at moments like that, just to make sure Carlos didn't let the snake element of his brain overwhelm his common sense. But he needn't have worried. Morales was slouched, staring at the tile floor as if he hadn't even heard Corben's verbal attack.

"Any idea how they found out about the Sanctum?" Goodman asked.

"I just didn't feel like asking Walden that question," the lieutenant said. "I didn't want the bastard to get any more smug about this than he already was."

"They talk to Willins?" Goodman asked.

"That's why the D.A. called. They'd like you two to do that. If you think you can handle it."

* * *

The major crimes detectives met with the district attorney's investigators, Laboe and Green, in their cubicle on the eighteenth floor of the CCB. When Goodman remarked that the atmosphere of the D.A.'s offices seemed even more tense than usual, Laboe, a short, balding man who could have shaved twice a day but didn't, told him that one of the deputies, Dimitra Shaw, had just been killed in a hit-and-run.

"She was hard to work with," Laboe said, "but it's still a lousy thing. Walden's gone nuts. Callin' out the guard. Word is he was dickin' her."

"Maybe we better take care of our own business, huh?" Morales said.

"Your partner asked," Laboe said. He then explained how they'd found out about the Sanctum. Ray Wise had had them phone every upscale romantic hideaway in a hundred-mile radius of the city. Pretending to be employees of Willins, they attempted to reserve his "usual" room. The Sanctum was the first to accept the reservation without question.

The investigators then visited the Sanctum armed with the proper papers. They were able to demand a copy of the spa's computerized booking files and to force statements from two clerks who reluctantly admitted that Willins had spent quite a few evenings there in the company of Madeleine Gray.

Green, a stocky black man with a modified Afro, said, as they headed for the elevators, "This guy Willins is gonna freak big time when he discovers he's been outed."

"I think we can assume he already knows," Goodman said.

"No way," Laboe said. "Not with the scare we threw into those peckers at the Sanctum."

When the quartet of lawmen was ushered into Willins's

office at Monitor Records, they discovered another person was present—Jesse Fallon.

"I assume you're here to discuss Mr. Willins's relationship to the late Ms. Madeleine Gray," the lawyer said, handing Goodman a sheet of paper. "This should save us all a little time."

It was a neatly typed statement. "Madeleine Gray and I began a romantic liaison approximately a year ago that continued for nearly eight months. Approximately four months ago she informed me she wished to end the affair and I agreed to do so. We parted amicably.

"I further testify that, to my knowledge, my wife was 100 percent unaware of this relationship at the time Ms. Gray met her unfortunate end."

It was signed by Willins and notarized.

"Any idea why Maddie gave you your walking papers?" Goodman asked.

Willins consulted his lawyer, who nodded his approval. "She was going on a quick trip to Europe. Part vacation, part business. She wanted me to fly over and meet her, but that was impossible, not only because Dyana would have heard about it, but because I have a business to run. When Maddie returned, she said she thought it would be a good idea if we stopped seeing each another. Frankly, I'd come to that same conclusion, myself."

"She meet somebody on the trip, you think?" Goodman asked.

"I'm sure she did. Maddie didn't like to be alone."

"It says here your wife didn't know about you and Maddie. That still true?"

"I—"

"Mr. Willins has confirmed the fact that he and the deceased were involved romantically," Fallon said, "and that Mrs. Willins was not aware of this relationship at the time of the Gray murder. Beyond that, we are not prepared to venture. Thank you gentlemen for your time. I know you will do your best to respect Mr. Willins's privacy and will keep this very personal information confidential, if at all possible."

≡ FIFTY-NINE ≡

The problem, Nikki realized, was that she'd never liked the woman. That was why she was so deeply affected by Dimitra's death. Strange how emotions did their number on you. Although she and Joe Walden seemed to be sharing the same symptoms—anger, frustration, guilt—they were coming at them from different angles. He was reacting to the loss of a lover, she to an unwanted sister whom she'd rejected.

Virgil helped with her grief.

They spent the night at his place. He even invited Bird, knowing how comforting she found the big dog. He prepared their dinner efficiently and silently while she rested on the sofa in his living room. Bird lay at her feet, so tuned to her mood that he remained quiet and passive even when Virgil joined her and put his arms around her and held her close.

After dinner, she wandered into the bedroom and fell into the deepest sleep she could recall.

*　*　*

She was still in her clothes when she awoke. Virgil's side of the bed remained unused.

The apartment was empty.

She went to the front door and looked out on the sunny courtyard. Virgil, in his workout clothes, was sitting on the steps, reading the morning paper. Bird's leash was beside him. The big dog was standing at the fishpond communing with the koi.

It was such a lovely scene she hesitated to enter it.

Bird took the decision out of her hands. He suddenly shifted his attention to her, gave a little "yip," and trotted up the steps to greet her. Virgil grabbed the leash and stood. "How you doing?" he asked.

"I'm okay. Did you sleep?"

He nodded. "On the sofa. Didn't want to disturb you. Bird and I did some bonding. Now we're both hungry. How about you?"

While he fixed scrambled eggs and bacon, she sipped her coffee and read the morning paper. A photo of Dimitra and an account of her brief life and hit-and-run death shared the front page with an assortment of stories about John Willins's affair with the late Madeleine Gray.

She skimmed most of the reportage, a history of the Willins-Cooper marriage (complete with wedding picture), a survey of his recording empire, her previous declarations of love for him. Columnists speculated on the effect Willins's adultery would have on the trial, the marriage, and Monitor Records. A short, vague history of the "secluded and somewhat mysterious spa known as the Sanctum" was offered, as well as profiles of the two "dedicated D.A.'s men who uncovered the secret romance," detectives Matthew Laboe and Horace Greene. The coverage seemed as complete as the judge's ban on public discussion allowed.

Finally, when she felt she could avoid it no longer, she took a deep breath and read what the reporters had to say about Dimitra. The police had no witnesses and no leads. Paint flecks adhering to Dimitra's belt buckle had been identified as a standard black enamel used by most vehicle manufacturers. The article ended with the statement that "an emotional District Attorney Joseph Walden, with a catch in his voice, vowed to find the person responsible for the accident."

Accident? Nikki supposed that's what it was, though Dimitra had used the word "life-threatening." "She was afraid."

"Say what?" Virgil was staring at her. So was Bird.

"Sorry," she said. "I was thinking out loud. Dimitra was afraid of something."

"You think what, she was murdered?"

Nikki shook her head. "No. I think Joe hit it right, when I told him about her phone call. He said he knew something was bothering her. He thought maybe her health problem was worse than she let on. Her doctor claims not to know about any medical problem, although Dimitra may have gone to some specialist on her own. Joe thinks she was worrying about that when she walked out in front of a car without looking."

"There you go," Virgil said. "Feel sad as you want. I feel sad myself. But she's gone, and you just ain't the reason."

That was what she wanted to believe.

The image of Dimitra's broken body haunted her all morning. Trying to dispel it, she threw herself completely into a strategy meeting, taking a contrarian approach to the use of the Willins-Gray tie-in.

The potential benefit of the revelation was obvious: it gave them a go ticket on the jealousy motive. Unlike Joe and Ray and most of the team, however, Nikki remained cautious. They still would have to prove Dyana Cooper's foreknowledge of the affair for it to have any legal significance. And Willins's betrayal might lead jurors to feel protective toward Dyana. She reminded them that a jury had recently awarded a ditched wife a million dollars in damages from the woman who had "lured" her husband away.

"Don't analyze this to death," Wise said. "Let's just grab this cherry that's been tossed in our laps and beat Dyana and her smart-ass lawyer into the ground with it."

"Love the imagery, Ray," Nikki said. She checked her wristwatch. "Whoa, I've got an appointment. Have to run."

The D.A. nodded. "They're burying Dimitra tomorrow morning."

"Yeah," Nikki said. "I got the notice."

"Where you headed?" Wise asked.

She'd scheduled a meeting at the home of Nita Morgan, the woman who'd accused Ed Goodman of blackmail. But that wasn't any of Wise's business. "Personal stuff, Ray. Nothing you'd want to analyze to death."

≡ SIXTY ≡

Goodman sat at a back booth at the Saratoga, anxiously nursing a glass of iced tea. For the last ten minutes, he'd been checking the front door each time it opened, so he saw Nikki enter, survey the late lunchers and the loiterers, and finally spot him at the rear. As she walked toward him, he tried to read the expression on her face. Success? Failure?

She took the seat across from him and said, "Lunch is on you, detective. We ought to be having it at Spago."

"It went well?"

She opened her briefcase and removed a sheet of paper. It was a document exonerating him from all blame in the matter of blackmail. It was signed by Nita Morgan.

He couldn't believe it. "How the hell . . . ?"

"She looks like a loon, with that long jet-black hair and the evening gown. Addams Family–time. But she didn't get that house in Beverly Hills being eccentric. She knows what she's doing. I spotted that right away. Her vampire TV series from the sixties is being repackaged for cable and she owns a big piece of it. She's also writing a book. She's looking for publicity."

"And that's why she came after me?"

"Not exactly," Nikki said. "She came after you because she got a new agent. For the past five years, she's been paying Maddie Gray three thousand dollars a month to act as her public relations counselor. That's a euphemism for blackmailer. Her agent convinced her that times have changed. Her sexual preference is no longer a big deal. It might even be good for her career if she comes out of the closet. They were trying to figure out how best to do it when you blundered into her life."

"So she invented the phone call?" Goodman asked.

Nikki shook her head. "She swears somebody tried to shake her down using Maddie's files."

"Arthur Lydon."

"Probably," Nikki said. "In any case, you're damn lucky the call was made while you were in the box with Dyana Cooper."

"What about her claim that she'd made a mistake about the time?"

"She says somebody from Internal Affairs told her to change her story. But that's unlikely."

"I bet it was the same jagoffs nosing around my apartment building," he said.

"You didn't mention that before," Nikki said.

"A couple guys posing as Internal Affairs shooflies. Talked to my neighbors."

"They find out anything we should know?"

He hesitated, then said, "Years ago I, ah, got involved with this lady who worked for Madame Sonya."

"How many years, exactly?"

"Seven."

"How involved?" she asked.

"We lived together for nearly a year."

"She in the life during that year?"

"Not while we were together," he said. "At least, not that I knew about."

"Why'd you break up?"

Smiling Edie. So sweet and agreeable. So easy to be with.

"Detective?"

"We drifted. I ain't that easy to live with."

"She go back hooking?"

"I heard she took up with some real estate guy and stayed with him for a while."

"Any idea what she's up to today?"

He hesitated, then said, "Last I heard she was back in her hometown with a husband and a couple rug rats."

"Name?"

"Edie . . Edith Jastrup. Her married name's Peterson."

"Doesn't ring any bells. I'll check the witness list."

Edie, a witness? Goodman hadn't considered that possibility. The thought of little Edie on the stand getting her past life thrown in her face turned his stomach.

"You know, Nikki, being a cop just isn't so much fun anymore."

She gave him a wry smile and said, "Let's order. I've gotta get back to the office."

She was so quiet while they dined on the Saratoga's chiliburgers that he asked, "Something on your mind?"

"I was thinking about Dimitra Shaw."

"I was sorry to read about it," he said. "You were close?"

"More than I thought," Nikki said, and told him about just missing the hit-and-run.

"She was lying on the curb?" he asked. "They didn't mention that in the paper."

"Her feet were in the street," Nikki said.

He scowled. "She was crossing the street to go to Jonah's.

She wound up on the curb in front of the place. It's a two-lane. That means she was past the middle of the street when she was hit. The driver had to have seen her. Unless he was drunk. Or stoned."

"Dimitra was afraid of something," Nikki said. "She warned me that Dyana Cooper had dirty tricksters trying to make our lives miserable."

"Tell me about that," Goodman said.

"She said they were just annoyances. Not 'life-threatening.' That's the exact word she used."

"Maybe she was wrong. No. It had to be an accident. Why would Cooper's people have gone after her? She'd resigned from the case."

"I don't know," Nikki said.

"Jesus," he said. "I just realized . . . it was my phone call to you that made you late to your meeting with her."

She'd forgotten his call. "What was it you were trying to tell me? Something about my father?"

"A vice cop named Lattimer has been asking about homicide cases involving William Hill."

"Were there any?"

He nodded. "Rudy Martinez, the son of a Latin movie star."

The name meant nothing to her. "Why would he check up on my father?"

"The dirty trickster theory," Goodman replied. "Carlos is being bothered by repo men. People are asking my neighbors questions about me."

"Ray and I have been having our problems, too. Who do you suppose the trickster is? Doyle?"

"He gets my vote." Goodman felt a strange tingle vibrate through him. It took a few seconds for him to realize it was anger.

"If Lattimer's on Doyle's payroll," Nikki said, "it would

explain how the fake Internal Affairs guys found out that Nita Morgan accused you of blackmail. Lattimer could have picked that up in your squadroom."

Goodman nodded, his mind making a slight detour. If Lattimer was working for Doyle, where did Gwen fit in? His heart started beating double time. His anxiety must have shown because Nikki reached out and pressed her fingertips against the back of his hand, as if to calm him.

"You okay?"

"Yeah, fine." He wanted a crack at Doyle, wanted to see the guy up close. See if he could make the fat boy sweat. Maybe even bleed.

Nikki read him like a book. "I just shook you loose of one sticky situation, detective. Don't get yourself in another. Not with the trial starting in two days."

"Right," he said. "It's just that I know how guys like Doyle work. They think they don't have to play by the rules. There's only one way to deal with 'em."

"This Doyle asshole isn't very high on my love meter, either," she said. "But breaking rules now will only make Anna Marie Dayne's job easier when she gets you on the stand."

Relaxing just a little, he said, "Dayne's tough, huh?"

"Tough? You can bet she'll be going for your throat," Nikki said. "But if you do anything boneheaded that messes up our case, like starting some bullshit vendetta against Doyle, I'll tear out your heart."

≡ SIXTY-ONE ≡

The Culver City branch of the Bank of California was jammed with customers, but William Hill stood a head taller than most. Stiff of back and firm of jaw, with his neatly barbered hair and his dark suit immaculately pressed, he looked more like a vice president of the bank than a part-time security guard.

He spotted Nikki as soon as she entered. His eyes seemed to dull as she approached him. "Hello, Nicolette," he said. "You doin' your banking here now?"

"We have to talk."

"I'm working, case you didn't notice."

She saw him shift his weight, ready to move away, to leave her once more. "Rudy Martinez," she said.

His eyes widened at the name. "W-who?"

"One of your old cases," she said. "I looked it up before coming here. Rudy was the son of a movie star. Got himself shot. You were the first policeman on the scene."

His eyes went to the clock at the rear of the bank. "I go on my break in seventeen minutes. There's a coffee shop in the middle of the block."

He was there in exactly eighteen minutes by Nikki's watch.

He barely had time to sit down across from her when the waitress put a cup of coffee before him.

"Come here a lot, huh?" Nikki asked.

"It's convenient," he said. "What's your interest in the Martinez case?"

"Tell me about it."

"Why should I?"

She realized once again that he would never play the father's role for her. The only reason he was sitting there having coffee was because something about the death of Rudy Martinez was important enough for him to tolerate her presence.

"This was a mistake," she said, rising.

"No. Wait," he said. "What do you wanna know?"

"Anything you can tell me," she said, sitting down again.

"Not much to tell. Me and Fred Dugan got there minutes after the shooting. This was maybe two years before old Fred dropped dead with a coronary."

"Who shot the boy?"

"Young Martinez was acting as middleman, buying guns for kids at his private school. The sellers were three army men who'd stolen the weapons from the Fort Collins armory. They said the boy tried to shortchange 'em. So they blew him away and took the money and the guns."

"That's all there was to it?"

He didn't reply.

"Well?"

"Why you asking these questions?"

"Meeting like this isn't any easier for me than it is for

you," Nikki said. "That should give you an idea of how important it is for me to find out what you know."

He took a sip of coffee and slumped a little in his chair. "The boy was lying in his own blood on the dirty warehouse floor. I had to shift him to get at a pulse, to see if he was still alive, which he wasn't. A stack of bills poked out of his shirt. I guess it was the money he was holding out on those soldiers."

He lowered his voice until it became almost a bass rumble. "Fred saw the money and he took it. Just reached down and grabbed it off that dead boy's body."

"What'd you do?"

"My partner had just stolen money, evidence in a murder. What could I do? It was tough enough being a black cop back in those days. If I'd turned on Fred, that would have been the end for me."

"Fred do anything like that before?" Nikki asked.

"Not before. Not after. The one time was enough for the both of us."

She wanted to ask a question, but couldn't. He must have seen it on her face. "No, Nicolette," he said. "I didn't take a penny. Thirty hundred-dollar bills. Fred wanted me to take half. Not exactly a fortune, but Tricia was in the hospital having your sister—"

"Half sister."

"Anyway, the insurance wasn't covering it all. Expenses were mounting up. Still, I've never been a thief. I couldn't take that boy's blood money."

"Was there an inquiry?"

Her father shook his head. "No. Nobody said anything about money, except the soldiers who shot him. They didn't know the boy was carrying it or they'd have taken it along with the rest. The other schoolboys in on the deal didn't say anything about it, if they knew. They were too busy talking to their daddies' lawyers."

"What if somebody was looking for a way of making trouble?" Nikki asked. "Could they find out about the missing money?"

"It was so long ago, and it isn't anybody's lost millions we're talking about. Dugan is six feet under. So's Nestor Martinez. What's to find out? Anyway, why would anybody want to make trouble for me?" His eyes met hers. "Oh. Of course, it's not me. I'm not the one in the newspaper every day."

"Sins of the father," she said.

"I knew the moment Fred picked up that money I should have grabbed it out of his fist and stuck it back in the dead boy's shirt. I just stood by and pretended it didn't happen."

"Like you pretended I didn't happen."

He sat frozen for a few seconds. "I have to get back to work," he said, starting to rise.

"Please." She reached out to him, placed a hand on his arm. "I know what it's like when somebody you love dies. After Blackie was killed I was full of sorrow and self-pity and anger. I wanted somebody to blame. Not the little punk who stuck a gun to his head. That was too easy. I started thinking: Why was Blackie in that tavern at that very moment when he could have been with me? I blamed him. Then I blamed myself. It took me a while to get past that, to see the situation as it was. Dumb bad luck. No rhyme, no reason. Mama died bringing me into the world. I'm thirty-three years old. That's how long Mama's been gone. You can't still blame me."

He slumped against the seat, suddenly showing his age. "You never knew her," he said. "Never knew how good . . ." He waved a hand as if to dismiss the thought. "I never blamed you."

"What was it, then? Where have you been my whole life?"

"I lost the woman I loved," he said, shifting on his chair. "I couldn't hardly take care of myself, much less this little . . . creature I couldn't even stop from crying. You were better off with your grandma. I thought so then and, seeing the way you turned out, I know I did the right thing."

"That's bullshit. You dumped me on Grandma and that was that. A dinky little toy at Christmas and on my birthday, most of 'em dropped off when I wasn't home."

"It was the best I could do," he said. "I worked nights, Christmas, Easter, whatever shifts my white police brothers didn't want."

"You believe what you're saying?"

"If I didn't, I'd have to admit to myself I was a coward who screwed up my daughter's life and my own."

"Funny," she said, "I don't recall you ever calling me your daughter before."

"My failing. My most-grievous failing." He grabbed her hand and squeezed it. "I really do have to get back to work now," he said. He stood, removing a thin, creased wallet from his pocket.

"Let me take care of it," she said.

He gave her a rueful smile and dropped a few dollars on the table. "Least a man can do is treat his daughter to a cup of coffee every thirty years or so."

≡ SIXTY-TWO ≡

Ray Wise was throwing a fit. "Where the hell have you been?" he demanded, standing in the doorway to her office.

"Had some errands that couldn't wait."

"We're starting a trial in two days with the eyes of the whole damned world on us and you're off running around doing bullshit errands."

She flashed on her father calling her his daughter for the first time in known history. "Let's get this straight, Ray," she said. "I don't have to justify to you how I spend my time. At least I don't waste it running around whining like a baby with a chafed butt. Calm down. You're right about the eyes of the world being on us, and you're looking like a loser."

He wrinkled his face as if he were tasting her words, then the fight went out of him, like air escaping a tire. He nodded meekly and eased onto a chair. "I made the deadbeat dad list today. I'm supposed to owe forty-two thousand dollars in back child support."

"Forty-two thousand? You got that kind of money?"

"I don't owe any money. Even that penny-pinching witch

I married says she's up to date. It's a glitch in the computers."

"We'd better go talk to Joe."

"About my child support, for Christ's sake?"

"That and a few other similar matters," she said.

Walden and Wise listened in silence as Nikki presented a somewhat abridged list of the annoyances, minor and major, that recently had beset those connected with the prosecution of Dyana Cooper Willins. When she'd finished, she could see that Wise was a true believer, while the D.A. was withholding judgment.

"I've heard of dirty tricks," Wise said, "but this is bullshit."

"Just relax a minute, Ray," Walden said. "Nikki, nothing you've told us here has any solid substance. Not the comment poor Dimitra made to you, nor the fake IAD detectives looking for dirt at Detective Goodman's apartment, nor the computers giving you and Ray a hard time. There's no proof it all stems from one source."

"We might ask Ray's ex-housemaid what convinced her to go public."

"A waste of time," Walden said. "She's not going to admit anybody paid her off. I'd be very surprised if anyone did. She's an opportunist taking advantage of Ray's celebrity. It happens to everybody who winds up in the public eye."

"If I'm right, the tricks are going to get dirtier."

Walden nodded. "The upside of that is, whoever's playing them will have to show more of his hand."

≡ SIXTY-THREE ≡

Five hours later, Nikki sat on the steps just outside Virgil's open front door, observing the large moon floating over the darkened patio and trying to shove the day's events from her thoughts. She sipped her drink, a delicious rum concoction, and listened to Pharoah Sanders's version of Coltrane's "After the Rain" on the stereo. Soon the pungent smells of garlic and tomato sauce drifted through the door. Virgil harmonized with Marvin Gaye on "Feel All My Love Inside." A cat pranced across the patio, chasing something tiny in the shadows. Just as the steel clamps of tension completely relaxed their grip, a neighbor turned on a television. The measured speech of a news anchor began describing the "shifting attitudes toward Dyana Cooper as the trial date approaches."

She took a final deep breath of honeysuckle mixed with simmering dinner spices, stood and went inside the apartment.

Virgil was busy in the kitchenette. He grinned at her. "Come sample the wares."

She sat down on a leather barstool at the kitchenette counter. He dipped a toe of French bread into tomato sauce for her. "Courtboullion sauce," he said.

It was delicious, tangy with spices she couldn't begin to identify.

"My mama's Creole recipe."

"Lots of garlic," she said.

"Lovers' clove." He moved around the counter and embraced her. "We're not about to go kissing anybody else." He put that thought into action.

They'd just finished the redfish courtboullion. Virgil was doing something in the kitchen with ice cream and an orange liqueur when her cellular phone rang.

Lulled by the food and the company, she answered without a second's thought. The voice was tinny, vaguely masculine. "Nikki Hill?"

"Yes. Who's this?"

"Do the right thing about Dyana Cooper, Nikki, or there could be consequences. You could even wind up back in Compton. Or worse."

"Who is this?" The caller had hung up.

Virgil was placing a dish of ice cream in front of her. "What's up, Red?"

"I don't know," she said. "Some weird-sounding guy. Threatening me."

He grabbed the instrument from her hand and pressed star-six-nine. She watched as he listened for a beat, then, annoyed, clicked off the phone. "Call was made from a cellular. Can't trace it back. What'd he tell you, exactly?"

"He called me by name. Said for me to do the right thing about Dyana Cooper."

"The right thing being what?"

"I don't know," Nikki said. But of course, she did.

Cooper's thugs were zeroing in on her. What did they want her to do, throw the trial?

She stood suddenly, feeling the need to be in motion. Virgil caught up with her at the door. "Whoa. Slow down a minute, Red," he said.

"I want to walk."

He looked back at the dessert, and she made up her mind that if he paused to put the ice cream into the freezer, it didn't matter how wonderful he was, she'd leave and never talk to him again.

But he passed that test and together they walked down the steps, around the koi pond, and out of the complex. He hadn't even bothered to lock his door.

"What's really going on?" he asked as they strolled along a sidewalk broken by the roots of overhanging trees.

"Nasty games," she said. She described some of the things that had been happening to her and Ray Wise and the detectives.

"Kid tricks," he said. "Don't let it mess you up, Red. You're stronger than that."

"The voice warned I could wind up back in Compton."

"Hell," he said, trying to be lighthearted. "We all could."

"It has a special meaning, a special threat."

"What special meaning?"

Cars passed, but they were alone on the dark sidewalk. She turned to him, looked into his eyes, and could see nothing but concern for her. And love. If she was wrong about that, she was destined to be wrong about everything.

She told him about Mason Durant and the destroyed evidence.

He was silent for a minute and she began to feel she had acted too impulsively. Maybe hers was a secret he, as a police officer, would rather not have shared. Maybe he thought she was being foolish. Maybe it was enough to bring their brief romance to an end. Maybe . . .

"Your caller doesn't know shit about Durant," he said.

"How can you be so sure?"

"He was trying to rattle you hard. If he'd known about Durant, he would have used the name, not some vague reference to Compton."

"Why mention Compton at all?" she asked.

"It's a matter of record you spent time there," he said. "What prosecutor in her right mind would want to go back? That was the threat. Nothing else, Red. Trust me."

"I do trust you," she said. "Believe me, I do."

≡ SIXTY-FOUR ≡

At the end of the long day, Goodman decided he was not going to spend the evening alone, eating from an aluminum plate in front of the TV. He convinced Morales to accompany him to the Academy, their purpose being to drown their troubles. It was a good plan, but it didn't work. After two solid hours of hard drinking, Morales didn't seem to have even a buzz on, and while Goodman was about three fingers of Meyer's Rum shy of baying at the moon, he wasn't any less troubled than when he was stone sober.

"Wha' the hell's going on, Carlos?" he asked, for maybe the fourth time since the booze had hit him.

Morales sipped his Seagram's and Seven and nodded. "Bad stuff, amigo."

"Wha' do we do about it?"

"I got my plan," Morales said.

"Good. I could use a plan."

"No, man. It's *my* plan. You'd just get yo'self killed following *my* plan."

Gwen Harriman joined them at the crucial moment when

one sip more would have sent Goodman either into outer space or rushing to the men's head.

"Having fun?" she asked them.

"Define th' term," Goodman said. "I am un-fa-m-i-l-i-ar wi'thit."

"He's shit-faced," Morales said.

"Not," Goodman lied. He was definitely shit-faced. But he *was* coming around. Gwen did that to him.

"You boys sure seem to be having a night for yourselves," she said, looking at the empty glasses nearly covering the table.

"Eddie wanted to get drunk," Morales said.

Gwen seemed concerned. "Why the booze, Eddie?"

Goodman tried to focus his bleary eyes on her. "Just toastin' a few folks. A son'bitch named Doyle. An' your pal Lattimer."

She frowned.

"Jack Lattimer?" Morales asked.

"I doe know," Goodman said. "Izzit Jack, honey?"

"Yeah," she said, cautiously. "But he's not my friend. I barely know him."

"Jack Lattimer," Morales said. "Vice. I worked with him back in the long ago. He was okay, but he was partnered up with that prick Pete Sandoval."

"Sandoval?" Goodman was sobering fast, or thought he was. Peter Sandoval, who'd left the LAPD to start his own scumbag detective agency? Hadn't they been working at opposite ends of someth— Lobrano! A Golden State Savings and Loan VP named Martin Lobrano had blown the whistle on his boss, the bank's CEO, Leonard Quarles, for supposed securities frauds. Lobrano leaped from the eighteenth floor of his Wilshire apartment building just days before Quarles's trial.

Goodman had examined the death from every angle without finding even a hint of homicide. Sandoval had been working for the lawyers defending the S&L chairman. The detective leaned his head back and said, "I have seen th' glory."

"You seen what?" Morales asked.

Goodman waved away the question. He'd just remembered that the evening before leaping into the void, Lobrano had had dinner with a man named James Doyle. That's why Doyle had seemed so familiar at the Willins house. The Irishman had been almost skinny then, with longer hair, one of twenty or twenty-five people he and his partner had talked to about the suicide. Doyle had felt so bad about "poor Marty." The son of a bitch! The *son* of a bitch!

He was vaguely aware of Gwen saying something. "Huh?"

"C'mon, soldier," she said, taking his arm. "I'm driving you home."

"Whoa, amigo, this young gal hungers for you. She wants your sorry old ass."

Goodman allowed them to drag him from the establishment and out to Gwen's car. "See you tomorrow, amigo," Morales said. "Harriman, take it easy on this old fart."

As the old fart lay back on Gwen's too-soft bed, watching her undress in darkness, he asked, "What's the deal with Lattimer?"

She paused, stepping out of her slacks, then said, "Nothing."

"No," he said, marveling at the way her pale skin reflected the moonlight through the open window. "It's everything. Tell me about it."

"I can't."

"Does it involve a man named Doyle?"

"I don't know that name," she said.

He was silent while she removed her bra, then her panties. The sight of all that lovely youth was revving up his old carcass. Heart beating faster. Breathing getting slightly labored. Exquisite warmth flooded through his whole body, then gathered in his groin. The doctor had told him the blood pressure pills he'd just started taking might cause sexual dysfunction, but his body seemed to be functioning just fine.

Unfortunately, he couldn't enjoy the moment.

"What the hell kind of mess are you into?" he asked.

"You don't want to know," she said. She put on a brave smile and slipped beneath the covers beside him. He felt her press against him, cool hand moving across his chest, down over his stomach.

Her breath tickled his cheek. "I do want to know, honey," he said. "I want that very much."

"This is what I want," she said, covering his mouth with hers.

In the middle of their kiss the phone rang.

She tensed, then started to pull away. He held his arms out, away from her body, surrendering her to do as she chose.

The phone rang three times. Four.

She remained suspended, inches above him, the tips of her breasts barely touching his gray-haired chest. Making her decision, she relaxed and lowered her body atop his. The answering machine took over. The caller left no message.

The questions that had been plaguing Goodman's mind no longer seemed terribly important.

≡ SIXTY-FIVE ≡

At five A.M. on the morning of the trial, Nikki watched Bird lumber toward the wooden stairs, then began her ascent up the giant dune. There was enough light in the charcoal-gray, predawn sky for her to make out the prints of some previous climber who had been kind enough to pack the sand. Concentrating on placing her toes precisely on that person's footprints, she hoped to be able to zone out, using the time to sift through the jumble of information she'd be needing in court.

Instead, she reflected on Dimitra's funeral. The gathering had been small. Joe, who'd made the arrangements, had been there, of course. And Ray. Virgil. A few other deputies and clerks. Several men and women she did not know who'd been friends of the deceased. No family. Nikki wondered if her own funeral would be any better attended.

Dimitra had left instructions in her will that she be cremated. But the rather whimsical request that her ashes be scattered over the city from the top of the Criminal Courts Building surprised Nikki. Joe did the honors and they watched the wind add their colleague's remains to the general pollution of downtown L.A. Then the district attorney reached into his pocket and handed Nikki a bracelet. "She left a will. She wanted most of her things sold off, with the money donated to charity. But she specifically stated that this was for you."

It was an angular solid gold bracelet. "She wrote that she had it made in Taxco," Joe told her. "She was sure you wouldn't have anything like it."

Nikki blinked away the tears and kept moving up the dune. *Focus, damn it,* she demanded of herself. Near the midway point, her pacing became totally automatic and she began to concentrate on the trial. Their case, though not airtight, was pretty compelling. There was a strong motive. Blood evidence. Fibers from Madeleine Gray's rug found in Cooper's car. One witness, a gas station attendant, could place the Jaguar in the vicinity of Maddie's home at the approximate time of the murder. Another, young Missy Rosten, had seen the car parked at the murder site.

The sky was brightening. Nikki could make out the edge of the dune. Somewhere to her left, Bird stood at attention, watching over her. To her right, another early climber moved past. Nikki's thighs were burning, calves knotted. Her lungs gasped for air. Just a few more steps and she was over.

Bird trotted to her side.

Shaking out her limbs, waiting for her breath to return to normal, she thought about the ways Cooper's spin doctors were moving public opinion back in her favor. John Willins had made several public confessions of adultery on various television venues, pleading with audiences to think what they might of him, but to maintain their belief in the innocence of his wonderful wife whom he'd treated so shabbily.

At the same time, stories had broken in several leading magazines describing a prosecution team in disarray, scurrying to bolster a disintegrating case against Cooper.

The battle would be won in court, not in the press. Not this time. She gave Bird a comfort pat, then turned to slide back down the face of the dune. She was ready for the trial. Maybe she'd even take another run up this little hill.

Later, on her way to the Criminal Courts Building, she heard the same AM pundits who'd been talking about "Dyana's dark decision" just days before now commenting on her "nobility" and "innocent demeanor." *The gods of the airwaves taketh and giveth.*

She was just a few blocks from work when the AM station switched to a live report from the CCB's entrance on Temple Street. A hard-pressed reporter who was being pinballed by the anxious crowd described the "frenetic and frantic atmosphere on this morning of justice." He asked people why they had come; the obvious answer was repeated over and over, not only by the interview subjects, but by the crowds chanting "Dy-an-uh. Dy-an-uh."

Well, Nikki thought, *that's why I'm here, too.*

She could imagine the scene on Temple—a combination circus, soapbox, flea market. And a gauntlet for anyone participating in the main event.

She took the rear entrance to the employee parking lot.

She arrived at her office a little after seven A.M.

Wise was prowling the corridor. He looked terrible. Bags under bloodshot eyes. Hair poorly brushed. Little bits of white paper stuck to his jaw. "Where the hell are the clerks?" he asked her.

"I don't know," she said. "Talk to our case manager."

"She's got to get on top of things," Wise said, following

Nikki into her office. "We need clerks here by seven every morning. Maybe even earlier."

"They'll be here for us," she said as he dropped onto a chair. "Rough night?"

He rubbed his eyes. "We left here when? About nine?"

"About then."

"When I got home, the power was off. I should have gone straight to a hotel, but the electric company assured me the problem would be taken care of." He rolled his head around his shoulders, prompting a succession of pops and cracks. "Unfortunately, surprise surprise, it turned out that it was not an area problem, but one specific to my domicile and, evidently, I had to be awakened at the ungodly hour of three A.M. to be apprised of that fact."

"What caused it?"

"They thought some kid in the neighborhood might have stuck a penny in one of my main outlets in the garage and shorted everything out. You and I know that's bullshit, unless Willins has a kid on the payroll."

Nikki nodded in sympathy. "Ray, you know you've got paper stuck to your face?"

"Oh, crap!" He began brushing at the white flecks. "I'm used to my electric. I shaved down here with a blade and nearly cut my throat."

There was a noise out in the corridor. A junior clerk with coffee and doughnuts. Wise looked as though he might kiss the young man.

At a quarter to nine, Nikki and her slightly less askew co-counsel descended from the eighteenth floor to the ninth, worked their way past the assorted clerks, lawyers, gofers, members of the news pool, witnesses, guards, and court officials to enter Department 140.

Nikki paused just inside the swinging doors and surveyed

the partially carpeted, wood-paneled space that was smaller than the average Bel Air living room. She took in the four rows of spectator seats, filled by reporters, Dyana Cooper's immediate family, including her errant husband and her minister father, friends, associates of Anna Marie Dayne, and members of their own prosecution team. A handful of court watchers—retirees who were at the building all day, every day, watching trials—were lucky enough to have had their names drawn in the morning lottery.

Nikki wiggled her shoulders to shake the stress away. She took a deep breath and headed past the murmuring crowd. She pushed through the double half-door of the bar and followed Wise to their table on the right.

Once seated, she let her eyes wander the short distance to her left where Dayne and her client sat poised and confident. The attorney was wearing a conservative dark blue business suit that somehow complimented her Mowhawk haircut, and her trademark African hoop earrings. The accused was in a simple but elegant dress that might have been a Thiery Mugler. Nikki thought that if the jury were to take a vote that morning, based on just the appearance of the accused and the lawyers, Dyana would be set free and she and Wise would get life without possibility of parole.

Judge Rose Vetters arrived in a cloud of Shalimar that wafted from the bench. "Just what I need," Wise grumbled. "Dying for another cup of coffee and she gives us perfume."

It seemed impossible that the judge could hear him, but her head suddenly swiveled in their direction. For the occasion, in addition to the perfume, she'd altered her hair coloring from its usual cotton-candy pink to a silver-blue. She had also eschewed her beehive 'do for a 1950s helmet with flip. Nikki wondered why she hadn't gone the whole hog and included little barrettes with blue bows. "Morning, your honor," she said sweetly.

Judge Vetters nodded. In a spirit of fairness, she nodded to the defense table, too. There being no other business, she ordered the clerk to bring in the jury.

Twenty-two men and women, ranging in age from twenty-six to fifty-eight, filed in to occupy the padded executive chairs lined up at the right of the room. Nikki had not been involved in their selection, but she'd spent hours devouring every fact she could about them. For example, the tall black man with the little mustache—one of eight African-American jurors—worked for a shipping company in the Valley. Nikki had taken the trouble to find out that he played blues guitar in a club on weekends and despised the sort of rap music that Willins's company recorded.

The elderly woman who lived in the Angel's Flight Apartments with her unmarried daughter, one of six women judging Dyana Cooper's guilt, must have seemed like a dream juror to Wise and Dimitra. Educated, conservative, white, and apparently unawed by the accused. With minimal digging, Nikki had unearthed the information that she and her daughter had been deserted years ago by her husband, an experience that could very easily lead her to identify with the similarly mistreated Dyana.

So many expressionless faces, trying desperately to keep so many agendas hidden.

Judge Vetters suddenly rapped her gavel. The room quieted. Wise mumbled, "Magic time," not quite under his breath.

Nikki turned to him, surprised by this bit of whimsy. What she saw surprised her even more. He was sitting straight in his chair, alert and, if not exactly dynamic looking, close enough. The man who'd been moaning about lack of sleep and the absence of clerks only a short time before now seemed to have been replaced by an eager, self-possessed attorney. She'd seen so much of the unimpressive office version of Ray Wise she'd forgotten the man's success record in the courtroom.

The judge did her introduction, added a few original flourishes in presenting her admonitions, and turned the floor over to the prosecution.

Wise stood and, emphasizing his limp, moved from the table to present the twelve jurors and ten alternates a warm, sincere smile that was quite unlike anything Nikki had ever seen grace the man's face before. Evidently pleased by several returned smiles, he launched into Los Angeles County's case against Dyana C. Willins.

He began by describing the actress-singer's earlier visit to Madeleine Gray's home on the afternoon of the murder, where "a fight broke out, in the course of which, Ms. Willins has admitted, she picked up a nine-pound oval sculpture and smashed it against the skull of Madeleine Gray, drawing blood.

"These are not speculations open to dispute. They are facts as described by Ms. Willins to detectives assigned to the murder. It is also a fact that the blow, though powerful, did not kill Ms. Gray. At least not immediately.

"The coroner will tell you that Madeleine Gray died at sometime between the hours of eight P.M. and eleven P.M. that night, of damage to the skull. The wounds and contusions on her lifeless body offered glaring testimony to the brutality of her attacker. Her murderer was apparently so enraged at Ms. Gray that a beating and murder were not enough. The body was wrapped in a carpet, dragged from the Gray home, and transported all the way to downtown Los Angeles, to a grimy alley off Dalton Street, where it was thrown like so much refuse into a garbage receptacle.

"We will prove unequivocally that Dyana Willins's very distinctive car was at Madeleine Gray's home at the approximate time Ms. Gray died. We will present you with evidence indicating that this same car was used to transport Ms. Gray's body.

"The defense will be calling many people who will tell you that Ms. Willins is a wonderful woman who couldn't have committed this horrible crime. I admit having that same feeling myself, until the evidence began to mount higher and higher and I was forced to accept the fact, as you will come to accept it, that no other possibility exists.

"I know you're probably looking at Ms. Willins sitting at the table over there and thinking: This is an upstanding, honorable, one may even say admirable, wife and mother and beloved entertainer. How could she possibly take the life of another human being, and take it in such a violent manner?

"Before this trial is over, you will know how she did it and why she did it. You will have your proof, ladies and gentlemen. Proof, beyond a reasonable doubt.

"There are five elements to look for in establishing guilt." Wise held up his right hand, fingers extended. "Identity," he said, bending his little finger in toward his palm. "Motive." The next finger folded. "Evidence." The middle finger joined the others. "The crime must be willful. And with malice aforethought." Wise's thumb closed, leaving him with a fist in the air.

"All five are present in this case," he added, punctuating the sentence with the movement of his upraised fist. "Dyana Willins willfully took the life of Madeleine Gray in a brutal and callous manner. We who are assembled here, seeking justice in a difficult world, will see to it that she is punished for her crime."

He returned to the prosecution table. "How'd it look?" he whispered to Nikki.

"Great," she told him. "But I think you went a little over the top with that black power salute you kept flashing the jury."

Wise looked at his still-clasped fist and grinned sheepishly.

Anna Marie Dayne wiped the smile from his face. "Contrary to what Mr. Wise has just been telling you," she began, "we're going to provide you with proof that Dyana Cooper had no opportunity to murder Madeleine Gray and no motive to do so. We will present witnesses who will show you precisely how makeshift and frail the prosecution's case really is. You will hear testimony that casts doubt on the credibility of the prosecution's key witnesses, including the two policemen who concocted this absurd case against Dyana Cooper.

"You will hear from Mr. Jamal Deschamps, who was the first African-American to be drawn into this murder case with absolutely no legal justification except that he happened to be in the wrong place at the wrong time.

"You will hear from associates and friends and, yes, even people who are not so friendly with the accused, who will tell you that it is impossible to think of her committing so heinous a crime as this.

"Finally, you will hear from just a few of an endless list of people who knew the deceased for what she really was, an apparently heartless woman of no conscience who seemed to delight in adding to the misery and misfortune of others, even to the point of receiving money from them to keep their most devastating secrets hidden.

"I tell you these things, ladies and gentlemen of the jury, not to speak ill of the dead, but to open your eyes to the fact that Madeleine Gray was a woman with a vast army of enemies. The prosecution, for reasons we will explore, has chosen to ignore them all—all the rich and powerful and brutal people who can order a murder as easily as one orders a pizza for dinner—and concentrate on just one courageous, deeply religious African-American wife and mother."

When Dayne took her seat, Judge Vetters asked, "Mr. Wise, Ms. Hill, are you prepared to begin the case for the prosecution?"

"We are, your honor."

"Good, good," the judge said. "Please call your first witness."

"The prosecution calls Dr. Ann Fugitsu to the stand," Ray Wise said.

Nikki realized that she'd been holding her breath.

≡ SIXTY-SIX ≡

On the third day of the trial, Goodman was called to the stand.

He'd gone over his testimony with Nikki several times, the last being the previous evening. Now she took him smoothly through the various stages by which the LAPD had amassed the information leading to Dyana Cooper's arrest.

Goodman answered Nikki's questions confidently and unhesitatingly. The courtroom experience wasn't new to him. He couldn't count the number of times he'd occupied a chair in the shadow of an imposing judicial figure, staring at the hopeful face of an optimistic prosecutor or the patent sneer of a defense attorney. But those had all been simply part of the job. This was different. Doyle, the bastard, had made it personal. He was having a difficult time keeping his resentment and anger in check.

To combat precisely that sort of stress his doctor had recommended the calming effect of slow, deep in-and-out breathing. He had been trying that on and off during the hour he'd been on the stand, with the main result being that his lungs were full of the judge's Shalimar. Meanwhile, Nikki had covered most of the territory—the evidence, the automobile, Willins's letter in which he admitted adultery, and the fact that Dyana had lied to them during their initial visit to her home. Finally, they arrived at the point Nikki had chosen to end their courtroom duet.

"In the course of that interrogation," she said, "Ms. Willins admitted that she had attacked Madeleine—"

"Objection to the word 'attacked.'"

"Could you rephrase, Ms. Hill?"

Nikki returned to the prosecution table, picked up a sheet of paper, and walked back to Goodman. "Why not just read Ms. Willins's own words, detective."

He looked at the page and found it to be mainly a blur. He swallowed, blinked, and the words came into focus. *Jesus!* His head felt like a balloon about to pop. His blood pressure must've been rocketing to the moon.

Nikki pointed to a line. "You can start there, detective. Read down to there."

"Okay." He squinted. He was used to a more direct light when reading. "'Ms. Willins said, "I hit her."'

"'"Hit Madeleine Gray?" I asked. "With your hand?"'

"'And she said, "No. With some sort of sculpture that was on the table."'"

Nikki took the transcript away from him, returned it to her other papers. "You're familiar with the sculpture Ms. Willins mentioned?"

"Yes."

"Why is that, detective?"

"Because it's the same sculpture that was used to beat Madeleine Gray to death."

Nikki paused while a murmur passed through the courtroom. Then she said, "Thank you, detective. Your witness."

As Anna Marie Dayne approached, her smile sent a chill up his spine. She carried a section of trial transcript, opened to a specific page. "Detective Goodman, let's clarify a point. You say the piece of sculpture the defendant used to protect herself from Madeleine Gray is the murder weapon. On what do you base that opinion?"

"On a statement by an expert, Dr. Ann Fugitsu," Goodman said.

"You're speaking of her testimony in this courtroom?"

"I wasn't present in the courtroom when Dr. Fugitsu was on the stand."

"No. You weren't. So I suppose it was a statement she made directly to you?"

"In my presence."

"Which would make it hearsay." She handed him the transcript. "Would you read what Dr. Fugitsu actually said in this courtroom, detective? Begin with Mr. Wise's question about the murder weapon."

Goodman looked at the blurry lines, saw the name Wise swim before his eyes. He held the transcript farther away, blinking. He read aloud: " 'Mr. Wise: "Could you please look at Exhibit D and tell us if this is the instrument used to murder Madeleine Gray." Dr. Fugitsu: "Since it matches the physical requirements—that is, the proper heft, the smoothness of surface—to cause the fatal wound, and since traces of the deceased's blood were found on its surface, I would say Exhibit D to be the likely murder weapon, yes." ' "

"Does that sound like an unequivocal statement to you, detective?" Dayne asked.

"Object, your honor," Nikki said. "Calls for speculation and Detective Goodman is not an expert on linguistics."

"Withdraw the question," Dayne said, reclaiming the transcript and taking her time returning it to her table.

She walked back to Goodman and asked a few apparently

harmless questions about his career as a police officer, the number of homicide cases he'd investigated, the number of times he'd appeared in court. Then she shifted gears.

"You a married man, detective?"

"Objection," Nikki called out. "Relevance?"

"Goes to character, your honor."

Judge Vetters looked dubious. "I'll let you take a few steps down this path, Ms. Dayne. But only a few."

"Thank you, your honor. Detective?"

"I'm divorced," he said.

"Bachelor, huh?"

"A single man, if that's what you mean."

"Been a single man quite a while?"

"Your honor?" Nikki complained.

"This is a courtroom, Ms. Dayne, not a dating bureau," Judge Vetters said. "Move on, please."

"All right, your honor. Detective, have you ever consorted with felons?"

" 'Consort' is a little strong. I've met them, in my line of work."

"Your work as one of L.A.'s finest," Dayne said, not without sarcasm. "Well, in or out of your line of work, have you ever cohabited with felons?"

"Not to my knowledge."

"Are you familiar with a woman named Edith 'Edie' Jastrup?"

He'd been expecting the question, but still his heart sank.

"Yes," he replied, his face showing nothing.

"Did you not live with Miss Edith Jastrup for a period of . . . nine months and twelve days?"

"Sounds like you've got a better record of it than I do, but that seems about right."

"Objection, your honor," Nikki said. "What's the relevance of Detective Goodman's personal life?"

"An excellent question, Ms. Dayne."

"Sidebar, your honor?"

Goodman's calming breaths didn't seem to be working. He felt lightheaded as he watched Nikki and the defense attorney standing a few yards away.

Anna Marie Dayne handed the judge a document. "I'm going to put this in evidence, your honor." It was too far away for Goodman to see.

"What is it?" Nikki asked. "You've submitted nothing to our office."

"It came into our possession yesterday afternoon," Goodman heard Dayne reply. "A copy was hand delivered to the district attorney's office last night at seven P.M., and we have a receipt for the delivery, if you want to look at it."

"What's its significance, Ms. Dayne?" the judge asked.

The defense attorney shot Goodman a look, then leaned closer to the judge, whispering something that the detective couldn't hope to hear. Instead, he concentrated on Nikki's face and could tell by her knit brows that he was in for a rocky ride.

"We haven't had the opportunity to check the authenticity of this document," Nikki objected. "Show me the provenance."

"It's authentic," Dayne said. "There's the stamp. There are his initials."

"It's a copy," Nikki said. "Where's the original?"

"In the interest of moving along," Judge Vetters said, "I'm inclined to allow this to be placed into evidence with the proviso that the defense provide this court proper identification within forty-eight hours. But I warn you, Ms. Dayne, if such identification is not forthcoming, I will do considerably more than merely expunge the applicable section of Detective Goodman's testimony."

"Understood, your honor."

Dayne resumed her cross-examination by placing her document into evidence, with Nikki objecting for the record.

The defense attorney handed Goodman the document and asked, "Could you describe that item to the court please?"

"It looks like a copy of an arrest warrant," Goodman said.

"Are there any names on that warrant that ring any bells, detective?"

Goodman took his time reading the list of women's names.

"Yes," he said.

"Could you tell us the familiar names?"

"Edith Jastrup and Evelyn Jastrup," he said, his throat as dry as noonday sand.

"The same Edith Jastrup you lived with?"

"I imagine."

"And Evelyn is . . . ?"

"Her sister."

"How did this woman you lived with for more than nine months and her sister earn their daily bread, detective?"

"They said they were models."

"But you know differently."

"No, I do not," Goodman answered.

For the first time, Anna Marie Dayne seemed a bit surprised. "What are they accused of on this warrant?"

"It says Code Section 647b."

"What crime are we talking about?"

"Prostitution," Goodman said calmly.

"So I ask you again, detective, how did the Jastrup sisters earn their money?"

"As far as I knew they modeled clothes."

Dayne seemed frustrated. "In spite of what this warrant says?"

"This just seems to be a warrant," he said. "I'm not sure

that constitutes proof of guilt. We served your client with a warrant."

Dayne turned to look out into the courtroom. Goodman tried to follow her line of sight, but couldn't, because, almost immediately, she was back at him. "Aren't those your initials on the warrant?"

"No, they are not."

"How can you be so certain?"

"Why would I have signed a warrant involving a prostitution case? Seven years ago, the date on this warrant, I was working homicide."

"Let's say you knew one or two of the parties involved and you wanted to take a look at the warrant, you might have been asked to initial it. Right?"

"Maybe. But that didn't happen. I've never seen this warrant before." Goodman realized this was clearly contrary to what Dayne had been expecting. Which meant she was convinced the warrant was genuine.

She stood there, staring at him for what seemed like an eternity, saying nothing.

"Ms. Dayne?" the judge inquired.

"Sorry, your honor." She took the copy of the warrant from the detective and handed it to the judge. Then she moved back to her table. "I'd like to return to Ms. Cooper's interrogation by Detectives Goodman and Morales." She picked up her copy of the transcript and carried it to Goodman. "Would you please read the section indicated by the arrows, detective?"

Goodman blinked at the page. He was still thinking about Edie. He said, " 'I asked the defendant, "Did you murder Madeleine Gray?" ' "

"What was Ms. Cooper's exact reply?"

" 'No, I did not.' "

"Thank you, detective. That's all."

"You're excused, Detective Goodman," Judge Vetters said. "Unless my watch is fast, it's about time for lunch."

Nikki stopped Goodman in the hall. She said, very seriously, "Upstairs. Now."

"What's the matter?" he asked. "I thought it went okay."

"We'll talk in my office."

The wait for an elevator was painful. Neither of them spoke.

Finally, they made it to the eighteenth floor, past the barriers, down the hall, and into her office. She closed the door and turned to him. "You may have blown the case for us today, detective."

"What are you talking about?"

"I'm talking about perjury."

"You got me all wrong, Nikki," he said, disappointed by her lack of faith.

"You'd never seen that warrant before?" she asked, wanting to believe, but not quite up to the task.

"I may have seen a similar one," he said. "But not that one. That one's bogus. Somebody whipped it up for the trial, and they neglected to tell Dayne it was fake."

"How can you be so positive?"

"Because," Goodman said, "I set fire to the original seven years ago."

≡ SIXTY-SEVEN ≡

An hour later, Goodman entered Robbery-Homicide to find Morales sitting at his desk, moodily staring into space. A shiny blue murder book rested open in front of him. He shook himself out of his trance long enough to ask, "How'd it go in court?"

"You didn't miss anything," Goodman said. He swung his chair around and sat, facing Morales. "There's something I gotta do, partner."

"Get lunch?"

"No. I'm gonna take a run at this Doyle bastard, try to shake him up. You with me?"

"Not today." Morales stood up. "I got plans."

"Now?"

"Cover for me, huh?"

"Where you headed?"

"In due time, amigo," Morales told him. "In due time."

Goodman watched him saunter from the room. Then he rolled his chair to his partner's desk. The Madeleine Gray murder book was open to a page of Jamal Deschamps's initial interrogation.

Goodman was trying to decipher his partner's less-than-expert typing when Lieutenant Corben yelled their names across the squad room.

"Where's Morales?" the lieutenant asked as Goodman entered the office.

"Dentist, I think. Bad wisdom."

"Yeah?" Corben asked, as if he assumed Goodman was lying but didn't give a damn. "We got some action on the Lydon murder. Lab finally got around to sending us a list of prints found at his apartment."

Goodman looked at the list. Stephen Palmer made it, of course. Two-thirds of the other male names would probably be more of the deceased's romances, one-night stands in the main. Then he saw a name that rang all the bells. The guy's fingerprint had been found on a color snapshot of Maddie Gray located inside Lydon's locked safe.

"Something?" Corben asked.

Goodman nodded.

"Gonna keep it to yourself?" Corben asked.

≡ SIXTY-EIGHT ≡

That night, Jimmy Doyle was in bed, getting a hand job from the beautiful but disdainful Zorina, when the phone rang. The young woman, whose hair was now a raspberry shade, didn't call what she was doing a hand job. It was a sensuous massage. She sat on the bed next to Doyle, naked, massaging him sensuously while watching Jay Leno do one of his Iron Jay routines.

Doyle scowled, annoyed that the phone had broken the mood. He shifted his aural attention from the TV to the answering machine. After a few clicks and whirs and wheezes, he heard Pete Sandoval say, "If you're there, Jimmy, pick up."

With a grunt, Doyle shifted, daintily removed Zorina's hand from his penis, and lifted the phone. "I'm here," he said.

"Jimmy, thank God. I'm in the shit, buddy."

"Minute," Doyle told him. He covered the phone and said, "Zor, honey, could you and Jay move it to the living room?"

She shrugged. "I'll just give myself a sensuous massage," she said. It was one of the things he loved about her. She simply didn't give a damn about anything.

He watched her move languidly toward the door, a full-breasted woman with raspberry hair and, as if anyone in their right mind could mistake it for her natural color, a matching pubic thatch.

"Where the hell are you?" he asked Sandoval as he clicked off the TV. "You said you'd call before five to let me know how you were progressing on Walden."

"Sorry, Jimmy. I didn't have time to work on that."

"Didn't have time? What are you talking about?"

"I . . . I'm on the run. I only had minutes to pack."

Doyle couldn't believe it. If you couldn't count on Sandoval . . . "Tell me about it."

"When I, ah, visited that certain party's apartment, I left something behind."

"Talk English, damn it. I check for taps every hour."

"I left a print at Lydon's place. The cops have made it."

"You're shattering my faith in your professionalism," Doyle said, mind awhirl.

"The little bastard had an International TL-30 in his matchbox pad. Too much safe for average use. I had to take my right glove off to feel the combination. There were photos inside. I guess I picked one up before I put the glove back on."

Doyle didn't care about any of that. "How clean a break did you make?"

"Ten minutes after Lattimer called about the fingerprint, somebody was knocking on my office door. I barely got out of there with my laptop and Fuck You money."

"Leaving behind what?"

"Nothing much. I took your advice and converted to computer files years ago."

"Any link to the clients or to me?"

"Not that I can think of."

"That's not totally reassuring," Doyle told him.

"It's the best I can do, Jimmy, under the circumstances."

"And your plan is . . . ?"

"Take a vacation for a while."

Doyle was boiling. "I thought you owned this town," he said, sticking the knife in.

"You know why I'm running, don't you?" Sandoval asked.

"Just a guess, but maybe you don't have an alibi for the Lydon murder. And there's a bloody machete under your bed for the cops to find."

"Aw, Jimmy. You know fucking well that kind of weapon isn't my style at all. No. I'm leaving because of you."

Now this was worthy of the Sandoval Doyle had come to love. "Elucidate on that one, Peter."

"The fingerprint won't mean much in the long run. It might let some people I've fucked over through the years have a little fun with me. But nothing serious'll come of it. Not with *my* lawyers. On the other hand, it's enough to give the cops license to ask me certain questions, like why I was in Lydon's apartment. Eventually the questions could get around to our association."

"In other words, you feel I should keep you on the payroll while you're having fun in the sun down South or wherever. Maybe even pop for your expenses."

"Nothing like that. I screwed up and I cover my own ass. I just want you to know I'm doing the Polanski out of respect for our longtime relationship, Jimmy. That's all."

"Then *vaya con Dios*, old son," Doyle told him. "*Vaya con Dios*."

≡ SIXTY-NINE ≡

"So Sandoval is in the wind?" Lieutenant Corben asked Goodman.

"Must've just missed him last night. The paper shredder was still warm," Goodman said. He and Morales were in Corben's office, watching him feed his goldfish breakfast.

"Any salvageable material?"

Goodman shook his head. "They're poking around, and maybe they can tape some of it together," he said. "But the pieces are smaller than confetti."

"Was he tipped?" Corben asked.

"Looks that way."

"Any suggestions on who did the tipping?"

"Sandoval used to be a cop," Goodman said. "Maybe his partner, if he's still around."

Corben nodded. "I'll look into it myself," he said. "You seriously think Sandoval cut down Lydon?"

"I think Lydon's death was connected to the Maddie Gray murder," Goodman said. "And I believe I can tie Sandoval to Dyana Cooper."

Corben put down the box of fish food and returned to his desk. "Let's hear it."

"A while back, I investigated the death of a guy named Martin Lobrano who was an exec at Golden State Savings."

"I remember that," Corben said. "The head man was Leonard Quarles. I had money in his goddamn S&L when it went bust."

"Sandoval was working for Quarles at the time," Goodman said. "And so was a character named James Doyle. Doyle's in tight with the Willins family."

"You figure Doyle set up Lydon's murder?" Corben asked.

"All I know is that we've got a connection from Sandoval, whose fingerprint was in Lydon's apartment, to Doyle to Dyana Cooper, who we assume killed Madeleine Gray."

"What do you know about Doyle?"

Goodman had done some phoning and had pieced together a short bio that went from Doyle's birth forty-nine years before in Boston, Massachusetts, to the present. In between were a Harvard MBA, a short apprenticeship at a D.C. public relations firm, and some years as an effective lobbyist before moving on to handle the successful congressional campaign of a local businessman. Since then, he had assisted in the election of a Democratic president and two Republican governors and had signed on as a hired gun for a number of people in the public and private sectors who were in extreme need of image polishing. Included were a U.S. Army general who'd been accused of murdering his wife, and Leonard Quarles, who, it was assumed, had drained millions of dollars out of Golden State Savings and Loan before it went belly-up. Both the general and Quarles were free as the breeze.

"And Doyle?" Corben asked.

"No wants, no warrants."

Corben hummed a bar of some music Goodman was unable to identify, then turned to Morales. "What's your take on Doyle?"

"Man don't blink."

Corben scowled as if he didn't consider that to be proof positive. "I'll put somebody on Doyle's case. Meanwhile, I been thinking of assigning another team to help you out with Lydon."

"Could you hold up on that, chief?" Goodman asked. "At least until Carlos and I take a run at Doyle?"

"What kind of a run?"

"Shake his cage a little. See what falls out."

"Nothing extreme, understand?"

They started to go.

"How's your wisdom tooth, Morales?" Corben asked.

"Think I'm gonna have to yank the fucker," the detective replied.

In Morales's car, Goodman noticed a little Day of the Dead figurine stuck to the dash. The skeleton was wearing a dark suit and had a packet of money sticking out of his coat pocket.

"What's this?" he asked.

"Lawyer."

"From the Palmers' shop?" Goodman asked.

"I dropped by there yesterday."

"Without me?" Goodman sounded hurt. "You conducting your own investigation in Lydon's death?"

"Not 'zackly."

"What's that mean?"

"If I tole you, I know what you'd say. That I'm wastin' my time. So we gonna go talk with your man Doyle or not?"

"I suppose so," Goodman said, wondering why, suddenly, he was out of everybody's loop.

Nearly two hours later, Jimmy Doyle bounced down the steps from the house in the hills, got in his rental Lexus, and drove off. Morales and Goodman followed.

He led them to a sun-baked minimall just off La Brea. Cars filled the parking area before four storefronts—Tip-Top Costumes (For All Occasions), Slip'n'Spin Rollerballs, Vic's Video Repairs, and Wu Seafoo, the "d" in the name lost to the ages, apparently.

Doyle turned over his keys to a lot attendant in a Hawaiian shirt. Parked in a bus zone, the two detectives watched the stocky man saunter past a Rolls into Wu Seafoo.

"Look at the low riders on that lot," Morales said. The automobiles were mainly Benzes, BMWs, and Lexuses, with the odd Jaguar and Suburban making up the mix. "What the hell goes on at Wu's?"

"Guys eating seafoo," Goodman said. During the period when he'd provided technical advice to a television series, he'd been taken there a couple of times by the genial young owner of the production company, who was addicted to risks and who eventually embarked on a fatal sky dive headfirst into the Mojave.

Wu's had not been the detective's idea of a real restaurant. Real restaurants had tablecloths and waiters in tuxes and menus and a cocktail area. Wu's was an establishment frequented by men—primarily Asians and jaded Americans—who delighted in paying top dollar to sit at a Formica counter and dine on exotic and sometimes potentially lethal denizens of the sea.

When Goodman and Morales entered the air-conditioned, brightly-lit room, the counter customer nearest the door, a plump Asian gentleman, was dropping something with dangling tentacles into his mouth. Morales seemed fascinated by the spectacle.

Doyle was at the rear of the room, sitting at one of only three tables in the place. There was a tall, dignified man with him. They were chatting good-naturedly with their aged waiter. Goodman wondered if the old man might be Wu himself.

As they brushed past, the jabbering maître'd, the two young guys in chef's hats behind the long counter, a waiter beside the first table, and the one who was possibly Wu near the Doyle party all zeroed in on them. Goodman had seen their kind of eyes before—deceptively emotionless, maybe a bit curious, but, ultimately, expecting the worst from the barbarians. That might be exactly what they were going to get.

Doyle recognized them immediately. He slid his chair back a few inches. To give him room to swing? No. He stood up and reached out a hand. "Detective Goodman, isn't it? And . . ." He seemed to be searching his memory. "Morales."

When it became obvious that neither of them was going to accept his offered hand, he withdrew it. Goodman looked at the distinguished man. "You an associate of Mr. Doyle?" he asked.

"Hobie," Doyle said, "these are the detectives working the Madeleine Gray murder. Gentlemen, Hobart Adler."

The tall man nodded agreeably. Goodman knew the name. The guy was a hotshot talent agent. What would he and Doyle be discussing? The detective smiled and threw out a fishing line. "Dyana Cooper's agent, right?"

"Hobie is everybody's agent," Doyle said.

"I believe I saw you in the news a few nights ago, Detective Goodman," Adler said. "You were leaving the courtroom. Everything went well, I hope."

The smarmy-smooth bastard. "Everything went like roses," Goodman replied. "The defense attorney tried to run some fake evidence past us, but she got nailed. I hear the judge is going to sanction her. Imagine trying a dumb stunt like that?"

"We were about to have lunch, detective," Doyle said. "I know you'll excuse us."

"Actually, Jamey," Goodman said, "it's you we're here to see."

Doyle's face broke into a dangerous smile. "Jamey? Nobody's called me that in a long time."

"Your mom, wasn't it?" Goodman asked.

"Yeah. My mom." Doyle was staring at him now.

The ancient waiter stepped into the scene. "You gentlemen wish to be seated?"

"No," Morales said, flashing his badge. "And I ain't so sure we're gen'l'men."

"Jimmy," Adler said, "if you've some business with these fellows, why don't we have our lunch some other time?"

"Hey, don't run off," Morales said, blocking Adler's exit. "You gotta eat. You oughta try one of them sticker fish that kill you dead if they cook it wrong."

"Sounds delightful, but I think I'll be leaving," Adler said, barely ruffled, if at all.

"We're just going to ask Jamey a few questions about some stuff we found at the home of a friend of his, Peter Sandoval."

Adler blinked. *The bastard blinked!* Goodman was ashamed at the delight he felt over so slight an achievement. "Sorry you can't stay," he said.

The agent seemed torn.

Morales sent him on his way with "So long, Jobart, see you aroun'."

As Adler made his exit, a remarkably graceful one considering the circumstances, Doyle sat down at his table and said, "You boys don't want to rile him for no reason."

"Hobie?" Goodman said, taking Adler's chair. "Hell, he's an old prom queen."

Doyle watched Morales drag a chair over from another table. Then he turned his head toward Goodman. "You look a little long in the tooth to be behaving like such an asshole."

"That's the beauty of age," Goodman said. "You reach a point where you can get away with anything. And if not, what difference does it make?"

"If you say so," Doyle said. "You guys want some fish? On me."

"Naw," Morales said. "These people put MSG on everything."

"Well, here we are," Doyle said. "You got a question about Sandoval?"

"We were wondering if you knew his whereabouts," Goodman asked.

"Peter's a blithe spirit," Doyle said. "What do you want with him?"

"Robbery, murder, interfering with an investigation," Goodman said. "Maybe even racketeering. Pick a topic. We haven't gone through all his stuff yet. The guy was like a pack rat. His place is full of hidey-holes jammed with material. I'm particularly interested in his files on Leonard Quarles. You knew Quarles, didn't you?"

"In passing," Doyle said. "You sure about Peter? It doesn't sound like him at all."

"What's Sandoval been doing for you?" Goodman asked.

"Nothing. Like you said, he's a friend."

"Oh?" Goodman put on his surprised look. "Then he wasn't working on Dyana Cooper's behalf when he black-bagged Arthur Lydon's place?"

"Boys, I think you must be talking about some other Peter

Sandoval. The one I know used to be a policeman, just like you."

"Maybe a little different," Goodman said, rising. "Love to sit around all day and chat with you, Jamey. But we've got other puffer fish to fry."

Morales got to his feet, too.

"You did some research on me, huh?" Doyle asked Goodman. "Found out my sainted mom called me 'Jamey'?"

Goodman had located a Boston cop whose family had grown up on the same block as Doyle's. He looked the smirking man in the eye and said, "Just something I spotted in one of Sandoval's files. You have a nice lunch now."

≡ SEVENTY ≡

It was about four P.M. when Nikki finished up with her witness, Milan Jabhad, the night manager at Quik-E-Gas on Sunset and La Brea. Jabhad had seen a tan Jaguar XKE pull up to his pumps at approximately 9:05 P.M. on the night of the Gray murder. Since the car was on the other side of the pumps, he'd been unable to identify the person who got out to fill the tank, but, as he informed the courtroom, he'd watched the car drive away. He added that he thought there may have been two people in it.

The nervous little man had failed to mention that during the several hours of interrogation at the D.A.'s offices the previous evening. Stung by the unexpected revelation, which cast doubt on the prosecution's theory that Dyana Cooper had acted alone, Nikki tried to get back on track. Knowing the man's indecision, she asked, "But you can't be sure you saw two people?"

"Objection. Leading her own witness."

"Sustained."

"How many people are you absolutely certain you saw, Mr. Jabhad?"

"I only saw part of one," he replied, eyes as wide and full of alarm as a runaway horse. "When she pumped the gas."

The night before, the little man had told her that he could not identify Dyana Cooper, could not, in fact, say if the person had been a male or a female. Nikki felt it a personal triumph that he was now referring to the pumper as "she."

"So if you had to answer yes or no to the question about seeing two people . . . ?"

"I would have to say no. I saw just the one."

Nikki then led him to explain how his credit card setup worked, with the card being applied to a slot just beside the pump. The coded information on the card, plus the date and time and amount, were then transmitted to a machine in the bulletproof glass booth where he sat through the night.

Nikki entered into evidence the slip stating that a credit card assigned to Dyana Cooper Willins had been used to purchase $28.47 worth of gas at Quick-E-Gas on the night of the murder.

When she returned to the table, Wise passed her a note. "Lousy preparation."

"How'd you like my foot up your ass?" she whispered to him, smiling all the while.

The first question Anna Marie Dayne asked in her cross-examination was, "Mr. Jabhad, you know what Ms. Cooper looks like, don't you?"

"Of course."

"Can you state without question that she was the person in that Jaguar?"

"No."

"So it could have been two people, neither of whom was Ms. Cooper?"

"Objection. Mr. Jabhad has stated that he saw only one person."

"Mr. Jabhad," Dayne said, consulting her notes, "you said you had the impression there might have been two people. What was it that gave you that impression?"

The little man didn't answer at once. His body tensed and he seemed to be staring down at his shiny but pressed dark blue trousers. Then he brightened. "A shadow. I saw the shadow of someone next to the passenger window, as the car drove away."

"And neither of these two people resembled Dyana Cooper?"

"I didn't get a good look. But her credit card—"

"Did you see her use the card?"

"No."

"And her signature is not on the sales slip?"

"Our system does not require—"

"Yes or no."

"No. She didn't sign the slip."

"So two other people could have been in that car, using a card stolen from Dyana Cooper?"

"Objection. Calls for speculation."

"Sustained."

"I'm finished with this witness," Dayne said.

"Redirect, your honor," Nikki said.

This was what it was always about. The thousand and one little impressions the jurors got of how the trial was progressing. Time to leave them with something to chew on. "Mr. Jabhad, just to clarify, how many people were in the car?"

"Two. I am sure of that now."

"Couldn't the two have been Dyana Cooper and, in the

seat beside her, the wrapped body of her victim, Madeleine Gray?"

"Objection, your honor."

"Question withdrawn," Nikki said, filled with the satisfaction of seeing most of the jurors scribbling away on their tablets.

Then she was back in her office, scribbling on her own, prepping for the next day. At eight P.M., she and Wise dined for a leisurely fifteen minutes—two Whoppers, fries, diet Coke for him, Sprite and a shot of tequila for her—during which time they also managed to work out a full week's game plan.

At a little after ten that night, Nikki put her automatic garage opener to work and eased the Mazda into a niche created by boxes filled with books and old clothes still unopened from the move. Wearily, she clicked the garage door closed and dragged herself from the car.

She yawned while unlocking the door to the house.

She was surprised that Bird wasn't there to meet her. But it was late.

She walked down the hall toward the front of the house, depositing her briefcase on the kitchen counter. The moon was shining through the glass doors, providing enough illumination that she didn't even bother to turn on the lights.

She poked her head into the living room. Bird's plaid mattress was empty.

Something else caught her eye: an outline of light around the front door, caused by the street lamp outside.

The front door was open!

Could Loreen have been that careless when she dropped by to feed Bird?

Nikki ran to the door, the adrenaline rush chasing away any thought of sleep.

The street in front of the house was empty. The dog wouldn't have run away.

She stepped back into the house. "Bird?" she called.

From somewhere at the rear of the house came a reassuring growl.

Relaxing, she slammed the front door.

A shadow flitted past the doorway leading to the kitchen. "Bird?"

The responding bark came from too far away.

She stepped into the kitchen, her hand going out to the light switch.

Powerful fingers grabbed her wrist.

The intruder was trim, dressed in black, face covered by a ski mask. "Shhhh," it said, letting her wrist go.

"Shush, your ass," she said. "BIRD! BE!"

There was a crash at the rear of the house and more barking.

Another figure appeared, taller, dressed like the first. As if some silent message passed between them, both reached into their pockets and withdrew metal objects. With graceful flips of their wrists, shiny blades clicked into place, glistening in the moonlight.

Nikki uttered an involuntary sound, something between a whimper and a gasp.

The dog continued to smash against the door confining him.

Her briefcase rested on the counter only a few feet away. In it was her police special. The two figures advanced, blocking her way to the counter. The smaller one was too close, gesturing with the knife, carving horizontal figure eights in the air.

One more step and he was near enough for her to hear breath rustle against the cloth mask. Suddenly, the knife was shoved at her stomach. It was a feint. As she lowered her hands to protect her torso, the masked figure's other hand shot out, pressing a moist object against the side of her face, slashing down with it across her neck.

She stumbled backward, banging hard against the wall.

The figure moved in on her again, paused menacingly, and emitted a guttural "Hahhhhh."

Another crash, louder this time, came from the rear. The barking seemed less muffled.

The two figures exchanged looks. As Bird's feet pounded down the hall, they raced to the front door.

Nikki staggered to the counter, fumbled with the briefcase. The big dog brushed her side as he lumbered past her, racing for the now open door. Then she had the gun in her hand, clicking off the safety as she ran.

Bird was half a block away, racing full out, rounding a corner.

As she approached the corner, she heard a car start up, its engine racing, then wheels screeching.

Rounding the corner, she saw her dog standing in the center of the street, barking furiously. The dark sedan, its lights off, was roaring directly at him.

"BIRD!" she screamed. "BOP!"

The dog held his ground truculently until the very last second. Then, in an almost miraculous movement, he leaped sideways, avoiding the rushing vehicle.

The driver of the car was so stunned by the leap he lost control of the wheel for a second. The sedan swerved and bounced over the curb. Then the driver found his way back to the street, made a U-turn, and sped away.

Nikki ran to the dog. The animal aimed a final bark at the departing car, then turned to her. He sniffed at the gun in her hand. "Yeah, I guess I coulda used it," she said.

Bird moved closer and began to whimper. He seemed to

be studying her forehead. She touched the spot with her free hand. It felt sticky. Her fingertips came away red.

She raced back to the house, Bird at her heels. She locked the door, turned on the overhead light, and realized with relief that the red wasn't blood. It was . . . she sniffed her fingers. It was lipstick.

She ran to the kitchen and scooped up the cordless phone from the counter. She dialed the "9" and the "1" before she realized that the room was basically untouched. The gadgets were all in place. The little Sony TV was still on its shelf. The two masked intruders hadn't been burglars.

What had they been?

She clicked off the phone. She could call the police later.

The bedroom, the only other place where she kept anything of value, didn't look any different than it had that morning. Still messy as hell. The fifty-dollar bill she'd set aside for two cases of Bird's special food was still on top of the dresser.

They'd locked him in a closet off the empty second bedroom. Bird had smashed the door open. She bent down to hug the animal. "My big brave boy," she said. "How in the world were they able to jam you up in that closet?"

Bird yipped, drawing her attention to strands of raw hamburger caught in his beard. She gave him a look of disappointment. "What'd they do? Pick the front door lock and toss in some doctored food? You scarfed it down and woke up in the closet."

Bird pretended not to understand.

She headed for the bathroom to wash off the lipstick. When she turned on the light, she discovered the real reason the intruders had broken in.

Scrawled on the bathroom mirror in her own lipstick were the words "Remember Mason Durant."

Dazed, she sat down on the closed toilet, her head spinning. Could Mace have set this whole thing up? No, that was crazy. Not even he knew about her finding the hot dog. But who did? Tom Gleason was dead. Wise knew, of course, but what reason would he have to rattle her cage?

The phone rang, startling her.

She stumbled past a concerned Bird into her bedroom.

"Hope I'm not keeping you up." It was not the same man who'd called her at Virgil's, but this one's gruff whisper was just as intimidating, as if the caller were doing a bad Clint Eastwood imitation.

"Are you James Doyle?" she asked.

A pause. "No, my name is Justice. That's what I seek."

"We all do."

"I'll be sure to tell that to Mason Durant."

"You know him?"

"I know about him. And I know you could wind up taking his place if you refuse my request."

"What the hell do you want from me?" Nikki shouted.

"It's what I don't want. I don't want you to call Simon Bayliss to the stand tomorrow. Or ever." Bayliss was the manager of the Sanctum. Wise had scheduled his testimony for the following day.

"That's not my decision."

"Tell Raymond Wise he has as much to lose as you do if Durant's story is told."

"Tell him yourself," Nikki said.

"Do you want my people to return, Nikki? They won't be as friendly next time."

"Who are you?" she demanded.

The line went dead.

She quickly dialed Virgil's number. She needed his help. She needed him.

What she got was his answering machine.

"Oh, baby, please pick up. Please."

He didn't.

She slipped to the floor. Loreen. She'd call Loreen.

Why? So she could lay her misery on her friend? She'd done enough of that over the years.

Bird sat down beside her, leaning against her. She put her arm around him and thanked the good Lord she wasn't completely alone.

≡ SEVENTY-ONE ≡

"How long must this damned weight hang over my head?" Wise moaned.

"If you're looking for sympathy," Nikki replied, "try somebody who didn't have the message delivered in her face."

"You don't have a burglar alarm?"

"I don't even have a dining room table."

"We all have our priorities, I guess."

They were in her office at eight-fifteen the following morning. She'd just told him about the break-in and the caller's threat to publicize the facts of the Mason Durant trial.

"We could dump Bayliss," Wise said. "He's such a pain in the ass we're probably going to have to declare him a hostile witness anyway. We've already introduced Willins's statement about the affair. Bayliss is just another reminder to the jury."

"Then why doesn't Mr. Mystery want us to call him?"

Wise shrugged. "Maybe he's got some information we don't know about."

"It could be a test," Nikki said. "We go along with this, we get pushed more."

"How the hell could they know about Durant?"

"It doesn't matter," Nikki said. "We have two options: do the job or quit."

"I've got too much time in grade to quit," Wise said. "So screw Mr. Mystery and his threats."

She was afraid she was starting to actually like this miserable man.

They agreed that Walden had to be apprised of the break-in and the fact that someone was trying to control the trial. This was accomplished (with no mention made of the Mason Durant case) during a ten-minute window of opportunity between the district attorney's arrival at work and the start of the trial day.

He seemed stunned by the attack on Nikki. "This will not be tolerated," he said, pacing about his office. "I will not have my staff threatened and physically abused. You should have called me last night, Nikki. I'll send a forensic team to your apartment—"

"Please don't," she said. "Very little was disturbed and they were wearing gloves. You'd be upsetting my dog for nothing."

"If that's what you want," Walden said, pausing midpace to lean against the edge of the desk. "But I insist on you both having round-the-clock protection."

His plan also called for them to attach tape recorders to their office and home phones. "I want to hear the bastard myself. Judge Vetters might find it interesting, too."

He began pacing again, slowly at first. "We'll have to establish a code for when we need to reach you by cellular. Otherwise, use those phones for outgoing only."

"It's time we went downstairs," Wise said.

Walden glanced at his watch and nodded. He put his arm around his deputy's thin shoulders and walked him to the door. "More than ever now, Ray, we must win this case."

Meg Fisher was waiting when they emerged. She darted in and before she closed the door, they heard her nattering about the Af-Am Leadership dinner.

"Next time your mystery man calls," Wise said, "give him Meg's number."

Simon Bayliss, manager of the Sanctum, sat in the witness chair with his slightly hooked nose lifted in the air, as if he found Judge Vetters's perfume a bit vulgar.

He was a trim man of average height, dressed in an immaculate dark blue blazer and gray trousers with pleats sharp enough to draw blood. His face was tanned, barbered, and, though he was probably in his mid to late forties, as wrinkle-free as a preadolescent boy's. He reminded Nikki of a well-tended parrot.

Not a nice polly.

He obviously resented his present situation and was not at all interested in cooperating with the prosecution. Nikki sympathized with her teammate.

"Do you recognize Ms. Willins?" Wise asked him.

"Of course."

"From her movies?"

"Yes."

"And from seeing her in person?"

A hesitation. Then, "Yes."

"Have you seen her often in person?"

"What is often?" He spoke in a clipped British accent. David Niven without the charm, Nikki thought.

"Four times. Five times."

"Perhaps."

"This would be at the Sanctum?"

"Mainly, yes."

"With her husband?"

"I suppose."

"And have you seen Mr. Willins without Ms. Willins being present?"

"Yes."

"Was he alone?"

"Sometimes."

"What about the other times?"

"Not alone," the manager said.

Wise sighed. "Who was with him?"

"Which time?"

"Any time. Just give us the full list."

"I believe he visited with his company executives. I could get their names for you."

"What about women other than his wife?"

"Objection. Relevance?" This from Anna Marie Dayne.

"Goes to motive, your honor."

"Overruled. Please answer the question, Mr. Bayliss."

"What was the question?"

"Did Mr. Willins visit the Sanctum with women other than his wife?"

"Visit? I suppose."

"Would that be 'yes'?"

"Yes."

"Was one of these other women Madeleine Gray?"

"That's possible."

"Were they there together, sir?" Wise asked, not hiding his impatience.

"Mr. Willins used the facilities of the Sanctum. As did Ms. Gray. And Ms. Cooper. And most of the upper strata of Hollywood society. We on the staff are seldom privy to the specific details of their visits."

"For those of us not in Hollywood's upper strata," Wise said, "could you please explain how you can provide services and still be ignorant of what your guests are up to?"

Bayliss replied in a bored monotone, "The reason for the Sanctum's success is that it offers absolute privacy. Each unit is a separate cottage with its own entry and exit. Our landscaping has been designed to make it possible for our guests to arrive and depart without distracting other guests or staff members."

"You mean your guests can sneak in and out without being observed."

"Our guests don't sneak."

"What would you call it?" Wise asked.

"Your honor," Dayne said, "Mr. Wise seems to be badgering his own witness."

Judge Vetters, with some reluctance, Nikki thought, advised Wise to "use a bit more cordiality, even when it is seemingly undeserved."

"I'll try, your honor. I'd also like to designate Mr. Bayliss as a hostile witness."

"About time, too," the judge said.

"Mr. Bayliss," Wise said, "how many times did John Willins and Madeleine Gray spend the night in the same cottage at your establishment?"

Bayliss's eyes glazed. "You have our records. They're quite accurate."

"Your records indicate only that Mr. Willins rented cottages nineteen nights in the past twelve months. His guests aren't mentioned."

"As I thought I explained, we go out of our way not to inquire about such things."

"Your accurate records indicate that Mr. Willins's company paid for his stays."

"Then it must have," Bayliss said, as if the matter was of absolutely no concern.

"So his shacking up with Maddie Gray was business?"

"Object—"

"Withdrawn, your honor," Wise said. "Mr. Bayliss, according to your firsthand knowledge, how many times were John Willins and Madeleine Gray together in your establishment?"

"Five or six times, if memory serves."

"Thank you," Wise said, expelling a long exhausted breath. "Your witness."

Dayne rose from her chair but didn't bother to leave her table.

"Mr. Wise seems to have beaten this horse to the ground, so I'll make this short and sweet, Mr. Bayliss. Do you have any knowledge of the murder of Madeleine Gray?"

Bayliss apparently had not been expecting the question. His head jerked back and he momentarily dropped his arrogance. "The murder? I know nothing about that."

"Then we've wasted enough of your time and ours. Thank you."

She sat back down.

Bayliss, still a bit shaken, looked at the judge, who told him he could step down. As he walked past them, Nikki leaned toward Wise and whispered, "What just rocked Bayliss's world? Did we miss something?"

Wise was watching the table to their left. Nikki turned and saw a very annoyed Anna Marie Dayne speaking quickly into the ear of an apparently agitated assistant. "Whatever it was we overlooked," Wise said, "I think the defense is just as clueless."

≡ SEVENTY-TWO ≡

When Virgil arrived for dinner that night, Nikki was using one of her fancy machines to puree baked garlic cloves.

She moved quickly from behind the stove, but not quickly enough to head off the giant in the tight midnight-blue suit who had drawn his gun and was now unlocking the front door. Bird leaped from his cushion and stood poised, waiting for Nikki's command.

She was too busy watching the giant open the door and point his gun at Virgil.

"Sonny," she cried out. "He's okay. This is the man I told you about. "

Virgil, standing there holding a bottle of wine, looked from Sonny to Sonny's gun. Then he turned to Nikki and asked, "A story go with this, Red?"

"This is Sonny. My bodyguard."

"Nice gig," the detective said. He faced the big man and put out his free hand. "Virgil Sykes, Sonny," he said.

"Forgive me if I don't shake your hand, Virgil," Sonny

said, holstering his weapon, "but I like to keep mine empty and ready when I'm on duty."

Virgil shrugged, withdrew his hand, and turned to Nikki. "Okay, what now?"

"You folks 'scuse me," Sonny said, striding past the detective to make his exit.

"Sonny will be spending the evening in his car," Nikki said.

"Dinner, too?"

"Dinner, too," she said. "Feels he can survey the scene better out there."

"Bless his gun-totin' soul," Virgil said. He was suddenly very serious. "Got pretty rough last night, huh?"

"Oh, yeah."

"Hell of a time for me to be at a friend's place watching the Lakers," he said. "How'd they get in?"

"Popped the front door," she said. "My girlfriend came by to feed Bird and didn't know about putting on the double lock."

"Aw, baby," he said. He took her in his arms and kissed her.

Bird pushed his big head between them and eventually pried them apart.

"I thought we had an understanding," Virgil told the dog. He took something from his pocket and slipped it to the animal, who gobbled it down.

"What'd you give him?" Nikki asked.

"Dog treat," Virgil said. "New kinda dry burger meat. Part of my plan to win him over. What should I do with this human treat?" He held out the bottle of wine.

"Hey, no Ripple for us," Nikki said, noting the vintage and trying not to think about the strands of burger she'd found in Bird's beard the night before. "Pop the cork, mister."

They walked to the kitchen. He handed her something else from his pocket, a CD featuring the singer Erykah Badu. She fed it into her player while he rounded the counter looking for a corkscrew. "Umm-um." He inhaled loudly. "Smells like my sweet mama's kitchen. Don't know where you find the time to shop and cook, in court all day long."

She flashed on the race to the supermarket, the hunt for something, anything, that might make a dinner she could whip up quickly, the checkout lane that refused to move, Sonny at her heels the whole time. Then the rush to feed Bird, clean up the place, shower, dress. Cook. "Just got to take things in stride," she said as the singer-songwriter's odd mixture of soul and hip-hop filled the house.

"Wise musta had his work cut out for him today," he said, handing her a glass of white wine. "Dude on the radio said he just about had to jump down some guy's gullet to pull the answers out."

"Well, he got 'em out," Nikki said, taking the wine.

"To us, Red," he said, clinking glasses.

The wine was cool and crisp. She took a second sip and applied herself to the task of pan-searing their steaks, then covering them with a garlic cream sauce. "How'd the Lakers do, by the way?" she asked.

"Got their butts whipped by the Jazz." He looked at the steaks. "Just two, honey? What about old Sonny? Looks like he could eat these and a few more."

"Sonny fixed himself a salad. He's a vegetarian."

"He's something, that's for sure."

They dined sitting on wooden folding chairs facing one another over a card table covered by a red-and-white-checked cloth she'd bought at the supermarket. Virgil's comment, when he saw the table and chairs in the middle of her otherwise empty large dining room, was, "You got some monk doing your interior design, Red?"

Once the lights were lowered, the candles glowing, the food served, Bird taking it easy lying in the doorway and Gladys Knight communing with the Pips in the background, he amended his original statement. "This is sorta nice 'n' cozy."

She watched him devour his steak, nearly certain she was being foolish to suspect he could have had anything to do with the break-in. The food particles in the dog's beard had looked like regular hamburger, not anything dry. Virgil was too clever to waltz in and feed the dog the same thing that had knocked him out the night before. Anyway, she knew he wasn't either of the two housebreakers.

Why was she even thinking this nonsense? Because only a short time after she told him about Mason Durant, somebody had scrawled that name on her bathroom mirror. *You're behaving like a crazy woman. He was at a friend's house, like he said. Watching the Lakers. It's easy enough to check to see if the game really was televised.*

Stop, damn it, she commanded herself. Still, the suspicion was there.

"You're not eating," Virgil said. "I know some chefs can't eat their own cooking, but in this case, that'd be a crime. This is great."

"I'm just worn out," she said.

When they'd cleared the table, he asked, "Nightcap at my place?"

She shook her head. "Like I told you, I'm onstage tomorrow morning." She was glad that when she'd invited him to dinner, she'd warned that the evening would end early. She'd have to be up at the crack of dawn to prepare for court. Now she had an even stronger reason: she wanted to be alone to deal with her suspicions, to examine them and hopefully discard them before they did serious damage to the bond growing between them.

"Nightcap here, then?"

"Raincheck," she said.

"Sonny staying the night?"

"Jealous?" As confused as she was, she found the idea amusing.

"At least curious."

"There's another guy, Mark, who takes over at four."

"I could save the county the overtime. Keep the bad guys away for nothing."

"Who'd keep you away?" she asked.

She thought his smile faltered. But it was back almost immediately. "That's where the Bird dog comes in," he said as she walked him to the front door.

"You've corrupted him with your treats."

"Don't sell him short," Virgil said. "Takes more than a treat to turn that boy. See you tomorrow?"

She hesitated. "I'm having dinner with Loreen. I told you about her."

"Your best friend. Okay, if your plans change or you want to get together after your dinner, give me a call."

He leaned forward and pressed his lips against hers.

For the first time, she held back a little.

He sensed something was wrong. Gave her a wistful smile and said good night.

She stayed in the doorway, watching him stroll down the walk and give Sonny a two-fingered salute before getting into his car.

Am I being a fool? she wondered. *Or have I already been one?*

≡ SEVENTY-THREE ≡

Goodman watched Gwen's car disappear into the underground parking lot at a four-story building in Beverly Hills. He braked at the curb. Even without a night-light, he could make out the tasteful but shiny gold lettering on the building's glass front door. The Adler Agency.

Although any number of men worked for the talent agency, using his standard guide of worst-case scenario, Goodman knew exactly whom she'd come to see. Hobart Fucking Adler.

Just fifteen minutes before, he and Gwen and her partner, Manolo, had been drinking beer at the Short Stop, a cop hangout on Cesar Chavez Avenue. Her beeper had gone off and she'd left to use the pay phone. She was back almost immediately. "Sorry, guys, gotta run."

"I thought we were all gonna head out to Lucy's," Manolo had complained.

"Can't make it tonight," she'd said, looking at Goodman.

He'd watched her walk out of the bar. Then he'd followed

her out, vaguely conscious of the big Samoan yelling his name.

Now he sat in his car in front of the office building, surprised that on a warm Southern California night there could still be a chill in the air. He knew his next move. Was he thinking like a cop or a rejected lover? It didn't much matter in the long run. The hard fact was that Gwen was a policewoman involved with someone who had a lot riding on the Maddie Gray murder case. The case *he* was investigating.

He had to find out if she'd stepped over the line.

Gwen arrived at her apartment a little after one-thirty A.M. to discover Goodman slouched on her sofa, feet on her coffee table, bottle in hand.

"I used a pick to let myself in," he said. "Hope you don't mind."

"*Mi casa* and all that shit," she said testily. She kicked off her shoes and dropped her purse with a clunk on the floor. "See you found the tequila, huh?"

"Found this, too." He took a folded rectangle of paper from his pocket. It had been in a shoe box in her bedroom closet.

She sagged. She recognized it, of course. You don't not recognize a check made out to you in the sum of twenty thousand dollars.

"What's this Magna Productions, paying you all this loot?" he asked.

"A film company," she almost whispered, sitting beside him on the sofa. Picking up the tequila bottle. Purposely ignoring the check.

"New one on me. Magna. Says down here in the corner 'consultant's fee.' Back when I did my consulting, twenty large'd buy quite a bit of my time. Of course, that was a while ago. What's it buy now?"

She put the bottle to her lips and took a large gulp.

"Movie or TV?" he asked.

"Stop it," she hissed.

"Probably a feature film, that kind of dough."

"Stop it," she said again, louder.

"You must have a good agent."

"Stop it!" she screamed at him. She began to cry, pounding the tequila bottle on the couch beside her.

Goodman pried the bottle from her clenched hand, placed it on the table, and watched her cry. If it had been a movie, he'd have had a handkerchief to offer her. He wondered if anybody other than guys in movies ever carried one anymore.

He looked around the room for a Kleenex. The best he could find was a paper napkin. She threw it back at him, wiping her eyes on the sleeve of her cotton shirt. "You don't want any part of this, Eddie," she said. "These people don't play nice."

"Adler? Hell, I'm already on your boyfriend's shit list. Carlos and I fronted him and Doyle off at lunch the other day. Made him blink. He ain't so tough."

She was not amused. "Christ's sake, you don't play little cop games with somebody like Hobie. You try to catch him when he's asleep and drive a wooden stake through his heart."

"That's nice talk about your main squeeze."

"You don't know anything about it."

"That's why I'm here."

"I'm his mistress, okay?" she said harshly. "He gets horny, he calls me. I get him off, he sends me away."

"Sounds like a sweet deal for you," he said.

"Get out of here, Eddie."

He felt the blood building up in his veins, felt the slightly dizzy sensation caused by the pressure. He took a deep breath and exhaled it slowly. "Let's talk a little about the twenty grand," he said.

She shook her head.

"It's me or Corben."

"You wouldn't bring this to Corben?"

"Without batting an eye." He wondered if that was true. He thought it might be.

She grabbed the tequila. Dutch courage, or was she simply playing for time?

"I used to be pretty good at figuring things out," he said. "Let's see what I can deduce." Actually, he'd spent over an hour analyzing the facts.

He mock-studied the check. "This date's familiar. It's the day after Maddie's body turned up, the start of our investigation of the murder. I don't imagine that's a coincidence. So, let's see, what could you have done for your boyfriend to earn this loot? I guess we can rule out sex, since you were giving that away."

"Eddie . . ."

"What then? A running report on our progress? Not worth two gees, much less twenty. Something world-class. Something that Dyana Cooper really needed. Wanna know my guess?"

She watched him, saying nothing.

"The glass with her fingerprints that was missing from the room where we found the blood."

"You honestly believe I'd steal what I thought was crucial evidence from a crime scene?" she asked.

"At this point, Gwen, what I believe or don't believe is pretty immaterial. The facts speak for themselves. You took something from the crime scene, something big-time."

"You have to understand. Hobie is . . . well, Hobie.

Charming. Smooth. I wasn't . . . we weren't in love, or anything like that. It was kicks. He was great to be with. Exciting. Fun. He loved hearing stories about the job. He wanted me to start keeping a journal. Said he could sell it in a minute. But you know how I am, Eddie. I can't even get my reports done without a gun to my head."

Let her talk, he thought. *Keep listening and try to pretend she's just another suspect.*

"Anyhow, he asked me to do him a favor. Like a fool, I did. Everything changed. He gave me a check. A payoff. The fucker!"

"The check was for the so-called favor?" he asked, just to get it straight.

"I threw it in his face," she said. "He pushed it back at me. Said he didn't mean to insult me. I'd done something very important for him and he was just showing me his gratitude. It had nothing to do with our relationship.

"I tried to explain the only reason I'd done it was because of our relationship. I sure as hell didn't want to get paid. That made it seem like I was on his pad."

"That's the fact of it," Goodman said.

She gave him an anguished look. "Yeah. I figured that out. It's why I haven't cashed the check. If I did, it would put me in his pocket for all time."

"You took it."

"I had no choice."

"Well, there's 'yes' and 'no.' "

"You still don't get it, do you, Eddie? Let's see, how do I make you understand? You know the guy we work for. Not Corben; Chief Ahern. He's a client of Hobie's. And a personal friend. You see where I'm headed with this?"

"You saying *Ahern*'s on Adler's pad?"

"You're a sweet man, Eddie, but you're focused on the small picture. Ahern's not on anybody's pad. Still, that wouldn't stop him from burying me, or you, if his pal Hobie Adler whispered in his ear that we were bothering him."

"Adler told you this?"

"No. He told me that unless I behaved, in his words, 'like a good girl,' and took the check for a job well done, he'd be forced to 'do something unpleasant.' I didn't ask him to be more specific. I just took the check. But I didn't cash it."

Goodman mulled that over, then said, "Okay, tell me about the favor."

She shook her head.

"Let me explain something to you, kiddo. You stepped over the line. What we're doing here now is figuring out the price you're gonna have to pay for that. Answer my questions and maybe the worst that happens is that you quit the force. Clam up and I'll take everything I know to Corben. You can imagine how he'll handle it."

She finished off the tequila, dropped the empty bottle to the carpet, and said, "I stole Dyana Cooper's blackmail folder from Maddie Gray's cabinet."

Goodman stared at her, momentarily speechless.

"Hobie made it sound like no big thing. Maddie was blackmailing a close friend of his. His friend was worried that the information might become public. Couldn't I find the file at the Laurel Canyon house and remove it."

"And you said . . . ?" Goodman prompted.

"I told him I wouldn't steal evidence from a crime scene. Even for him."

"But you did."

"Hobie got where he is for one reason. He's the greatest salesman in the world. He said, 'What if I can convince you that it isn't evidence?' I hesitated and was lost."

"Why? What'd he say?"

"If his friend had killed Maddie, she would have taken the

file. Since it was still at the house, it meant she was not the murderer and therefore her file was not evidence."

It was the same bullshit line of reasoning he'd heard from the D.A. He was fed up with it. Fed up with everything. "Adler conned you," he said in disgust. "There are a hundred reasons why Cooper might have left the file behind. Maybe she panicked. Maybe she searched and couldn't find it."

"It's nothing I haven't figured out for myself," Gwen said.

"Okay, tell me about it."

"I just did."

"The file. Tell me what was in the file."

She wet her lips. "Hobie didn't mention whose file it was, just that it was labeled 'Soul Sister.' He ordered me to take it to him without looking inside."

"Sweet Jesus, he had you that buffaloed?"

"This isn't Disneyland, Eddie," she said and began to describe the contents. In essence there were photos, newspaper clippings, and a marriage certificate indicating that a decade before, Dyana Cooper, under her real name, "Diana Crosley," had married a young man named Isaac Hughes in her hometown of Hattiesburg, Mississippi. Hughes had subsequently murdered a man in a bar fight and taken flight to escape justice. He was apparently still a fugitive.

"Not evidence," Goodman said sarcastically. "Shit. Why the hell couldn't Dyana Cooper have found the damned file herself after she murdered Maddie, and kept you out of it?" He frowned. "How'd you know where to look for it?"

"It didn't take a rocket scientist," Gwen said. "I walked into that upstairs office and saw the file drawer hanging open."

He leaned forward. "*You* didn't pry the drawer open?"

"No. The murderer must have . . ." She stopped, realizing the same thing he did.

"Assuming the murderer jimmied the file drawer and left Dyana Cooper's folder behind," he said, "it means that prick Adler may not have been conning you after all. She didn't kill Maddie. What did he say when you told him about the busted drawer?"

"I didn't. He didn't want to know anything about the file or how I got it. He wants the whole thing done and over. That's why he's demanding I cash the check. That's what he was calling about the other night when I let the phone ring. And tonight."

"He sure took his time to tell you that."

"We got that out of the way right at the jump," she said.

"So you're still sleeping with the guy?"

"It's easier duty than telling him no."

He leaned his head back against the sofa and closed his eyes. "The answer to what you're wondering is this," he heard her say. "I hate the manipulating control-freak son of a bitch. I want out. Can you help me?"

"I don't know," he said, getting to his feet.

He reached for her phone.

"Who are you calling?" Gwen asked.

"My lawyer."

Nikki Hall answered on the fourth ring. He apologized for calling so late.

"It's okay. I was having a nightmare, anyway. What's up?"

"Do you and I still have a client-attorney relationship?"

"Wait a minute. Am I still in the nightmare?" she asked.

"I'm afraid not. Can we have some kind of privileged communication?"

"Damn. I'm not going to want to hear this, am I?"

"I don't think so."

"Then why don't you just keep it to yourself?"

"I have to talk to somebody at the D.A.'s office."

"Privilege only goes so far."

"What about trust?" he asked. "How far can I trust you?"

"I'm not about to answer that till I know what we're dealing with."

"I have some information about the Gray murder, but I can't tell you how I got it."

"Any other good news?"

"I don't have any evidence to back it up."

"I'll put on some coffee," Nikki said. "Come on over and we'll talk about it. See if it's as bad as it sounds."

He made a mental note of her address and hung up the phone. Gwen looked worried. "You'll come back after?"

"Will you be here?" he asked.

The biggest black man he'd ever seen slid out of a car and intercepted him before he reached the front door to Nikki's home. "Your name Goodman?" he asked, saving the detective the effort of trying to tear his gun out of his pocket.

He nodded.

"ID? Just use your fingertips, please."

Goodman plucked his leather-covered ID from his inside pocket, using thumb and forefinger. The big man backed to the street lamp, looked the official document over carefully, and handed it back. He walked the detective to the door and pressed the buzzer three times in quick succession.

Nikki answered the door wearing black sweats with white piping. "Thanks, Sonny," she said to the giant, who jogged back to his car.

The first thing Goodman noticed on entering the house was that there was no furniture. The second was a huge black hound about a foot to his left, glaring at him. "Better shake my hand, detective," Nikki said, "or you're liable to lose one of your limbs."

The handshake seemed to satisfy the dog, who followed them into the kitchen.

"Coffee smells great," Goodman told her.

"Pull up a stool and I'll pour us some. Then we can get right into this bad news you're bringing."

It didn't take him long to fill her in. When he'd finished, she said, "So we have to assume that on the night of the murder somebody other than Dyana Cooper pried open that drawer to get at a file that was not Dyana Cooper's."

"That's the bottom line," he said.

She was lost in thought for so long he began to feel uncomfortable. She turned to him. "Your informant was hired by Dyana Cooper to get her file?"

"Not directly by her."

"My point is: Dyana knows about her file being lifted."

Having no idea where she was going with this line of questioning, he nodded his assent. "She has to know it," he said.

Nikki seemed oddly relieved. "Then it isn't exactly the same," she muttered.

"What isn't?" he asked.

"Oh, nothing. I'm just cautious about the disclosure of evidence. In this case, we can be reasonably certain the defense has this information and has chosen not to use it. It would be tricky. Your informant would have to take the stand, say he stole evidence. He could then incriminate whoever put him up to it. But Dyana would walk. More coffee?"

"No, thanks."

"What I'd love to do, detective, is to kick your ass out of here and forget we've ever had this meeting. But I'm afraid I'm going to have to pass this information on to Joe Walden and let him decide what to do with it."

That was not good news. "I was hoping to retire in a couple of years," Goodman said. "If you tell Walden I'm withholding the name of someone who removed an item from a murder scene I'll be in Internal Affairs within an hour and out on the street in two."

"I understand," she said, picking up the phone and dialing. "I'll remove the middleman. That would be you . . . Oh, hello, Joe, hope I didn't wake you."

Goodman watched her stand and walk to the doors leading to the rear patio. "I just received another of those calls," she said. "No, no threat this time. Just some, ah, pertinent information we have to talk about."

She turned and winked at Goodman. "It's sketchy and there's not much substantiation, but it could have one hell of an effect on the trial."

Goodman took his empty cup to the sink, expecting to rinse it. But the sink was piled so high with dirty dishes he was afraid that if he turned on the water, it would splash onto the floor.

Nikki was in the midst of passing along the news about the "Soul Sister" file and its contents. Goodman waved his hand until she looked at him, then he mouthed the word "Thanks" and gestured toward the door.

The big dog watched him suspiciously as he walked across the living room. He let himself out, making sure the door clicked shut behind him.

Outside, the air had turned a little cooler and damper. The bodyguard was in his sedan, as alert as an owl. Goodman got in his own car and drove back to Gwen Harriman's apartment.

≡ SEVENTY-FOUR ≡

Saturday morning, shortly after nine, Nikki and Ray Wise were seated across the desk from the district attorney, who was turned partially away from them staring out of the window, thinking over the news she'd brought. News no one wanted to hear.

The scene was strikingly reminiscent of her terrible meeting four years before. The same office. The same kind of situation. The same three people. Well, not quite, but close enough. As she watched Joe Walden cock his head to the right in thought, she discovered an actual physical resemblance between him and his mentor, Tom Gleason. Not in looks, though Walden was approximately the same height as Gleason, but in general appearance and gesture. He favored the same smartly tailored suits, red ties, and bright suspenders that Gleason had worn. She wondered if they came from the same shop.

The more she studied Walden, the more obvious it became that Gleason was his role model. The way he spoke, the easy charm, even the quick anger. She wondered why she'd never noticed it before.

He spun around suddenly to face them. "It's just too bad we don't have a tape of the conversation," he said pointedly. "The police lab might've been able to use their fancy equipment to let us know how much of the story is true, if any."

"I didn't have time to set up the recorder," Nikki said.

"We have to assume the caller is someone in the employ of the Willinses," the D.A. said. "What do they hope to achieve by floating this information by us?"

"It's clever," Wise said. "According to Mr. X's 'confession,' Maddie's drawer full of blackmail goodies had already been broken into when he arrived for Dyana's file. The clear implication is that Dyana therefore could not be Maddie's murderer. I say this is all crap and we should ignore it. Any hint of this will send the jury into a tailspin."

"Nikki?" Walden asked.

Her discomfort was growing. Since she trusted Goodman, she supposed that the sequence of events had taken place exactly as he'd outlined them. It wasn't cast-iron proof that Dyana hadn't murdered Madeleine Gray, but it certainly raised a substantial doubt of her guilt.

To convince the D.A. and Wise, however, she'd have to tell them about Goodman. Then the detective would have to give up his source. It was always a bitch to try to work around the truth.

"Nikki?" the D.A. asked again.

Play the game, Gleason and everyone else had advised her. All she had to do was say she agreed with Wise. Just nod her head.

"We should at least consider the possibility that the story is straight," she said.

"Why?" Wise asked.

"If the story is true, we ought to be prepared should the

defense try to introduce it. It would be devastating to anyone involved in the theft of the evidence, but Dayne may use it anyway, with her back to the wall."

"Nikki's point is well taken," Walden said.

Wise begrudgingly admitted it was. "I suppose we could check out the bit about the earlier marriage," he said. "It'd be evidence of the woman's secretive nature and her longtime association with violent crime."

"Wouldn't it be lovely to find out Dyana Cooper had neglected to divorce her first husband?" Walden added. "It could void her present marriage, which in turn would remove Willins's protected spouse status."

Wise's smile was not a pretty sight. "I'd love a crack at that bad boy on the stand."

"Then we're in agreement?" Walden asked. "We investigate the previous marriage and keep our antennae tuned to every little change in the defense's presentation."

Nikki nodded.

"Good," he said. "I assume you two will be working the rest of the day?"

"I've got the Rosten girl coming in later to go over her testimony," Ray said. "I plan on starting with her on Monday morning."

"Fine, but don't forget the NAAL dinner. Tomorrow night. Hotel Balmoral. I expect all our tables to be filled."

As they headed toward their respective offices, Wise mumbled, "I suppose I'll be the token white."

"What'd you say?" she asked.

"I said, at this damned NAAL dinner, I'll probably be the token white."

Good, she thought. She was starting to hate him again, which meant all of her values hadn't deserted her.

* * *

She spent the rest of the day listening to the message on Goodman's answering machine, trying to convince herself that Dyana Cooper was indeed as guilty as sin and attempting to ignore the doubts she was feeling about Virgil. The remaining odd few minutes of each hour she used to prepare for her Monday afternoon in court with several of the Willinses' staff, who were all expected to testify that the woman had not been in the domicile during the complete time frame the coroner had established for Madeleine Gray's murder.

At a little after noon, a clerk interrupted her to drop off two tacos and a cola. She ate and drank with gusto, at the same time dialing her home number to access her messages. Nothing from Goodman or Virgil. But her friend Victoria Allard had called to inform her of the arrival of several new items of clothing in her size.

Victoria answered on the second ring, her usually upbeat saleswoman's voice strangely subdued. "I've got a Ralph Lauren, a Calvin, and some Escada."

"I really need a knockout evening dress," Nikki said. "There's this big shindig tomorrow night and that Halston I bought about a hundred years ago is definitely ready to retire."

Victoria said she had a very slinky Donna Karan that shouldn't require too much alteration, unless Nikki had been letting herself go.

She regarded the remaining few bites of taco guiltily and asked Victoria to set the Donna Karan aside for her. She was having dinner with Loreen. They'd both drop by at about seven-thirty.

"I have nothing for Loreen," Victoria said with an odd anxiousness. "No reason for her to waste her time. You come, try on the dress, and then you can pick her up later."

Nikki said she would.

Satisfied that she'd solved the problem of what to wear to

Joe's award dinner, she downed the remnants of the taco and dove back into her work.

At three, she was interrupted by the chirp of the phone. She answered it, hoping it would be Ed Goodman. Or Virgil. Instead, an operator asked if she'd accept a collect call.

"Figgered I'd catch you at work," the familiar hoarse voice said. "Hot and heavy in the middle of the trial and all."

"What's up, Mace?"

"Scout is out," he said.

"I don't understand."

"Scout is out," he repeated. "You got people watchin' you."

"No kidding," she said. "I'm dodging cameras every time I set foot outside."

"I ain't talkin' about reporters and shit. I'm talkin' about watchers. You know, spy boys, watchin' what you do, reportin' back to other people where you are. Like that."

"Spy boys," she said.

"Yeah, you know. Gang spy boys, notify the gang what's happenin' on the street."

She felt a chill. She was going to have to pull the plug on Mace soon, she thought. Before his paranoia spread to her.

"Thanks for the report, Mace. Gotta go."

"They come to Mace in the liberry. Wanted to know about my trial. About you."

That caught her. "Who's 'they'?"

"Gangsta punks. Do a lot of braggin'. Say they got the scout out on you. Been follerin' you aroun'. See, they think I hate your ass. They don't know we friends."

"We're not friends, Mace."

That earned her a wet chuckle. "Like you didn't he'p me get my liberry job."

"I didn't."

"You say so. Just you take care, huh. Mace can't afford to lose a friend."

She replaced the receiver. Take care? Damn right she was going to take care.

At a little after six, she put her notes and files in her briefcase and called it a day.

Sonny was in the waiting area reading a worn paperback. Nikki glanced at its title before he shoved it into his coat pocket: *The Healing Power of Prayer.*

"You a religious man, Sonny?" she asked as their elevator descended to the parking level.

"I keep an open mind," he said.

He instructed her to stay in the alcove while he surveyed the garage area. Then he led her to his Oldsmobile. As they bounced out of the underground garage, she turned to check out the sparse traffic in their wake. No spy boys that she could see, thank you very much, Mace.

≡ SEVENTY-FIVE ≡

"N ice neighborhood," Sonny said, later that night, as he drove Nikki and Loreen along a peaceful thoroughfare in the Malaga Hills section of the Palos Verdes Peninsula. In the twenties the area had been one huge estate. By the midthirties developers had split it up into good-sized lots, selling them with the slogan "Own your own dude ranch."

Most of the homes still had that ranch motif—sprawling, built close to the ground and topped with shake roofs, with enough surrounding property to raise horses, if that was your idea of the good life.

"I prefer being a little closer in to the city, know what I mean," Loreen said. She had decided to come along for the ride, even though Victoria had nothing for her. She sat in front, next to Sonny.

Nikki, in the rear, looked out at the family homes and said, "Works for Victoria."

They'd grown up with Victoria Allard, whose last name had been Martin in those days. The all-pro basketball star Ken Allard had moved her from the old neighborhood into

Malaga Hills. Moved her in, lived with her for five years and dumped her for some young tramp. Rather than give up her home, she'd transformed it into a clothing boutique.

"Not much crime out here," Sonny said.

"That what turns you on? Crime?" Loreen asked him.

"Not exactly," he answered. "But I'm ready to handle it if it comes my way."

"I bet you are, Wesley. I just bet you are." The moment Nikki had introduced them, Loreen had told Sonny he reminded her of the actor Wesley Snipes. Nikki, who saw no similarity, didn't know if her friend was just being pleasant or if she was coming on to Sonny. Time would tell on that score. Loreen wasn't what you'd call shy.

"I do my job," Sonny said. "This the place?"

He'd stopped the Olds in front of a large ranch home with a healthy green lawn and several cars, including a BMW station wagon, parked in the drive.

"You did good, Wesley," Loreen said, opening her door and struggling to get out.

"We won't be more than fifteen or twenty minutes," Nikki told him.

"My time is yours," Sonny said without emotion.

"Man is sooo poetic," Loreen said without a trace of sarcasm. Definitely coming on to him. "Sure you don't want to come in," she asked him, "have a pop?"

"I don't drink on the job," he said, his eyes patrolling the quiet street.

Nikki pulled her friend away from the car. "C'mon, Delilah. Samson's not going anywhere."

As they approached the front door, Loreen asked, "You ever wonder where Victoria gets her goods?"

Nikki pressed the doorbell. "She says she's got contacts at the factories. Considering my measly little paycheck, I'm not about to press—"

Victoria's front door was opened by someone Nikki had never seen before. He was very young. Handsome. Clean-cut. Dressed in an orange and black Nike tennis outfit too crisp to have ever been used in a game that showed off his muscular arms and legs to advantage. The only thing marring his college-net-star appearance was a thick scar that began at his left elbow and continued nearly to his wrist.

"Oh, two of you. Well, come on in, ladies," he said. "My name is Rupert. I'll take you back to the rooms. Victoria will be with you in a minute."

As he led the way down an off-white hall toward the rear of the house, Loreen made obscene gestures behind his back until Nikki nearly burst with laughter.

Victoria had turned two large bedrooms into her display areas. Each was filled with racks of women's clothes of all styles and colors, arranged according to size.

"Browse like always," he said. "Can I get you a cup of coffee or a Coke? Or something stronger?"

"I'll have a Remy," Loreen said.

"Victoria's holding an evening dress for me," Nikki told him.

"I'll check," Rupert said. "And a drink?"

She shook her head. When he'd gone, Loreen said, "Victoria's sure got herself a fine-looking . . . assistant." She laughed.

Smiling, Nikki moved on to the next room in search of her size.

She was examining a designer jacket marked down from $500 to $250 when she heard Loreen saying, in a surprisingly arch tone, "What the hell's going on, Victoria?"

Curious, but not alarmed, she tried on the jacket. It felt all right, but she thought it might make her hips look a little too large. She walked to the mirror on the back wall.

"That's too grandma for you." The speaker was a young

woman standing in the doorway. She was wearing a strange silver-colored wig, an orange T-shirt, and black tights patterned with orange question marks of varying sizes. Black running shoes with a splash of orange at the toe completed the ensemble. She held a leather case maybe two feet long and four inches across. She carried it like some women carry purses, clasped between arm and side with her hand holding it from underneath. "Get yourself something kickin'," the girl said.

"You work for Victoria?" Nikki asked.

"Yeah, like I'm a salesgirl." She took a step back into the other room and shouted, "She's in here, trying on some industrial-looking old folks shit."

Her call brought Rupert. He smiled at Nikki and said, "Let's go see Victoria."

"What?" Nikki asked, confused.

"Everybody's waiting," he said. "Come on. I got something to show you."

"Hey, whip it out, boyfriend," the girl said, giggling.

Rupert ignored her. "Come on," he said to Nikki. "Let's go."

Nikki removed the coat she'd been trying on. It probably was too old for her.

They moved aside for her to precede them.

Victoria's office was a space so immaculate it resembled Hollywood's idea of a germ-free environment. White walls. White rug. White, glistening furniture. Even the computer was bone white. Two young men engulfed by orange and black gangsta garb, one short, one average, stood on either side of an anxious-looking Loreen. A third leaned against a wall.

Victoria sat at her white desk. Like Nikki, she'd been an awkward girl who'd improved considerably with age. She was wearing a casual pantsuit that looked like it had been made for her. She wouldn't meet Nikki's eyes.

"Guess my evening dress isn't ready, huh, girlfriend?" Nikki said.

"This wasn't my idea, Nikki," Victoria said.

"It wasn't you who called to get me here tonight?"

Victoria continued to look away.

"She's cooperating with her number one supplier," Rupert said. "Like we explained to her, we just want to pass along some information you can use. Thought it might be easier in a friendly atmosphere than out on the street."

Suddenly, everybody had information for her. "This atmosphere's getting less friendly by the second," she told him. "Say what you have to and let us out of here."

"Take a walk, just me and you."

"Don't go off with that punk, girl," Loreen said. The short gangsta beside her reached deep into his pocket and withdrew a knife. He moved his wrist, making figure eights in the air with the blade, bringing it closer to Loreen, who watched it with alarm.

Nikki recognized that figure-eight gesture. "You bastards were in my house," she said.

Unruffled, Rupert replied, "There you go. Was anybody hurt?"

She was seeing red. "You violate my home. You threaten me. Try to run over my dog. And now you brag on how nobody got hurt?"

"That dog thing was my li'l bro'. He don't much care for dogs. Come on now. Let's take that walk."

"I'm not going anywhere with you, little smart-ass turkey trying to act like a man."

Rupert's lips twitched. She cursed herself for losing her temper. The others were looking at their leader expectantly.

Even if he'd been sincere about his peaceful intentions, she'd forced his hand.

"We were told not to harm you," he said to Nikki. "But your ugly friend is fair game." The girl in the silver wig held out the long case. Rupert shook his head. He nodded to the boy with the knife. "Waste of a blade to cut on that face. The woman's got nice hair. Scalp her."

Nikki saw Loreen's eyes widen. Her hands went to her hair protectively.

The police special was in Nikki's purse, but she wasn't exactly Jackie Brown when it came to guns. "Enough bullshit," she said. "You got business with me, let's finish it."

"Now you're talking," Rupert said. He gestured to the door. Silver wig followed, but he stopped her. "This is private," he told her. "Let's give that scalping thing some further thought. It's an amusing idea, right?"

Not even his gang knew how to answer.

Rupert walked Nikki down the hall to what appeared to be a guest bedroom. He gestured toward a chair beside a table. A Manila folder rested on the table, facedown.

"Let me get my reading glasses," she said, starting to open her purse.

The boy grabbed the purse, tossed it away from them onto the bed. "Your eyesight's fine."

She sat down on the chair and looked at the folder. There was a brown smudge on its surface. "Is that dried blood?" she asked.

He sat on the edge of the bed, his knees close to hers. "Madeleine Gray's," he said.

"You kill her?"

"No. That's the whole point here," he said. "To get it straight who did. Go ahead. Open the folder."

She reached out, but hesitated about touching it. He stood

impatiently, bent over her, and grabbed the file, dropping it on her lap. "Don't worry about fingerprints. This is just for your eyes. It's not gonna wind up in any court, I can guarantee."

The typed label on the folder read "Soul Sister." Inside, she found copies of the documents Goodman had described. The marriage certificate. Newspaper accounts of the trial and conviction of Dyana Cooper's husband. His mug shot.

She studied the pages carefully, then looked up at Rupert. "Okay. Now what?"

"Don't you have any questions?"

"No." It was a lie, of course. Her mind was buzzing. Could he possibly be Goodman's source? If not, how did he get the file?

Her apparent disinterest seemed to unnerve him. He took the folder, straightening the sheets almost prissily. "This came from Madeleine Gray's house after the murder."

"I figured that."

"I didn't take this. The person who did was working for Dyana Cooper, doing the cleanup for her after she did the murder."

"You saying Dyana Cooper killed Maddie Gray?"

"That's what I'm saying."

"I'd like to talk to this cleanup person," Nikki said. "In the other room?"

He shook his head. "No. We were not involved in the murder in any way."

"You're just trying to save somebody's ass by throwing the blame on Dyana Cooper," she said.

"You don't give a shit for the truth, do you?" He was bristling. "You put Mason Durant in the joint, even though you weren't totally convinced he was guilty. We're concerned you might go in the other direction with Dyana

Cooper. So we're giving you all the proof you need that she killed Maddie Gray."

"How do you know about Mason Durant?"

"There are ways of finding out everything. Maddie taught me that."

"You knew her?"

"We helped her with stuff. That's why we don't want her killer to go free."

There was a knock at the door. Silver wig. "Time to book," she said.

He consulted the fancy sports watch on his wrist. "You hang in here for five minutes, Nikki," he said. "And maybe we won't scalp your friend."

He folded the file and jammed it into the waistband of his shorts. Then he grabbed her puse. At the door, he turned to her and held it up. "I'll leave this with Victoria. Be cool. Don't be a fool."

Don't worry about that, you little pissant, she thought.

She waited about two minutes and left the room.

Victoria was in her office, alone. "Nikki, please understand—"

"Where's Loreen?" she asked, grabbing her purse from the desk, checking to see if the gun was still there. It was.

"I told you not to bring her."

"Where is she?" Nikki demanded.

"They took her. Rupert said he'd let her off at her shop. He's not a bad—"

"Rupert's as bad as they get," Nikki said, moving toward the door. "Just because he looks like Tiger Woods doesn't mean he won't slit your throat for a quarter. They could have killed us, and you, too, without cracking a frown. Your business partners."

She shook her head in disgust and left the room.

Victoria ran after her. "Nobody's gonna be hurt," she shouted.

"We don't know that yet, do we?" Nikki threw open the front door. "We go back to being kids together, Victoria, and you set us up for this kind of bullshit? I promise you: They put one little bruise on her, you're gonna wind up doing time. And you're out of the clothing business as of right now."

"Don't try messin' with my business, Nikki," Victoria shouted.

"Or what? You'll put your thugs on me. Been there, done that."

Sonny was getting out of the Olds, a look of confusion on his broad face. "What's goin' on? Where's Miss Loreen?"

"Let's go find out," Nikki said.

For the first half of the drive, she had to keep interrupting his questions to urge him to go faster. For the second half, she had to keep interrupting his apologies.

They arrived at the beauty parlor just in time to see a black Chevy driving away, leaving a bewildered Loreen standing on the sidewalk in its wake.

Nikki was out of the Olds almost before Sonny could stop it at the curb. Her arms went around her friend. "I'm okay," Loreen said, trying to catch her breath. "They didn't do anything. I was so scared, Nikki."

Sonny joined them, looking sheepish. "I blew it," he said. "I shoulda come in."

"It might have made things worse," Nikki said. "We're all okay."

"I really screwed up," Sonny said. "I didn't even check the perimeter to see if there was a rear way in and out. I would have seen their car parked back there."

Loreen was fanning herself with her hand. "I'll forgive

you, Wesley," she said, "if you just do two things. First, drive us somewhere quick where I can get a cigarette and a shot of cognac for my nerves."

"And the second thing?" Sonny asked.

"We can talk about that later," she said.

SEVENTY-SIX

≡ SEVENTY-SIX ≡

Jamal was still living large. Enjoying room service. Piling up tube time. But his shyster, the king of the comb-over, wasn't giving him the attention he thought a new millionaire deserved. The last time they'd talked, the lawyer had asked him a mess of questions about Madeleine Gray's ring. Like the ring being in his pocket might be a deal breaker or something.

The dumb-ass ring.

All he'd had to do was pass that ring on by. The cracker cops would still have busted him on general principal. Then his false arrest case would've been golden.

But he had to grab the ring.

The brass ring. Wasn't there something about grabbing the brass ring?

Shit, it didn't matter.

He walked barefoot across the thick carpet into the bathroom. The first thing he was going to do when the eagle flew was to get a place with a shit stall like this. Floor to ceiling mirrors. He struck a few poses. Front and rear view. Looked fly. Superfly. He chuckled. He had a picture of the original Superfly on the wall of his place. Just as a goof. Big floppy felt hat. Droopy-ass lip brush. A ton of metal on his fingers. What were they thinking back then?

He peeled the bandages from his knife wounds.

Shit, they were just little slits now. Pinpoints where the stitches used to be. Didn't look much worse than the sex marks that sweet-and-hot Dorothea left on his back. Some pucker, but not bad. Still had that war wound thing. Impress the hell out of the ladies.

He thought he might just take a trip up to the rooftop pool. Catch the sunset. See what was lying around having evening cocktails. Comb-over told him to stick to his room, but, shit, it was a nice evening. *Won't be any shank-waving assholes up by the pool. Nobody with machetes, neither. Just some fine ladies, maybe, waiting to hear a little jaw music.*

He studied the collection of swim trunks he'd charged to his room from the shop in the lobby and selected a little thong number. In honor of the European women he'd noticed seemed to be in the majority poolside.

He slipped into the thong, slapped some cologne (seventy-five dollars the ounce, from the hotel shop) on his face, and selected one of his five new pairs of Ray-Bans, the sleek, skinny pair that looked like the shades Will Smith wore in that alien movie. He grabbed the fluffy white terrycloth robe with the hotel's crest. He slipped his plastic room card into a pocket of the robe and marched out to sample the delights of the evening.

He'd just settled on a cushioned lounging chair, pillow behind his head, wine spritzer on the deck near his right hand, when there was a tap on his shoulder. He put on his best dude-of-the-world expression and sat up, twisting a little to show off his abs.

Carlos Morales stood beside his chair. "Been lookin' all over town for you, Jamal," he said. "How's about we have a little talk? Or would you rather get your bony ass tossed off this fucking roof?"

≡ SEVENTY-SEVEN ≡

Goodman spent the weekend at Gwen's apartment.

She didn't want to be by herself.

They ate, watched TV. Didn't talk much. Didn't make love.

It wasn't until Sunday morning that the detective decided to call home for messages.

He was surprised to hear the electronic voice say that he had nine. He rarely got more than two or three, especially on weekends. As they unspooled, he discovered that they'd come from only three people.

The winner with most calls, six, had been Nikki Hill. She'd started phoning Saturday morning and gone on until the early evening. Judging by the messages, she was in need of some sort of information or advice. As her messages tapered off, his partner's began. At a little after six P.M., Carlos had wanted Goodman to phone immediately. Something needed to be done and he wasn't sure he could handle it by himself.

The next Morales message, an hour later, was a bit more

profane and abusive, suggesting that Goodman disengage from a sexual activity that was unlawful in most of the United States and answer the damned phone. The final message, made at eleven-forty-three P.M., the night before, was from his depressed neighbor across the hall, Dennis Margolis, whispering that he could hear someone trying to break into Goodman's apartment. He thought it might be the fake policemen. "If you're in there asleep, Ed, better wake up," Dennis had cautioned.

With a curse, he dialed Dennis's number. Naturally, there was no answer. Second on the list was Nikki. Another frustrating miss. Finally, he phoned Morales's home and got his partner's wife, who began shouting at him in Spanish.

"Whoa, there, Estella," he said. "Tell me what the problem—"

"The pro'lem is my husban' not here this morning. I got no husban', no car, no way to get to Mass with the kids. The pro'lem is I doan see Carlos for two damn days. Where is the bastar'? He say he with you."

"I'm gonna have to get back to you on this, Estella," Goodman said. He dropped the receiver onto the cradle as if it had suddenly turned into a rattlesnake.

Gwen looked at him with raised eyebrows.

"Somebody broke into my place. I got to get over there, check the damage, see if anything needs doing. I want you to stay here until you hear from me."

"Why don't I come along and—"

"No good. I want you to be around to pull the plug on Doyle and Adler if anything happens to me."

"That's a great plan, Eddie," she said. "I can just hang out here, watching the tube and wondering if you're alive or dead."

"I'll call you from the apartment in thirty minutes," he said. "If I don't, send out the troops. Good enough?"

"Don't do anything brave or stupid," she said.

"Don't worry, honey, I have great plans for my remaining years," he told her.

The noonday sun was hot enough to melt rubber. Goodman parked behind his apartment building and entered through the back door. He took the rear stairwell two steps at a time but proceeded cautiously along the corridor leading to his door.

He touched a key to the lock and the door pushed open. He gave it a harder push and it swung inward, the still-extended slip lock moving through splintered wood.

His gun was in his hand as he stepped over the threshold.

Carlos Morales was lying on his couch, eating a handful of breakfast cereal. "'Bout time you showed up," he said. "Doan you ever come home anymore?"

"You been here all night?"

"Where else am I gonna go?"

"You broke the damned door," Goodman said, holstering his pistol.

"You doan keep no key on the molding or under the welcome mat. You doan answer the phone. What am I supposed to do? Hey, how long they been havin' these little pieces of breakfast food that taste like graham crackers?"

"Your wife's going nuts, Carlos."

"Tell me something new."

"Go home."

"Can't."

"Why not?"

He gestured with his chin toward the rear of the apartment. "Bedroom."

Hugely annoyed, Goodman stomped to the darkened bedroom. A black teenager in orange and black gangsta wear was lying on the floor, handcuffed to an iron bedpost. He glared up at Goodman and bared his teeth. He had cuts on his face and his right eye was swollen.

Morales stood at the door. "This here's Fupdup," he said.

"Your fuckin' ass is dead, man," the boy shouted in a high, hysterical voice.

"Why's he in my bedroom?"

Morales gestured with his head and led him back into the living room.

"I tole you this was all gang shit. Fupdup's a Crazy Eight."

"Why is he in my bedroom?" Goodman asked again.

"Because he's one of the ones dumped Maddie Gray in that alley."

Goodman saw a Corona bottle on the carpet. "Was that the last beer?"

"Couple more in the fridge," Morales said.

He followed Goodman into the kitchenette, continuing to talk while his partner opened a Corona. "Remember when Jamal was tellin' us about almos' catchin' his lunch from the gang in that alley?" Goodman nodded, taking his first sip of beer. "At the time, we forgot to ask him if he could ID any of the Eights in the car. So I been tryin' to get aholt of Mistah Deschamps to pose that question. Figured that lawyer had him hid away in a hotel, so I been checking 'em all, startin' with the most expensive."

"That's where you been disappearing to the last couple weeks?"

Morales nodded. "You can't do it by phone, amigo. You got to go and talk with the help. I foun' him yesterday. You know, I had Jamal all wrong. The man's a dude. He was happy to cooperate."

Goodman gave him a skeptical look.

"Well, maybe I had to twist his arm a little, but he tells me the banger who nearly nailed him is named Fupdup."

"He saw him?"

"No. He heard one of his asshole buddies call out to him. Anyways, Fupdup don' have much up here," he said, tapping his head, "but his big brother, Rupert, is runnin' the Eights these days and he don't want the bangers calling his li'l bro a fuckup, so he named him himself. Fupdup."

"Jamal told you all this?"

"I doan need Jamal for that kind of information. I know these *cucarachas*. I know every fuckin' one of 'em, where they live, where they eat and drink, and where they hang out. Took me less'n an hour to get my hands on Fupdup. He's a big gamblin' man. Loses 'bout a gran' a week back of the Ready-Burger on Western Avenue. 'Course, Lorenzo, th' dude runs the game, pays Rupert two gran' for the privilege of having Fupdup piss off the other players. Anyway, none of them seemed to mind me leavin' with the little bastard, not that they had any choice."

"What do you expect to do with him?" Goodman asked.

"I already did, amigo. C'mon, he'll tell you."

"Let me make a call first."

He made it quick, telling Gwen he and the apartment were fine and that she shouldn't worry. He suggested she stay in. He'd join her later. How much later? He wasn't sure.

"That a ring in your nose, amigo?" Morales asked him when he'd hung up.

Goodman just sighed.

In the bedroom, the boy glared at them furiously.

"Fupdup," Morales said, "tell *mi amigo* about Maddie Gray."

The boy squinted. "Fuck you!"

Morales removed his gun from his holster.

Goodman tensed. He hoped his partner wasn't going to shoot the boy.

"You know me," Morales said. "Crazy Cop?" The boy

nodded. "You held your mud longer than even your brother would have. But you already gave it up. All I'm askin' for is a repeat. Doan make us do that dance again."

The boy looked at Goodman. "We dump the white bitch in the alley," he said.

"You kill her?" Goodman asked.

"Shit no."

"Who did?"

Morales smiled, watching the boy.

"Don't know for sure. She dead, is all I know. We drive out to this place, put the dead bitch in the trunk and cart her off to the hood, dump her ass in the bucket. Then we remember the ring, go back and the fuckin' cops come along."

"Tell 'im where you picked up the body," Morales said.

"Place out o' town where honks go to dry out. The Sanktum."

Morales grinned at Goodman. "Nice, huh?"

"Who sent you out there to pick her up?" Goodman asked. "Rupert say it some Ninja Turtle we gotta help."

"What's the Ninja Turtle's name?" Goodman asked.

"I just tole you. Name like a Ninja Turtle."

Goodman turned to his partner.

"Don't ask me," Morales said. "This guy's Tap City in the brains. It's his brother who's got the answers."

"How do we find *him?*"

"I know where he lives, but he's got all these shooters around him there. We'll jus' hang here and wait for a better opportunity. Shouldn't be too long."

"What makes you think so?"

Morales put his hand to his belt, tapped something there. "Fupdup's beeper. Chirped a couple times yesterday evenin'. I let him return the call. It was Rupert. Big bro tole him they had some work to do last night. The Fup man was under my gun and behaved himself and said what I'd told him, that he was with a ladyfren' and couldn't make it. Rupert gave him a pass for last night, but said for him to be sure to be on call tonight. So I think we can expect a beep before too long."

Goodman asked the boy, "What's happening tonight?"

"Ooocie juicie," the boy said. "Rupert calls, tells me where to be for the ooocie juicie and that's where I be. Rupert's the man."

Goodman walked out of the bedroom in search of another Corona, Morales at his heels. "What do we do with him, Carlos?"

"Can't turn him in," Morales said. "He'd be out in ten minutes and I'd be spending the rest of my life explaining the cuts on his face."

"Speaking of that, how old is he?"

"Sixteen. So what?" Morales asked defensively. "He and his woman got two kids and Lorenzo tells me he and a buddy stomped a guy to death after a card game. You start thinking that's a little boy in there, you gonna wind up dead."

"Okay. So we can't arrest him."

"Anyway, we need him to lead us to Rupert."

Goodman nodded and swallowed his beer. "If we get Rupert and he opens up to us, you know what we're going to find out?"

"Sure," Morales said. "I knew that soon's Fupdup tole me Maddie's body was at the Sanctum. The wrong fuckin' Willins is standin' trial for murder."

≡ SEVENTY-EIGHT ≡

The previous night, Nikki had decided she no longer needed Sonny's "protection." If Rupert and his gang were inclined to harm her, they'd had every opportunity. The dispirited bodyguard had notified his alternate they were off the case.

His confidence was bolstered a little by Loreen's insistence that she'd feel much safer if he'd stick around and have dinner with them. Dinner and drinks at a nearby Mexican restaurant. A couple of margaritas later, Sonny began telling them stories from his crime file, some of them quite lurid.

By the end of dinner, Loreen was nearly her old self, her chair shifted so that she was almost in Sonny's lap. Nikki was starting to relax, too. She suggested she would take a cab home, but Sonny insisted on driving. He was not drunk, merely mellow.

The bodyguard and Loreen waited in the car until she unlocked her front door, and Bird eagerly took over the job as her protector.

She woke up a little after noon.

She'd had bizarre dreams, prompted by the evening's mixture of stress and alcohol. On awakening, she couldn't remember any of them. She lay on her back, her mind muddled, trying to sift through facts and theories. Top of the list was her belief that she was prosecuting an innocent woman. She wanted to simply close her eyes. Sleep was such a tempting alternative to real life. The hell of it was that you had to get up eventually or they'd bury you.

She fed Bird, made sure he took his pill. Then she prepared to burn off the tequilla-and-taco residue.

First stop was the dune. Then a run along the path at Manhattan Beach, slow enough for Bird not to overwork under the hot sun. The whole time her mind was a jumble of questions. Could Virgil possibly be tied in with Rupert and his gang? Would Rupert have any reason to harm Loreen? Did Loreen and Sonny get hooked up? Could she continue to prosecute Dyana Cooper? How much should she tell Joe Walden?

She stopped for a late lunch at an outdoor cantina where the owner, Rafael, didn't mind having Bird on the patio as long as he behaved himself. The big dog relaxed at his mistress's feet, watching her intently while she nibbled a salad and reshuffled the questions on her mind.

It was four-thirty when she returned home.

Almost by rote, she cleaned up the bedroom, sort of, showered, and, wrapped in a robe, with the great Aretha wailing through the sound system, she took the Sunday *L.A. Times* to the patio. Not until she went to the kitchen for a glass of milk did she notice the blinking light on her answering machine.

Virgil had phoned the night before at ten. At ten-thirty. At ten-forty-five. At eleven-fifteen. And again at midnight. His messages did not suggest annoyance. Merely resignation and disappointment.

She was about to stop the tape to call him when she heard Goodman's voice saying, "Sorry I didn't get back to you, I just got your messages. I'll try again." Recorded at 12:24 P.M., just after she'd left for the dune.

There were two more calls.

One was from Virgil. "Man, that musta been some dinner with your girlfriend. Later." One P.M.

The final was Goodman again, at 1:53 P.M. "We've got to talk. It looks like Maddie Gray didn't die at home after all. The murder took place at the Sanctum. I'll . . . " There was a loud crash in the background. Then angry shouting. "Sorry," Goodman said. "Got a situation here."

She dialed the detective's number and reached his answering machine.

Damn! How had he found out about the Sanctum? Did he have proof? What was the noise she'd heard? What the hell was he up to? That's what she needed: more questions.

The Sanctum! No wonder that stiff-necked manager had been so nervous on the stand. He must have been scared shitless trying not to perjure himself.

If the Sanctum was the scene of the crime almost everything Rupert had told her had been a lie. What he'd said, and what all of the evidence indicated, was that Dyana had murdered Maddie at the house in Laurel Canyon. Lose that location as the crime scene and the case against Dyana Cooper disintegrated.

A new, very strong suspect would then emerge. John Willins.

He and Maddie go to the Sanctum. They argue. He kills her and takes the body away, to the Dumpster. She frowned. *Why did they argue? Lovers' quarrel? Then who went to the house and pried open the file drawer?*

No. Not exactly a lovers' quarrel. She's been drunk and angry all day. She gets mad at him, tells him she has a file on him that could cause him grief. This so infuriates him that he kills her. Later, he has to retrieve the file.

He doesn't realize that Maddie also was keeping a file on his wife. Maybe he even flips past it, not knowing the significance of the title "Soul Sister." He goes home and the first thing Dyana tells him is how her day went, leading with the fight at Maddie's. Concerned that his wife might actually be implicated in the murder, he goes running to Hobart Adler, who, in turn, brings in his fixer, James Doyle.

Where do the gangstas fit in? Did they really work for Maddie? Possibly. Would they run the risk of terrorizing a district attorney just to seek revenge on Dyana through the court? No way. They wouldn't give a damn about the trial; they'd be more direct. Probably try to take her out in a drive-by.

Or a hit-and-run! God, is there any way Dimitra . . . ? It's possible. Why would they have done it, though? What danger did Dimitra pose? I can see the reason the gangstas would want Dyana to be found guilty: then the real murderer could rest easy. But if the real murderer is John Willins . . . ?

Even though she'd witnessed many examples of man's inhumanity throughout her career, the depth of her feeling about this one surprised her. She'd seen mothers blame their crimes on their daughters, fathers on sons, brothers on brothers. A husband setting up his wife to save his own worthless hide was par for the course. Nikki realized she'd fallen victim to the cult of celebrity; like the rest of the world, she'd been suckered by the media manipulators into believing that Dyana Cooper and John Willins were the ideal couple.

Now, she was convinced, the perfect husband was going to great lengths to make sure that his perfect wife was found guilty of a crime he had committed. Not that she could prove he'd done it. Even so, she had to tell her boss about this Sanctum development.

He wasn't at home, however, and he didn't respond to his beeper.

Then she remembered that in exactly—she looked at her watch—one hour and ten minutes he'd be attending a cocktail party at the Hotel Balmoral before going in to the dinner where he was to receive the African-American Leadership award.

She ran into her bedroom, threw open her jammed and jumbled closet, and began searching for the black Halston cocktail dress she'd hoped she'd never have to wear again. Double-damn that Victoria Allard.

≡ SEVENTY-NINE ≡

Two boys, neither older than nine or ten, circled a battered and rusty mud-brown panel truck that was parked, apparently untended, in the middle of a run-down block of Normandie Avenue. The cracked and sunbaked white lettering stating that the truck belonged to Adam's TV, had the boys wondering if Adam might be lame enough to have left his truck in that neighborhood with TV sets in the back.

They moved in on the double doors at the rear of the vehicle.

The taller boy reached out and tested the handle.

Suddenly, from inside the truck, a monster dog from hell started barking insanely. It rammed the rear doors, which were obviously just barely holding it in.

The boys ran off down the street.

"Still think Leander's a bonehead, amigo?" Morales asked as he turned off the tape recorder and duckwalked back to a canvas chair inside "Adam's" truck.

Goodman was sitting on a matching chair directly behind

the vehicle's forward panel. The window to the cab had been painted over, except for a tiny dot the size of a fingertip. A little device similar to a front door security scope had been Krazy-Glued to that spot. By applying an eye to the scope, Goodman got a windshield view of the street.

"I didn't say he was a bonehead," he clarified, "I said he was a fanatic. Who else but a fanatic would buy his old surveillance vehicle from the garage when he mustered out?" The owner of the truck was a retired vice cop named Al Leander. "Who else would have tapes of dogs barking?"

"You gotta admit, this stuff comes in handy."

"What's Leander need it for? He's retired."

"Let's be thankful he had it," Morales said. "Not many LAPD guys, retired or active, I'd trust with Fupdup. On one side, they'd kill the little bastard as soon as look at 'im. On the other, they'd feel sorry for him and let him go. Leander'll keep him chained up in his basement, but he'll feed him and maybe even let him listen to the friggin' ham radio. We're lucky we got Leander."

Goodman wasn't so sure. He wasn't so sure about any of Morales's fall-back plan.

The original plan hadn't been that great either, but at least they could have hung around the apartment until Rupert beeped his little brother. Sitting slumped in the canvas chair wasn't doing his back much good, and the intense heat was baking him. In fact, he'd stopped sweating, which he thought was a symptom of dehydration. The gangstas in the house on the corner, the one belonging to Rupert and Fupdup's auntie, weren't showing any signs of leaving.

If only Fupdup hadn't unscrewed the bedpost and tried to brain Morales with it, forcing Morales to bang into the wall and smash the kid's beeper, they could be relaxing with air-conditioning and a Corona.

"I'm thirsty," he complained.

"There's a mom-and-pop a couple blocks south got all the Cokes and beer you need. Big old honky like you never be noticed in the hood."

"There really a mom-and-pop around here?"

"Sure. Over on Denker."

"How do you know this neighborhood so well?"

Morales was using another of Leander's peepholes. "My sister Pilar lived a couple blocks away," he said.

Goodman was surprised. "A Chicana lived in this neighborhood by herself?"

"Not by herself. Pilar was a teacher, got assigned a school up on Western Avenue. She met this other teacher, black guy named Luther Bing. A little wimpy, but okay. Moved in with him."

"They don't live here anymore?" Goodman asked.

"They don't live anywhere anymore," Morales said, drawing back from his spy hole. "See, the Crazy Eights— not Rupert and his asshole buddies; this was some years ago—they didn't exactly approve of mixed couples on their turf. So they tole Luther, he wants to eat tamales, he should go live in East L.A. Luther picked a real bad time to brave it out. He said they couldn't chase him away. So they gutted him right on his front porch and went inside the house and raped and killed my sister."

Goodman stared at his partner.

"There were eight of 'em," Morales said. "Proud of what they did. Went around bragging about cleanin' up the neighborhood. My brother officers did what they was supposed to and pulled 'em in. That fucker Thomas J. Gleason was head deputy D.A. then. He said there wasn't enough evidence for a conviction. There was never enough evidence, as far as Big Tom was concerned.

"My ole man, he wouldn't accept that. He kept pushing for somebody to do something. He found one piece of evidence, a neckerchief they traced to this prick who was called Lee-O. The old man was the kind of guy who never let up. Finally the cops went after Lee-O. He died before they could nail him."

"Died how?" Goodman asked.

"Burned to death. Seven of 'em are dead. None by my hand, amigo. A couple OD'd, or maybe it was the Colombians sending a message to the Crazies that they were unhappy with their drug arrangement. One guy drowned. Another got shot in that big bank robbery in San Diego about six years ago. I don't know 'bout the other, 'cept he not around anymore. Maybe dead. Maybe moved away."

He resumed his position at the peephole.

Goodman was reeling: what must it have been like for his partner, being a cop and having to stand by while the punks who raped and—

"They're movin'," Morales said, doing a fast duckwalk to the rear door.

By the time he and Goodman had hopped into the cab of the truck, the black Chevy was nearly two blocks away. Morales stepped on the gas, smiling merrily. "We're on 'em like white on rice."

The Chevy was tearing down Exposition Boulevard, heading east to the Harbor Freeway.

Morales closed the gap a little. "Chevy look familiar, amigo?" he asked.

There was something about it, Goodman thought.

Morales brought it into focus for him. "On the day Arthur Lydon lost his guts to the pigeons, we went up to Maddie Gray's house to see if he was there."

"Right," Goodman said.

"That Chevy," Morales said as he moved the truck through the gathering traffic, "was coming down the hill from the Gray house when we were going up."

They entered the freeway and rolled north. The sun had set on the weekend, and several lanes of other motorists headed in the same direction, most of them thinking about dinner. Goodman was thinking about his partner, realizing how stupid it was to ever take anybody at face value.

"They might be headin' to your place," Morales reported just before their truck dipped down the exit leading to the Hollywood Freeway.

Headlights were blinking on as the Chevy barreled along. Goodman tried the radio. Cool jazz filled his head, each note as clear and precise as if the combo were in the truck with them. "Super-stereo," Morales noted. "Say what you want about Leander, amigo, the man knows what he likes."

"Too bad he didn't install a water fountain," Goodman said.

The Chevy left the freeway at Cahuenga and went south along that boulevard until Sunset, when it turned right. Dusk was rapidly segueing into night.

"Heading to Willins's office?" Goodman wondered.

The Chevy made a right before that, at Sunset Plaza Drive.

Goodman's heart was racing. He began his calming exercises. It would take more than steady breathing to still his excitement.

The Chevy was headed up the hill toward Jimmy Doyle's villa.

Morales downshifted and moved up the steep drive, catching the Chevy in his headlights as it kissed the curb and stopped. Passing by the black car, Goodman pushed his peripheral vision to the max, but still couldn't make out its shadowy passengers. "I don't get it," he said. "Why'd they park so far below Doyle's place?"

"Either he tole 'em he doan want a gangmobile parked in front of his house, or they payin' a surprise visit."

He eased the truck to a stop above the villa and the two detectives got out. They walked down the twisting drive until they found a section of the road that allowed them full view of the house Doyle was renting. Goodman's eyes were drawn to the sight of the Hollywood flats far below to their left, miles and miles of lights shimmering like zircons in the clear night.

He shifted his focus to the villa, then past it, squinting down the drive. "You see the Chevy?" he asked.

"Naw. Just one big shadow down there. You'd think these homeowners would spring for some streetlights."

They moved down until they were less than twenty yards from the villa. They could hear someone singing a cappella. Doyle. Wailing an Irish ditty about a politician named Dough-erty who won an election by a very large majority.

Down the hill, car doors slammed.

The detectives retreated from the villa into the shadows.

Goodman saw the young men sauntering up the hill. Four of them were typical gangstas, but the one in front was a real style setter. No baggy pants for him. He wore his colors in the form of a bright orange jacket and pleated black trousers. He carried a long, flat leather case.

When the group reached the villa, they spread out. Two explored the outer edges of the building, crawling over the waist-high wall and continuing toward the rear, where the structure cantilevered over the hill. While they skulked silently across the patio tiles, orange jacket and a sidekick strolled to the front door. The remaining gangsta took up a lookout position near the curb in front.

The doorbell chimed. Doyle's singing stopped briefly, then began again.

Goodman shifted his position and was able to get an angle

on the front door when it opened. The big vice cop, Lattimer, stood in the doorway. "Yeah?" he inquired of the two boys, his deep voice floating on the night.

"You Mr. Doyle?" orange jacket asked politely.

Lattimer stepped back out of Goodman's line of sight. The detective could hear him shout, "You expecting anybody, Jimmy?"

Orange jacket and his pal entered the villa. The pal closed the door.

"If she's a heartless lady with raspberry-colored hair, send her up," the detectives heard Doyle call out. He began to sing again. "Two by two, they marched into the dining hall. Young men and old men and girls who weren't men at—"

The singing ended abruptly with a sound resembling a cough and a gurgle.

"Shit," Goodman hissed and started forward.

Morales moved more quickly and more gracefully.

By the time the lookout heard the soft scrape of rubber sole to his right, the butt of Morales's pistol was on its way to that sweet spot above his ear.

Morales dragged the unconscious boy behind the waist-high wall while Goodman, his own gun drawn, circled the property to the left.

The main patio at the rear of the villa was in darkness, but faint light spilled out of open doors over the pale pink flagstones. Just beyond the doors was a dining room. The light came from a stairwell against the far wall.

Goodman, seeing no gangstas, slipped inside the villa, moving cautiously over the thick carpet toward the stairs. Conversation drifted down the stairwell. ". . . could cut your friend's ear off," a male voice was saying. "Better yet, I'm sorta fascinated by the idea of scalping someone. We could do that, to show you we mean business."

"I'll take your word for it," Doyle said, sounding surprisingly calm.

Goodman felt something jab into his back. "Drop it, mother-fucker," someone hissed.

The detective didn't hesitate. His gun hit the carpet without a sound.

"Wassup down there?" the voice shouted from above.

From behind Goodman, the gunman replied, "'S'okay, Rupert. We jus' messin' aroun'."

"Then stop it!"

Goodman turned. The boy was at least a foot shorter than he, dressed in baggy black and orange, baseball cap backward on his head. He had a Colt .45 in his small hand, pointed at Goodman's gut. Behind him, Morales's gun was pressed against the top of his baseball cap, persuading the boy to lie to Rupert. Goodman took the Colt from the little gangsta's fingers and picked up his own weapon from the carpet.

"So we're clear on the plan?" Rupert asked somebody upstairs.

"By tomorrow evening, I'll be long gone," Doyle replied, sounding like he meant it. "I don't suppose you'd tell me who sent you here. As a professional courtesy?"

Morales grabbed his gangsta and shoved him up the stairwell past Goodman.

They heard Rupert chuckle. "You've got brass, fatso."

"I'd just hate to think you and I might be working for the same folks and they picked this unfriendly way to cancel my contract."

"Guess that's a mystery you'll never solve."

Morales pushed the gangsta to the top of the stairs, using him as a shield. "Hey, everybody chill, huh?" Morales yelled.

Goodman entered the scene with caution. One of the

punks was sitting on a couch next to Lattimer, flash frozen with his pistol casually prodding the cop's side. Lattimer had an unhealthy-looking lump on his chin and a lightning bolt of blood extending down from the left corner of his mouth.

Doyle was standing at the foot of his bed, wearing only boxer shorts, black socks, and black wing tip shoes. His body was pale and puffy. A livid red welt extended from the bottom right of his jaw to his temple. He regarded Morales without expression.

Next to him was the obvious leader of the gang, brandishing an outsize knife with a long blade that was sleek and smooth and gently curved. It must have been resting inside the leather case Goodman had seen the boy carrying, which now lay open on the bed. The boy suddenly pressed the blade to Doyle's throat and said, "Another step, I'll slice him clean."

"Rupert, you make my mouth water," Morales told him.

The boy with the knife looked confused. "You know me?"

"I know shit when I see it."

"One's missing," Goodman said, walking past Morales, a gun in each hand. His weapon was pointed at Rupert, the banger's Colt aimed in the general vicinity of the boy with Lattimer.

"No," Morales said. "I popped that one on the way in."

Goodman edged toward the boy on the couch, giving Rupert a wide berth.

The boy watched him coming. He didn't know what the hell to do. He looked to Rupert for some clue, but Rupert was having his own moment of indecision. Lattimer broke the ice by grabbing the boy's gun and smacking the kid in the face with it. Blood gushed from the gangsta's broken nose.

As the vice cop drew back for another slam, Goodman said, "That's enough," pointing his guns at Lattimer now.

The vice cop looked at him, amazed. "What?"

"Hand over the weapon," Goodman ordered.

Lattimer snorted, hesitated, then presented the pistol to Goodman, grip first. "You gonna hear more about this," he said.

"Yeah, right," Goodman said. "Like you're gonna hear about swapping department secrets with the Irish tenor over there."

"I think we're leaving now," Rupert said, dragging Doyle a few feet toward the stairs. His blade nicked the short man's throat and a line of red formed immediately.

Without warning, Morales shoved his gangsta shield toward Rupert. His weapon now covered both of them.

"You're the one they call Crazy Cop," Rupert said. Morales grinned. "I hope you're not so crazy you force me to kill this guy."

"Do it," Morales said. "I'm tired of waitin'."

At that moment Rupert realized it was no bluff. As far as Morales was concerned, his hostage was worthless. "Shit," he said, and withdrew the blade from Doyle's neck.

"Drop the pigsticker, Rupert," Morales commanded.

Rupert raised the blade to his lips, kissed it, then turned and placed it in its case.

Doyle drove his fist into the boy's kidney. Rupert yelped and fell against the bed. Doyle straddled him, pounded his neck, and rode him to the carpet. He grabbed Rupert's ear in his fist and twisted it. The boy howled. "Who sent you here, you little prick?"

"Fuck you," Rupert replied between screams.

Doyle released his hold and stepped away. "Lovely city you guys got here," he said to Goodman. He grabbed a

Kleenex from the box at his bedside and began dabbing at the cut on his neck.

"Who do you think sent 'em?" Goodman asked.

Doyle shrugged. "Could be anybody. There's no loyalty anymore. Know who your only friends are, detective? The people you got the goods on. They respect you. Since they've got the goods on you, the feeling is mutual."

He moved to his dresser and started to reach into an open drawer.

"Hold it," Goodman ordered.

Doyle held it. He shook his head. "Just gettin' a shirt."

Goodman looked inside the drawer. He nodded and Doyle removed a starched white dress shirt. "It's the New Wild West," the Irishman said. "Everybody's carrying. I don't have a gun; I must be from out of town."

Morales ordered the three gangstas to eat the rug. When they were stretched out on the carpet, he patted them down, one by one, removing gravity knives, a palm-size Intratec 9 mm, pagers, thick rolls of cash, vials of cocaine.

Lattimer, who'd been watching Morales with bored indifference, seemed surprised when Goodman said to him, "Now you."

"What?"

"On the floor," Goodman said, pointing his gun at the vice cop.

Lattimer lowered himself in stages, cursing Goodman the whole time. The detective found no other weapon, but he did discover a computer disk in the vice cop's jacket pocket. "What's this?" Goodman asked.

"Work."

"Good," the detective said, slipping the disk into his pocket. "I'd like to see the kind of work you do."

Doyle had put on his pants. He pulled a suitcase from his

closet and placed it on the bed. "The LAPD," he said, shaking his head. "You think you got it all under control."

Goodman looked around the room. "Something we missed?"

"Do the math, bucko," Doyle said, pulling out handfuls of underwear and socks from the dresser. "Punks like these outnumber you two to one. They're all armed with superknives or Uzis." He dumped the clothing into the suitcase. "It takes eight or nine of you to subdue just one stoned asshole like Rodney King. And he didn't even have a weapon. So do the fucking math."

He shoved more clothes into the suitcase.

"You going somewhere?" Goodman asked.

"Count on it. This town's not for Jimmy Doyle."

"What's the deal, Jimmy?" Goodman asked. "Who'd you piss off, besides me?"

"Fuck if I know, Goodman. As you heard, young blood over there wasn't in a name-dropping mood."

"You do anything to annoy your client?"

"Dyana? She and I are solid."

"I meant her husband."

Doyle paused and gave it some thought. Then he shrugged and went back to his packing. "Who knows?" he said.

"Him," Goodman said, pointing to Rupert.

"Yeah, well . . ."

"Let's load up and vamoose, huh?" Morales said.

Goodman nodded. He spotted an empty cleaner's shirt box on the floor and began dumping the weapons, beepers, money, and drugs into it.

"Nice little haul, boys," Doyle said with a smirk. "Drugs, cash. A useful little throw-down. Cop's delight."

"You've been spending too much time with Lattimer," Goodman said.

Morales grabbed the back of Rupert's orange jacket and jerked him upright. The boy looked wobbly. "I'm not going anywhere with you," he said.

"Like you got a choice," Morales said, cackling. He pushed him toward the stairs.

"You guys can't just leave," Doyle said. "There are bodies all over this place."

"Let your cop take care of it," Goodman said. He took one of Doyle's neatly folded handkerchiefs and used it to pick up the case containing Rupert's long knife.

"Hey," Lattimer shouted. "Catch 'em."

Goodman watched as the two unguarded bangers raced out onto the balcony and clambered down over the rail. "That'll simplify your cleanup, Lattimer," he said.

"Some fucking city," Doyle said. "Get ready for Armageddon, boys. It's on your back doorstep." He followed them to the top of the stairs and shouted down. "Think of me when the revolution begins. I'll be three thousand miles away, watching you fuckers burn and die out here, courtesy of CNN."

"Talk, talk, talk," Morales grumbled, dragging Rupert past one of his unconscious gang brothers. "That fucking Doyle's got diarrhea of the mouth."

≡ EIGHTY ≡

"The elevator at the end goes directly to the Grand Ballroom, Ms. Hill," the concierge at the Hotel Balmoral said.

She thanked him, thinking not for the first time that celebrity might turn out to be a mixed blessing. On one hand, it was nice to be recognized. On the other, having everyone suddenly know your name was creepy.

Her fellow passengers on the elevator—the men in tuxes, the women elaborately gowned—greeted her with smiles of recognition. Though she assumed half of them despised her for what they considered to be the wrongful persecution of Dyana Cooper, she smiled back. After all, she thought, she probably *had* been wrongfully persecuting the woman.

The elevator opened to a noisy, milling crowd in the midst of a cocktail party. To the right were the closed doors of the Grand Ballroom, where the dinner would be held shortly. To the left were floor-to-ceiling windows offering a view of the moodily purple evening sky and the Pacific coastline to Malibu and beyond. In between were several hundred people in evening wear, networking, wheeling, dealing, and, in some rare instances, merely talking trash and enjoying themselves.

Nikki moved into the fray, searching for Joe Walden. She couldn't believe there were so many tall black men in one place. She began to think that height might be a requirement of the National Association of African-American Leadership when she spotted a woman no taller than five feet wearing the multicolored badge (red, white, blue, green, yellow, and black) that indicated she was a member rather than just a guest. She had Ray Wise backed against the wall and was shaking a finger in his face.

Sadistically, Nikki decided not to interrupt, continuing the search for her boss. She found him at a far corner of the room, talking animatedly with the mayor, the assistant police chief, and a few others. She stood on the periphery of the group and tried to catch his eye.

The crowd hushed suddenly. Nikki saw the people around her staring in the direction of the elevator. Joe, the mayor, and the others were staring, too. The assistant police chief's mouth was hanging open in surprise.

She turned to find out what could possibly provoke such a reaction.

The elevator had just disgorged a group of newcomers. In their midst, looking like they had just stepped from the cover of *Entertainment Weekly*, were Mr. and Mrs. John Willins.

≡ EIGHTY-ONE ≡

Alvin Leander had taken to smoking a pipe in retirement. Its acrid fumes filled the clean little room attached to his garage. Other than the smoke, it was, Goodman thought, the ideal place to piddle away your declining years. One side of the small, well-insulated, windowless space was devoted to an elaborate ham radio setup where he assumed the ex-cop spent many a happy hour talking with other old men with too much time on their hands.

Across from that was Leander's remarkably well outfitted tool and woodworking station. Its main element was a solid hardwood workbench that, thanks to Goodman and Morales, now had the Crazy Eights siblings, Rupert and Fupdup, firmly tied to its opposite ends.

Leander, whom Goodman guessed to be no more than five years older than he, had put on a little weight around his middle, and his dark brown skull was showing through a cap of wiry gray hair. But he was still the same deliberate and cautious Leander who had driven several partners bat-shit during his long career on the LAPD.

"Carlos," he said, his forehead wrinkled in genuine concern, "you're not going to mistreat these boys, I hope."

"Naw, Leander," Morales said, paying particular interest to a chainsaw hanging from a wall hook. "Jus' gonna have a talk with 'em. Maybe you and Eddie can work on that computer thing."

Leander looked at the floppy disk in Goodman's hand. "Computer's in the house."

"Go. I can handle things out here," Morales said.

Leander wasn't certain he wanted Morales to handle things, but he reluctantly led Goodman into the house. His wife, who was sipping coffee in the kitchen, stopped him with a steely glance and pointed to the pipe. "Sorry, sweet pea," he replied and retraced his steps to the backyard. Goodman, who remained in the kitchen being glared at by the wife, heard him beating the pipe against his heel.

An eternity later he returned, showed his wife the now empty pipe bowl, winked at Goodman, and led him to another room that bore his unique touches.

Like his workspace behind the garage, his computer room was spotlessly clean. The machine itself rested atop a Formica table, alongside two printers, a scanner, a fax, and various little connected gadgets the purposes for which Goodman couldn't imagine. "What do you do with all this stuff, Leander?" he asked.

"Keep up my presence on the Web," Leander said seriously. "I'm the list manager of the L.A. Crime Beat Newsgroup."

Goodman didn't have any idea what that was and he didn't want to. So he just said, "Mmmm," and handed over the disk he'd taken from Lattimer.

Leander took his place at the computer. Goodman grabbed a chair and placed it beside Leander's.

"You're looking at a five hundred megahertz, Pentium II

processor with a six-point-four-gigabyte hard drive, Eddie," Leander said proudly as he booted up.

"Hell of a thing," Goodman said. He was of two minds—curious to see what was on the floppy, but also wanting to occupy Leander long enough for Carlos to get Rupert to start singing. He hoped that the boy would open up quickly. He didn't really think his partner would seriously hurt either of the gangstas, regardless of the debt he felt he owed the gang. At the same time, he wasn't sure what Carlos might do if push came to shove.

"Could be a little tricky," Leander said, looking at a message on the screen that read "Access Denied." "What we'd better do is copy this disk right away, in case there's some sort of cleanwipe that goes into effect after a few access tries."

"If you say so," Goodman said.

Leander copied the disk, then took a few more runs at unlocking its secret.

"You going to be able to do anything with that?" Goodman asked.

"It's just a matter of elimination," Leander said. "You don't know much about computers, do you, Eddie?"

"Not much."

"They can keep you going once you're retired," Leander said. "Activate your mind. Keep you plugged into the world."

"I thought that's why you had the ham radio."

"Whatever gets you through the day. I like to keep busy."

While Leander nattered on about his cures for retirement, Goodman tuned out. He tried to reconstruct the events of the Madeleine Gray murder using the new crime scene. *Maddie and Willins are at the spa, screwing around,* he thought. *She pisses him off. Why, I'm not . . . No, she pisses him off by telling him she's ditching him for some . . . No, that's probably wrong, too. She pisses him off* by telling him she knows his secret. *Sure. She's a blackmailer. Just because she's banging the guy doesn't mean she's giving him a free pass on the blackmail. She knows his secret.*

The secret. He's . . . what? He uses gangstas in his record business? Who doesn't? He . . . Goodman felt he was on the verge of some great understanding, but it just wouldn't come. *Okay. Move on. He gets the Crazy Eights to clean up the place and take care of Maddie's body. What is the connection with the Crazies? They sell drugs and rob banks. Willins probably wouldn't be involved in robbery. But drugs? In the music business?*

Anyway, they take the body disposal and cleanup off his hands. Willins drives to Maddie's house (Using her key? Was her key among her effects?) and looks for his file.

No, let me backtrack a bit. He tells Rupert or whoever to stay with the body until he gives the go-ahead. That way, he has all the time he needs to find the blackmail stash. He breaks open the cabinet, grabs his file. Because Maddie used nicknames, he has no reason to know his wife's got a file there, too, labeled "Soul Sister."

He gets away clean. Wait! His wife's car was seen at the house around that time. Okay, he was using the Jag that night. Yeah. That works. Then he—

"Sandoval?" Leander's voice interrupted his mental meandering. "I know that name."

"What about Sandoval?" Goodman asked.

"It's all here," Leander said. "He was using Word for Windows and a simple encryption."

On the monitor screen, Goodman read:

Sandoval Agency Case 427; Report #3
Client: James Doyle

Billing Address: 2912 Dumbarton Street NW
                 Washington, D.C. 20007
Background Check (BC)—addendum to original
Subject: various

Below that was a list of people Peter Sandoval had been
investigating for Doyle. An addendum to his original reports, it also included notes to himself and avenues left not
pursued (due to his flight from the police). Lattimer was
probably going to try to complete the job.

The security-conscious private detective had identified
his subjects by initials only. Topping the alphabetized list
was "J.D.," whom Goodman identified from Sandoval's
notes ("flaky . . . eager to sue . . . cabin fever in hotel . . .
can't keep it in pants") as Jamal Deschamps. "E.G." ("possible burnout . . . check med. record") was his own listing.
"N.H." ("lives alone . . . check papa . . . killer dog . . .
Compton why?") was Nikki Hill.

"Let's see more," he said.

Leander began a screen scroll and initials drifted by.
Some the detective recognized, some not. "Coming near the
end of the file," Leander told him.

Goodman blinked. "Back up a notch."

There, below "R.W." ("check old trials for impropri-
eties") were the initials he was looking for. "J.W." John "I
Love My Wife" Willins. That paranoid sleazebag Doyle! Investigating his own client. How had he put it: "Your only
friends are the people you've got the goods on."

Sandoval's notes on "J.W." were intriguing. "Deep-check
early bio. Carver, CA. Parents' death by fire; accident? . . .
See Emory at Eternal Light re: #1232." There was a telephone number.

"Got a pencil and paper?" Goodman asked. "I need to
make some notes."

Leander gave him a pitying look and pressed a button on his keyboard. One of the printers came alive with a laser copy of the file in under ten seconds. He handed it to Goodman and said solemnly, "You know, Eddie, computers aren't for everybody."

Goodman folded the sheet and put it in his pocket. "Why don't you erase that copy you made, Leander? Then we ought to look in on Carlos and the boys."

As they passed back through the kitchen, Leander's wife asked, "Who's in the workroom using the chainsaw?"

Instead of answering her, Leander headed from the house faster than Goodman had ever seen him move.

They found Morales sitting on a chair in front of the workbench, looking even more pissed off than usual. He'd moved both Fupdup and Rupert. The two boys were seated on top of the workbench. Ropes connected to their bound wrists had been tossed over a rafter and tightened until their arms were raised above their heads. More rope had been used to secure their ankles to the front legs of the bench, forcing their legs to spread.

Sawdust marred Leander's immaculate floor directly under each of them. Ridges were cut in the bench beginning at its lip and continuing until they almost kissed the V of their open legs. More sawdust had been spun up the boys' pants. Goodman saw that the crotch of Rupert's black silk trousers had been ripped.

Leander's main concern was his chainsaw, which Morales had replaced on the wall. The ex-cop ran a knobby black hand over it as if it were his child. "Baby needs oil."

"All I get from 'em is bullshit," Morales said, glaring at the brothers. "This one," he said, indicating Rupert, "doan say nuthin'. I threaten to saw off his brother's dick, he doan care. I threaten to saw off his dick. He still doan care."

Rupert glared at Morales venomously. Fupdup was crying. Goodman wondered if the boy might be in shock. "You okay?" he asked.

"I tole him all I know," Fupdup said hysterically. "I remembered the name."

"Shut up," Rupert ordered.

"The little creep tries to tell me the Crazies have been run by the same guy for as long as he can remember. That guy's known as Lee-O. Lee-O killed Maddie Gray. Lee-O calls all the shots for the Crazies."

"Isn't Lee-O the one who—"

"Yeah," Morales cut him off. "And he got fried in a fire twenty years ago."

"Maybe another Lee-O?" Goodman said, looking at Rupert.

"You gonna find out the hard way, assholes," Rupert said.

"What was Lee-O's real name?" Goodman asked Morales.

"Leonardo Broches."

Goodman turned to Fupdup. "That your Lee-O?"

Tears glistened in the boy's eyes. His head moved up and down. "Ninja Turtle. Leonardo. Yeah."

"What's he look like? Old? Young?"

"I never see him. Rupert's the only one sees him."

"You're dead, Fup," Rupert told his brother.

"That's it," Morales roared. Apparently out of control, he pushed Leander aside and grabbed the chainsaw. He gave a yank to its starter. The loud rattling engine filled the small room, nearly deafening Goodman.

Rupert's eyes widened. He tried to climb up the workbench on his back. "Call him off," he shouted at Goodman. "Fucker's mental."

Leander grabbed Morales's arm. "That's enough."

Morales hesitated, then killed the chainsaw's motor. Leander grabbed it from him and took it to the other side of the room, holding it protectively.

"Can't be the same fuckin' Lee-O," Morales said. "I know for a fact he's dead. Like I told you, after what happened to . . . after what happened, the cops were looking for him, so he left town to stay with relatives. Their place caught fire and they all burned."

Goodman took his partner's arm and led him away from the two boys. He showed him the printout of Sandoval's file. "Look under Willins's entry, 'J.W.'"

Morales's eyes opened wide as he read the words: "Carver, CA. Parents' death by fire; accident?"

"Suppose, when their place burned," Goodman said, "John Willins and his parents had a relative staying with them, a young thug from L.A. who suddenly dropped in? They all die but one. That boy leaves Carver, comes back to Los Angeles, gets in the music business. He claims to be the Willinses' son, but maybe he was really their nephew or something, a gangbanger who found a way to get the police off his back and start clean again."

Morales nodded, seeing it. "So he set fire to their place."

"Let's find out for sure."

"Any idea where Carver, California, is?" Morales asked Leander.

The old man strolled over to his radio station and pulled down a book. They waited while he slowly turned pages. Finally, he said, "About a hundred fifty miles to the east. Just this side of Joshua Tree. Past Desert Hot Springs. I could print out a map—"

"Thanks, Leander, for all your help," Goodman said.

"What you gonna do with them?" Leander asked, pointing to the brothers.

"We can throw the little one back," Morales said. Fupdup licked his lips nervously, afraid to believe it. "The other one we turn in, 'cause I'm pretty sure he used that big-ass knife of his to cut up Arthur Lydon."

"You'll never prove it," Rupert said. "I'll be out in an hour."

"You might want to stay in, Rupe," Goodman said. "If your pal Lee-O is as strong as you think, when he hears how you gave him up, he might be real mad at you."

"He knows me better than that." But the boy looked shaken.

"You'd be wise to let us deal with him."

"Fuck you," Rupert said.

"You really lettin' me go?" Fupdup asked.

"Why not?" Morales said. "We ain't doin' the Crazies no favor, leavin' an asshole like you on their team."

≡ Eighty-two ≡

Joe Walden was at the podium, in the middle of his acceptance speech, when Nikki's cellular phone chirped. She grabbed her noisy purse and made a quick, and she hoped unobserved, exit from the ballroom.

She was actually annoyed at missing the speech. She'd never heard Joe address a crowd before and had been tremendously impressed by his eloquence. Here was a man who actually believed that racial parity could be achieved without social disorder or revolutionary tactics. Moreover, he was capable of making his beliefs clearly understood.

Just as impressive, he'd apparently been able to ignore the totally improper presence of Dyana Cooper and John Willins, whom the organizers of the dinner at least had had the intelligence to seat on the opposite side of the room from the county tables. She found it impossible to even look in Willins's direction, knowing that he was not only a murderer, but a coward willing to let his wife pay for his crime.

Walden's eyes had opened wide at the news about the Sanctum.

As the others had filed into the ballroom for dinner, Nikki had managed to have a few moments alone with him in an alcove past the kitchen. Worried that a waiter would interrupt them at any moment, she'd rapidly paraphrased Goodman's phone message and its implication—that Willins had murdered Madeleine Gray. "I can't wait to get that smart-ass manager of the place, Simon Bayliss, back on the stand," Nikki had said.

"He'll just deny it," Walden told her. "We need concrete evidence. Let's meet tonight at the office, when we're finished here."

"I'll tell Ray."

"No," he'd said. "I learned something about Ray today that's almost as disquieting as the news you've brought me. I think we'd better keep Ray in the dark about this, until I can figure out precisely where we're headed with the Willins trial."

"What's up with Ray?" she asked.

"We'll talk about it tonight."

Without another word, he'd led her into the ballroom and to their table, where they were greeted by Ray, Meg Fisher, and an assortment of familiar office faces. She'd purposely taken a seat several places away from Ray, even though it meant listening to Meg rant on about the importance of the award.

Standing in the now nearly unoccupied cocktail area, she answered the phone warily, hoping it was Goodman and not another threat. Hoping also that it would not be Virgil. She hadn't figured out what to do about him. About them.

It was Ed Goodman, speaking fast with lots of background noise. "What?" she said, "I can't—"

"Sorry," he said. "We're at the lockup. Dumping the

gangsta who killed Arthur Lydon. But that's not why I called."

He told her an amazing theory that he and Morales had conceived, the gist of which was that John Willins was living a lie. He was, in fact, one of the founders of the Crazy Eights and was still very much connected to them. He had probably murdered members of his own family to escape prison and establish a new life for himself. When Maddie Gray discovered his secret, he'd killed her.

As incredulous as Nikki was, she understood that it was possible. L.A. was like a Hindu heaven. People arrived from all over the country to begin life anew. Con men were transformed overnight into respected business tycoons. Vegas hookers became actresses with off-Broadway experience. Hospital orderlies automatically graduated to the ranks of prominent physicians. She herself had discovered that several L.A. lawyers boasting Harvard degrees had never even visited that august university. Names were changed, histories manufactured. In the city's rarefied laid-back atmosphere, résumés were rarely checked and when they were, so what? One merely moved on to apply somewhere less uptight.

That a ruthless South Central gangbanger would emerge as John Willins, multimillionaire music impresario, was not beyond belief. Hell, he probably bought the company with profits from crack cocaine peddled by the Crazy Eights.

"This is starting to sound like a litany, but do you have any proof, detective?" she asked.

"I'm hoping to find some in the town where Willins's family burned to death," Goodman said. "There should be records, people who knew them, photographs of the real John Willins. Carlos and I are driving there tonight. We'll be a hundred miles or so out of our jurisdiction, so we'll need some sort of paper to flash. Can you put together documentation for us?"

"I'll do better than that," Nikki said. "I'll come with you."

Sensing his hesitation, she added, "Otherwise, it'll be tomorrow before I can get the paperwork started."

"We're nearly through here," he said. "We'll swing by the hotel for you in about twenty minutes."

She looked down at her cocktail dress, her high heels. "I'll be waiting."

She returned in time to hear Joe Walden end his speech on a high note. "Over a century ago, abolitionist Frederick Douglass declared, 'The destiny of the colored American . . . is the destiny of America.' Three decades ago, the Reverend Martin Luther King, Jr., elaborated on that thought when he wrote, 'Because the goal of America is freedom, abused and scorned though we may be, our destiny is tied up with America's destiny.' I stand before you tonight, brothers and sisters, to reiterate what both of these great patriots have stated so eloquently, and to add my own heartfelt belief that we alone are responsible for the fate of ourselves, our families, our cities, our country. We alone are masters of our own destiny and the destiny of all Americans."

Applause and exuberant cries of approval rang from the crowd, and Nikki cheered as loudly as anyone. So stirring had been the district attorney's words that even Dyana Cooper and John Willins were standing and clapping.

Walden, clasping his award, a carved wooden statue of a tribal warrior, descended from the stage and walked back to his table, shaking hands along the way. Meg Fisher was ecstatic, exhorting her two photographers to "Keep clicking, boys."

Nikki waited as long as she felt she could, then waded

through the crowd to the D.A. Over the congratulations and well-wishings, she shouted, "We have to talk now."

He nodded and continued pressing the flesh for another few minutes, then gestured with his award toward a door beside the stage. It led to a dimly lighted unused portion of the ballroom. Chairs were piled atop tables. Everything was powdered with dust.

"Is this the reason you left in the middle of my speech?" Joe Walden asked.

"Sorry about that," she said. "What I heard of it was wonderful."

He smiled. "I think I even got through to the Willins table."

"It's John Willins we have to talk about."

"As I said, we can talk later at the office."

"This can't wait," she said. She told him Goodman's theory.

His reaction dismayed her. "It's too bizarre," he said. "Willins may have murdered Madeleine Gray. But the rest of it. Escaping from a fire. Assuming the identity of one of its victims. It's like a Robert Ludlum thriller."

"I'll let you know if there's any truth to it," she said.

"What do you mean?"

"The detectives should be here for me any minute. We're driving to Carver, California, tonight to check out the story."

"I'm surprised Lieutenant Corben permitted them to notify our office."

"I got the impression they're hoping to get something more solid before they try any of this out on Lieutenant Corben."

"Yet Detective Goodman tried it out on you."

"I . . . we've had a good working relationship," she said. "He trusts me."

"Excellent," Walden said. "Maybe this time we can stay

in step with the LAPD. If not slightly ahead of them. Are you scheduled for court tomorrow?"

"Ray was going to do the cross on the Willinses' security guards."

"Ray, yes. Well—"

"You said there was a problem about Ray?"

"Nothing for us to get into now."

"We should ask for a continuance," Nikki said. "At least until we know the status of our case against Dyana Cooper."

Walden nodded. "All right. I just hope this doesn't turn out to be yet one more fiasco to blow up in our faces." He smiled and shook his wooden warrior at her. "I trust you won't let that happen. Keep me informed."

They reentered the ballroom together, just in time to have a flashbulb explode in their faces. When Nikki regained her sight, she saw that John Willins had been standing just to their right, near the door. Had he been eavesdropping on their conversation?

Walden saw him, too, scowled, and strode past him. Nikki's eyes met Willins's for a brief moment, but she could read nothing there. He turned and walked away in the direction of his table.

Members of the NAAL and their guests were impatiently awaiting their cars and limos in front of the hotel. When Nikki got through the crowd, she saw no sign of Goodman and Morales.

Abruptly, a beige Mercedes limousine swung in to the curb, cutting off a departing vehicle. The chauffeur rushed to open the rear door, just as Dyana Cooper exited from the hotel, followed by her husband.

Willins ducked into the limo after Dyana and slammed the door shut himself. The chauffeur quickly returned to his seat. Nikki watched the sleek vehicle disappear from sight.

When the detectives arrived, Goodman said, "Hope we didn't keep you waiting too long."

"I hope so, too," she told them as she got into the rear of their sedan, "because Willins may know what we're up to, and he tore out of here ten minutes ago."

EIGHTY-THREE

≡ EIGHTY-THREE ≡

Goodman had been hesitant about the scrupulous deputy
D.A. joining their hunt for truth since he wasn't sure how
fast or how loose they'd have to play it in Carver. The one-
hundred-seventy-five-mile trip was not easing his mind on
that score. While Morales sped them through San
Bernardino and Victorville and Barstow, Nikki decided to
use the time to ask questions. Some they answered truthfully, some not so truthfully, and some they couldn't answer
at all.

She began by taking Goodman through the business of
Dyana Cooper's stolen file once more. Like a dentist probing a particularly sensitive spot, she asked again how he'd
come by his information. He still refused to identify his
source.

She moved on to the Sanctum. Were they sure that the information about it being the crime scene was reliable? Who
was his source?

Goodman looked at Morales. "Les' sorta simplify the
story," his partner said, meaning that he should leave

Fupdup out of it and put his information into Rupert's mouth. "It was a member of the Crazy Eights, the one we arrested for the murder of Arthur Lydon."

"You said you were booking him just before you picked me up. You left word about the Sanctum hours ago."

"These things take time," Goodman said. "The boy gave up the info about the Sanctum right off the bat. He didn't personally kill Maddie Gray. He and his pals merely cleaned up the murder scene and removed the body."

"That's enough to put them all away for quite a while," she said.

"Right. But at the time Rupert wasn't thinking about that."

"Rupert?" She seemed startled by the name.

"You know him?"

She told them about a confrontation with the clean-cut gangsta at the home of her former friend Victoria Allard. "He had a copy of Dyana Cooper's file."

"He must've got it from Arthur Lydon before he . . . Did he have a long leather case with him when he fronted you?" She nodded. "Inside was the machete he used on Lydon."

Nikki shivered, then said, "Tell me you didn't use force or interfere with his rights in getting his confession."

Morales made a noise that might have been a sneeze or a belch. Goodman said, "I think the weapon will speak for itself."

"How did you obtain it?" she asked flatly, as if she no longer had confidence in their methods.

"We were on our way to talk with James Doyle," Goodman said, "when we observed Rupert and several other members of the gang parking near Doyle's temporary residence. We watched the gangstas enter the building—"

"They break in?" she asked hopefully.

"Not exactly," he replied. "They rang the bell. A friend of Doyle's opened up. They hit him and entered."

"You saw them hit the guy and that's when you went in?"

"Uh huh," Morales said.

"We found the punks in Doyle's bedroom," Goodman said. "Rupert had the machete at Doyle's throat. But Carlos read the kid pretty well and took a chance that he wouldn't actually cut Doyle."

Goodman wasn't happy with the spare-me-the-horseshit look she was giving him. "Are the other gangstas in custody, too?" she asked.

"No," Morales replied. "They beat it and we didn't feel right about shooting them in the back."

"Why stop at that?" she asked sarcastically.

"Too much paperwork," Morales said.

"So Rupert told you Willins got them to clean up his murder and dump the body?"

"He used Willins's gang ID," Goodman said. "Lee-O."

"Lee-O? I know that name." The connection she made obviously annoyed her, and she took it out on them. "Let's see if I got this straight. This punk-ass Rupert, who makes up lies faster than most people breathe, told you Lee-O killed Maddie at the Sanctum. We all know John Willins whooped it up with her at that spa. Therefore Lee-O equals Willins."

"That more or less covers it," Goodman said.

"For the sake of argument, let me remind you that the miserable manager of the place said Maddie was a customer there, too. Suppose she took a liking to some dude she met and brought *him* to the spa for fun and games. And the games got rough. And he was just Lee-O, the old gangsta, and not John Willins at all."

"The spa manager would know the truth," Goodman said, growing sorrier and sorrier that he'd asked her along.

"The spa manager is a slimy weasel who is not about to cooperate in any way. We can't count on anything he has to say."

Goodman took the copy of Sandoval's decrypted notes from his pocket. "This is information that Doyle's private peeper was gathering."

She glanced at the page. "These initials are . . . oh, I see. 'J.D.' is Jamal Deschamps. 'E.G.,' 'N.H.,' 'C.M.' And 'D.S.'" She frowned at the page. Goodman assumed she was reading about "D.S."pulling the plug on her aunt and using the inheritance to attend law school.

"The John Willins material is down near the end," Goodman said.

He watched her eyes go down to the bottom of the sheet and absorb the information. "Hmmm. These are just Sandoval's speculations," she said. "Maybe Willins's parents did die by accident."

"That's what we're going to Carver to find out," Goodman said.

"What's this 'Emory at Eternal Light' and the phone number?"

"I don't know exactly. A funeral home? I've called the number a bunch of times. Nobody answers."

Nikki dialed the number on her cellular. Again, no one answered.

"Can I hang on to this sheet?" she asked.

He nodded.

"This trip better be fruitful, detectives," she said. "Because if all we have to go on is what you just told me, we'll be damn lucky to get a conviction on Rupert. Willins? He'll be as free as O. J. Simpson." She smiled. "The part about Lee-O being in charge of the Crazy Eights confirms something an old . . . associate told me. It also explains the bracelet with the lion charm. Lee-O the lion. Which suggests Maddie knew his past.

"Except," Nikki went on, "if Maddie was murdered at the Sanctum, why was the bracelet found at her home?"

"It was in the room where she'd had the scuffle with Dyana Cooper," Goodman said. "Knowing what we do about Maddie, it's possible she might have been amused to flaunt a bracelet Willins had given her right under his wife's nose."

Morales interrupted the discussion. "We're here," he said.

≡ EIGHTY-FOUR ≡

Nikki looked out of the car window to discover that the Barstow Freeway had been replaced by a dark narrow road between fenced-in fields that went on as far the eye could see in the moonlight. No town was in sight.

"This is Carver?" she asked.

"Naw. This is *cacahuates*," Morales said. "Peanuts."

"Carver's the only town in California where it gets hot enough to grow peanuts," Goodman said. "Almost as many harvested as down in Georgia on Jimmy Carter's farm."

"Tha's why they call the place Carver," Morales said. "After one of your people. George Washington Carver. The peanut guy."

Nikki wasn't sure how she felt about Carver being referred to as "the peanut guy," but she was amused by the detectives' knowledge of the territory. "You aren't putting me on?"

"Absolutely not," Goodman insisted.

"You did some research?"

"A friend of ours had a book."

"George Washington Carver, huh?" Nikki said. "Not too many towns named after black men."

The road continued for several miles without a break in the peanut fields. They reached the end of the fenced-in acreage, rolled past a farmhouse or two, and crossed railroad tracks. A sign by the side of the road informed them that they were entering "Carver, California. Population: 14,325 and growing fast as peanuts."

Downtown Carver, such as it was, was just around a bend in the road. It consisted of the local version of a 7-Eleven, called simply QuickBuy, with a pale light glowing over the front door and an eerie neon sign illumintating the interior; a gas station closed for the night; a former movie house, named—What else? the Carver Theatre—that had been converted to a ninety-nine-cent-or-less store. Finally, there was the probable reason for the conversion of the theater, a video rental shop with a hand-printed sign tacked to a slot that said "Return Videos Here."

No people were visible anywhere.

Morales drove along at a clip, looking for some sign of life. Ten or fifteen minutes later they found it. Headlights, moving their way from a road to their right. Morales parked the sedan across the road, blocking the truck's egress.

"Not the friendliest of gestures," Nikki said.

"It's doin' the job," Morales said as the truck ground to halt.

The black man who swung out of its cab was well over six feet, heavily muscled, and, judging by his expression, not predisposed to liking strangers.

Goodman opened his door to meet the man.

"We need a little hel—"

"Mind getting out of my way?" the driver of the truck growled.

Nikki edged over to the window and said, "We just need some help."

The trucker eyed her suspiciously or appraisingly, she couldn't tell. "Where can we find your police chief?" she asked.

"What's wrong?"

"These two men are policemen from Los Angeles. I'm—"

"I know you, don't I?"

"I don't think we've met. Can you direct us to your lawman?"

He continued to gawk at her. "That'd be Parnell. Southwest edge of town, near the railroad station. He's gonna love gettin' waked up."

Chuckling, the man returned to his truck.

Goodman got back into the sedan. Morales made a U-turn, kicked up some dust, and went back the way they'd come.

It didn't take them long to find the small brick building with the sign out front that read "Jail and Police Station." A light glowed over the door. Parked in front was a five-year-old, brown and white Ford Taurus with a gold star on the door and the words "Carver Police Dept." hand-lettered in the center of the star.

Parnell Jefferson was a small, wiry black man with a mustache who apparently slept in his uniform shirt and trousers when he was on duty. He opened the door of the jail and police station in his sock feet, yawning. He seemed unimpressed by the two detectives, but when he saw Nikki, he tried unsuccessfully to tuck his shirt into his trousers.

"What can I do for you folks?" he asked.

Goodman showed him his badge and said, "We're looking for information about some people who used to live in Carver. The Willins family?"

Chief Jefferson shrugged. "Name's kinda familiar. But I don't recall—"

"Burned in a fire, twenty years ago?"

Jefferson smiled. "Twenty years ago," he said, "I was fourteen and living very happy with my mama and daddy on the South Side of Chicago, Illinois."

"Anybody been around long enough to have known the Willinses?" Nikki asked.

"Reverend Wilmot's been here a while. Roosevelt Styles, who owns the peanut plant. I suppose somebody'll remember the name. Old Emory Moten, of course. The oldest citizen in these parts. He surely knows everybody who's dead."

"Why's that, chief?" Nikki asked, recalling Emory's name from Sandoval's notes.

"He's the caretaker at Eternal Light. Cranky old man, except when he's drunk, which is most of the time. Then he's just stiff."

"Eternal Light would be . . . ?"

"Carver's only cemetery," the chief said. "Of course, we've got a boot hill for people can't afford Eternal Light. If these folks are worth your coming all the way here from L.A., they probably wouldn't be buried in Boot Hill, now would they?"

≡ EIGHTY-FIVE ≡

Eternal Light Cemetery, at the southern tip of Carver, just a few miles from the start of the Mojave Desert, covered the equivalent of several city blocks, enclosed by a high white-washed wall that had been structurally altered by earth-quakes in the area.

Possibly because of the sudden drop in temperature in the desert, a fog was settling in. Seeing its wisps float in front of the sedan's headlights, Nikki said, "That's an over-the-top touch, isn't it? Graveyard's not going to be spooky enough, we've got to have fog, too?"

Morales parked the sedan near a wrought-iron gate.

In just the short drive from the police station, the air had turned cold. Nikki was freezing in her cocktail dress. To her surprise, Morales put his coat around her.

Goodman tried the gate and it creaked open.

Inside the wall, the area was nearly pitch black. The absence of moon or stars and the presence of fog made it almost impossible to see anything clearly past a foot away. They had two flashlights, which could accomplish only so much in the fog. At least they provided enough illumination to keep them from stepping into an open grave.

It was no place to be wearing high heels, Nikki decided as she stumbled beside Morales, sharing the light from his flash. Goodman wandered off to their right in search of the caretaker. It wasn't long before he called them to join him.

Emory Moten's cottage was a rustic affair with a smooth stucco base and what appeared to be a Spanish tile roof. A faint light shone behind a circular window built into the front door.

Goodman knocked a few times. When that didn't work, Morales took his turn pounding on the wood.

No response from inside the cottage.

"What now?" Nikki asked.

Morales tried the doorknob. Locked. "Old dude's sleeping it off inside, probably."

"Try again," Goodman said.

Morales banged even louder, yelling, "Hey, open up in there!"

Nothing.

"I sure didn't drive all this way to spend the night in a motel," Goodman said. He handed his flashlight to his partner and slipped a small leather case from his pocket. He unzipped it and removed two thin metal picks. "Shine some light over here," he said to Morales.

Nikki turned away as Goodman worked the picks into Emory Moten's lock. She could barely make out the shape of tombstones in the fog. She shivered inside Morales's coat.

The sound of the door creaking open drew her attention back to the detectives as they entered the cottage. "Yo, Mr. Moten," Goodman called. "Anybody here?"

No reply.

She walked to the door and looked in on a cluttered,

rough-hewn room dimly lit by a brass lamp on a desk against the wall. Everything was old and worn—the heavy desk, the wooden chair with its tattered cushion, a faded and stained maroon couch. There was a filing cabinet with rust poking through its dark green paint, an ancient floor-model TV with an antenna enhanced by a ball of tinfoil stuck on one rabbit ear, and a deep blue plastic container near the door almost filled with empty beer and whiskey bottles and tin cans.

"Guy really knows how to live," Nikki said.

"I'll see if he's in the back," Morales said.

Goodman strolled to a grimy framed map that decorated the wall above the desk. "This looks like the ticket," he said.

As Nikki moved closer she could see that it was a schematic drawing of the cemetery, broken down into rows of lots numbered consecutively from 1 to 2050. The lots were of different sizes, which meant there was no consistency in the number per row. "According to Sandoval's notes, we want 1232," she said.

The detective ran a finger along the map, from the spot marked "Office" to Lot 1232. It was in roughly the center of the graveyard. "Twenty-two rows up," he said. "Even knowing that, it could be a bear finding it in the fog."

"Nobody home but us chickens," Morales announced, joining them.

"Where would he go?" Nikki asked.

"Hangin' with relatives, prob'ly," Morales said, looking at the map. "Can't blame him. This place is a rat's nest. Bedroom smelled like bad cabbage."

"Let's get our business done," Goodman suggested.

As they walked out into the cold, foggy night, Nikki said, "The visiting gangsta should be included on the headstone. What was Lee-O's real name?"

"Leonardo Broches," Goodman said.

"If it's there, it'll definitely tie Willins to the Crazy Eights and to Maddie Gray's murder."

Nikki's heels kept sinking into the ground as they made their way through the fog, counting rows. At the twenty-second, they began concentrating on the tombstones. They moved slowly and carefully but they didn't find the final resting place of the Willins family.

"What now?" Morales asked.

"It was an old map," Goodman said. "Maybe they've added rows. Or maybe Sandoval got it wrong."

"As long as we're here, let's check a few rows up and back," Nikki said.

They split up, Goodman taking the lower rows, Nikki and Morales the ones above.

"Fog's getting thicker," Morales grumbled, as his partner disappeared from sight.

Colder, too, Nikki thought. She hoped Morales wasn't freezing in just his shirt. "Let's get this over with," she said.

They began checking the names on the tombstones. They were almost at the end of the row when they heard the shot.

Morales clicked off the flash. Nikki was almost over-whelmed by the fog and the darkness. "You okay?" he whispered. She could barely make out his white shirt.

"Uh huh," she said. "It's Willins, isn't it?"

"That'd be my guess," he said. "I doan think he was shooting at us."

She didn't either. The noise had come from the other side of the cemetery.

"Stay here," Morales said. "I gotta go check on Eddie."

The vague image of his white shirt disappeared in the fog.

She hunkered beside a headstone, staring off into the dark cemetery and straining to see something that would offer a clue as to what was going on.

Another two shots, in quick succession.

Who was shooting and who was being shot at, she couldn't tell.

She saw a flash of light. Then another. Then, nothing but darkness.

She thought she heard a footstep.

The detectives should be calling out to her any second. Telling her not to worry, everything was all right.

All was silent, the fog masking even the ordinary sounds of night.

She began edging back, keeping the headstones between her and the pathway. Her high heel sunk deep into a mound of loose dirt. Before the implication of that could make its way to her brain, she took another step backward. Into emptiness.

She tried to shift her weight, but she was too far gone. She fell awkwardly into a deep gravesite, smashing her head against a wall of packed earth. Her foot was twisted beneath her.

She lay on her back, dazed, staring up at the sky filtered by fog. Pain shot up her leg from her ankle. She rolled onto her side so that she could straighten the leg. The pain coming from her ankle was excruciating. It was broken. She'd just have to endure it. She forced herself not to cry or moan as she sat up, though the raw pain radiated along her leg like a fireball coursing under her skin.

Maybe Willins hadn't seen her fall. Maybe he'd pass her by. Then she could somehow climb out of the grave. Those hours spent struggling up the sand dune should count for something. Maybe she could make it to the car and the gun and cellular phone in her purse.

That pleasant scenario was abruptly canceled by the sensation of something slimy crawling on her hand. She shook it away. *Worms. Oh, God.*

A beam of light swept the top of the grave.

It was bright enough to give her a sense of the deep hole she was in. It also showed her a weapon. A pickax rested within reach. She blessed the careless gravedigger. Of course, because of her ankle and her position, it seemed impossible for her to take advantage of her discovery.

The light shined directly down into the grave. Into her eyes.

Practically blinded, she could make out very little of the features of the man standing above her at the edge of the grave. She was able to tell that he was big and, judging by his pant legs and shoes, still in his tux. Hadn't taken the time to change, of course. Too anxious to find out what they were up to in Carver.

"So there you are," he said. "I was worried over nothing. You don't have a gun, do you?"

He chuckled.

"The headstone you were looking for is right over there," he told her. "Auntie and uncle and my dear little cousin, crispy critters all. Just a few plots over. Of course the family name on the stone isn't the one you were expecting."

She knew that now, just as surely as she knew that the man standing beside the grave was her boss, District Attorney Joseph Walden.

≡ EIGHTY-SIX ≡

I 'd rather not shoot you just yet," he said, sitting on a high mound of dirt beside the open grave. He clicked off the flash and assumed a ghostly image in the fog. "It'll be a while before the gang arrives to do the cleanup. I don't like spending time alone. I've always been a people person."

He was squatting up there, sounding so smug and satisfied with himself. He'd assumed she'd given up. He always had underestimated her.

"Are the detectives dead?" she asked, her left hand feeling for the handle of the pickax. She didn't think she could even lift the thing, much less swing it in an upward arc faster than he could aim and pull a trigger. But she wasn't about to just lie there and let the bastard kill her at his leisure.

"Dead or dying," he said.

"My God, Joe, how many people have you killed?"

"Quite a few. My aunt and uncle and cousin. Maddie, of course. We could count Dimitra. I didn't actually do that one myself, but I ordered it done."

"Why? I thought you and she—"

"Oh, she was a great piece of ass, just too curious for her own good. Anyway, back to the list. The old caretaker here—"

"He's dead?"

"Certainly. I'd just choked the life out of him when you people started knocking on his door. I didn't think that you, an officer of the court, would let them break in like that. I barely had time to drag the old buzzard's body into a closet before Morales came snooping into the bedroom."

"Sorry we inconvenienced you."

"No problem. I just roll with the punches. I've always had a knack for murder. Especially close work. My marksmanship is only so-so; though, as tonight proves, it gets the job done. I imagine I'd have made a damn good hired assassin, if Tom Gleason hadn't shown me my true calling."

The tips of her fingers touched the ax handle. "What's Gleason got to do with it?"

"Tom was a genius. He created the Crazy Eights, you know? We were just a bunch of punks. Eight of us. Petty thieves, barely in our teens. Tom was head deputy D.A. under Pendleton. He knew our juvie records and he handpicked us. Brought us to his place in Pasadena, fed us steak and ale, told us his plan for our future. We were to become the new gang in town. Gang? Two of us couldn't stay in a room together for more than ten minutes without fighting. Tom was patient. He spent a year shaping us up, making sure we stayed out of jail."

"What was his point?" She grasped the ax handle.

"His point? His point was he needed distributors for his product."

"Drugs?"

"He'd cut a deal with a local bigwig whose son had been arrested for running a penny-ante import operation. Tom told me it was one of the old California families, going back several generations, but he never uttered the name in my presence. It'd been a snap for him to find enough mistakes the cops had made to dirty the evidence and let the kid roam. The boy was sent to a school in Switzerland as punishment for his crime. Tom and the boy's father took over the operation and expanded it.

"Tom had vision. He saw a vast market that their white-bread pushers weren't able to penetrate. The gangs in the hood were nickel-and-diming, but there was no organized distribution. That's where we came in. Eight tough kids who knew the territory and who were a little smarter than the other gangstas. Plus we had a head deputy D.A. on our side."

"Tom Gleason," Nikki said, "the black man's friend."

"He was. His dedication to inner-city youths is one of the main things that helped him get elected over that jive-ass racist Pendleton."

Nikki tried to lift the ax. It was too heavy. She dragged it closer to her body. Maybe with both hands . . .

"Tom was sincere about helping black kids."

"Sure," Nikki said, "he helped 'em by turning 'em into crackheads."

"You don't understand. Some kids are born to self-destruct. If it's not drugs, it's booze or guns. They're weak and worthless and they give up. What's wrong with using these losers to allow ambitious young people to do something with their lives?"

"In other words, what's wrong with a couple hundred kids, including babies not even born, dying of crack and smack so you can get your law degree? Right?"

"Of course," he said without irony. "The things I'm capable of achieving are worth the lives of a hundred drug burnouts. Tom saw that. He handpicked me. He saw your potential, too."

"Mine?"

"Sure. He thought you had the stuff to be a great prosecutor."

"He told you that?"

"He told me everything. I was his protégé. Dick Grayson to his Bruce Wayne. He was grooming me to be him. He thought you were bright and ambitious and tough. You let him down with Mason Durant."

Of course Walden knew about Durant. How foolish she'd been to think Virgil might have betrayed her confidence. How sad she might never see him again to make it up to him. She had both hands on the ax handle now. She'd have to stand to reach Walden with the weapon. She wasn't sure she could move.

While he droned on, recalling time spent in the company of the great Tom Gleason, she tried sliding her body up the wall of packed earth. Each little movement sent a searing bolt of pain from her damaged ankle. She positioned the top of the ax blade against the grave floor and used the upright handle as a cane.

". . . when you sent me your letter asking to be reinstated, I suddenly realized, of course, I had to have you back downtown. I needed prosecutors I could control. I was sleeping with Dimitra. And thanks to the Mason Durant screwup, I had something to hang over both your head and Ray's."

She was several inches off the ground now. The wall of earth was pitted with rocks and she was glad poor Carlos Morales's coat was blunting some of their sharper edges. She halted her progress because he'd stopped talking. "So how did a smart guy like you do something so stupid," she asked, "killing a high-profile celebrity?"

"It's my one failing. My bloody temper. I'd handled it pretty well for more than twenty years, but that night Maddie was an unholy bitch. She was drunk when I got to her place. Drunk and insulting. I'd brought her a present that she threw back in my face."

"The charm bracelet," Nikki said.

"It was . . . a sentimental gift. She was wearing an expensive ring I assumed had been given her by some bastard she was fucking. She hadn't thrown that back in anybody's face. We shouted a bit. I may have slapped her a couple of times. Then, she went through one of her mood swings and began to act like a loving woman should. She told me she'd arranged for us to go out. This was surprising. Until then, she'd insisted our romance be kept a secret."

"She didn't want her fans to know she was seeing a black man?" Nikki asked.

"Nothing like that. Whatever else she was, Maddie was certainly not a racist. She'd sewn some wild oats in the past and almost lost her show because of it, so she was determined to keep her private life private. And I think secrecy turned her on. Anyway, what she'd planned that night wasn't any public declaration of our relationship. She'd booked an overnight at one of the Sanctum's more secluded cabanas. She even made me hide in the bathroom when they delivered our dinner, the dinner that we never go to eat."

"What happened?"

"She was a very nasty drunk. I'm afraid I was moved to beat the hell out of her. She retaliated by informing me that she'd discovered a notebook in my coat pocket one night. She'd thought it was my little black book and copied several pages while I was sleeping. It didn't take her long to realize the numbers were for beepers. In even less time she'd discovered whose beepers they were."

"If you wanted to keep your connection to the Crazy Eights a secret, why did you tease her with the lion charm?" Nikki asked.

"The charm?"

"A lion. Lee-O."

"That never occurred to me," he said. "No. The lion was a reference to a sex show we caught in Paris—lion and trainer."

"She was the one you told me about during my interview lunch," Nikki said. "The one you met on your vacation."

"Precisely. From the first moment I saw her, I was blinded by love. But when she was screeching at me, threatening to expose my gang connection unless I gave her one hundred thousand dollars, the scales fell from my eyes. I understood I had to kill her. I couldn't have picked a better place to do it. I used a bust of Julius Caesar. Nothing at all like the metal sculpture everyone was so satisfied with."

"Why'd you take the rug from her house?" Nikki asked.

"In the course of our earlier altercation, I dropped my glass and it shattered. Pieces of it caught in the rug. I didn't want to risk leaving any prints or saliva for the lab to play with. So when I returned to get the file she'd been keeping on me, I cleaned up the broken glass from the floor and took it and the rug when I left.

"Not that it was easy to make my getaway. In the midst of my cleanup, the door buzzer sounded. I moved quietly to a window and saw a man and a woman—John Willins and his wife, though I didn't know it at the time, it was too dark. When no one answered, they went back to their damned Jaguar and just sat there for nearly an hour. I waited with them, eager to be on my way down the road to where I'd parked my car."

"They probably were there to pay blackmail," Nikki said.

"Maybe they were there to kill Maddie and I saved them the trouble."

"You planted the rug fibers in Dyana Cooper's car?"

"No," he said. "That was a pleasant surprise. I imagine when she had her fight with Maddie, she must have picked up the fibers on her clothes and carried them back to her car."

He paused. Getting ready to end their little chat?

"So you're carrying on the Tom Gleason tradition," she said.

"What tradition is that?" he asked suspiciously.

"He picked you as his protégé," she said. "You've picked Rupert as yours."

"He's a great kid, isn't he?" Walden said proudly. "You should have seen him just three years ago. A gutter rat with delusions of grandeur. Not much smarter than his brother. Jacking cars and calling himself Mr. Caviar. Why? Because he thought it sounded classy. He's got a sharp mind and he learns fast. I was telling him about James Doyle's tricks helping Dyana Cooper's defense, and Rupert said, 'Don't worry about it; I'll handle Doyle.' Just like that."

She couldn't see his face, but she knew it was wearing the sappy proud grin of an ersatz father. She decided to wipe it away. "You shouldn't have let him try to take on Doyle," she said.

"What are you talking about?"

"Goodman and Morales busted him at Doyle's place. He was carrying the machete he used on Arthur Lydon. He's behind bars."

"Damn, that's why I couldn't reach him," Walden said. "When was he arrested?"

"Just before we left. He's the one told the detectives all about Lee-O."

"No. Not Rupert. He knows enough to keep quiet, and I'll figure out a way to free him. That's the beauty of my job. He'll be getting out. Dyana Cooper will be going in."

He fell silent. Eager to keep him talking, Nikki asked, "What happened twenty years ago?"

"What?"

"You said you'd kept your temper under control for more than twenty years."

"Oh, yes. God, Tom was a generous man. I damn near destroyed his whole operation, and still he kept his faith in me."

"What happened?"

"Temper again. I was young. Black was beautiful. A brother had the gall to bring his tamale pie to live in the hood. I warned him. He got pushy and I got pissed off. I talked the others into a little neighborhood ethnic cleansing. It was an idiotic thing to do, a thing you do when you're a kid and full of fire. The police were all over me. That's what sent me out here to my aunt and uncle—to escape their clutches. So I guess, in the long run, it was the right thing to do after all."

She'd got her good leg under her body and was in a crouching position. Just a few inches more.

Walden stood up.

"I hear someone coming. My cleanup squad has arrived, earlier than I'd expected." He moved to the edge of the grave. "I'm glad we had this time to ourselves, Nikki"—he raised his gun and pointed it down at her—"before we had to say good-bye."

≡ EIGHTY-SEVEN ≡

Goodman awoke tasting dirt, with a fire in the lower part of his back. When he tried to move the fire grew hotter.

He'd been shot.

The stories were correct. You don't hear the shot that kills you, and he'd heard this one. Felt it too, as it knocked him to the ground.

The shooter had approached him cautiously. Had taken the useless gun from his fingertips, had prodded him with the toe of his shoe.

Goodman had remained still as death, and the man, Willins he presumed, had wandered off in the fog to do more damage.

He and the shooter must have heard Carlos approaching at the same instant. He'd opened his mouth to shout a warning just as two shots rang out. He'd kept silent, praying that the next sound he'd hear would be his partner's gruff voice calling his name.

He'd heard nothing, so he'd lowered his head to the earth

and let the combination of shock and pain do their thing to his body.

"Hey, 'migo."

It was Carlos, but it wasn't. The words sounded strangled, weak, high-pitched.

Goodman moved his head in their direction.

Carlos was kneeling beside him. His left arm was hanging uselessly, his white shirt stained red from neck to waist on the left side. "You 'live, 'migo?"

"Barely."

"You see 'im? See the fucker?"

"Willins?"

"Not Willins. Walden." Carlos said. "Joe Walden. The other J.W."

Goodman closed his eyes. "Take me now, Lord, I'm ready."

"Can you move?"

Goodman tried to get his feet under him and was chilled by the realization that he had no feeling at all in the lower part of his body. He fought the fear long enough to reply, "No. I don't think I can."

"Tha's okay. You gonna make it, man," Carlos said. He staggered to his feet.

"Hold on, partner. Take it easy."

"No time. Caught me high in the chest. Hit a vein or somethin'. Losin' lots o' blood. Gotta go now 'fore it all runs out."

Goodman watched him moving into the fog, looking like the hunchback of Notre Dame.

He doubted he'd ever see him again. Certainly not in this world.

≡ EIGHTY-EIGHT ≡

Walden aimed the pistol at Nikki at point-blank range.

Even as she lifted the ax she knew it was a hopeless gesture. Still, as long as there was a second of life left . . .

A figure appeared, smashing into Walden just as his gun discharged.

Nikki threw herself to the floor of the grave, eyes shut tight, ears ringing from the sound. When she realized she hadn't felt the impact of the bullet, just the agonizing pain from her ankle, she opened her eyes. Walden was tottering on the lip of the grave, trying to free his gun hand from the grip of Carlos Morales.

Then both men were tumbling into the grave with her. Fueled by a combination of adrenaline, anger, and self-preservation, she pushed clear of their grunting and flailing bodies.

Walden was under the detective, pushing at him with both hands. He'd dropped his gun in the fall. Morales was screaming Spanish curses. He was covered in blood, straddling the D.A., his good hand grabbing the big man's throat, squeezing, pressing. Walden suddenly bucked and twisted, throwing the weakened detective against the side of the grave, where he cried out in pain and sank to the ground.

Walden bent over and Nikki saw him find his gun. As he pointed it at Morales's head, she grabbed the ax with both hands and swung it forcefully and unerringly into Joe Walden's broad back. With an animal roar, he fell across Morales's body, writhing, his hands trying to reach behind him. As she watched, his wiggling slowly quieted. A gurgling noise sounded in his throat and the life went out of him.

Morales looked up at her. "We got the fucker, didn't we?"

"We sure did, Carlos," she said. "We put him in a grave where he belongs."

Morales's face registered a satisfied grin. Then he closed his eyes.

≡ EIGHTY-NINE ≡

Nikki sat in the caretaker's office, phone to her ear, growing more and more furious with each unanswered ring. Finally, a sleepy voice said, "Police station."

"You awake, Chief Jefferson?"

"Awake? Sure I'm awake. Who's this?"

"Deputy D.A. Nikki Hill. I was in your office a couple hours ago."

"Sure, I re—"

"Listen up. There's not much time. I'm out at Eternal Light with a bunch of dead men and maybe one still alive."

"Hold on, I—"

"Just listen," she said. "You've got to do two things. First, get as many lawmen as you can out here. Highway patrol, sheriffs, whatever. There's at least one carload of L.A. gangstas who'll be showing up any minute and they'll be armed and dangerous. You also have to get some kind of doctor or paramedic or whatever you can find out here. You reading me, chief?"

"Yeah, but—"

"Damn it, I've had to climb over two dead men to get out of a grave, then walk across a cemetery on a broken ankle just to make this phone call. So don't give me any 'yeah, but.' Just do it. Please."

"I hear you," he said, and she broke the connection.

Chief Jefferson did his job.

By the time two gang Chevys approached Carver, he had assembled an impressive collection of highway patrolmen and other lawmen from the nearby towns of Barstow, Midway, Harvard, and Baker. Roadblocks, a first for Carver, were in position.

There was no confrontation to speak of. Shots were fired. One by a gangsta in the second car, the rest by the lawmen, blowing out the vehicles' tires and radiators.

An astonishing collection of guns and knives were tossed from the windows of the two Chevys. Then their occupants emerged, one at a time, hands over heads, to lie down on the macadam to await a pat-down from the police.

Nikki heard about this the next morning from Chief Jefferson, who insisted she call him Parnell, as all of his friends did. They were in her room at Barstow General, the hospital where the ambulances had taken her and the detectives. "There are about fifty newspaper and TV people outside wanting to talk to you," he said.

"You can give 'em the story," she said.

"I'd be happy to," he said, "but I don't know it."

"Then they'll just have to make it up the way they always do," she said.

She was ready to leave. Her badly sprained but not broken ankle had been x-rayed and taped. All that remained was for someone to drive her back to Los Angeles. That someone, Virgil, was on the way.

The situation with Goodman and Morales was considerably more dire. Both detectives were in the hospital's intensive care section awaiting surgery. The bullet in Goodman's back was pressed against the spine and the X rays offered no clue as to how much damage it had done. The doctors had temporarily stanched the bleeding in Morales's chest and were replenishing his blood supply, but the general outlook was gloomy. An operation was necessary, but he was too weak to undergo it. Surgeons used by the LAPD were flying in from Los Angeles to make their own recommendations.

Virgil arrived just after ten A.M. to find her sitting in a wheelchair reading the morning paper.

"Hiya, Red."

She tossed the paper aside and looked at him joyfully, spreading her arms wide.

He dropped to one knee and enfolded her, pulling her, chair and all, toward him.

"Oh, baby, it's good to see you," he said.

"Help me out of this thing."

He reached under her arms and pulled her to her feet, holding her awkwardly. "I ain't gonna break," she told him. "Kiss me, damn it."

He obeyed with such exuberance that the wheelchair was thrown back against a wall.

Neither of them noticed.

"Now that's medicine," she said.

"I didn't make the trip by myself," he said.

He carried her to a window overlooking the parking lot. She saw Bird's huge head poking out of the window of Virgil's sedan.

"They stopped me from bringing him in," he said. "No animals."

"If that's how they feel, let's leave," she said.

* * *

Before they did, they stopped by Intensive Care, where they were allowed to look through the glass at the two detectives, resting side by side under the apparatus. From where she stood, Nikki couldn't tell which was which.

≡ NINETY ≡

The bullet was successfully removed from Ed Goodman's spine less than twenty-four hours after it was put there by the man they'd known as Joe Walden. The prognosis was that he would eventually regain the use of his legs, assuming that he adhered to an intense physical therapy program. When Nikki heard that Detective Gwen Harriman had resigned from the department to care for him she wondered why a resignation had been necessary, but marked it off as one of the inexplicable decisions people make when they are in love.

To the surprise of all the medical experts, Carlos Morales survived two operations, though he lost one of his lungs and a good deal of his attitude. Nearly two months after the shooting, Nikki visited him at his home and found him sitting in a wheelchair, thin and frail. His hair and mustache had turned gray and he seemed to have aged twenty years.

He grinned at what he read on her face. "Hey, I thought you were tougher than that," he said. "It's okay. Carlos is still here, under this old man."

"I came to thank you for saving my life," she told him.

"You saved mine, too," he said. "But I owe you more than just my life. Because of you, the *maricón* who called himself Lee-O is finally and truly dead."

She didn't understand why that would be worth more than his life, but she knew better than to ask. "I owe you a coat," she said. "I think yours got left behind at the hospital."

"Hey, quiet about that," he said. "Estella'd go nuts if she heard I gave my coat away to a beautiful woman."

She walked to the chair, bent down, and kissed him on the cheek.

He looked up at her. "You know, Nikki, a while back I tole you Virgil Sykes wasn't so nice. That was jus' bullshit. I mean, the guy was a player, but I unnerstan' he's settlin' down."

She smiled. "Yes. I think he is."

"He's one lucky *hombre*."

"Estella's doing pretty well in the luck department, herself," she said.

≡ EPILOGUE ≡

Within six months, interest began to wane in *The Maddie Gray Murders* and *The Joseph Walden Deception,* to quote the titles of best-selling instant book accounts of the events (both woefully inaccurate). Jamal Deschamps's suit against the county was settled quietly for an undisclosed sum. (Nikki discovered it to be two hundred thousand dollars.) The untelevised trial and eventual conviction of Rupert Williams and five other Crazy Eights, one of them a young woman, for the murder of Arthur Lydon rated only slightly more space than the average gangsta news reports.

Before long, the restless media had scurried off to other big stories, such as Dyana Cooper's divorce from John Willins and Hobart Adler's departure from the agency he had founded to become the CEO of the world's fourth largest international entertainment conglomerate. One of his first executive announcements, Nikki noted, was the appointment of James Doyle as the head of worldwide acquisitions. She wondered if the top three conglomerates knew what they were in for.

Jack Lattimer took early retirement from the LAPD and just weeks later was diagnosed with cancer of the prostate. Peter Sandoval was never heard of again, at least not by that name.

An appeals court accepted the recommendation of the district attorney's office that Mason Durant be retried for the murder of street vendor Ellis Hawke. The trial, with acting district attorney Raymond Wise handling the case for the prosecution, was a strictly file-and-forget item that resulted in another guilty verdict for Durant.

The district attorney's office was almost back to normal, though its reputation would be in question for some time to come. Wise was behind the big desk, at least until the next election, and probably thereafter. The top job hadn't seemed to change him much. He was still rude and annoying and at times unbearable. As far as Nikki could tell, he was an honorable man, in his own odd way. As long as she did her job and got the proper number of convictions, he treated her with respect.

She and Virgil were maintaining a steady relationship that, both of them agreed, should be allowed to progress slowly. They attended church regularly and on more than one occasion had had cordial, if brief, conversations after the services with her father and her step-relations.

Loreen Battles's romance with Sonny the bodyguard lasted for only that one night of bliss. As she later confided to Nikki, "The man is a splendid physical specimen, but he's so wrapped up in his bodyguard bullshit he doesn't know anything else is going on in the world. He's so out of it he thinks Boyz II Men is a day-care center."

Nikki began to experience something rare for her, an almost ordinary life. A last wrinkle was ironed out one afternoon when she answered her office phone and heard that familiar voice. "Hi, Nikki, how's it goin'?"

"Pretty good, Mace. How about you?"

"Same-o. Thought I might see daylight there for a while. But here I still am."

"You do the crime, you do the time."

"Yeah, but guys come and go all around me. Man raped a young woman and cut off both her arms. Did eight and was out. I got no chance of parole until ten, and all I did was get rid of a worthless, piece-of-shit bad-food pusher."

His admission of guilt was like a curtain being pulled back from a window and the sunlight shining through. She felt so blissfully happy she had to fight to keep her voice neutral. "What is it you want, Mace?"

"Uh, well, I been enjoying our little talks over the years," he said. "But I think I got to move on now."

"That's good, Mace," she said. "That sounds like a positive step."

"I got one last favor to ask."

"Uh huh," she said, suspiciously. "What might that be?"

"Could you see it in your heart . . . to give me Mr. Wise's direct phone number?"

She was barely able to put her hand over the phone's mouthpiece before she burst out laughing.

A few moments later, her giddiness under control, she told Mason Durant she thought she could do that one last, little thing.

CHRISTOPHER DARDEN was a key prosecutor in the O. J. Simpson criminal trial. He is the bestselling author of *In Contempt*.

DICK LOCHTE is an acclaimed mystery writer and screenwriter. His first novel, *Sleeping Dog*, was nominated for an Edgar Award.